All right are reserved, no part of this pu
reproduced or photocopied or stored in ..., ...
system or be transmitted in any form without prior
permission in writing from the publisher nor be otherwise
circulated in any form or cover other than that which it is
published.

Copyright and all rights are reserved by T.A. BIRD2020

All characters and events are products of the author's imagination in this publication other than those clearly in the public domain, are fictitious and any resemblance to any real person living or dead is purely coincidental.

The Guardians of the light and the brotherhood of the knight

BY

Tina Ann Bird

This book is dedicated to my beautiful loving mother Christine Beeden Bird and to the memory of my late beloved father
Leslie Norman Bird

My first book

The Guardians of the light and the brotherhood of the knight

I would like to thank

Anneli Bird

Carolyn Jones

Charlotte Bird

Chapter one

Dark sun rising

Phillip Bagbie was sat at home in his room just passing time, bored of playing on his computer games, his last college classes had finished yesterday. He and his twin sister were brought up by their Auntie Christine as both of their parents burnt to death in a hotel fire along with 53 other guests 18 years ago.

Their auntie had been babysitting them at her house on the night of the fire, they were aged one at the time. For as long as he could remember his aunt had two male visitors every year that always left an envelope with her. She never opened the envelopes she would just say "thank you". The two male visitors were always very polite and would ask if we were all ok and could they do anything to help. Their aunt would just say "no but thank you anyway". The men would say the same thing each visit, if you or the children, ever need us, please contact us and someone will come. They always left the envelope on the table and never spoke to him or his sister unless their aunt nodded her head in approval, and then it was to say hello and good bye or how are you and that kind of thing it had always been that way.

Phillip would ask his aunty Christine, who the men were, she would say they were friends of your parents from the pension company your dad use to work for. He got the feeling that she blamed them in some way for the death of his parents because she would always say, if it was not for them, they would not have been at the wedding reception at the hotel, when they died. But mainly because the police never arrested anyone for it, she had obviously felt the need to blame someone.

But today was different, Phillip heard his aunt come home and a strange feeling came over him, he sensed she was flustered. He came down the stairs to see that his aunt was home from shopping and went to her sitting room and came out with one of her envelopes, in her hand, she did look very flustered, Phillip asked her if she was ok, could you put the kettle on and lock the front and back door. Is someone giving you hassle Aunty Chris because I will give them a slap. No, she replied and picked up the phone and went in to the living room and closed the door behind her.

Christine dialed the number that was on the card, that she got from inside one of the envelopes she had ripped opened; she ignored the money in it. After a few rings a man picked up. Hello may I help. Hello yes, she replied this is Christine Bagbie and I think I need help; I am not sure, I think I saw someone today and I don't know who to ask or tell or even if I am doing the right thing, maybe I am being silly. The man replied by saying, stay calm is any one there with you now, yes, Phillip, but I don't want to worry him. Don't worry Christine I am on my way and I will have one or two people with me when I come, lock the door and don't answer it until we arrive. My name is Marcus, I will be about ten minutes. Christine started to tell him her address, don't worry Christine we know where you live and swiftly put the phone down.

Marcus stood up from sitting at his desk in his office at the brotherhood of the Knights, He glanced over to his companion who was no longer sat on the black leather sofa, to the left of him. Kirk had stood up knowing that something was wrong. Come brother, get the Bagbie file, as he opened his phone and called Paul and asked him to get the car as they were going to the Bagbie's house. By the time they arrived at the car Paul was waiting holding the Black Mercedes car door open for them. Once in the car Kirk said what is it brother you look concerned, tell me Marcus said, from your point of view first, not what the file say's as you have done some yearly visits to the Bagbie's house, what is Christine Bagbie like. From what I have observed, she is a very strong woman that knows her own mind, she is like a lioness with her cubs, she is not an alarmist and she has never asked for help in anyway, she was Peter's twin sister.

Yes, there are not many immortals that are reborn with a twin and a female, it's very rare if at all. Right what does the file say, we don't have long we will be there soon. Peter Bagbie was born and not sent to us he was born first, 2,176 years ago to Nathaniel he was his only child, as normal in Egypt. His first death was in France over 1,347 years ago he was not married and did not have any children, he was believed to have been beheaded at the battle of Calais, we don't know who killed him, anyway he was reborn 1,346 years ago to Banner. Your joking said Marcus. No why, oh yes that's right names are your thing aren't they? As you well know and it means father of Light. If I may continue, Marcus raised an eye brow at him. His 2nd death was a beheading again 586 years ago at the siege of Jerusalem, he was sent with 9 others to stop and capture and detain Crispin, by order of the brother hood, at Xander's request, the order was witnessed by our King no less. It was reported that also lost was Stephen, Crispin and Frederick at the same time. He was born 585 years ago to Jared, Kirk looked at Marcus, one who descends from a decedent.

Again, he was an only child not married, no children. His 3rd death was in England in 1969, he was killed by an explosion, a suspected gas leak, it was not proven how the leak occurred, his 4th birth was in 1970 to Nathaniel again and this was a rare event as twins and one was a female, Christine, this time in England. Now that's interesting Marcus said a gift from god, Marcus raised his eye brows again, Nathaniel means gift of god. And then 20 years ago Nathaniel was reported missing, believed to be dead, then 18 years ago Peter's finale death with wife Leah and 53 others all died in a fire, at a hotel, cause unknown and of course it's one of your investigation cases. He and Nathaniel have not been reported as being reborn anywhere. Peter did ask permission to marry Leah, they then had twins, again one boy and one girl. His son Phillip is not known to be immortal nor is Christine, Peters sister who took the children in and brought them up as her own, the girl is Jessie, she is also human. But 2 females born within 20 odd `years of each other, both twins both in the same family. Females are never immortal and it's very rare, born to an immortal. So, is father trying to tell us something and if he is what is it? Kirk said lots of questions were asked when Christine was born. We are missing something Kirk, something that somebody else knows.

Phillip knocked the living room door and said tea's ready Aunty Chris. Christine opened the living room door, you better come in, there is something I need to tell you now you're old enough to know. Phillip put the tea down on the coffee table and sat down on the sofa with his aunt. Where to start, well today I think I saw someone, no I am sure that I saw someone, a few times now, someone I first saw 18 years ago, the night your parents died, he was outside in a car in the road and your mother was sure he followed them from their house.

When she dropped you off here, your father went across the road to speak to him but he drove off and I am sure I caught a glimpse of him at the church when your parents were buried and today, I am sure he followed me home from town again.

Phillip jumped up and ran over to the window. He stopped at the end of the road; please don't go outside Phillip. Marcus is on his way over, who the hell is Marcus and is this something to do with those envelops? Please sit down and let me tell you. Do you remember the two men that come once a year? Yeah, the men from dad's old pension company he belonged to or worked with, they bring you those envelopes. Yes and no, they bring the envelopes but they also come to check on us, to make sure we are ok and to make sure we have everything that we need. The envelopes they give me are full of money. I have always saved every penny, for you and your sister, just in case you ever need anything and I have never touched a penny, I am saving it for you both, to give you a little nest egg each.

Yeah, I know it's not normal for someone to have envelopes full of cash stuffed in the sideboard, I am not blind, and well I opened one once to see what the men brought you, as you never opened them or threw the letters a way. Phillip really! I brought you up better than that. Yes, aunt but you still have not told me who those men are? They are not from your dad's pension company, your dad was in a club, so to speak, a private members club, and I think they are called brothers of the Knight or something. Just then the doorbell rang and they both jumped up. I will get the door wait here, Phillip. Like hell, it could be anybody. Just then a man's voice called from the letter box, Christine its Marcus are you ok? coming she called.

She walked over and opened the front door, after looking through the spy hole, she recognized one of the men from his visit last year, Kirk. Do you know him Auntie Chris? Yes, I do and Christine opened the door. Please come in, Christine and Phillip stood back and let Marcus and Kirk come in.

There was another man, sat in a black Mercedes outside of their house, Christine closed the door behind them and walked into the living room Marcus and Kirk looked at her, Phillip was frowning trying to be the man of the house and said please sit down, aunty Chris have your tea, you still look very shaken .Marcus said yes, please sit and have your tea Christine, your all safe now. She was safe with me in the house. Marcus looked at his associate and raised an eye brow, to stop him from saying anything; of course, I can see that she is very well looked after. I only meant to reassure her, not to offend you, sorry. Marcus held his hand out to Phillip and said let me introduce myself I am Marcus Dewdney and this is my associate known as Kirk and the gentleman in the car is Paul. Christine gave Phillip her do as your told look; Phillip shook Marcus's hand then sat down next to his aunt.

Phillip, Marcus asked where is your sister, will, she be ok? Why should my sister be in any danger my aunt only thought she saw someone from the past? Marcus looked at Christine, she's at St Mary's College it's her last day today, she's due to come out in about 20 minutes. We can send someone to collect her Marcus said but before he could finish, Phillip said no you bloody will not, you will frighten her and she does not know you. I will go with your friend outside in the car, so I can get there before she comes out and you can stay with Aunty Chris.

Will you be ok with these men aunty Chris while I am gone? Yes, and when I get back, we will all have a little chat. Before Phillip knew it, Marcus had stood up and had his phone out and was giving the driver instructions. Phillip got his coat and took one more uncertain look at Marcus and gave his aunt a kiss on the cheek and left.

Christine said if anything happens to me please look after them, promise me please. Marcus sat down next to Christine and patted her hand, now why don't you tell me, what or who has you so frightened and tell us why you think anyone is going to hurt this family. And yes, I promise to look after all of you ok. Kirk, Marcus said without looking away from Christine, can you make Christine a fresh cup of tea and check the house, to make sure it's secure, while I chat with Christine, thank you. Kirk left the room without a word.

Can you tell me why you called Christine; take your time. Well the night my brother died, he had brought the kids around for me to babysit and my sister in-law went back to the car to get the nappies, she came back from the car and said that there was a man out there, that she had seen outside of their house earlier in the day. She also added that he was following her and would just sit in his car watching them outside, so Peter went out to speak to the man, but he just drove off, after a few words. Peter came in and said everything was ok and they left to go to their friend's wedding reception and never came back, those poor children. Anyway, I saw him the same man my sister in-law pointed out, outside the house last week, he was parked outside the cemetery once when we went to lay some flowers and today, he followed me home again, that's twice this week. Jessie said she thought some man followed her yesterday, it scared her and today I panicked, I did not know who else to call.

You did the right thing by calling me. Christine gave a description of the man to Marcus.
Don't worry and don't worry about the children. Phillip is very much like his father and he is very protective over his family. Oh yes, he has always been the man of the house, he tried to carry all the shopping bags home from the corner shop when he was seven and a one-minute walk took about ten, as he kept putting the bags down and refused to let me or his sister carry even one. Bless him, after that I did the shopping while he was at school and his sister is just as bad. I would protect them both with my life. That will not be necessary, that's what I am here for. Would you all be more comfortable in a hotel, of course I would pay. Christine just looked at him, are you mad after their parents dying in a hotel fire and when that man was last seen following my sister in-law here and maybe to the hotel, do you really think that will happen. Over my dead body forget it. I am very sorry, not a smart thing to say please forgive me.

Christine eyed him; can I ask you something while the children are not here. Marcus nodded, did Peter and Leah really die in that fire and was it really an accidental fire? How do you fit in to all of this? Just then Kirk came in with another cup of tea and nodded to Marcus. I have checked the windows and doors and all is ok. Marcus, raised his eyebrow, I will keep an eye out for their return, he then turned and walked out of the room closing the door behind him.

Marcus continued, yes, they did die in that fire along with many of my other friends and yes it was a very sad accident and I look out for all of my friends and their families its part of what I do, my role within the brotherhood. So, I get paid for doing something that is my calling and duty and honor. So, for me it's a win, win.

And again, you did the right thing about this man. It sounds like he is up to no good and he is frightening you and that's not right and by the sound of it he did the same thing to Peter and Leah this is something I will not have; we need to find out why.

Christine would it be ok if one of my men stay here with you for a few days, so we can get a good look at him or even catch him and find out what he wants, would that be ok with you?Christine thought about it for a second, then said, would you be able to stay. Just then Marcus took a long look at Christine and could see her fear, yes Christine that's fine don't worry. Do you have a spare room, if not I will be more than happy to take the sofa? I am sorry but it's the sofa. Just then Kirk came in the living room, they have returned and he nodded.

Jessie was sat in her last class in college recalling the past few weeks of her life with her friend Stella. Things where not going Jessie's way at all, her lifelong best friend left to go home to her dads before starting university after the summer, and her boyfriend of two years had dumped her because she wouldn't have sex with him, perhaps it was for the best as it never felt right. He had said some nasty things to her and he was quick to take up with the school slut Lindsey Carter and to top that she had a letter yesterday telling that her new job she was due to start was no more, due to cut backs and no university for her as grade placements were cut too. Now Stella could not go into town to help her buy a dress this weekend for the dance and without a date to go to the end of term dance with, yep things just gets better and better, what a downward turn her life had taken. Look Stella said you don't need a date for the dance there are loads of people going without a date and don't worry about a job something will turn up and we can still meet up every weekend for a drink.

There were a few other girls in her class that she got on with and there are a few boys that might take her to the dance if she asked but that would look like an act of desperation. She just needed to go home curl up and die. What would life hold for her now, it was the end of the world, and the college bell rang out for the last time. She got up and dragged her bag off the floor and filled it with all of her belongings and put her I pod on, she walked out slowly taking in everything and everyone. When she walked to the gate her brother was stood there with a few girls stood around him. He put his arm out to pull her to him and she smiled at the girls, they walked to a black car where a man stood in a suit and opened the door for them, Jessie stopped and looked at Phillip he said its ok get in he is a friend of auntie Christine.

They drove home in the back of the black car Jessie asked her brother what was going on. He replied we will have a chat at home. They sat in silence for the rest of the trip home. They pulled up outside their house and the driver got out of the car and came around the car and opened the door for Jessie. Jessie wondered if they had won the lottery but should have known her luck was on the down. A man she did not know opened the front door Jessie stopped her heart was pounding and she grabbed her brother and said, is it Aunty Christine, is she dead because I can't go in if she is. Hot tears ran down Jessies face, Phillip cuddled her. She was shaking. Phillip was talking but she could only hear her heart beat. Her aunt must have heard them coming in as she was at the door with her arms open and Jessie pushed Phillip aside and ran to Christine and she put her arms around her, Jessie had never been so relived and cried.

Christine was pulling Jessie in to the living room where there was another man on the phone with his back to Jessie, stood in the far corner of the room. Jessie stopped crying she had no idea what was going on. Phillip was shouting at the man saying that all this was his fault and said I told you that your men would frighten her. Phillip that's enough! She thought you were dead because of all the men. The man in the corner closed his phone and turned around and looked at Jessie their eye's locked for a second and she'd swear she saw spark of bright white light come from his eye's, it drew her to him with a jolt and that's all she remembered as everything went blank.

Marcus felt like he had been hit by a bolt of lightning, never had he felt anything like it in his life, he had not even realized that he had let out a gasp until Kirk had asked him if all was ok.
Kirk had opened the front door and followed Jessie and Phillip in, behind Christine into the living room had caught Jessie when she fainted, Kirk looked more concerned that Marcus had made a noise and did not move to catch Jessie, the fact that Jessie had fainted and it was Kirk who laid Jessie on the sofa and shepherded, Marcus and Phillip from the room leaving Christine to tend to Jessie.

The next thing Jessie knew is that there someone holding her hand and there was quiet. Jessie then opened her eyes, she was laid down on the sofa with the curtains closed and aunty Christine was sat on the edge of the sofa holding her hand and wiping her head with a cold wet flannel, see darling you're fine don't say anything I will go and get you a drink try not to get up just yet darling and we will have a chat in a bit. Christine went into the kitchen and looked at the three men, they were all sat around at the kitchen table looking at each other and they all looked red faced.

I am sorry aunty Chris is Jessie ok? Oh, come here you and she gave Phillip a hug, she's fine she's just woken up. I will make everyone a cup of tea and then we will all sit down together and have a chat this is nobody's fault but mine. Marcus stood up if anyone is to blame it's me, this is down to me and for that I am truly sorry. Phillip was just protecting his family. Men! Christine said and started handing out the tea, right she said looking at Phillip I will give Jessie her cup of tea and when we come back there will be no shouting and arguing I will not have it.

Christine came back with a cup of tea for Jessie and she sat up slowly and said I am so sorry, I did not know what's going on I thought something had happened to you, I was so upset, I'm sorry. Oh, you silly Billy, drink your tea, have you eaten today? I had a packet of crisps at lunch time. Oh, that's not good enough, drink your tea and when you're ready come in to the kitchen for that chat. When Christine went back into the kitchen, she looked at the three men again and said will one of you please be good enough to go to the local take way and get some food, I don't feel like cooking after the day I have had and times getting on. Christine went to retrieve her purse but Marcus stood up again and said this is on me it's the least I can do! Phillip you can go to the take away with Marcus. Kirk just looked at Christine as if she just slapped him, Marcus just smiled, Kirk you can help Christine get the table ready while we are gone. Phillip eyed his aunt, but knew better not to say anything and left with Marcus.

When Jessie heard the front door close she went into the kitchen and found her aunt with a man laying the table ready for teatime, I am just going to wash up and get changed aunty ok?, Christine looked up, that's fine darling and continued what she was doing the man just nodded at her and Jessie smiled and went to her room and had a quick wash and got changed into a red v neck cotton t shirt with white writing on it, put her jeans on and white fluffy slippers, she took her pony tail down and brushing her long dark hair through then set off downstairs, she walked into the kitchen.

Christine said Jessie this is Kirk and he works for Marcus the man who was in the living room with me, she shook her head as if to say she did not remember anything, apart from the darkest most beautiful eyes she had ever seen and that spark but Jessie could sense something about Kirk, she could not put her finger on what it was. They will be back in a minute he has gone with your brother to the take away, good Jessie said I love take away smiling back at them both and sat down at the table. Just then the doorbell rang and Kirk was already out of the kitchen going down the hall, Jessie just looked at her aunt as she had not moved for a few seconds, Phillip came in the kitchen with Kirk and another man. Well this was different from all the shouting and confusion earlier Jessie thought, she stood up and Christine stood next to Jessie and put her arm around her, Christine said this is Marcus.

Marcus just stood for a second taking in the sight of Jessie he was stunned trying to hold on to the shock as earlier she had taken him by surprise and he was sure she had the power to see the spark escape from inside of him which all immortals had. He had been unguarded and foolish and she had paid the price for it, could she be the one.

This confirmed her innocents because only the pure could draw out the light and then she had to be bonded to someone to use it. So, there was hope he said sorry and held out his hand to Jessie and said my name is Marcus Dewdney. She took his hand and he kissed the back her hand and said I am your servant madam looking at her the whole time. God Jessie thought she was going to faint again. He released her hand as he did so Jessie felt electricity surge through his fingers, he pulled her chair back out and said please sit. She moved forward to do as he asked and he pushed her chair in behind her and then he took a seat next to her.

They all had tea together and Christine told everyone about what had happened with the man who had followed her brother and sister in-law and now Jessie and her. She explained to Phillip and Jessie why Marcus and Kirk would be staying at their house until they could find out what this man wanted and why when any of them wanted to go out, they had to have someone with them until they caught this man.

Jessie just kept nodding and could not take her eyes off of Marcus she was drawn to him never had she ever felt anything like it she could smell his aftershave and felt very attracted to him like a pulling from within side of her. God it felt like his body was hypnotizing her, boy it had to be that aftershave and whatever it was it was expensive and definitely working for him. He looked like a solid man he definitely had big muscles as they were pressing through his shirt when he moved, she knew because she was sat so close to him.

He had the darkest creamiest brown eyes and long eye lashes he was closely shaven and had very good skin and short dark black hair, oh yeah he looked after himself and when he stood up to excuse himself from the table she nearly followed him he must have been about six foot two if not taller and this trouser suit was tailor made to fit his well fit frame. Jessie helped her aunt to clear the table.

When Marcus came out of the loo he went to the sitting room with Kirk and closed the door, Phillip said he was going to his room to do some work on his computer Christine said are you ok with all of this Jess as you have been very quiet you know? Yes, I am fine Jessie said and smiled at the aunt again. She thought to herself oh yeah, she had been taking in Marcus all of him and he is all ok with me, but she said I need to get my college dance dress tomorrow, and I don't have anyone to come with me you know a girlfriend. Don't worry darling I know I am not as young as I use to be and fashions changed but I will go with you darling, if you want? Jessie smiled and gave her a big hug, she felt bad about fainting and worrying her, that would be great, thank you Aunty Chris. She then went upstairs to see what her brother was up to, he had his bedroom door open, come in sis and look at this.

Phillip had a web page on the screen of his computer and it had a picture of Marcus on it. She said what is this about Phillip? When Marcus told us his name at the table, it rang a bell, so I put his name in the computer and this is the result, it says he is a member of the Brotherhood of the Knight, the same as dad was, so that checks out but, look at this, it says his family name is one of the oldest in England and his family are decedents from a long line of fighting king's from the East, his family line can be traced back to 828 AD, and he and his family are very, very wealthy and powerful and own some very large estates around the country and in Europe, there is not much about family members or him or any of or the brotherhood of the knight. There are a few small articles in the society pages about Marcus and his family and not a lot else, except for the fact he is the only sole living heir and will inherit millions upon millions when his grandfather dies, as his parents died when he was a baby, so his parents are dead to, just like ours Phillip. Yes. Phillip can you find out more about what this brotherhood does and let me know because the more we know the more we can understand what's going on. Yes, sure sis great minds think alike, yes that they do Phillip yes, they do, Good night brother.

Marcus said I think I have might have discovered something in Jessie. Yes, I noticed earlier Kirk said and I think I felt something while you were out, I think she sensed something about me, I am not sure you felt something from Jessie, Marcus said that's interesting and it adds up we will see. Marcus and Kirk had just finished discussing the shift arrangements for tomorrow and the next few days, they would need to put a plan together to catch this man, when Marcus's phone rang, it was Paul from the car, Marcus there is a red Honda car with two men in, they have driven past the house three times now and are parked just about four houses down, to your right, they are watching the house and they are not a where that I am here, I am parked across the road about four house's back to your left. Do nothing, get the registration on the car and a description of the two men if you can, if their status changes call me and he closed his phone.

Kirk said what now, yes now, bring Christine in and close the door, sit in the kitchen but be ready for anything and re check both doors, don't move any curtains. Don't alert the others look natural. Marcus opened the living room door and Christine came to ask if they would like a cup of tea,

Kirk said I will do that why don't you sit down and take a load off. Christine smiled, why thank you Kirk, that would be lovely. Kirk left the room and closed the door quietly behind him.

Marcus said, can you tell me your normal routine for every day of the week and what you all normally do at night. She went thought their routine, but said everything will change now they have both left college, there's a big college dance next week and we have to go ladies shopping tomorrow for Jessie dress. Phillip has his dad's tux ready, so he's ok.

So, we will need a lady to go shopping with you tomorrow, I know just the girl, her name is Amanda, she is very good at close protection and it will look natural, we have used her as part of our team from time to time. What time do you want her here? she will drive there and park outside and drive you both to where you need to go, do not go anywhere alone or away from here, you must advise Jessie to do the same. Just like three girls on a day out and if you see our friend or if something does not seem right, then tell Amanda straight away. And one of us will be with Phillip all day, so don't worry, just make sure you all have your phones and there all turned on. Just then Kirk came in with the tea for both of them, if you don't mind, I will go and read the newspaper in the kitchen.

Just to let you know Kirk will stay with us, just for tonight, we will take shifts is that ok? Yes, of course that's fine, I feel a little silly now, I think I may have over reacted by phoning you today and I feel I have put you to all of this trouble for nothing. No, don't be silly you have very good protective instincts as a mother and it's no trouble to us at all Christine. She finished her tea and said good night and went to her room. Marcus picked up his phone and hit the speed dial number marked X.

In the night duty masters office of the Brotherhood of the Knight Victor was on duty, he had held his office for many years and in the last twenty years the black telephone with the with dial and red center had only ever rang once, when there was a fire which killed other members of his brotherhood and tonight was the second, he picked the phone up, hello this is Victor.

Victor this is Marcus, Victor did not say anything for a second or two, then said, how I may help sir. I need you to wake up Xander, tell him that I think the dark sun is rising and I need you to call Amanda and tell her to come to the Bagbie's address for 9am, tell her it's a girls shopping day and tell her to come armed, I have a meet and greet team with me, we are being watched, we will stay, Kirk is inside with me and Paul is in the car outside, watching the two men as we speak. Can you also call Simon and update him? I will wait for Xander's call? Yes, Sir. Marcus hung up.

Victor put the black telephone receiver down and lent over to the white telephone, on the other side of his desk and pressed the red button, after a few rings a male voice said, this is Xander, My lord Marcus called, he said to tell you that he thinks the Dark sun is rising, he awaits your call sir, he also asked me to alert Amanda and Simon. Yes, do so, tell me Victor where and who. The Bagbie's sir, there was silence both ends of the phone, it is my wish to convene my council Knights. When Sir? now tonight and Xander put the phone down. Victor got up from his seat and opened his office door, called his security officer Joshua over, I need you to start making calls to the council of knight's, yes sir, which one's sir, all of them, for tonight, go now, he then turned and walked back into his office and closed the door.

Marcus walked into the kitchen and Kirk was sat in the dark, with his chair in the corner of the room facing the back door. All is well my friend. Kirk did not move, yes, all is well my friend. Good, I will check upstairs, just then Marcus's phone vibrated, he answered with a swift yes. Paul's voice said, there out of the car and it looks like they are walking down to the foot path, by the corner shop, there going around the back. Marcus clicked his fingers and pointed towards the back-door, Kirk swiftly stood and produced a small sword, knife and long bread knife from the kitchen draw and threw the knife at Marcus, who caught it one handed.

He told Paul to stay where he was and shut his phone. Marcus nodded and Kirk un locked the back door, both men moved into the garden, closing the door very quietly. Kirk stood in the shadow of the shed and had a good view of all the walls, Marcus stood by the drainpipe by back door, not moving. The two men from the red Honda where starting to climb over the back wall. Then they both stopped half way over, as the kitchen light came on and Jessie was at the sink in front of the kitchen window, getting a drink of water, one of the men whispered, that bitch is mine, I am going to fuck that then slit her throat. Yeah well just as long as Crispin gets her first, yeah, he wants her more than anything, I have ever seen. Whatever is left you can have. Marcus fought back the urge to kill them both now and slit their throat's, he knew, Kirk would not move unless he did first, or the two men moved with in arms reach, he would have killed them both before Marcus would get to them. The house behind them put it lights on and they were shouting at each other, the two men jumped down off the wall and said to each other, We'll come back tomorrow, then walked back down the footpath.

They did not follow the men as the Bagbie's where their priority and now they had to find Crispin, was it possible he had survived and was here in this country. And why did he want Jessie, any man would have to be dead not to want her, how had he known and how had he found them, did he know about Phillip. Within a few seconds Marcus's phone vibrated, it was Paul's voice saying, the two men were waking back to their car and were now getting back in it and now driving off.

Follow them, keep your distant, they are armed killers. And shut his phone once again. Kirk moved from his position to go back into the house. Marcus followed him in, they locked the back door and Kirk put the knife on the side, where he was sat and took his position back up. Jessie had already gone back to her room. I will check the house, then he put the knife up the sleeve of his shirt and put his jacket on. He went to check the front room and front door, he climbed the stairs quietly, the first room was Jessie's she was laying in her bed with her long dark hair splayed across her pillow and down her back and was hanging over the bed, she was laid on her side facing the window, she had a slim firm frame, he could see the curve of the hip even with the sheet on her, she looked so beautiful and innocent, for the first time in many years he felt want, lust, desire and then a huge streak of pain went through his body, just at the thought of what the men had said, followed by a wave of anger, he would see them all dead and chopped into bit's, if they even harmed one hair on her head. He had never felt anything like it in his life, he could hardly breathe.

He checked on Phillip, he was asleep on top of his bed with his computer on, he looked as young as his sister, he pulled his door to and listened at Christine's door, she was snoring lightly. He returned to his post. Two hours later Paul phoned to say, the two men were now in a house in Winchester.

Good get as much information as you can, then update Simon's team, then come back. Marcus closed his phone and pushed X on his phone, he could not wait for Xander to call him back, this has to be dealt with now. Again, Victor looked shocked that the phone with the red dial rang out again, for the second time that night, hello this is Victor. Victor, I need to speak to Xander, please hold sir I will see if he is free. Again, Victor lent over to the white phone and picked the receiver up and pushed the red button. Xander's body guard, James picked the phone up, this is James. Marcus needs to speak to Xander. James was shocked, it must be very important. Please hold, after a minute Xander picked up the phone, please connect me to Marcus.

There were three clicks on the phone and Xander was put through to Marcus. Hello Xander, there was a silence, Crispin is alive and I think he is here in this country, he want's Jessie Bagbie badly. I think that she is the guardian of light, I was not sure earlier but then I overheard a conversation, I feel lots of emotion when I am close to her and she sensed something about Kirk as well, the two men who were watching the house were from Crispin, I don't think he knows about Phillip, and I don't know how he found out about Jessie. The reason I think that is, I am sure, she may have, well seen my light, it was my fault, I was not guarded, I thought after all this time that there would never be another, ever. I am truly sorry, she was upset, it was a split second and then she fainted. She has the power I felt it, I was sure she seemed to pull a spark out of me.
But I was not aware of her power until after, she is shielding it somehow.

Xander was quiet, is she of age now? Yes, they are both 18, she is innocent, I am not sure about Phillip, but he is very protective of Jessie. Was he in the room with his sister when she saw your light? Yes, he was. Is it possible, that he was shielding her without knowing it, which is why you did not pick up her ability? Yes, but Christine was in the room as well. So, one of them could be shielding her without knowing it, our father's word of truth is faith Marcus and our hope is, that these are the lost guardians.

Have you told anyone about the spark? No, only you and Kirk knew something, as he was here, let's keep it that way for now, I am meeting my Knight 's tonight. The Bagbie's, are now your full and only responsibility, I don't have to tell you what's at stake, if she is the doorway for our kind to go home, then our father is calling us and has sent his doorway for us to come.

You were made to do this job Marcus; I don't have to tell you what could happen if she fall's in to Crispin's hands. We had better hope that her brother reaches his full potential, to protect his sister, before anything happens and if she is slain. If she is, slain he will kill them all, he will not stop just at them. He would kill all of the brother hood and could kill all for miles around him.

Once she was his wife, some of the brother hood were drawn to her and raped her to death. Father sent his holy massager to take him back, as the door had been closed when they killed her. And now he has been sent, in the form of her brother, she must have a pre-selected mate and we must find him, or perhaps she has found her mate. If anything happens to her, then you must kill him, or he will bring about the end of all humanity. You must kill him first, if it looks like she has no hope of surviving. Hope is with us and soon I will see my father. And with that Xander put the phone down.

About seven thirty a.m., Christine came down the stairs to find that Kirk and Marcus had laid the table for breakfast and had a pot of tea on the go, both looking like they had just walked off a move set, it was not fair some people just looked good no matter what. What would you like for breakfast asked Kirk? we will all have bacon, eggs and toast as it Saturday, I will call Phillip and Jessie, as it takes them at least ten minutes to rise from there pits.

After breakfast and after the cleaning up had been done, Marcus explained that Amanda would be going with the girls, to make it look like there's nothing wrong and Simon's team would do the rest and there would be a companion for Phillip as well He and Kirk would be back this evening, the doorbell went and Kirk answered it. Amanda nodded at Kirk and walked into the living room and introduced herself to Jessie and Christine, hi my name is Amanda and I hear we are going shopping today. She was at least five foot ten maybe eleven long blonde hair, blue eyes and she looked about twenty-five next to Marcus, as he looked like he was in his mid-thirty's. She was dressed in black leather boots, jeans, T-shirt and a small black leather fitted jacket and a designer handbag of course, she smiled and kissed Marcus on the cheek. Jessie felt a pang of jealousy shoot threw her.

Marcus asked if they were ready, he turned to Amanda, everything is on my account and gave her his card. Jessie beamed a big smile like a Cheshire cat, Christine said, Marcus you can't do that, it's too much, it's my pleasure; please let me do this for you. Then Amanda said come on girls, the shops are open, time is a wasting. I am driving so let's go. See you guys later. Jessie said Thank you to Marcus and took a step towards him gave him, with the biggest smile that lit up her face, she looked in to his eye's, she was drawn to him and there was something in his eyes, he was trying to fight something, she stopped herself, he looked uncomfortable. Perhaps he thought she was just a child or perhaps he had a thing with Amanda. Well she would change his mind, she just nodded and left.

Marcus had to take a few breaths. She was strong, he had felt it pull her towards him and he towards her. He would have to be very strong around her. So, it was Phillip shielding, he could feel her power when he was close to her, when Phillip was not there. Kirk came in and said Simon is here, good you may go and tell Paul to stand down, I will see you both tonight at 7 pm, be well brother.

Simon walked in to the Bagbie's living room, well this is the biggest alert that has ever been, in all of my years eyeing him carefully. Xander has taken only me in to his confidence and ordered me to find her mate and protect him with all I have, including my life. As I believe her brother of all people is her protector. Simon moved a little closer to Marcus still eyeing him and still managing to keep his distance, in all my one thousand years on this earth I have never see you look, how shall I say, look flustered at best. I know your older than me brother and I mean you no disrespect, but I can see her effect on you and she does not know. No Marcus said she is aware of something, but of what she knows nothing. So, they really are the guardians and as if she had chosen you. They are very young to this world; you must bond with her brother Phillip, draw his power to keep him calm as he shield's his sister's power, when he is close. I could not even detect it when he is close, they are upset at the moment, so we need to keep them very calm and try and keep this as normal as possible.

Simon asked, he is hear? Yes, in his room waiting, to go to meet his friend in Mill street, off of the high street and we need a plan of action for their prom next week.

He is taking his sister, whether he wants to or not, if he is close then I can do my job with a clear head. Who else is back up? Amanda is with Jessie. Mathew's teams with you and Joshua's team with Jessie, Peter and his team are outside and all teams will rotate 24/7. Did X tell you Crispin is a live and I think he is hearing. Yes, X gave me a full update, took a deep breath, I am to be your second brother, if we don't find her mate, she has drawn your light, you must be her first choice and I to be her second choice.

Marcus stomach muscles tightened, just the thought of Simon even being close to her, or trying to mate with her. If he could not find her mate or she refused Marcus, Simon would have to step in. Marcus would rip the skin off of him and impale him, Marcus clenched his fingers. Simon backed slowly out of the room as he had never known Marcus show, or feel emotion before, and it felt strange to feel the emotion coming off Marcus. I mean you no harm bother, be at peace. Just then Phillip came down the stairs, I am ready.

He looked at Simon and felt oddly at peace. Simon introduced himself, let's go and just nodded at Marcus they left him stood in Christine's living room. Marcus had never felt anything like the power he had felt from Jessie and it was affecting him strongly, yes, he had many women in his very long life, but he had never felt urges or emotions, his kind never did, it was only when someone very powerful were near them and that's why the brotherhood stayed close to each other, they shared a bonding a peace. Like a sense of peace and comfort. Some were given permission to get married, to make up any lost numbers but, their offspring were half human and became venerable to the others, like Crispin, who would kill and rape and did not value human life, Crispin just wanted to go home, if he died he would be reborn and his sole and sprit would be old, he would not die of old age, he would be weak as strength came with their long age. If, however you managed to survive, the only way to go home would be through the guardian, you would be with father and at peace and young again. But on a very rare occasion a messenger would bring you or take you, or the guardian, she was the second ever sent. She was to be treasured and guarded with all of our life's, that was the brother hood's job to protect her and complete father's wishes, as she was the doorway and if was to bring forth and release that power within her, he has to help her to contain it and show her how to control it. But you have to be very close and trusted like her mate. He would be hers, for all time until he was called, if she wanted him.

When Marcus had calmed himself down, he went home and packed his clothing, his sword and knives and showered, he tried to sleep and for the first time in his long life he felt uneasy, and restless, at just thought of Jessie asleep in her bed, with her dark hair hanging down.

After a long full day of shopping Jessie had got her evening dress, shoes, and make up and Aunty Christine even managed to get a new outfit, that Amanda had talked her in to. Amanda had taken them to one of the best restaurants in Southampton, for a long lunch and now they were all looking for underwear, as Amanda had said every woman needs to look and feel beautiful and of course you had to have matching underwear for that. While aunty Chris was trying on a peach bra, Amanda picked up some black silk and lace all in one set's and lace thongs in every colour, black lace stocking's and some stretch lace body stocking, four in different colours and matching bra's, that looked like they were not worth stitching together, as there was not a lot of material and looked see through and two silk dressing gowns.

Amanda said to Jessie, that will make your boyfriends eye's pop out. What that lots for me, I already have a dress. This little lots, to top our trip off for the day and she dumped the lot on the counter, we will take the lot. It's a shame I don't have a boyfriend. That will change, good-looking woman like you. Jessie had worked up the courage to ask Amanda if Marcus was her boyfriend. Amanda looked at Jessie and smiled. No, he is my boss and work colleague that's all. The casher had to ring her bell to get help to pack it all up, Amanda took Aunty Christine's bra out of her hands, that to please and smiled triumphantly.

They were all loaded down with their bags of shopping and made their way back to Amanda's car. The man parked next to Amanda's car was taking his suite jacket off and was putting it into his boot. Amanda told Jessie and Christine, to get in the car, she would put the bags in the boot. As Jessie and Christine where putting their seat belts on, they heard a click and whooshing sound twice, they could not see anything because Amanda's boot was up, and the then sound of a man's voice and the car boot slamming. Amanda got in, you girls ok? Jessie and Christine looked at each other, yes, we're fine thanks. Christine asked Amanda, are you ok? yes, she said as she turned to smile at them both, the side of her face was covered in blood. Don't worry it's not mine. she pulled some baby wipes out of the glove compartment and wiped her face, looked in the rear-view mirror and smiled, started the car and drove off.

After a few minutes Christine asked what happened Amanda? Oh, nothing much me and the man in the next car had a disagreement and I won, with a little help from a friend, don't worry everything's fine, we will all go home and have a nice cup of tea. How does that sound. She, kept smiling, driving and she even put the radio on.
All they could do was sit there and wonder. As they pulled

up outside of our house, she pulled out her mobile phone and spoke to someone called Simon, oh good you're at the house now with Phillip, um could you come out to the car and give us a hand in with the shopping please, as I am not in a fit state for the neighbors to see me and I don't want to alarm Phillip, there was a few seconds silence, no they are fine and I am fine. She then shut her phone.

As they pulled up outside their house a big man of solid muscle and short blond hair, came out, followed by Phillip, he opened Christine's door and the big blonde guy opened Jessie's. Hello I am Simon, please allow me to help you, he took her hand and helped her out of the car, he asked Phillip if he could grab the shopping from the boot. It was only then that Jessie saw the full state of Amanda, blood covered the front seat. Amanda had wiped most of the blood off, her face but her clothing was blood stained, she smiled at Jessie, today was great, catch you soon, thanks' yeah, thanks, but then left her to speak to Simon for a second while Jessie staggered into the house in shock, still not sure what had happened.

Simon asked Amanda what had happened. Well as we approached the car, there was a man waiting for us so I got the Bagbie's in the car, opened the boot to put the shopping in, grabbed my gun with the silencer on it and he pulled a knife, I put one in this heart, Joshua shot him in the back of the head, I got sprayed with blood and he fell on me, we dumped him in his boot. I threw the rest of the bags in the boot and got the hell out of there, as quick as I could, I left Joshua's team to clean up after we left. A good day shopping then, did you recognize him? No, low rent scums. Ok, well you better go and get cleaned up, I will speak to Joshua later and thank you Amanda. She then nodded and left. Simon went back into the house and closed the door.

Simon went into the kitchen and found Phillip hugging his Aunt and sister. Poor Amanda, said Christine, is she ok. Simon looked at Phillip, then looked at the woman, sorry hello Christine my name is Simon, Amanda is fine she did her job and none of you are hurt, I will put the kettle on and you can show me what you lovely ladies have been buying. Phillip can show you what we have been buying. Simon handed Christine a cup of tea and then handed Phillip a cup of tea, to give to Jessie, as he had no wish to be near her, if she was upset. He would let her brother soothe her, while he stood near to Phillip to use his calming influence.

After they had their cups of tea everyone had calmed down enough to sit at the table and showed Simon their purchases. Jessie showed him her dress for Friday, wow lovely dress and Christine showed him her new outfit, then Phillip showed his aunt and sister his new laptop. Really Simon, that is too much money, let me pay you for it, Christine asked, nonsense's it's a gift from me, as he is a very bright young man, it was my pleasure. While Phillip showed Christine how to work his, wireless laptop, Jessie put her dress, make up and shoes away and was holding up some of her new under ware, how was she ever going to ware any of it, some of it looked tiny and very skimpy, a hot flush of embarrassment ran up her cheeks, what if someone was to see her in it and who would that be! Had Amanda meant for someone to see Jessie in it, or did she think Jessie needed to grow up or had she meant her to feel special. She put the underwear in her draw and went down to her have tea.

Christine had made chicken salad and mash potatoes, after

they all cleaned up. Jessie said I am going for a bath and went up stars. Simon was watching Phillip trying to teach Christine how to use the internet, when Simon's phone rang, Phillip looked up at Simon, as he answered his phone, ok he said and shut his phone, Marcus and Kirk are here. Simon stood up and went to the front door, to let Marcus and Kirk in. The three men then went into the kitchen. Marcus eyed Simon, what is the update brother. Simon gave him a full up date, from what the ladies brought, to what happened at the car with Amanda and what they had for tea. Marcus said, we have enough kit to stay for a few days, is there a team in place tonight for any unwelcome visitors, return. Yes, and everything you and X asked for is in place and ready.

Where is everyone Marcus said? Phillip is in the living room, giving Christine computer lessons and Jessie is in the bath. I will take my leave, he nodded at Kirk and Marcus. Thank you, Brother, be at peace. Simon said, good bye to Christine, Phillip stood with a big smile and said, thank you, are you coming back tomorrow, Simon looked at Marcus who nodded in agreement. Yes, I will come back tomorrow, we can go and do something if you would like, say good night to Jessie for me. Then left. Marcus and Kirk put their bag's in the sitting room and went into the living room where Christine was looking frazzled by Phillip's computer. They sat opposite Christine and Phillip.

Jessie had a good soak in the bath, washed her hair then tried on one of her new tiny black lace bra's and matching thong, she twisted her wet hair and pinned it up and put on her new black silk robe, after she painted her nails, soft pink and went downstairs, she went into the living room, can we go down the pub tonight, all of us?

Christine couldn't see why not, I think I need a drink after my computer lesson, Phillip smiled, yeah, why not, I have to put my laptop away and change. What about you two, Marcus?

Marcus could not speak, he thought he was going to choke, that dressing gown was stuck to her body, her underwear or lack of it was pressing against her dressing gown, she looked like a super model. Kirk spoke for Marcus as he was having difficulty speaking English, we would love to accompany you all the pub. Good, there is a quiz on and Stella might be there, I have to dry my hair and dress, I should be ready in about 20 minutes, Jessie said and turned around and ran up the stairs, Marcus thought he was going to have a heart attack, when she turned around to go upstairs, it was very obvious that she had a thong on. He was so relieved when she said she was going to put clothing on. Christine and Phillip both went upstairs, to wash up and get ready. Kirk slapped Marcus across the back and laughed, are you ok? It's a good job we are going to the pub because after that I need a drink, I am going to put my jeans on, I will be back in a sec.

When Jessie came down the stairs 20 minutes later, she walked in the living room, Marcus was stood there with body hugging male jeans a belt and black shirt. He looked and smelt gorgeous, his muscles where pressed against every part of his clothing, she was drawn to him, she felt hot, she wanted him to kiss her, she stopped where she was because he was staring at her, he was unable to move, not only had she dried her hair she had it down, flowing about her face, she had the smallest tightest black t shirt on and sprayed on, low cut jeans the type with no waist band on, you could see her midriff and navel, she had hi heeled shoes and make up on. What was a man supposed to do with that, she smelt like an angel?
 If she came any closer, he would be at her mercy, she

wanted him but she looked unsure. He said, very quietly, you look like a super model.

Thank you and beamed a massive big bright smile at him, she was just an innocent child, trying to be a woman, he did not know what he should feel if she choose him, he would be honorable, but she was killing him because her power was drawing him closer, he could not walk past her if she wanted him, he would have to fight his morals and level headedness and give into her desire and then he would not be in control of himself. She had to learn how to control it. The heat was building up inside of him. Just then Kirk came into the living room and stood in between them, blocking some of her pull, he must have felt Marcus's unease because he asked if all was ok.

Just then Christine and Phillip came down the stairs, are we already then Christine asked? Yes, Jessie said. Good, Paul is waiting outside to take us all, shall we go? Kirk Sheppard them to the front door, giving Marcus a minute to regain himself. Kirk sat in the back with them and Marcus sat in the front with Paul.

After the quiz at the pub which, they won, Phillip went over to the other end of the bar, to talk to small group of friends who were all trying not to stare at Jessie, who was talking to two other girls about the prom, nearly every red-blooded male in the pub was eyeing her up. Marcus just smiled in her direction, as the two girls were more interested in Marcus than talking about what they were going to ware to the prom. Marcus asked Christine and Kirk if they would like another drink, they both said yes. He rose from his seat and walked to the bar; Jessie's two friends made a B line for Marcus.
All the girls were smiling and trying to introduce

themselves to him, Hi I am Stella and this is Penney, Jessie did not look, none too happy about it, they were trying to come on to Marcus and she felt a huge pang of jealousy. Marcus asked the girls if they would like a drink. They all said yes, and raised he's head towards Phillip who raised his glass, so Marcus could see he needed a new drink, Marcus gave the bar tender his order, he took Christine and Kirk's drink over to them. They looked like they were getting on, pretty well. Marcus noticed that the more Jessie drank alcohol the less power that came out of her, it was to his relief, this was his chance to find out if it was her or the power that wanted him. He gave her a big smile and walked back to the bar. One of Jessie's friends Stella, boldly asked him in front of Jessie if he would like to take her to the prom, as her date, as she did not have one, if not would he meet her for a drink.

Marcus eyed Jessie who was looking furious. I am sorry, but I hope to take another lady, tears welled up in Jessie eye's, she said she was going to the ladies, Stella asked Penny, Is she ok or is it the fact she is going with her brother to the prom, her ex-boyfriend said she was a frigid cow because she would not let him sleep with her? then said to Marcus, you're a bit up market to be hanging around with her. Well you're her friend and you hang around with her, what does that say about you. Phillip came over to claim his pint of larger, well said Marcus. Jessie came out of the loo and stood behind Marcus. What went well Jessie asked, giving her two friends and evil look? Marcus was just telling your friends, that he was escorting you to the prom and I was just hitching a lift, with the two of you. I mean after all, Marcus paid for a very expensive designer dress today, I am sure that he would like to see you in it.

Marcus said, I was just telling the girls, I am already

spoken for, as I was going to ask you Jessie, if you would do me the honor, of letting me take you to your prom. Yes, she said putting her arm around Marcus's waist, he let her do that, she beamed a big bright smile at the girls. I am going to sit with Aunty Chris, said Phillip and left the bar. Marcus passed the girls their drinks and as he bent forward to do it, Jessie took her chance and hoped Marcus would go along with it, as he had done so already, she slid around the front of him, now trapped between him and the bar, with her back to the girls, she curled her arms around his neck and pulled his head down and kissed him. God, he smelt great, tasted even better and kissed like a god, what was wrong with her, she never did this, she was not drunk, she was enjoying the moment.

Christine looked up to Phillip, what is your sister playing at? Nothing, Marcus is going along with my plan, as her so-called friend are total bitches. Poor bloke deserves a big drink, he was sticking up very politely for her, But I think she's pushing her luck now. Look at those bitch's face's, their gob smacked and it looks like their catching fly's, good for Marcus, he is a standup guy.

Marcus had seen the hurt in Jessie face and the that tears welled up in her eyes, when she went to the loo and her so called friends did not deserve her loyalty. Phillip had given him his chance, he felt Jessie touch, when she slid her possessive arm around him, what man would not feel honored, but Jessie has slid in front of him and pressed herself in to his body, she was kissing him possessively, he slid his strong arm around her and lifted her, to him, welcoming her. Her body felt light and hot and she was driving him crazy. He tried to slow the kiss, she slid her hand down his chest, if she went any further everyone in the pub would see just how much he wanted her.
So, he put her down. Stella said, um we are here, Marcus

leaned back, I am sorry please forgive me, I am taking up your time, not looking at Jessie's face, he whispered into her ear, I will wait with your Aunt and brother, then smiled at the girls, kissed Jessie on the cheek, while looking at the girls and returned to the table.

Phillip said, put it there my friend, stood up and they bumped knuckles, thanks for taking Jessie's side, I am sorry I dropped you in it but those girls are total bitches. Could you take her to the prom Friday or she's goanna look pretty stupid if you don't and she will never hear the end of it?

Well done, you shut them up, exclaimed Kirk. Marcus looked at Christine she looked at him and said, she's an adult now, she can choose for herself. Jessie's could not look at Marcus, he tasted as good as he looked and she must have looked flustered. Boy she wanted more. When everyone was ready to leave, they all got back in the car and Paul drove them all back.

At home Phillip announced that he was going to bed, see you all in the morning. Kirk asked if anyone would like a cup of tea? Yes, I would love one thank you, replied Christine. They both went into the kitchen. That left Paul outside in the car and Jessie and Marcus in the hallway.

Marcus said, we need to talk Jessie; yes, she hung her head. Marcus closed the living room door, pleases don't look like that, she didn't look at him, if you would like me to take you to your dance, then I would be very honored to do that, if that is what you want. I just assumed that such a beautiful lady would have a mate or boyfriend, I am 33 so I thought my age might be an issue.

Jessie please speak to me, tell me I am not what you want,

if you're going to kiss men like that, then you need to be mature enough, to be talking about it, because I don't want any miss understanding, you must know what you're doing, tell me what you want, after that kiss, he smiled, it's all of you I want, not just for kissing, I mean sexually.

Jessie looked up at him her face was flushed red, full of embarrassment, I do want more of you, but I don't know what to do. He already knew she was an innocent, but he needed her to tell him.
I have never been with a man, I have never let anyone touch me, it never felt right, till now. I want you sexually to, all of you, but just for me and no one else. Marcus said the same applies to you, there can only be me, you are mine now. Yes, she said stepping into his embrace.

He put his arms around her and slid his arm to her neck and pull her head back gently, then kissed her, she kissed him back, his other hand slid down her back and he slowly and gently gripped her bum, she made a little whimper noise, which made him kiss her harder, he drew back, she was driving him crazy, I think that's enough for one evening ,he released her slowly, goodnight she said, her face was flushed and she left the room, calling out goodnight aunty Christine. Christine called back good night love.

Marcus went to the kitchen in search of a cup of coffee, Christine got up, I am going to turn in for the night, thank you for keeping us all safe and thank you for all the stuff you brought, and a lovely evening, goodnight, she left the kitchen. You two look like you're getting close. Kirk smiled, yes, we are but we are not the only ones, are we? No, me and Jessie have reached an understanding, tonight when we got back from the pub, she has agreed to be mine. Well, I thought the two of you had a very good understand, of stamping ownership on each other in the pub. Marcus looked at Kirk, I found that when she drink's, it reduces her influence on me greatly.

Chapter Two
New beginnings

When the two men had finished their drinks, locked up, checked the house and switched all of the lights off it was 12.20am. They both went into the sitting room and sat down in the dark waiting. Marcus was sat with his sword on his lap and a knife strapped to his leg, Kirk was sat with a machete and a smaller knife. Be calm brother be at peace. Yes, Marcus said, the bonding process has started with in me, and well you can feel how it is, sorry I just keep thinking about what our two uninvited guests said yesterday and the urge to rip them apart, well's up inside me. Once the bonding process is complete it will burden you less brother.

At 2.53am, Marcus's phone vibrated. It was Paul, outside in the car, The Red Honda car is back and there are three men inside, they have parked two spaces back from where they were yesterday, one man is with the car and two are coming your way. Paul's team is about, they are hidden well. Stay where you are. Marcus closed his phone, let 's shows our unwelcome guest's some good manners. Be ready brother, there are two and one in the car.

Kirk unlocked the back door and took up the same position as he did the other night, Marcus took up his and waited, the two men stopped the other side of the wall, saying we will have to carry her out of the front door, did you bring the syringe, yep ready to go. The two men then, started to climb over the wall, jumped down to the other side, the first man over, took one step forward and Kirk brought his machete down and chopped his head off, in one swoop. Marcus threw his knife and killed the second. Marcus pulled out his phone and called Paul, secure the one in the car, I want him alive, take him and the car to Victor. I want him questioned. There are two bodies in the back garden, one of them has a syringe in one of his pockets, find out what's in it and I want the cleanup done tonight. Marcus closed his phone and Kirk retrieved Marcus's knife from one of the body's and wiped the blood in the body's clothing. It's a good clean accurate throw in the dark and very fast, you still have it Kirk said. They went back into the house and locked the door. Kirk took his shirt off and wrapped it in a plastic bag, he took a tea towel and wiped the blood from his body, then put the tea towel in the bag.

Marcus checked himself for any blood, you're messy with a knife! Marcus's phone vibrated, it was Paul from the car; they have secured the third man and there bringing the van around to the path now. Ok good, stay put and closed his phone. Kirk had gone to put a t shirt on, after they then had a cup of tea and made up their beds, on the living room sofas, knowing that Paul's team were outside.

Marcus was woken by his sense, that Jessie was near, he could feel her power, he did not move as he could feel she was standing, looking over him. He did not want to startle her, she was looking at his body, taking him in, and she was inquisitive. He was laid stretched out on his back with his black designer boxer shorts on and his sleeping bag was pushed down, to the top of his hips. His hand went under the back of his head, he just laid there trying not to move or laugh. When the heat started to stir, he said is there something crawling across me or are you checking me out, he opened his eyes, I suppose it's only fair after your little parade with that black silk gown yesterday.

She stepped back, as he moved slowly to push himself up

into a sitting position, so his sleeping bag was now past his knees, he was trying not to grin, she turned away to be modest, her face was bright red. He asked, what can I can do for you, on this lovely morning Jessie? Kirk asked me to wake you up. Before she could say another word, he was up off the sofa and had hold of Jessie, he pushed her behind him looking for danger. Then Jessie saw her chance to get her own back, nice butt, but breakfast is ready and she slapped his butt. He spun around, I have better assets, if you wish to see the them, he grabbed the top of his boxer shorts and she ran from the room. Two minutes later, everyone was sat at the kitchen table, this is very nice of you Christine thank you, can I use your shower after breakfast, asked Marcus? Don't, thank me, Kirk made breakfast, the tea and the table was already laid and he used the shower. Christine just smiled at Marcus. She sipped her tea. Phillip burst out laughing and slapped Kirk's back. Marcus just held his hands up, and bit his toast.

After breakfast, while Marcus was in the shower, the front door bell rang. Kirk answered the door it was Simon, I am here at Marcus's request to bond with Phillip and Phillip asked me to come today. Peace brother and he stood back to let Simon enter. They went into the kitchen, the Bagbie's were all sat round the table, trying to decide what they were all going to do for the day. By the time Marcus had come down, looking dazzling all the family were laughing together. Marcus stopped when he saw Simon, sitting right next to Jessie, sipping tea, with his arm around the back of Jessie's chair. For a second it looked like Simon was trying to use his calming and bonding on Jessie because he was so close to her.

Kirk stood and nodded at Marcus; we were just trying to

plan our day. Well how about we take the lovely ladies to London, do a little sightseeing, a light lunch somewhere and then we could take in a show, or evening meal and if it gets late, we could stay, at my family's house in London. Or we could come back after lunch. Your welcome to come Phillip, but I thought as you got on so well with Simon, he might take you to the brotherhood of the knight's hall and show you our museum.

It's a very big place, it has a private apartment, it's like a mini palace, and he could tell you a bit about our history and about the brotherhood, then perhaps a movie and pizza or drink, how does that sound? Maybe if we stay in London then Simon could fix you a deluxe suite in one of our apartments, for tonight, that way your Aunt and Sister would not worry, as one of my men will be with you, at all times. That would be great to see what dad did, and to know more about what you do, I will grab my jacket and overnight bag.

Jessie and Christine went up to change, to go to London and get their overnight bag's, leaving the three men in the kitchen. Marcus moved so quick, he grabbed Simon, pulling him out of the chair and pushed him face first up against the wall and had a knife to his throat. Kirk did not move. You maybe my second, until I am fully bonded, but that's all you are, know your place. You stay away from Jessie, she is mine. There will not be a next time because I will skin you alive. Be at peace brother, I am following X orders he still wants me to bond with her, just in case you are not her mate. Marcus released him just as quick as he grabbed him. Kirk took one step towards Simon, you are old enough to know better, I have seen Jessie make her choice and she and Marcus are bonding, she is his mate.

Marcus will be very protective until the process is

complete, so I would advise to keep your distance, as he is not himself, he has feelings and feelings affect us, as you have found out first hand. Be at peace brother, Simon said? Kirk took a step towards Simon, who knew he was in over his head, if anything should happen to Phillip while in your care, there is no place on this earth, that I would not find you and even X could not protect you from me. Because we are brothers together, we fight for each other, not for one-person's greed. Be at peace brother, because you're doing a very good job of bonding with Phillip. I will call later for an update, who is watching the house while we are a way? Joshua's team, good Kirk said.

It took just under two hours to get to the middle of London. Marcus took them all into Buckwell's a large department store, where they split off in to pairs. Kirk took Christine and Marcus took Jessie. After an hour they all met back up and Christine was telling Jessie what Kirk had brought her, while the men were talking. Christine looked so happy, like she was in love; Kirk had brought her a pair of pear earrings and some perfume. Marcus had brought Jessie some very expensive perfume and a long lace white evening dress, that stretched all over her body like a skin tight glove, when you put it on, but you could not, wear any under wear with it, well that's what the ladies in the dressing room said, when Jessie tried it on. Marcus also brought her a sliver hair clip and matching sliver hair slide, and a pair of silver high heeled sandals, when they had finished talking, he said lady's we will go to my family home in Kensington, rooms have been arranged for us there, as well as lunch and then tonight we are having dinner at the famous London restaurant the great White Moon , we also have use of the royal box, at the royal theatre tonight. So, shall we go? They were led back to there waiting car.

The big black gate's, said, the Dewdney Estate. As they drove passed them, up the drive to the biggest house Jessie had ever seen, a house that looked like a mini Buckingham palace, a butler opened the house door, then came over and opened the car door, Master Marcus, it's good to have you home, I have followed all of your instruction's sir, they all went into the house, where there was another butler. Who said, to Christine, may I show you to your room madam and lunch is in 45 minutes madam? Kirk and Christine went off with him. Jessie and Marcus followed the first butler, who was called William, carrying Jessie's bags. He led them to, what must have been the penthouse rooms as there was a balcony that seemed to go on forever, you could see the whole of London, as one wall was made completely of glass, There was a living room and the biggest bedroom, Jessie had ever seen, it had the biggest bed she had ever seen and a small leather sofa, a dressing room off each side of the bed and a massive bathroom joined, both dressing rooms at the end. While she was having a look around the butler left.

Marcus was stood by the foot of the bed, come here Jessie he said, in a very masculine voice. Marcus and been very close to Jessie, the heat had built up in him, to a point, he needed release, he was wound up so tight from need; it was killing him, he was losing his grip. Jessie smiled up at him, he smelled great as always, his aftershave seemed to drug her, his eye's looked like they were on fire, he just put his arms around her and kissed her slow and hard, he slid her coat off, then ran his hands down her back and squeezed her bum, he ran his hands back up to her hair and pulled her head back and kissed her neck, then stopped, he was breathing heavy, he took a step back and undid his suit jacket and slid it off, dropping it to the floor, she took a step closer to him, sliding her hand up his shirt,
then she unbuttoning each button, one at a time, her hand

started to shake, it felt like her hands would not work, so she leaned forward and kissed, each place on his chest, where the buttons had been by the time, she had undone his last button, his breathing was so heavy, he was panting. Jessie started un- tucking the bottom of his shirt, it seemed like he was struggling to breathe now. As she looked up to see his face, she licked her lips, which were dry from all that kissing and her tongue touched his skin, just above his belt.

He pulled her arms, kissed her, fast, he then made a sound that came from down, within his chest and ripped her blouse in two with his hands and discarded it on the floor, he then ran his hands over her bra, rubbing the pads of his thumbs, over the place where her nipples were pushing the lace, she let out a whimper that she had never heard before, he growled in response. Jessie was hot and light headed, a pulse between them, building up getting faster and faster, he pulled one of her bra straps down, kissing her shoulder, he did the same to the other side, pulling her bra down, exposing both of her breasts, she did not know what to do, no one had ever seen her, or touched her like this, he slowed his kisses and just looked at her. Jessie, you're so beautiful, he then ran his hands over her breasts, circled her nipples with his thumb pad's, bent his head and licked her nipple, she threw her head back, he sucked it gently and all she could do was gasp out his name, the pulse within her had now built up so fast, it was thudding inside of her.

Her thong felt wet and Jessie was now the one breathing heavy. Marcus picked Jessie up and laid her on the bed; she was calling his name again and closed her eyes. He laid on top of her, but taking his own weight, this forced her skirt to rise exposing the tops of her stocking 's and both of his legs were between hers, so her legs were spread apart. Marcus said, don't close your eyes, look at me Jessie, I want to see you. He slid his hand up her stocking and up under her skirt, he bent his head and slowly licked her nipples, she started to make a whimpering sound, he looked at her face and then he touched her wet thong, gently sliding his thumb under it touching her hot, wet silk nub. She came instantly, she was bucking under him, Jessie was grabbing and scratching his back, calling his name, he kissed her hard, she was still bucking under him. He kissed her until she stopped bucking under him, then she was just gasping for breath. She felt so embarrass, she had never felt anything like that ever and he knew it. He rolled off her, he was gasping, he was struggling just as much as she was, that was good to know.

Marcus could not believe what he had just done and he could not believe how she had responded to him; she was so fucking hot, never in all of his life had he ever had a woman responded to him in that way. A few more seconds and he would have taken her. He never meant for it to go that far, he was laid on his back and he was harder than Hell.

Jessie looked at Marcus. She looked so beautiful; she was staring at him. She slid over the bed and straddled him, sitting on his stomach. Jessie my arms are trapped by my shirt, under my back honey, and I can't touch you like this. Jessie just smiled at him. if she decided to take him, then he could do nothing about it, this was not how he had planned things. Jessie leaned down to kiss him gently, her nipples grazed his chest softly and then she moved down his body, kissing him, he was trapped and couldn't do anything, she licked his skin just above his belt again and he bucked against her. She slid down and sat on his knees, undone his belt, then slid off the end on the bed and pulled his trousers and boxers down, she pushed his legs apart,
   she was taken back by the sheer size of him and his beauty.

She thought to herself, that was never going to fit anywhere.

Marcus tried to sit up, to loosen his shirt but wished he had not, as Jessie crawled up his body and was pushing his shoulders back down and was kissing his chest, then she went to sit up and straddle him again but, she slid back down Marcus's body until his hot think very hard shaft touched her wet thong, where Marcus had slid his thumb. Jessie stopped and looked unsure of what she was doing, and then she rubbed herself against him, making a very wanting sound, she was so wet. Marcus could not fight her, he just bucked under her and groaned out aloud, calling her name. His breathing was so fast. She liked that and the effect it was having on him, she did it again slower and he begin to shake. Marcus whispered to Jessie; I can't hold on honey.

She then moved, she slid herself down the bed and keeled on the floor, wrapped her hand gentle around the bottom of his shaft and looked at Marcus while she licked the top gently, and then, plunged her mouth over the end and sucked, taking him in her mouth deeper and he began to buck against her. It felt like a hot salty tomato bursting in to her mouth, the only thing she could do was swallow it. Unsure what to do with it she sucked gently again, she felt Marcus slump back down on the bed as he was trying to sit up. She then stopped and wiped the back of her hand across her mouth to make sure there was nothing on her lip. She then stood up and walked to the bathroom to clean up a bit.

Jessie looked at herself in the mirror and could not believe what she had just done. She felt very brazen. She washed herself and brushed her teeth, she slid the bath robe on. When she came back, a few minutes later, his shirt was on the floor in bits and he put his trousers back on and was laid on the bed. She walked slowly to the bed, he grabbed her, come here you little minks. He rolled her over so she was on her side and he was laid behind her, he grabbed the end of the bed cover and covered them both, cuddling her from behind, she fell asleep very quickly.

Marcus felt at total peace with himself. He didn't sleep, he just laid next to her stroking her hair and listen to her breathing. The telephone by the bed was flashing. He looked at his watch, it had been over an hour since they had entered the room, he lifted the cover and slid off the bed and covered Jessie, he would let her sleep. He walked into the other room and picked up the silently flashing phone.
Yes, William he said, Sir would you like to have lunch severed in your room, as master Kirk and his guest are having lunch in their room's sir. Are they now! Yes, Sir. Also, sir there is a messenger here from you grandfather, he is waiting to see you, he has something for you, he was ordered to give it to you only. he is waiting in the lobby sir. Right William please tell Kirk and Christine, that we will be ready to go the great White Moon at 7pm, followed by the theatre and don't bring lunch up to my room, Jessie is not to be disturbed, we will call if we need anything and I will be right down to see the Messenger. Very well sir, Marcus put the phone down and went down to his visitor.

His visitor was a man called Royce, he had been with Xander a very long time and a member of the brotherhood. Marcus reached out to hug the man, but Royce stood back and tilted his head and looked at Marcus in shock, so it is true then, I can sense a change in you, brother, tell me I am not too late. No. Royce produced a wooden box and gave it to Marcus, he opened it slowly there was a metal case inside, a smaller one, he gave Royce the box, so he could open the metal one. Marcus just looked at the pair of rings in wonder. Royce said, please my I look, I have never seen it, I have long thought it a myth. Marcus picked up the bloodiest, reddest Ruby on a solid gold ring. This is the Blood of Jerusalem and it's just over three thousand years old, it was taken from the dead body of the last Guardian, buy her husband and placed in a box after his killing spree, Yes Royce said.

There is more to the story, the Guardian of the light is the door way back to heaven, it is always female, she was said to have been so pure that when she had found and chosen her mate, they were bound by blood, a cut to the finger and words exchanged and that was it they were married. He did want to take his wife, he loved her so much, he could not hurt her in any way. He just wanted to look upon his beauty. But the first was so jealous, of her beauty and the fact that, once an immortal had taken her the doorway would open and the power would release, she would take his light and he would be back in heaven. So, the first ordered him to take her as a test, to make sure it was her, they waited, because she would draw a spark of light from her chosen mate and if he would not, then he would order a second immortal to take her. But he wanted proof of this, that the deed had been done, which is how funny enough a best man came about for today's weddings, but that's another story. Anyway, the second, would have to take her in front of him and the other as proof, then they could return to our father. So, her husband prayed to our father, in the dust on the floor, asking for a sign, his advice, he thought that he would not be forgiven and that his sole would be marked, to take something so pure just the thought of it made him weak, he cried while he prayed.

He cried three tiers of blood that dripped from his face and landed in the dust, as he put his hand down to touch where the blood had landed, the earth moved, he picked up a hand full of dust to scoop up the tears and the blood turned into a big ruby, he held it and was amazed, that was the sign, for the father, as proof for everyone to see. He forged a gold ring and mounted the stone on it as a gift to his wife, in exchange for him taking her virginity. But as he did so, three chips came off the ruby and he made another ring for him, as proof of his tears. So, the husband went home and gave her the ring and took her virginity, he prayed to god for forgiveness, for taking something so sacred and heavenly away from her body. The next day he told the first what had happened and showed him his ring, as proof that he taken his wife and she now had a ring as proof, not only proof but a sign from the father.

Very well the first said, bring her tonight and we will bring forth the light. But while the husband was at the temple, the first had sent the second, to kidnap the wife and bring her to the temple. So, the first sent the husband home and the others chained the wife up in the temple, they were all taken by her power, it drew them to her, but her power did not affect her husband because he was a guardian as well. They all raped her to death, they could not stop themselves, they did not realize that the second male Guardian had to be there to protect her and them from the power within.

When he found out the wife was not at home, he knew the

first had kidnapped her, so he went back to the temple and saw them taking her dead body, all of them naked, her blood everywhere, he went crazy and brought forth his own power and killed the all men, but did not stop there he killer all the men, for miles in range, until a messenger from father came, the massager took him back to his wife's body, he cleaned her body and took their rings off and told him, that this was not fathers wish, it was the firsts doing and the husband placed the ring in a box and gave them to a boy who live at the temple. Xander said Royce, yes, but there's more.

The messenger told Xander that now the female Guardian was dead the father was sad and unhappy and for this, all the immortals would pay the price for her death and learn their lesson, now the dark sun had set, because of the death of the guardian had brought darkness, as she brought light to them, when she lived, they would now be in the dark, they would not see fathers light, to take them back to him and only when the dark sun could rise again would he allow them to go back to him in heaven and see his light once more, the massager took her body, so no one could look upon her and the messenger, took the husband, willingly back to the light in heaven. Father has punished the immortals by not sending another guardian until now. And now I give it to my wife as she is the Guardian. Then Marcus put the ring back and produced a matching man's ring, a thick solid gold band with three smaller stones the same color, and this is the second ring. It is called the tears of Jerusalem. I have never heard the full story before but that ring is legend to us and I never knew of the second rings existence before today, Royce said.

As far as I know the story of this ring has only been told to six people ever, so please remember your place here today, your name is now historic Royce, one for seeing it and two delivering it. Royce bowed at Marcus then he hugged him and said, thank you brother, please take the wooden box back to Xander, for safe keeping. Royce nodded then left. Jessie had woken up, Marcus was not there, so she got up and walked into the living room with the glass wall, she opened the door and took some breaths of fresh air, it cleared her head, she left the window open and walked back into the bathroom and looked at the glass shower room and thought yes. She slipped off her dressing gown and looked at all the soap and shampoo's, she didn't know what to use first, she felt like a child in a sweet shop.

Marcus made his way back to his room, when he entered the room, it felt cold and the door was open, he looked outside, Jessie was not out there so he closed the door, he could not hear anything so he walked into the bedroom to find the bed looking a mess and no Jessie, his heart jumped at about a hundred beats a second and fear rake over him, he ran to the bathroom and Jessie was in the shower.

The room was filled with steam he could see her and she looked like a water nymph with bubbles in her hair and bubbles dripping down her back and water spraying all over her, he stepped back and had to hold on the vanity unity, he was mesmerized and he was rock hard again, she turned around unaware he was stood there watching her, he was taking in all of her body and beauty, the bubbles had dripped down her front spilling over her breasts, they slid down like a waterfall between her legs and down her legs . She turned around again.

He was still stood there, he wanted to strip off and join her, but there would be no doubt that he would take her over and over, he closed his eyes and walked back in the bedroom and closed the door behind him, he had to, it hurt him to leave her there.

After an hour Jessie had washed every inch of her and had dried her hair, put it up with her sliver clips and slide, they really shone in her dark hair. She had applied her make up, just eye liner, mascara, lip gloss and her new perfume. She then put her robe back on, she was not ready to put her dress on, just yet. She went in search of Mucus. He must have showered in another room because he too, was in a dressing gown, sat at the table with a bucket of Campaign and some food. What's all this? Jessie, he stood, I wanted to wait till later, but I can't it seems, control myself around you, so I want to do this now because tonight I am going to take you Jessie, with no interruptions and nothing between us and in every way. There was a thudding between her legs again. But I am an honorable man, you say you want me and only me well, you showed me that you want me today, and I want only you. Then Marcus got down on one knee and said, will you honor me and be my wife. If you consent to me now, we must share a blood bond. Then in my world we are married, we will have a wedding ceremony later on or whenever you wish, but from this time on, from the moment we exchanged our blood and rings, you are mine, always and forever and if you're not sure or you don't want this or you don't want me, then tell me now.

Jessie launched herself at Marcus, pushing him on floor straddling him again. Twice in one day, he was stuck. She stopped kissing him and screamed, yes. He had to lift her off him, very quickly, as like her had no clothing on under his dressing gown. They both stood and Marcus untied her dressing gown, slid it to the floor, he took her all in, for a second, she was shaking, then untied his dressing gown and let it slide to the floor, Jessie looked at him, he was a well-built specimen of a man. She had seen her friend's mags with naked men in but never any with a body like that. He then turned picked up the two rings, picked up her hand from her side and said, I am yours and pushed the ring on her, it fitted perfectly.

For eternity, my body is yours, I will fight for your life and honor you with my body, he then kissed the ring Jessie took the other ring from Marcus and she repeated his words. Then kissed his ring. Marcus picked a small gold knife, up, it had a diamond on the hilt of it. He held Jessie's hand up and drew the knife across the top of the same finger he had put the ring on, blood ran down her hand finger and across her ring, Marcus cut his ring finger and waited for the blood to drip down his finger and across his ring, he touched his cut finger to her and held them together with his other hand until the blood dripped as one.

He then let go of her fingers and turned and poured a glass of Champaign out, and handed her a glass to toast, after their toast to each other he retrieved their dressing gown's and helped Jessie on with hers, then put his on and with blood still on their hands he kissed her deep and hard and said, we are man and wife; we now are married and share that bond and now share a blood bond, tonight we will share a physical one. Would you like some food my wife, no thank you Husband and she smiled, I would love more Champaign?
Yes, my wife, but not too much, I want you to know what you're doing tonight. After a cuddle Jessie went to wash up

again, got dressed and put some more perfume on, just in case she did not have enough on already. She put her hi heeled shoes on and slid her halter neck dress that fitted like a skin tight glove on, the lace stretched over her slim hips and went all the way down to her ankles. She had no under ware on, just her shoes and dress, the dress also had a slit each side of her legs, she turned around to have a look, the dress was backless and hugged her skin, her bum and showed little bits of her legs when she walked, one long thin peace of her dark hair had come down, but it clung to her body, it snaked down her neck and between her shoulders and finished where her bra would have been, it looked amazing, so she left it there . She kept looking at her ring it was a very big ruby, it was beautiful and she was married, wow and tonight she would be a woman. She walked out of her dressing room and Marcus stopped dead and looked at her, his mouth had dropped open and his eyes nearly popped out of his head.

He was speechless. Jessie touched her neck she felt awkward and bit her lip, don't you like it, it's the dress you brought me today, I can change. He shook his head; she looked like a vision, pure beauty and innocents. You're so beautiful, I only stare out of amazement, I will be fighting men off tonight, my wife. She beamed a big smile and his heart melted. May I say you look like a god, my husband and I will be fighting woman off you too, you look like a male model when you wear a black suite with a with shirt it drives me crazy and that aftershave, it just makes me want you so much, she blushed a pink flush across her face. I have a wedding gift for you. He gave her a box with a ruby necklace and matching earrings. I am sorry, I don't have anything to give you she said.

He whispered into her ear as he put her necklace on, oh yes you do and its nothing you can buy with money and you can only give it once, you're giving it to me tonight remember and that dress just makes me want to take you now, he growled into Jessie ear. Jessie just walked over and leaned over the table to get her purse, Marcus had to stop himself from ripping that dress off her, he was never going to make it down the stairs. He grabbed her shawl and placed it around her shoulders and ushered her down the stairs and into the lobby, where Kirk and Christine where both looking very elegant.

Christine spoke first, oh my Jessie, you look so beautiful and then spotted the ring on Jessie's finger and your engaged, wow that was quick, yes we are Marcus said, sorry I had to do it, he held Jessie's hand, we would like to ask your permission, for us to marry, when Jessie is ready. Is this want you want Jessie because marriage is a big step and it's for life. Yes, it is. Then I give you both my blessing, I just wish your brother was here. Christine went forward and kissed Jessie and Marcus. Kirk looked at the ring and looked at Marcus and knew the truth, well done you two congratulations to you both, he shook Marcus's hand and kissed Jessie on the cheek. William who was stood at the door waiting to open it said, may I congratulate the happy couple sir, yes you may and thank you. With that they all went outside; William opened the door for everyone to get in the car.

In no time they were at the Great White Moon and a door man opened the door and escorted them in, then someone escorted them to their table on upper level, where everyone looked at them and at Jessie, when she took her shawl off every set of male eyes were on her and even three Arabian gentlemen sat at the next table stood up and nodded at Jessie and waited until she was seated before they sat back down themselves. Marcus eyed the gentlemen carefully, then he took his own seat next to Jessie. There waiter came over and asked what they would like to drink, Marcus said a bottle of your finest. They all ordered their food and their champagne arrived, Jessie remembered what Marcus had said about drink tonight, so she sipped hers slowly. While waiting for the deserts to come, Kirk over heard the Arabs speaking to each other, they were looking at Jessie, they were disrespecting her saying she was a jewel and how much they would pay to possess her. Kirk stood up and stepped over to the Arab's tables, my friends wife is not for sale at any price and if this was not their wedding day and my family was sat not two feet from me I would draw my sword and kill all of you dogs, you are from my home land and you dishonor me and my family, and if you wish to test me then I am ready . The Arabs looked at each other and apologized, nodded their heads in respected, then left very quickly.

Kirk returned to his seat and nodded to Marcus, Christine said if you excuse me, I need the powder room and Kirk and Marcus stood like gentlemen to excuse her, Jessie said wait up Auntie Chris, I need the powder room to. As the ladies walked towards the powder room nearly all the men in the room had their eyes on Jessie, Marcus could not take his eyes from her, the way her hips swayed and the lace moved with it, her bare back and that bum. He was getting hard just watching her. Kirk said, do you not want to sit brother? what oh yes sure. Kirk let out a little laugh. It's been a very long time since I have seen the blood of Jerusalem and its mate the tears of Jerusalem, it suits you both and you look very proud and happy. Your feelings will settle soon. And if I may say, she has chosen well she is very taken with you. Marcus was still looking at the powder room, yes, thank you brother and when did you get to see the rings Kirk?

I recovered them for Xander after they were stolen, about two thousand years ago. Are you bonding with Christine because you seem very relaxed in her company brother and very at home, with her? Yes, she has a calming effect on me and I have not had female comfort and calming in many years, sometimes it just like being human.

Jessie and Christine came out of the powder room admiring Jessie's ring when out of nowhere a young man in his late twenties, who looked like a playboy, stepped in front of Jessie and invited her back to his table. Marcus could see Jessie shake her head in refusal and tried to step around the man, when he moved again to block her, Marcus was out of his chair and stood behind the man in seconds he could see Christine was trapped behind Jessie and Jessie was holding her Aunts hand for reassurance, as the man was not taking no for an answer, Jessie looked at Marcus, she looked frightened and unsure, Christine was telling the man to leave them alone. Marcus said to the man, you are frightening my wife and my mother in law. The man turned around to see Marcus who looked like a huge mountain of muscle stood next to the play boy. Marcus, had now pushed the man against the wall with one arm, Jessie ran in to Marcus's other arm. Kirk then stepped forward and stood squashing the man against the wall, while he held his hand out to Christine and said, are you ok darling? He gave the man a good hard elbow in the ribs and Marcus let go of him, the man fell to the floor where Kirk left him.

They all returned to the table, let's all have another drink as we are celebrating, said Marcus. Then the band started to play love songs, would you like dance Jessie, she looked at Marcus and smiled, yes, but I am not very good. He took her hand and led her to the dance floor, there were a few couples already there when they took the floor.

Marcus held her to him and they moved together as one, Jessie unbuttoned Marcus's jacket so she could be closer and feel his warmth, smelled him and felt his muscles move when they danced. Jessie looked up at Marcus, he kissed her possessively he held her so close and tightly, while his other arm hand held her neck, her hips moving against his. Then a man said to Marcus may I have the honor of dancing with your lady sir. Marcus stopped kissing Jessie and Jessie tried to pull Marcus closer. No, my wife does not want to dance with you so find your own woman.

Marcus put his head on top of Jessie as she was still hugging him. And he kissed the top of her head. After a few minutes of dancing Kirk and Christine join them on the floor and where dancing, when Kirk stopped next to Marcus, would you mind if I dance with you lovely lady kind sir? Marcus could feel Jessie's smile against his shirt, she lifted her head from his jacket, exchange is no robbery, if you would let me dance with you lovely lady. Marcus surrender Jessie to Kirk saying, no one else gets a turn with her, in a deep voice. Kirk smiled and kissed the back of Jessie's hand, men to day don't know how to treat women and he took her in his arms and moved quickly around the dance floor. Kirk was twirling her round and she was laughing like a little girl. He has a lot of energy for an older man, observed Marcus, Christine burst out laughing at Marcus's jealousy. He could give you a run for your money. It was Marcus's turn to laugh. and spun Christine around. By the time they made their way back to the table, everyone was full of laughter, they tried to outdo each other on the dance floor and time had gotten away from them, it was nearly eleven o clock and they had missed the theatre, but they didn't care.

They finished their drinks and made their way back to the waiting car, that took them back to the Dewdney house.

They said good night in the lobby and Jessie gave Christine a big hug, love you mum. Christine's heart melted and tears welled up in her eyes, Jessie gave Kirk a hug, thank you for a lovely evening and kissed him on the check. I think if your sharing the kisses, then you missed someone, said Marcus. Oh yes, sorry or course and Jessie leaned over and kissed William the old butler on the cheek, everyone laughed and with that. Marcus picked Jessie up and carried her up to their bedroom and kicked the door shut behind them, he laid Jessie on the bed and kissed her gently on her mouth and turned around and sat on the leather sofa by the bed, Jessie sat up and looked at Marcus and smiled at him.

Come to me Jessie and walk slowly, Jessie did as he asked, she slid off the bed and walked to him slowly, her heart started to beat so fast, he slid his jacket off and handed it to her, she bent down slightly to take it, he asked her to put it on the little table by the bed, his eyes never leaving her body as she walked to the table. Jessie could feel him watching her so she put a little swing in her hips and slowed down, then bent slowly to place his jacket on the table, she could hear him growl from across the room, she walked back slowly and his eyes were full of fever, she stopped in front of him, and bent over again, took her hi heels off, she then stood in front of him, she wanted him. She was blushing.

He just watched her, he wanted to savor this moment and keep it forever, she was a girl, Untouched, a virgin and he was going to make her a woman, his woman he would take her virginity and show her how a real man makes love to a woman, he would teach her everything. She looked like desire, smelt like an angle and she was driving him crazy. She was his, he had waited all of his life for her and in a little while, she would never be the same, she would be his completely.

He was on his feet and kissing her with need and desire, heat shot through his body.
Jessie ran her hands down the front of his shirt; she looked up at him, her eyes shining and full of excitement and uncertainty. She was so beautiful, she started to unbutton his shirt. He was not getting caught twice. She kissed his chest and licked his nipples and undid all of his buttons, he then took his shirt off and threw it on the floor. He unclipped Jessie's dress and peeled it off her and let it drop to the floor, he stood back and looked at her naked body and undid his belt and took some condom's out of his pocket, took of his trousers and under ware and stood before Jessie, pure male and fully hard. Jessie looked at the condoms, I want you, all of you, I want to feel everything with nothing between us, I don't want to feel rubber on my first time, and I want all of you inside me.

I want to know what that feels like. You could conceive a child, if you're not on the pill, no I am not and if we are married then, there's no problem, unless you don't want children Marcus. He had a vision in his head, off her asleep naked on his bed and of her belly full with his child and her breasts full of milk, he liked it very much. He dropped the condoms and picked her up, pulled the cover back and placed her on the bed and got in next to her and covered them both. They both turned on their sides, to face each other. They kissed each other and Marcus pulled her on top of him, she straddled him, he let her have her way until she grasped him with her hand and he bucked.

In one quick movement, she was underneath and he was on top of her, he kissed her hard, she made a sound of need, his breathing was deep and hard, he dipped his head and licked and sucked her nipples, one at a time, he kissed his way down her body until his tongue found her wet hot bud between her leg, he groaned and licked her slowly, she was shaking he tasted her with his tongue, licking every inch between her legs, she began to thrashing about calling out breathlessly, Marcus please, she was pulling his hair.

He stopped he wanted her, like no other woman and she wanted him. He laid her back against the pillow, open your eyes Jessie I want to see you, he then spread her legs apart and laid between them, he kissed her mouth, I love you Jessie and thrust forward quickly entering her for the first time, he did not want to linger and hurt her more, he could feel her heat within, then he felt her flesh rip around his shaft and stopped, she was so tight he had taken her virginity, he had to steady himself and take another breath, he thrust forward taking more of her, ripping her flesh inside her apart, to accommodate him. Jessie had screamed out, hot tears ran down her face and he withdrew from her, he felt her hot blood run down his shaft. Her innocents would stain his sole forever. And to see the pain as he took her body, that he could never forget.

He kissed Jessie gently, he was shaking himself, Jessie he said, please open your eyes and look at me. She did and he kissed her again, the worst is over, do you want me to stop, she was shaking. She could feel his rock-hard shaft and knew he wanted more, please she said quietly don't stop, it will hurt a little each time we make love, but it will be easier, I promise honey. He entered her again, slower this time, he was gasping, she was so tight he could feel her muscles tighten around him and her flesh rip again and he groaned out loud. Say my name Jessie honey, say your mine, as she did Marcus thrusts got quicker, he was pushing himself all the way into her, she was bucking and grabbing his back calling his name out in gasps of breath, he felt her red hot liquid sweep over his shaft, sparks of light shot out of her eyes and he lost it, he called out her name and filled her with his hot seed, he tried to keep his weight off her but could not, he slumped gasping for breath, kissing her, then eased himself slowly out of her and laid on his side facing her. When they could both breathe again, he said Jessie, are you ok honey, please look at me baby. Jessie opened her eyes and looked at Marcus and touched his face, her eyes full of wonder. He pulled her to him and kissed her again, turned her over and cuddled her close to him.

They fell asleep together. When Marcus woke he felt complete, he had never slept so soundly, he reached out for Jessie, she was not there, he pulled back the cover to get out of bed and there was blood on the sheets, he closed his eyes not only proof of her pure innocents, not that he needed that, her body had ripped to make room for him, shit he must have hurt her. He got out of bed and changed the sheet, he did not want Jessie seeing that, then he walked to the shower where once again, she was surrounded in bubbles and steam, but this time, when he went in, she turned around to face him. Its ok, let me wash you, she stepped back against the wall unsure of what he wanted, she smiled, don't worry Jessie, you will need a day or so to heal first, before we try that again. He looked at her again, what in the world are you washing yourself with, you smell like everything, she laughed, I tried every bottle. He laughed loudly and helped her wash the bubbles off, and she helped wash him, a bit too well. She was more than washing, she was touching him, she put her arms around his neck and kissed him, Jessie please honey.

I am trying, his breathing was heavy, he put his arms on the shower room wall behind her, trapping her, he just gazed at her with love and desire. So, she slid her arms down grasping him in her palm and pulled gently, he groaned out loud and rested his head on top of hers, she then slid down onto her knees and took him in her mouth and sucked, he loved that, his release was hot and fast and lots. When they were dry and dressed, they went down to the kitchen, it was ten o clock in the morning Kirk and Christine where in the garden. William made the breakfast and Marcus went into another room and came back with two pain killers and gave them to Jessie with a glass of water, which she took. We have lots to talk about and discuss, when we get home to you Aunts house Jess, like where we are going to live and there's things you're going to need to know, you will have a bodyguard not just because of the brother hood of the knight, but because your now a very wealthy woman, to my family fortune and most of all, because you're so beautiful, men will want you and what men can't have they tend to take.

By twelve o'clock they were home at Christine's. Phillip and Simon had just got back from their overnight stay at the Brother of the knight's visit. They all sat around the table with a cup of tea, while Marcus, Simon and Kirk went into the living room and closed the door. Marcus asked, for an update, Simon informed him that, Phillip is very interested in the brotherhood and wants to become one of us and take up his dad's old post, he is up to date on the book history of the brother hood but not the rest, I did not know how much you wanted me to tell him and Joshua's team are outside. Phillip and I have bonded, his is very calm round me, he is getting the hang of it, we watched movies and had a take away. We have had no unwelcome visitors and no one has come looking for the three men yet. They will, said Marcus, so be ready, now more than ever. Victor still has the one we caught, he is alive when he is done, he will report to X, what of your news Marcus. Jessie and I are married and are fully bonded, so I no longer need a second brother. As you wish I will take my leave, Simon said goodbye to everyone and went to congratulate Jessie, he lifted her hand to kiss it and asked, is that what I think it is? Yes, my ring has a name it's called, Simon finished her sentence "the blood of Jerusalem" Yes, and Marcus has a ring and it has a name to. Simon looked stunned; this time Marcus finished the sentence by saying it's called "the tears of Jerusalem" it was made from the same stone. Well you learn something new every day, I wish you both all my best and kissed Jessie's hand and slapped Phillip on the back, catch you later and left.

So, Phillip said, what is the score with you and Jessie then? Yesterday I asked your Aunts permission to marry Jessie and she said yes, of course with you being the man of the house and Jessie's brother I would like your permission to marry you sister. Well then, brother in law to be, you better put it there because it's a yes and Phillip walked around the kitchen table and shook Marcus's hand, slapped him on his back and kissed Jessie on the cheek. Christine cuddled Kirk, out of happiness, Phillip looked, but did not say anything to his Aunty but said to Kirk, since its going around, welcome to the family, he reached across the table and shook Kirks hand, please don't go out of the house together again will you. Why, asked Jessie, well you might come back married or something. Jessie went red and gave a little laugh, Phillip looked at Jessie's ring, wow is that real? Yes, it is Marcus said. Phillip whistled.

Marcus said, while we are all talking marriage and the value of things, everyone please sit. I need to discuss things now, while we are all together and it's a lot to take in, so please ask as many questions as you like. Firstly, Jessie and I are married according to my faith, we will marry publicly and as soon as possible, second, apart from me, Jessie is now the only other living heir to the Dewdney fortune and estates, some hundreds of millions if not more and when Xander passes on, it comes to us and if anything happened to me it all goes to Jessie and any children we may have. I don't have any previous wives or children. If anything should happen to us, Christine and Phillip, I leave it all to you, my solicitors will have this drawn up by the end of the week and we will sign the documents, Kirk is our witness he knows my wishes and thirdly, the newspapers will be all over this like a bad rash, I want to protect you all, it is my duty as I am bringing you all in to the light, so to speak. We have managed to keep most family things private, you will all have to have your own bodyguards purely to stop people abducting you and hurting you. Kirk are you happy with me giving Christine a female bodyguard? when you're not with me, you can have time to relax with Christine as I want you to continue with me old friend but I will release you if you wish.

No, I will never leave you. Then that's settled Jessie will have two bodyguards one male and one female. Phillip will also have a male bodyguard and you will have full use of any Dewdney estates, house's and castle's, transport or staff. Which brings me to the fact that this is your family home and I would never ask you to sell it? But for security reasons, you all cannot stay here, today we had a discussion about everything, I am going to buy you a family home and put it in Christine's name and staff if you wish and all bills will be paid by our estate. The other option is any brotherhood hall luxury apartments, you all are welcome to have one but it's your decision, you're a family, you should stay together but we always try and keep a low profile to a point, you will have a car and driver.
Above all we protect each other. You will have your chance to say goodbye to your friends from collage, they

cannot know anything, just that we are engaged. I know I'm asking a lot from you all, I am going to make a few calls in the other room so you can talk in private, but I need to plan either way, for whatever you all decide

Your security as my family, is now my priority. Phillip spoke first, you are our family now, so it's ok with me if you want to stay. Kirk stood to leave, Christine grabbed his hand, stay there a few things I need the kids to hear. Kirk nodded and sat back down. I still need to make my calls, so pleases start without me, Marcus stood up and kissed Jessie on the mouth and left the room.

Marcus went into the living room, sat down on the sofa and called his grandfather, the phone rang three times, Xander said, yes! Thank you for sending the rings, we are married and we will have a public wedding soon. Good, well done is she the guardian? Yes, it is her. Then her security is paramount, whatever it takes. Have her ready, we will start the ceremonies soon; I have longed to see father for so long. You have my permission to tell her everything because she will need to know. I have something to ask of you, Marcus said, there is to be no second to me, Kirk will protect her if I should ever fall. She does not want another, and she has Phillip as well. No, exclaimed Xander, there must be a second, No, she has chosen me, we are mated, I will never let another man touch her, she is my wife, we are fully bonded in every way and she could be carrying your great grandchild.

Do not cross me Marcus said in a raised voice. I have done everything you have ever asked; do not let history repeat its self. For I will kill everyone, who would even think about touching her, until the last breath in my body I swear this and do not try and force her into anything, as you don't want to push her into doing something, we all will regret.

And I have released, Simon as my second this is my will. Xander was quiet for a few seconds, forgive me Marcus I forget what it is to feel love and emotion and I forget what that bond brings with it, very well if that is her request and what you both want. Marcus was silent, thank you. I need you to send Royce to me and the family solicitor for tomorrow. It's good to see you are thinking ahead and making arrangements, Royce is the best, he will help you with all of that, and when do I get to meet my new granddaughter in law? Soon. Don't worry about Crispin or anything else at the moment, get yourselves settled and sorted out and leave everything to me and Victor. Thanks Marcus said and closed his phone.

Marcus went back to the kitchen and stood behind Jessie, he put his hands on her shoulders and kissed her on the top of her head, have you made any head way yet. Christine said yes, yes we have and we would like to take you up on the offer of the family home, for all of us and this house will be kept and rented out, until a time when the children can decide if they want to sell or do whatever they wish, as Phillip and Jessie grew up here and don't want to give it up just yet. Also, I want bodyguards as these two are the only family I have left, I want them protected. I have seen horrid things on the television, and the newspapers. We are quite happy to go along with your plan as you have the most experience in these things. Good, he said. They all had lunch at Christine's and Marcus called Victor and made arrangements for bodyguards, for the next day and, they spent the afternoon at Chilworth in Southampton, viewing private homes and estates.

Marcus had Paul drop off everyone except Jessie and him, as they were going back to one of the brotherhood apartments for some privacy, they would be back in the morning. Joshua's team was still in place and Kirk was with them.

When they arrived at the apartment Jessie went for a bath, in the huge bathroom, with marble everywhere and thoughts taps looked like real gold. She tipped at least three different bubble baths into the water and laid back and let the water wash over her, she did hurt a little, Marcus had felt so big, she did not think he was going to fit, it hurt like hell, but the pleasure he had given her, just thinking about it now, made her nipples go hard. Marcus had taken his suite of and went to the guest bathroom to shower, as he did not trust himself with Jessie and hot water, so soon. He came out refreshed and put on some blue jeans, he had not buttoned them up all the way, he had done 3 of the 5 buttons up, he did not bother putting any boxers on, he was towel drying his wet hair and went back into their bedroom,

Jessie had on a black stretch lace all in one piece of under ware. Her pink rose bud nipples, where trying to push through the fabric, she was killing him. He licked his lips, like he was looking at food. She slipped on, her spray on jeans again, brushed her long dark hair and clipped it up. What was the point in getting dressed? he dropped the towel, she looked over at him and that pulse between her legs started hammering, he looked like a male pin up model? And he was all hers. She smiled a big smile and asked, what, do I have bubbles in my hair still? she turned around and bent over and looked in a little mirror to check her hair, the sight of her bent over with tiny stretch jeans on was enough for him, what was a man to do.

He was over that bed and lifted her up and took her to the dressing room, where he put her down in front of the vanity unit, so she could see herself and see him stood behind her, he butted against her gently leaning her forward slightly, then kissed her neck and pressed himself against her bum, he put both of her hands against the wall and slid both of his hands around the front of her, filling his hands with her breasts and the lace, he was watching her the whole time. He unclipped her hair with one hand. Jessie started to groan and her tilted her head back, he kissed her mouth hot, fast and hard, while still feeling her breasts in his other hand He stopped kissing her, slid his hands down to her jeans and un zipped them slowly. Jessie's breathing was getting harder and deeper, she was still looking at him in the mirror. He pushed her jeans down her leg as far as he could with his hand and did the rest with his foot, he then unbuttoned his three button and his jeans fell to the floor and stepped so close to Jessie she could feel his rock hard shaft against her lower back, his chest touched her shoulders, he was breathing fast.

He slid his fingers from her hips, around the front of the lace all in one and pulled it to one side then slid his fingers in and found her very hot and wet, she closed her eyes and let go of the mirror with one hand and put it on the side. Marcus stopped, look at me Jess, you do this to me, I only have to look at you and I want you. If you don't want me to go on then pleases, say now. Because I will not be able to stop myself in a minute and I don't want to hurt you. You are driving me crazy Jess. Jessie looked at Marcus, don't stop. Marcus stepped back and grabbed her all in one at the back and pulled it to one side of her soft peach bum and lent her forward a bit more, he entered her with one hot wet hard thrust. She called out making all kinds of little noises. God, he said that just makes me want to take you harder,
he held her to him, he had a handful of her hair he was like a man possessed, she was gasping for breath and calling his

name, god, he thrust into her again and again, over and over, harder and harder, he was taking her with his whole length, she was so tight. Jessie could see the need to possess her all over his face and the way he was looking at her and the feel of him thrusting in her was just too much, she bucked and she pushed her self-back on to him hard, as she came. It was too much for him and his body gave her what she wanted.

After a few second, he slumped over her. He kissed her back and withdrew himself from her, then lifted her up and carried her to the bed. He laid her down and got in next to her and whispered, I love you Jess; I love you to Marcus.
Marcus woke up with the sound of Jessie talking to someone but he could not make out what she was saying. She was dreaming and she sounded afraid of someone or something, she started to whimper. So, he pulled her to him and pulled her on to his chest and covered her over with the cover, he put his arm around her and held her there, whispering its ok jess, its ok honey, she stopped whimpering. He drifted back off to sleep. He woke again to find Jessie's head laid on his neck, her body on his chest with her hair everywhere and legs apart straddled over him, hugging him, she was talking into his neck, her nipples where pushing against his chest, she was sweating in the lace, and once again he was hard as rock.

Jess honey, but she gripped him harder she was still dreaming, so he went to sit up, she slid down his body a bit, now her mouth was over his nipple and her bum was on his lap, he groaned when she wiggled, trying to get comfortable, he laid back down to give her more room, I love you to, she was saying, he heard that ok, she licked his nipple and he let out a little groan, he could feel her smile into his chest and she wiggled up him a bit, she was talking again, his heart would die if she said someone else's name.

Jess honey, no, she said I am staying. Jess baby please, he whispered. She wiggled back down him, a bit too far and his rock-hard shaft was between her legs pressing against the black lace. If she had not had that lace all in one on, she would have pushed herself on to him, she was nearly there now. He did not move, what was he going to do, he could feel her heat. Men did not take woman who did not know what they were doing. So, unless she woke up, there was nothing, he could do except be a man about it and take what she was doing. She rocked forward slightly, it pulled the lace along his shaft and her nipples got even harder, she was licking him again. I love you, she said again. God, he hoped she was having a dream about their love making or at least dreaming of him. She wiggled again and the lace pulled back, the tip of his shaft was on her silky hot, very wet bud, she was having a wet dream, and she groaned out, his shaft hurt from being so hard and she pushed back again, I love you to, she said again.

He would give everything to know who she was talking to in her dream; Marcus ran a hand down her back and said in a masculine rasping breath, Jessie honey. He tried to pull her up this body again but she was stuck to him like a limpet, then she said Marcus I love you to, and reached up and touched his face. He smiled with relief, that she had said his name. Her body started to tremble and she rubbed herself against his shaft again and this time she came, hot liquid rolled over him, she was whimpering and wiggling on his chest, her nipples grazing his chest when she moved. He was so close to coming, he could barely breathe. He never wanted her so much, but it would have been so wrong to take her. After her wiggling stopped and she released her grip, he rolled over as quickly as he could and laid her down to sprawl out over the bed. He had to go and finish himself off in the bathroom because his need for her was hurting him, it did not take him long at all.

When he returned, he looked at her, she looked so young and he felt pleased to take part in her dreams, he had felt like a king when she had whispered his name. He got back in the bed pulling the covers over both of them and cuddled her till he found the peace of sleep. When he opened his eyes, he saw Jessie's big dark brown eyes staring at him smiling, good morning husband. I had a horrible dream last night. Did you, why don't you tell me about it, honey? She told him, this horrible creepy man wanted to take me away from you, but you would not let him, you put a shield around me and saved me and then my dream got better, how so, he said, well you kept telling me you loved me, so I kept telling you that I loved you to, did you now he said, yes, then what happened, she went red in the face and said well I was showing you how much I loved you. Do you think you could show me, how you were showing me, how much you love me? Yes, she said and jumped on him and straddled him, he went hard immediately, power surged up in Jessie, it felt like red hot fire, she had no control over it, it came from deep inside of her and flowed out from her and into Marcus, shooting through his body, like red hot fire, sparks were taking control of him a feeling of hot need and desire, he then sat up and ripped the lace all in one off her, grabbed her hips and entered her with some force, need swept through him. He was sucking, biting her nipples hard and he was pulling her down on him so hard, she was screaming his name over and over, he could feel her tight hot flesh rip to make way for his sheer size, he said your mine and he drove into her again hard and fast.

She grabbed him and held his head to her breast, with both of her arms around him to stop him biting her more. While he took what was his over and over it was over quickly, he was grabbing her bum cheeks and squeezing them hard, pulling them apart until he convulsed, violently in her, they were both covered in sweat and Jessie was sobbing his name, pleading. The power had left his body, that had never happened before, he had never lost control ever and he had never taken a woman with such violent need and force, what the fuck was wrong with him, Jessie was shaking and tears where coming down her face. He felt like he had just raped her. He let go of her gently, she was still getting use to his body, and he had hurt her again.

He went to lift her off of him but she was shaking so much he could not, Jessie he said in a low voice, I am so sorry honey, I never meant to hurt you and never meant to take you with such force, I never meant to do that, I lost control and I will never do that again, I am so sorry, please forgive me it was nothing you did, I could not control myself, I have never needed, wanted or loved someone so much before. Jess please forgive me, please say something, she had driven him to it, she hurt everywhere, she let go of him, slowly. He could see her body as she pulled back away from him a bit.

Blood was dripping from one of her nipples where he had bitten her, she had teeth marks and red marks all over her. He did not want to think, what she would look like tomorrow; he closed his eyes, he did not want to see what he had done to her, she winced in pain as she tried to move but he was still in her. He lay back slowly to give her more room to move off of him, she cried out as she did, pain shot threw her again. He tried to be still as he could for her. Blood spilled out of Jessie and ran over Marcus's body as she lifted herself off of him, it then ran down her leg's she tried to stand to make it to the bathroom. She got as far as the door when Marcus could bring himself to look at what he had done to her, there was blood all over her and dripping down her, he was covered in it, her back had marks and scratches down it, as did her bum from where he was pulling her down on to him with some force. God what had he done. There was blood everywhere, on him, the bed, the carpet and on Jessie. He stood and Jessie's blood ran off his body and he followed her.

Jessie had stopped in the dressing room now where he had taken her last night. What had made him do it, was it her power over taking him, it had to be. Jess honey are you ok, do you need a doctor or nurse, you lost a lot of blood? she shook her head to say, no. I can't tell you how sorry I am, she could not walk anymore, it just hurt so much, she still had not turned too looked at him. Don't worry Jessie, I am not going to hurt you, I am going to pick you up and carry you to the shower, I will not do anything ok, I am just going to take you to the shower, ok honey, she nodded. He picked up a towel and wrapped it around her, before he picked her up, she was like a limp doll, and he was worried. He stood in the shower holding her. He turned the tap on and just held her under the shower and just cradled her to him. He knelt down after a while, still holding her, she held on to him and just cried. When she stopped crying, he gently sat her up against the shower wall, I am going to get some pain killers, I think you need to see a nurse. Jessie shook her head to say, no.

Ok, Jessie honey, I am just going to get some pain killers and the first aid kit, I won't be a second. When he came back, he had his jeans on and a first aid kit and a glass of brandy for her. Marcus turned the shower off and reached into his pocket and pulled out two tablets and gave her the glass of brandy, take these and have a big swig of the brandy, we need to get you dry and I need to look at the bite marks and scratches, ok jess. She nodded. He went off and came back with a chair, towels and a dressing gown. He helped her stand and took the wet towel off her, he dabbed her all over very gently to dry her, I need you to lean on the chair so I can do the back first, he put antiseptic healing cream on her scratches, then helped her on with the dressing gown, sit down and have another swig of brandy honey, he handed the glass to her, she had another big swig. I need to take a look at you breasts and your nipples; it may need stitching! It might hurt, I need you to lean forward and put your left arm on my shoulder, I will be as gentle and as quick as I can. She nodded, again. He put antiseptic cleaner on the bites and cream on the scratches and put stick-on plaster stitches on the deep bite, where he bit into her skin. He had to fight the urge to kiss it better. He closed her dressing gown and combed her hair. While she got dressed, he cleaned the bathroom up.

It was 10.30 am and his phone was vibrating. He opened it; it was Kirk, is everything ok as we are ready Kirk said? Marcus had to fight back the hurt in his voice and say, yes. Kirk, I needed you to take over everything for me today and I mean everything. Kirk listened and did not say a word, Royce should be downstairs, here at the apartments somewhere or with Victor, and the solicitor is somewhere, sort out the meet and greet with the bodyguards for today and take Royce and the solicitor and buy a house that Christine selects, get everyone to sign my will and paper work. Jessie will not need her bodyguards today and we will sign our bits tomorrow, get Phillip and Christine a car and driver, Victor or Royce will help and book the wedding.

Kirk was still silent for a second, taking in everything that Marcus was saying and then said, what do you want me to say about you being absent today? Just say we got overly jolly celebrating last night and that we have hang over's today, make our apologies and that they will see us tomorrow ok... Can I do anything for you Marcus, or Jessie? No, I just need you to be me for today, please my friend.

Kirk understood and felt Marcus's pain, I will sort everything out, don't worry, you sound up set is everything alright Marcus? Don't worry about me and thank you my old friend, he had to swallow back a tear and closed his phone.

He walked into the bedroom, he was nearly sick, Jessie's blood was everywhere, he had seen blood before in battle from men but never like this from a woman, his woman, what had driven him! He had done this, he felt sick to his stomach. He went into the kitchen to find some rubbish bags and went back into the bedroom and stripped the bed off, picked up her bits of black lace that he had ripped from her body, guilt washed over him. He would need a cleanup team, to replace the carpet, sheets and towels. He sat on the end of the bed holding his head in his hands and cried, he was ashamed to be called a man, for the first time in his very long life.

Jessie looked at herself, she had driven him to it, she too had felt the fire and power burning in her, she felt it flow from her body, driving him further, controlling him, she could not stop it. She could barely walk, now she knew what men wanted from her. Never would she let another man touch her or take her like that, she would kill herself first. He must feel terrible, but it was her fault.

At least she knows his limit and knew whatever happened that was the worse it could ever be. She could hear it in his voice when he spoken to her after and then by the way he had helped her and now by the way he was crying, in the other room. She had dried her hair, put some make up on and managed to get dressed, it hurt to put jeans on, but she did it. She had to put padding in her bra and pants until she got to a chemist, she then put a t shirt and an off the shoulder jumper on top, it hurt more to bend over, she could not put her shoes on, so she threw them on the floor and wiggled into them. He had not really taken her against her will, she had wanted him and she was on top of him, he had not hit her, he just got carried away and could not control himself, her fire and power had driven him on, he had said that last night when he had taken her from behind, in front of the mirror.

Marcus had to pull himself together for Jessie, he went into the guest bathroom, had a shower and got dressed in jeans, t shirt, trainers and a jumper then went in to the living room. Jessie was sat there looking at him. She looked like her old self. How are you feeling now? I am a bit sore and hungry and I need to go to a chemist. Jessie, I am so sorry, please forgive me, I still think you should let me call one of our doctors or a nurse, we have a female doctor.

We need to have a talk this afternoon, there are something's you need to know; it might at least help you, to start to forgive me. I don't know about forgiveness Marcus but I will let you make it up to me, please just tell me I will do anything, I will let you know when I have time to think about it more. There was hope for him, that was good enough for now.

He knelt on one knee and kissed the ring on her hand. Can, we go to the chemist now? of course let's go and he held his hand out to help her? She got up carefully and walked to the door. He gently picked her up and walked down; to Paul, he held the car door open and Marcus placed her in it gently, then got in himself. Paul stopped at a chemist as ordered so Jessie and Marcus could go in. Buy anything you need he said and gave her £100.00 he waited by the door, as he made a short phone call, while she brought sanitary towels and some small wound dressing, she spoke to the female pharmacist and got some decent pain killers and some healing bath soak and a pregnancy test kit. She paid with the cash that Marcus had given her.

What would you like for lunch honey? A takeout she said, Paul drove them to the local shopping mall and they went in, she had to use the ladies' room first, she changed the padding in her pants and put a dressing over her nipple? At lunch she took more pain killers and then went back to the apartment. Marcus picked her up and carried her to another apartment, all of their stuff had been moved from the other places and there were red roses everywhere and a box of French chocolates on the table. He settled her on the sofa and took her shoes off, so she did not have to bend. He poured her a glass of wine and told her the whole story about him, the brotherhood, the lost guardian and the messenger, about Xander and her brother Phillip and his calming effect on him, covering her power, and the power of the wedding rings, the power and feelings and effect she had on him and the fact that the effect of it all built up in him, that could have been, part of what happened this morning, he told her what happened about her dream and her on top on him, everything.

She realized it was not him, not one bit of it, he just carried the guilt of it all, it was her. What had she done to him? She had taken in everything he was telling her, including his age and there where others that where older than Xander himself, he told her what he had seen in his life time, she said, if all that's true then what about your parents dying in a plane crash in the 1970s. No, they died hundreds of years ago every 50 or 60 years we release a statement, so people don't get suspicious about our age and we try and stay out of the papers as much as possible. She had more wine and pain killers, it was gone one o'clock in the morning when they had finished talking, she went to the bathroom and put a long t shirt on and changed all of her padding, she would have a bath in the morning. He said good night and left her in the bedroom alone.

She walked to the guest bedroom, he was taking his clothes off, he had just his jeans on again. Jess is everything ok? No, what are you doing? I thought after this morning, that you would not want to share a bed with me again. Oh, I know of a way to make all this go away, but it requires one hundred percent truth from you. He looked at her, yes! Did you marry me and bond with me because you were ordered to, or because I am the guardian? Or because you wanted me, you wanted to make love to me and you wanted me and me alone forever, because for me there will never be another, I love you and you are my husband.

But I will still do my part for the brother hood and I understand if you only did it for them and you don't really want me, that you had sex with me because of that, then if so, I release you from me to love another. He looked shocked, No! I would never do that, I married because I want you and only you, I love you, and you are my wife. Right ok then, do you think you meant to hurt me, the way you did because I don't, but what is done is done, do you think that it was my power inside doing it. Yes, I never ever wanted to hurt you in any way, ever and I am ashamed to be called a man. Then come to bed and cuddle me, hold me as a husband should, I can't blame you if, I or the power drove you to it. She held out her hand, he kissed it, got up and they went to bed and cuddled, till they both fell asleep.

The next morning she still hurt a lot, she had a bath, with her healing bath soak, she was stiffer today but the bath had helped and at least she had stopped bleeding, she treated her bite marks and put cream on her bottom, it felt better, but she had bright yellow, red and black marks up her back, finger print marks across her lower back, bum, hips and black with red marks across her breasts. She then dressed. Marcus had breakfast on the table. Once ready, they went to Christine's.

Things had changed, there were lots of people there and cars everywhere. Jessie went into the kitchen with Marcus behind her, Christine stood up and gave her a hug and kissed her on the check, Kirk who was stood behind Christine came over and looked at the pair of them and gave Jessie a hug and nodded at Marcus. Where's Phillip, Jessie said? Christine rolled her eyes; he is upstairs with his bodyguard packing. Two other men that were sat at the table stood and Marcus said, let me introduce Royce, he is here to help things go smoothly, he bowed and kissed her ring and this is the Dewdney family solicitor Eric Black. Mrs. Dewdney, he said and shook her hand. Jessie questioned, who the very large man in the back garden reading the paper was? Oh, Christine said, that's my bodyguard, his name is Kevin and the poor love is a bit big to be in here with us bless him, Kirk had a disagreement with someone called Victor and Kirk won, he insisted that I need the incredible hulk because of my tiny size and rolled her eyes again, Jessie tried not to laugh. Oh, you think that's funny do your young lady, your two are in the living room waiting for you.

Please sit-down Jess, said Marcus, everyone looked at him, they only sat when Jessie did. Jessie signed all the papers, wills and wedding forms, which was in four days at the register office. Royce explained that, Xander and some members of the brother hood and us here, will be at the wedding, is there anyone you would like to invite Mrs Dewdney. No, but I would like to speak to my brother alone please. How do I do that? she looked at Marcus who nodded at Kirk, who got out his phone and said, come down please.

A man came down the stairs and went into the living room and Jessie went upstairs. She walked into his bedroom, sis, she threw herself at him and he gave her a hug, I am sorry about all this, shut up you're off your head this is so great. I want to ask you something, what, he said, I want you to give me away, well dad, would have. Tears welled up in her eyes and he hugged her again. It is my duty and honor, I would love to, thank you sis and hugged her again, tears rolled down her cheeks. When she stopped crying, they went downstairs and stood in the hall, Phillip had his arm tightly around Jessie. Kirk stood immediately and looked at Marcus.

We have news; I am to give Jessie away, Christine stood up again and cuddled the pair of them. Marcus stood and Christine grabbed him and pulled him in for a cuddle. After he said why don't we all go and have a look at the house Christine has brought for us all to live and then go for lunch, but first you must meet your two bodyguards, he opened the living room door, every one stood.

Phillips bodyguard left the room and closed it behind him, leaving Marcus and Jessie. The two bodyguards bowed at her, Jessie already knew Amanda and hugged her, the man stepped forward and held his hand out and said Mrs. Dewdney, I am Robert. They will be with you 24 hours a day 7 days a week. When my wife is out of my sight, she is in yours and Amanda's hands, Amanda will go into the ladies' room with her, the doctors and so on, Robert will be outside the door at that point and at any other time, he is to be next to or behind you at all times, and Jessie you should never be anywhere without them. I will sort a phone out for you, so you can call anyone of us at any time and you should get to know all the other bodyguards because they should not change, that way you can spot some who should not be around you ok? All bodyguards have money, cards and are fully armed. For now, Paul is our driver until we find you a driver, now let's have a look at this house then.

Jessie asked, what is Phillips bodyguard called? Peter, Marcus said, Amanda and Robert just looked at each other puzzled. Oh! and she left the room. Marcus said it was her father's name. They left the Bagbie's house in a fleet of cars. They arrived at the new family estate in Chilworth, there were hundreds of workmen everywhere. The house was surrounded by a wall, about ten feet tall and it was having new security gates fitted with a security office as well. They were putting cameras up everywhere. When the cars stopped Paul opened the door to the car and by the time Jessie had gotten out of the car there must have been twenty men in black suites everywhere, they were all the brotherhood security and bodyguards, Jessie and her family all had their bodyguard's around them.

A man came over and bowed at Marcus and then came over to Jessie and said Mrs. Dewdney, I am Victor and it my honor to meet you, he took her hand and kissed her ring, then turned and clicked his fingers and a path way was made clear for them to go into the house.

The work men were not allowed near Jessie. Christine said, to Kirk we only brought it yesterday, it will be ready Saturday, we can all move in then Kirk said and Marcus slapped his back and smiled at him. You and Marcus don't have to live with us, if you don't want to. No, nonsense we are a family Marcus said, safety in numbers and all that. Well I am giving you and Jessie the whole top floor, it has a master bedroom, bathroom, dressing room, a nursery room, living room, office and guest bedroom. Kirk and I will have the west wing and Phillip will have the east wing, there will be a shared family living room, kitchen and hall.

Victor's phone rang; he spoke very quickly, so all Jessie could make out was" keep me updated". Well it seems all the cars and men in situ have sparked the media off, there are reporters outside of the Bagbie's and a TV crew waiting for you, if you go back. Victor took Marcus's arm, let's take a walk, if everyone could make their way back to the cars, as the workmen do need to finish, thank you.

When everyone was outside Marcus asked, what is it, has Crispin showed up in person? Joshua's team were ready to take him and the press showed up and scared him off, shit said Marcus and they could not get a tail on him. Ok thanks. We will stay at the Brotherhood apartments until the house is ready. Good, Xander and his party are close, they're at the Brotherhood house in Winchester and we will put the other wedding guests there until the wedding. The reception will be at brotherhood hall, where you are in Southampton, away from the cameras.
Marcus said, can you arrange someone to collect their clothing and stuff and have it taken to the apartments, all

the rest of the stuff will be packed up and brought here. Also, after the wedding and on the day of the ceremony of light we will need Phillip in the room with them and not outside because, she has a lot of power, so he will need to be stood very close to her. That is unexpected we knew he had to be near, but not that near to her, do you really think it is necessary asked Victor, yes, I do, very well I will alert Xander to this, thank you, they shook hands and left.

In the car Marcus explained, now the press are alert to our presence, we cannot go back to Christine's, so how about lunch as promised at the pub, all together up the road and a trip to buy wedding gowns for the girls and suits for us men, so we don't draw lots of attentions we will be shopping in two parties and I am afraid that as best man Kirk you are going to have to come with me shopping. Kirk smile, I am honored my old friend, thank you, well Marcus said, when you marry Christine you will be family so you might as well start now, as my best man and then father in law to be, every one cheered.

After lunch they spilt into two groups, the girls got into Paul's limousine on Marcus's insistence. Jessie was worried, she didn't have any money, don't worry Marcus said you signed the papers this morning, you will have your own card and account within two days and you will have you phone by tonight, Marcus clicked his fingers at Robert who then stepped forward. My wife does not carry money, so put anything she wants on your card and she doesn't have her phone, so stay close, but that is a given and she can use your phone if she needs to ok.

You are now in trusted with my most loved and treasured possession, my wife and if anything should happen to her, I promise you a very painful and very slow death, just so we are clear, you call me first about anything, do you understand me. Yes, Sir, Robert said and stepped back.

Marcus just stood there for a second, unsure he wanted to kiss her, but he did not want to hurt her. Jessie read his thought's and reached up and cupped Marcus's face and kissed him slow, wet and deep. He had to hold himself back, and he did, just raising his hands to her face, he saw her back and bum this morning when she was drying herself, she looked like she was badly attacked and guilt again washed over him.

Kirk had already kissed Christine and they were now on their way into town to buy a wedding dress and out fits, they stopped at one of the high street wedding dress shops and Kevin got out and opened the door, by the time Jessie had gotten out behind her bodyguards and Aunt there was a small crowd around them, just people seeing what all the fuss was about. Amanda had Jessie's hand and Robert was behind her, Paul stood outside the shop door stopping anyone else going into the shop. Kevin said to the manager, you are going to have to lock the door and put your closed sign up, while we are in the shop madam. Ok, and she bolted the door and put the closed sign up. How may I help you? by now the three other shop assistance had come out from the back room.

I need to check your back room and exit doors. Sarah the manager called, show this man what he needs to see, Kevin turned and nodded at Robert and went off with Sarah to check the shop.

Christine announced, my daughter needs a wedding dress today and I need an outfit to, can you help us? Yes of course what would you like to see, Amanda said just bring us a range of your most expensive dresses and money is no object? What color, would you like jess? Oh yes, nothing white, ivory or cream please, and Christine knew what she was getting at and just raised an eye brow, the manager just waved her hand at one of the girls, she went off and then the manager enquired, what would the mother of the bride like? I think a knee length dress and jacket and hat please, ok, what color would you like to see? What other colors are you going to have Jess? Oh, I don't know, what are the men buying, they never said, Amanda pulled out her phone and pushed a button, Marcus answered after one ring.

Please hold she said and passed the phone to Jessie, hello, Marcus sounded relived are you ok honey? yes, um we want to know what color suits you are buying, so we can match. She could hear Marcus's smile on the phone, he whispered what would you like to see me in Jess, Marcus, Jessie gasped, then she giggled, I love that jet black suit you took me to the Great White moon in and that white shirt, it just did things to me, seeing you in that it made my knees go weak. Ok darling then that's what we will buy and we will wear the color of your flowers honey.

I love you darling she said, I love you to jess, bye and he waited till she put the phone down before he closed his. Two hours later they left with dresses, shoes, hats, wedding under wear and Jessie picked some French lace bits up, they spent £18,200.00 By now there was a large crowd of people that had gathered outside of the shop and some press. Oh my god, exclaimed Christine, how are we going to get to the car now.

Amanda said, Joshua has a second team not far from us but we don't want to make headlines if we can help it, so

Robert is there a back door and where does it go, can you get Jess out that way? Yes. Kevin will open the door, Paul will be in front and I will have hold of you Christine, we will walk to the car just like when we came in, Paul will open the door you will get in first and then I will, Paul will lock the back doors and Kevin and Paul will get in the front, we will drive around and pick up Robert and Jessie. That way it gives them a diversion to get out the back when the world is watching us.

Amanda said to the manager a man called Simon, a big chap with blonde hair, we will be around to collect our bags in one hour. Right, Robert you go out the back with Jessie and then go to the next street and we will pick you up there, have your phone ready and your eyes peeled, Ok, go now Jessie and do everything that Robert says to do. Jessie nodded and they left through the back of the shop, while the rest went out the front.

Robert went first holding Jessie's small hand in his big hand. They were nearly at the end of the ally way when two men walked down the alley towards them, they had long knives, Robert stopped and gave Jessie his phone and pulled out a small sword, he faced the two men who kept walking towards him, he told Jessie, open my phone and press one now. She did as she was told, he also took his gun out and gave it to her, a voice said hello. This is Jessie Dewdney and there are some bad men coming towards Robert and I, with long knives, in the alley behind a wedding dress shop we have been in, and we need help now! Ok, honey I need you to crouch down on the floor and stay down, the men will not hurt you, so don't run anywhere, we are not far from you, my name is Joshua, can you tell me what's happening now.
   Jessie looked up, there's lots of blood, Robert is fighting a man with his sword and he gave me his gun. Ok, honey

you're doing really well stay down, hold on one second Jessie stay on the line. Can you shout to Robert, yes, good do not stand up? Remember I need you to stay down yes, she said. After the count of three, shout to Robert "down" can you do that for me honey, yes, she said, ok count to three. Jessie counted one, two, three, "Down Now Robert". Robert dropped to the ground and the man he was fighting went to jump over Robert towards Jessie, she curled up in a small ball and heard click, thud, click thud, click thud.

The first man was laid across Robert and there was blood everywhere, there were two holes clean threw the bad man's head and the other man was already dead, they put a hole in his head. The man on the phone was talking again, hello Jessie honey are you ok are you hurt? No, No. I'm fine; the two bad men are dead, and Robert, Joshua said down the phone. Robert, Jessie said are you ok? I am ok, just a few cuts, he is ok a few cuts I think, Robert pushed the dead man off him and stood up and took the phone from Jessie.

Robert said call Kevin and tell him to take Christine back now, we don't want to frighten her as well, and there could be more, send a cleanup crew and a car for us, also a blanket, for Jessie is cold, in shock and covered in blood from myself and from the two body's, Marcus is going to freak. Joshua advised them to stay where they were just in case their friends showed up, one of my men is covering you, so if they come back you will have help, we will not be long brother and he closed his phone.

Robert picked up his sword and put all the body's together and tried to cover them the best he could. He held his hand out and Jessie gave him his gun back, she was shaking, he was right it had turned cold. He helped her to get up, she winced in pain, he pulled her to her feet and a sharp pain shot through her and she bent over, Jessie talk to me. Its ok I hurt myself the other day and it still hurts a bit that's all. I need you to try and rest against the wall, I need to check you. No, I won't take your clothing off, I am just going to check to make sure you don't have any holes in your clothing. Ok. He checked her; you look ok except your covered in blood. Jessie felt dizzy and the last thing she remembers was Robert saying, oh shit. And darkness took her.

Marcus and the men had finished their wedding shopping feeling that their duty was done, they were in the car and were going to have a male bonding drink together. Marcus's phone rang it was Joshua with the worse news he could imagine, telling him that Jessie was on the other phone stuck in an ally way on the floor and that Robert was fighting two men to save her life. Hold on, Joshua said he was taking to Jessie now on the other phone he could hear her on Joshua's loud speaker, he could hear the sword fighting and she sounded scared, Joshua was giving her instructions to save her life, Marcus gave him the address on the street they were near. I have to go I have a hit team now trying to help is there anything else, I need to be one hundred percent for Jessie, I have to go, Yes, Marcus said call her honey she responds to that he closed his phone and he then shouted new direction to the driver and said its a matter of life and death, go faster.

The car swung around in the road, they were not far, Marcus quickly told the other's what was happening and said be to be ready, Phillip you will have to wait in the car with the driver there will be a lot going on and I don't want something else to go wrong. As the car stopped, they saw the ally way he opened his phone and called Joshua and said tell them not to shoot we are coming up the ally he drew his sword ready. It was getting dark.

Marcus spotted the bodies on the floor and then saw Robert just standing there holding Jessie's lifeless body. He drops his sword and started screaming no, no, no and ran towards them. Kirk and Paul had to hold Marcus back; he looked at Jessie's face she was covered in lots of blood again. Robert was saying she ok, she's ok she just fainted she seemed to be in a lot of pain.
They released Marcus and he took her from him and held her too him.

Chapter Three

Old Friends

When Jessie opened her eyes, she was in a room that looked like a hospital room there were machines beeping, a drip, bp monitor, oxygen and a pain killer hooked up to her and it was dark, she did not have her clothing on, she was in a hospital gown. She tried to move and sit up but felt a little woozy, someone stood up and walked over to the bed it was Amanda, she said how are you feeling, she opened her phone and spoke so someone, she's awake and closed her phone. Marcus is outside with the doctor he will be right in and everyone is out there, everyone's been very worried, where am I Jessie asked, you're in the brother hood medical facility and Marcus insisted on a female doctor, he has been frantic.

Where is Robert he saved my life, he's in the next room, a few stitches, two broken ribs and a few cuts, but he is alright, worried Marcus is going to kill him. Your aunt and brother came in to see you with Kirk they are outside and Xander is here with James, Victor is here and a few other bigwigs from the brother hood, Joshua popped in to make sure you were ok. You did well. No, I did not Jessie said I fainted. This is the first time Marcus has left your side, when the doctor took him to the other room to speak to him. All the wedding stuff has been delivered by Simon it's all in your Aunt's apartment, at her bequest as she did not want anyone seeing your dress. What's the time Jessie asked. Amanda looked at her watch and said, it's one twenty-three am. What Jessie said, you have been out of it for about nine hours and the doctors been very worried they were going to move you to a private hospital if you were not awake by two, they still might that's what Marcus is discussing with the doctor now.

Just then the door opened and Marcus came in and nodded

to Amanda, she left the room. Marcus went over to Jessie and kissed her gently on the head, I have been so worried. I am so sorry about all this, no, stop Jessie I am the one who is sorry not you darling. Jessie lifted her hand to try and touch his face but she felt so weak, Jessie told him, Robert saved my life and so did the man on the phone Joshua. I have to thank them. It's their job, but I will thank them if that's what you wish. So why did I faint, I feel so weak what's wrong. He held her hand and said when I brought you in, they put all this stuff on you I was so worried and they took blood, they wanted to do a female internal exam and I refused. So, they gave you a full body scan instead, it took two hours.

The doctor and I have just spoken she is just waiting on some more test results any time now and said that when I was a bit ruff with you her words not mine, that the ripping inside you caused a tare to a big blood vessel which is why you bleed a lot the other day which made you weak and because it was a lot of blood it takes time to build it back up and is very painful, because you did not have a lot of blood your heart had to work faster and not enough blood means not enough oxygen and when you were cold the blood went to your heart and you suffered shock as well and shock can kill. They found something out on the scan, what Jessie said. Marcus pulled out a scan picture and showed it to Jessie. what is it she asked? our baby he said it is tiny only a few cells the size of a grain of rice a good few days, so you conceived the first time, but a lot can happen, the drugs they had to give you to save your life could affect the baby and you might miscarry, they don't know they are worried you could lose more blood, if that happens then, Marcus held his breath for a second and said in a low voice Jessie you will die.
He quickly moved on and said they are looking at Phillip or Christine to see it they are a match to give you blood they

even took my blood. Marcus smiled and kissed her on the head again, he asked, are you up to a few visitors there are a few people that want to see you they just want to see for themselves. Just then the female doctor came back in and introduced herself to Jessie, I am doctor Adams, it's good to see that you're awake, how do you feel now, Jessie said I feel funny woozy. Ok can I talk to you again Markus please and she walked to the door and held it open.

Amanda came back in and Marcus said I will send them in, I won't be long honey. The door closed and Marcus told Christine and Phillip that they could go in. He nodded at them. Doctor Adams said I think you better bring someone with you a family member Marcus just looked at Xander and he got up and followed Marcus and the doctor into the room. James followed them and waited outside the door while Kirk watched everyone as he was stood guard outside of Jessie's room.

What is it doctor Marcus said, she looked at Marcus and at Xander, its ok doctor this is my grandfather? We just got the last lot of blood tests back and I am afraid it is very bad news, I am very sorry but your wife can't make enough blood quick enough and it's too late to give her blood now her hormone level has dropped which means her body cannot function and the fetus will die within the next half an hour or so. I am so sorry, but your wife will become unconscious at this point she may fall into a coma and she could die. She is too weak to be moved. If you have a priest, then may I suggest you might want to get him here now.

Marcus just fell to his knees and cried "no, no". Xander asked is there no hope at all? No, she said the heart has sustained to much damage and it is affecting the brain which is why she feeling woozy. I can up the pain killers but they will just put her to sleep and she would never wake up sorry. You need to tell her family and say your good buys to her. She then left Xander with his hand on Marcus shoulder. Marcus stood, tears where rolling down his face and for the first time in many, many years Xander put his arms around him and cuddled him to sooth him, Marcus could feel Xander's soothing power working on him. Xander said come my son we need to be strong for her. Xander and Marcus left the room, the crowd of people fell silent and just looked at Marcus's face, with his red eyes and tears still on his face.

They walked to Jessie's room, Kirk opened the door to let them in, come brother Marcus touched his arm Christine will need you. Kirk walked in with them and Peter, Phillips body guard took Kirks post and James stood next to him. Christine and Phillip stood back from Jessie's bed. Marcus walked to her bed and said Jessie this is my grandfather Xander Dewdney. Xander lent forward and picked up her hand and kissed her ring, he said it is my honor to meet you Jessie. He stared at her he could feel her power draining from her body. Marcus took Christine, Phillip and Kirk to the corner of the room and told them what the doctor had just told him they all started to cry even Kirk, they all hugged each other and Marcus said we have to be strong for Jessie. Please make your peace with her now, she has no time.

Xander kissed Jessie head and stood back Christine and Phillip both kissed her and Marcus stood over her holding her hand telling her he loved her tears started to roll down Jessie's face she was in a lot of pain the baby was dying and Marcus knelt at her side still holding her hand and prayed for the life of his unborn baby and for Jessie's life and the lord to be merciful to both as they were true innocence's in this world. He would gladly give his body, sole and life in exchange for theirs. Xander knelt beside him and prayed to and put one of his hands-on Marcus's shoulder, Phillip and Kirk did the same on the other side, as Christine went around the other side of the bed and held Jessie other hand. Her machines where beeping and Jessie started to scream out in pain, the doctor came back into the room and said I am sorry, I am going to give Jessie a pain killer now so she won't hurt anymore. I am very sorry.

Marcus started to shake and hot tears where rolling down his face. Phillip could feel his sister's pain and he felt hot, like sweating hot and could feel power oozing into his body from everyone else. He started to shake violently. The doctor gave Jessie an injection then waited by the door. Be at ease brother, Kirk said to Phillip, I can feel it building in you. But he was shaking, he let go of Marcus. Kirk stood and Christine stepped back from the bed and walked around to Kirk. Be at ease Xander said and stood. Marcus never moved. Then Phillip fell back on to his heels and a bright white and blue light shot out from his eyes and mouth and the light filled the room, as it started to shake like they were in the middle of an earth quake. The door opened James and Peter came in leaving the door open, Marcus stood and covered Jessie body with his, he was still whispering I love you my wife.

Kirk pushed Christine back in the corner of the room where Amanda was stood and he stood in front of them, a thick white haze filled the room, there was a very loud clap of thunder in the room then there were two figures that stood next to Jessie bed. They were huge at least seven feet tall and they were in the form of two men but one of the men seemed to grow taller to a least nine feet and had a staff in his hand that grew with him.

The shorter one of the two seemed to have another being inside of him, making an awfully screaming noise like a hiss that filled the room, and their skin moved, it was like milky water and marble, their eyes were like blue diamonds. The taller one stood and looked out towards the door and looked at everyone outside and inside the room. He pulled up his staff and hit it on the floor, the floor cracked dust went up in the air and light shone out from the room, everyone out side of the room fell to their knees. The little one walked around the bed and screamed out like it was in pain. Marcus stood up from over Jessie's body and stood back, the movement made the big one turn, he looked at Marcus the marble face seemed to look at him with sadness in his eyes it then nodded at Marcus and he understood that it wanted him to step back, but he did not want to leave Jessie, the smaller one hissed and Marcus moved back reluctantly.

He looked down at Phillip who was still sat back on his heels on the floor the light still coming out of his eyes, he was still staring at the ceiling, had he summoned the messenger or had father sent him! The smaller messenger lent over the bed and kissed Jessie on the forehead and Marcus stepped forward, the taller one moved and stood between Marcus and the bed and he looked down at Marcus. The smaller one ran his hand down Jessie's body.

It stopped its hand over her abdomen, screamed and hissed the being inside him moved. The smaller one took his hand off Jessie and slid off her hospital gown and covers her body was in a blue light so no one could see her. The smaller one pointed at Phillip and the big one touched his staff and it disappeared he bent down and picked Phillip up and laid him on the bed next to Jessie, pulled a long knife of sliver out and cut Phillips hand, he let the blood run on to Jessie. The smaller one ran his hand back over Jessie again and looked confused he screamed at Marcus and then pointed at him, the big one grabbed Marcus's hand, cut his hand and collected the blood on his own and let the small one touch it. He hissed again and the big one pushed Marcus onto his knees. Marcus said take me and leave her. The big one smiled at him Kirk moved but the big one just turned before he could get one step and grabbed Kirk around the neck.

Kirk did not resist but just looked at the Messenger. The messenger looked behind Kirk at the two women and the massager nodded at Kirk and let him go, pushing him back towards the two women. The smaller one wrapped Jessie's body in the sheet on the bed. He kissed her on the mouth and pushed the light into her, then stepped back and hissed at the big one again and the being inside the little one screamed out. The big messenger picked up Jessie wrapped in the sheet and kissed her on the forehead then laid her in Marcus's arms. He cuddled her to him kissing her. The big one then picked Phillip up and laid him on the floor next to Marcus and Jessie. Phillip now had his eyes closed and the big one now had his staff again, he hit the floor with it again and a red light rose from the ground and covered Jessie, Marcus and Phillip.

The smaller one walked over to Xander and touched his face it seemed to be communicating with Xander.

It then stepped back from him and bowed down towards him and the big one smiled at Kirk and nodded, the two beings stood together and the big one struck the floor and a big clap of thunder came and in a second all the light from everywhere went and the haze with it the machine that Jessie was still wired to started to beep like mad then evened out into a regular beep. She opened her eyes and looked at Marcus and said I love you. Tears were running down his face and I love you to and kissed her gently, the red light shone, Xander and Kirk tried to approached Jessie and Marcus with the doctor but none of them could get near to them until, the red light faded.

After the ruckus died down and order had been brought about by Xander, and everyone had been left in no doubt that they had been visited by a heavenly massager Marcus insisted that the doctor give Jessie a second body scan right away. Which she did. After one-hour Marcus could hear the machine finish, he had stood outside the door not wanting to be away from Jessie. the doctor opened the door and said gather your family I have news. Marcus picked Jessie up and carried her to another room where Phillip had now come around and was sat with Kirk, Christine, Amanda, Xander and James, Peter and Robert where outside of the room. He gently laid her on the bed. Doctor Adams came in with scan pictures. She said I have unbelievable news; she closed the door behind her. Is Jessie ok Marcus said looking worried? The doctor said well yes, she is in one hundred percent perfect health, not a mark, scratch or bites, and no brain or heart problems, no blood problems she looked at Marcus, but she does have something that is truly a gift and I am bit worried. What is it? Marcus said.

The doctor held up the scan picture and said your wife is pregnant, the fetus survived Marcus said! The doctor said I don't know, Xander said what you mean you don't know. Jessie was a good, few days pregnant we have the early scan to prove it.

Yes, Marcus said I have a copy I showed Jessie, that was before your visitors, now she is at least three months pregnant, there is no mistake we have checked the scan and here is your copy. Congratulations. If the baby grows normally, it will be here in about six months. We want to keep you in for a few more tests Jessie. Just till tomorrow, then you are free to go we will just monitor you just to check the baby has not grown any quicker. You are free to eat and drink normally. Take it easy as you are three months pregnant now and now, I will leave you all to it and she left the room closing the door behind her.

Marcus put his hand on Jessie's abdomen where the messenger had touched and Jessie said she knows you're here protecting us, Jessie put her hand on Marcus. Your daughter she said she loves you and she can feel you close to her she feels warm? As I do. You know it's a girl Jessie, Marcus said. Yes, I do and everyone looked at Jessie. She is speaking to me; I can hear her.

Xander approached Jessie unsure, ooh Jessie said she knows who you are Xander she can feel you approaching and she likes it. Xander asked, what else does she say child, she said you have spoken to the angles and you knew one of them. Is that right you have seen one before? Yes, Xander said when I was a child, I was given a box in a temple by an angel and a guardian at the time, that was over three thousand years ago.

How could you possibly know that? She said the angel told her he had seen you before and that father missed you and your love by him but he has one more job for you, did the angel tell you she said. Yes, Xander said and he put out his hand to touch her stomach, Jessie looked at Marcus and nodded then Xander touched her abdomen and felt power and heat and a calming feeling. Xander asked what's wrong with her, Marcus looked at Jessie, I think she's gone to sleep. Good idea Marcus said. Let's leave them to it let her rest and you can come back later said Phillip as he shepherded every one out of the room Amanda went with a nod from Marcus.

When she closed the door, Marcus climbed on the bed with Jessie and cuddle her to him gently and kept kissing her gently on the mouth, when he stopped, she said there was something else I have to tell you, what is it Jess? Well she said the angle spoke to me to, although I don't know what he said to our daughter, he told me that you love me so much you offered your life for mine. Don't worry about that now honey just rest. No I want to tell you in case I forget, the angle told me that you had meant to hurt me and the burst of life from our little angle even though she was a grain of rice was enough for her power to take you by surprise so to speak and to stop her doing it again the angle took that power away because when she grows it would have happened a lot so they gave her another gift, the one she used today, she can feel people like you and the brotherhood and Phillip and she has an addition she can talk to me she tried to talk to Xander but she got tired . So now you don't have to feel guilty, none of this is your fault. That's good to know replied Marcus. They both cuddle up to each other and slept.

They were awoken by the doctor to take blood from Jessie and then the doctor scanned Jessie's tummy, everything is fine the baby is growing at the normal rate so have your normal checks and I will be quite happy and very interested in delivering the baby when it's ready in about six months. Um doctor! yes what is it Jessie, is it ok to have sex is it safe with the baby? There is no reason why not your perfectly healthy and sex will not hurt the baby provided you're not so ruff with each other; you know what I am talking about she pointed at Marcus and he held his hands up. Ok! he said. Then go home and have sex, goodbye and she shook Jessie and Marcus's hands and left.

Marcus helped Jessie get dressed and picked her up and walked to their apartment leaving Robert and Amanda to open the doors and carry Jessie's bag as the medical fertility unit was under the brotherhood apartments. They all got in the lift and went to their apartment. Marcus put Jessie on the sofa and Christine, Kirk and Phillip came, all the bodyguards went back to their posts.
Kirk said how about a cup of tea for everyone. Oh, yes please replied Jessie. As Kirk went off to make the tea Christine went and sat next to Jessie and gave her a big hug and said she is not talking to day then? No, I can feel her get hot when Marcus is close to me, she was really existed to speak to me and Xander but I think she will sleep or stay quiet until she's ready to come out.

I was looking forward to speaking to her said Phillip, don't worry about it she is going to have a lot to say when she's older, I could feel her taking you all in she is very strong. You will start to show by the end of this month Jessie. It's a good job the wedding is on Monday. That's tomorrow Kirk said as he gave Jessie her tea.

Oh my god I have not done anything. Don't worry Jess, Marcus said Christine and Royce are sorting it you have just got to put your dress on honey and Jessie smiled at him.

Marcus's phone buzzed and he opened it, ok thanks and closed it. Xander's here, the door opened and Xander and James walked in with Royce.
Xander went straight over to Marcus and hugged him, Marcus looked surprised, Xander said it's been to long I, have sat back waiting, wanting to leave this world and now everything has come at once, all of you ladies have drawn my interest and I have not been living a real human life, now you have given me that chance, I thank you. Jessie went to stand and he said no my dear. How are you both today? We are both fine she said. Has she spoken to you again, no, she scenes when you are near it comforts her, she feels hot when your near and she was so existed yesterday? I get the feeling she might be silent till she is ready to come out. she will let us know when she is ready. Good he said.

Everyone please sit down I have some things to discuss, Royce get your pad and pencil out. I am having an account linked to you for the little one and I am giving you personally five million pounds so you can buy anything you need for yourself or her. I am making provision in my will for her and any other great grandchildren that come along. I will also be buying the whole Chilworth manor estate just up the road, not far from you so we can be close, as I do not want you having to drive everywhere, when I want to see her or them. I am not forgetting you Phillip, you helped to save Jessie's, life and my great granddaughters life as well I would like to invite you to be one of my Knights!

It will take you many years to get up to speed and no human man has ever been invited before, but because you have very good credentials there will not be a problem.

Then Xander turned and smiled at Christine and said we are family, is there anything I can do for you? Oh, yes, Christine said get rid of that horrid man who is trying to kill my family. We are working on that don't worry. Jessie is there anything I can do for you. Yes, she said can you be around more, it's good to see my family together and when she comes, I think she will talk your ears off all the time if yesterday is anything is to go by. Yes, you all are very gifted and I have been told that you missed your dance, so, I have an arranged a honeymoon for the two of you.

Just time away to recover, you have been through a lot, a yacht, just around the med you can have it as long as you need it, I am sending a doctor and a full security team with you, Victor has taken care of moving all of your stuff to your new home and Joshua is putting extra security in, he is very good at his job. Yes, Jessie said if it had not been for him and Robert, I would be dead now, I owe them my life. I will make sure that they are thanked and looked after. There is another reason for my visit to day. I know you have the rings they are from me to you two and it is your right to have them. But I would like you to have something that belonged to my wife and then Marcus's mother and now if its ok with Marcus I want to give them to you, I would be very honored if you wore them at your wedding. He clicked his fingers and James produced a long gold box and handed it to Xander. Who gave it to Jessie, she opened the box and it was a diamond necklace the stones where huge, bigger than her ruby and there were five giant stones on a gold chain with a pair of diamond tear drop earrings? Marcus explained, they once belonged to Cleopatra.

Thank you I will be very honored to wear them, she said. She stood up and hugged Xander, he could feel love and warmth from Jessie and James looked at them as he too felt it come from Xander. Oh, Jessie exclaimed as she took Xander's hand and placed it on her belly. She giggling she has so much love. Yes, Xander said I feel it from her, Marcus felt a pang of jealousy and walked over to Jessie can the father and husband get in on the action? Christine and Kirk smiled and giggled at Marcus's jealousy. Yes, she really likes Xander she is drawn to him I think it's his age or strength. Oh, Marcus listen she put his hand on her tummy and Marcus could hear a faint little word Daddy. He was on his knees kissing Jessie belly with tears in his eyes. She knows who you are Marcus she gets warm when you are near. Why can't I hear her? She's gone back to sleep; it takes a lot out of us. Are you ok Jessie, yes, but I am hungry? He stood and Xander stepped away.

Where do you want to go? Jessie looked scared and put her hand on her tummy, are you ok Xander said, he looked at Marcus. Yes, she said, but I am afraid for us with that man out there. Don't worrying darling no one can hurt you when you're with me, but what about the reporters she said, what about them, let them photograph me with my beloved family they will not get near you darling, where would you like to for this meal before your public wedding. I really fancy a take out! Jessie kissed Marcus slow and deep. Let's go he said and they all left for the restaurant with six black cars, bodyguards and a full security team in tow.

Christine said if you eat anymore you will not be able to get into that dress tomorrow. Its ok, I am full now I am totally stuffed; I could do with a sleep. Ok, honey, Marcus gave her hug. Let's get you back said Xander. James stepped forward and whispered into Xander's ear. Xander said ok. It seems the press are outside don't worry it's all in hand. We will go and get into our cars and take you home for your sleep. He touched her hand and she smiled.

Jessie looked over to see all the bodyguards move closer there was Amanda, Robert, Kevin, Peter James, and ten other bodyguards all dressed in black, they came up to stand behind them and of course, Kirk is more like family now. Jessie's family was growing by the day. They all managed to get to their cars and drive away with hardly any effort as everybody moved together.

Jessie fell asleep in the car and Marcus pulled her onto his lap and cradled her to him, he kissed her head.
He let Phillip bend down and take her from him so he could get out of the car and then Phillip gave her straight back. They all walked in to their apartments Kirk, said Christine, will be in to get Jessie at 6pm tonight as she is going to the house and you're staying with me see you at 6pm. I know it's going to be hard to be apart for one night but it will soon be over. Marcus nodded would you, Christine and Phillip join us on the yacht. I know Jessie would need time with you all, please come, see you at 6 pm and Kirk closed the door behind them.

Marcus pulled the cover back on the bed and laid Jessie down, took off her shoes and loosened her jeans, she grabbed his hands and said I am not tired, I just wanted you all to myself-doing this, taking our clothes off, why you, little minks said Marcus. Jessie took her jeans and top off; Marcus did not need to be asked twice he started stripped his clothing off and Jessie said take them off slowly and look at me. He did and was fully aroused by the time he got into bed. He lay next to her and kissed her with hunger, pulling her gently on top of him, he said she's not going to wake up is she, no, Jessie laughed she won't wake again today. Good, he pulled Jessie down on his hard-wet hot shaft, slowly and they both growled, Jessie flung her head back and rocked forward and Marcus slowly sat up and gently took her breast in his mouth and eased her back fully on to his shaft, Jessie came out of sheer need for him. He rocked her again and filled her. They both fell asleep holding each other.

Marcus woke up at 4.30pm and went into the shower, Jessie woke up to the sound of the water running, she went into the bathroom and Marcus looked like a god he was stood naked and his body was completely wet which made his mussels look even bigger and well defined, he was washing his dark hair, whilst stood with his back to her, his head tilted back with the shower running onto his face he steed back and turned around. Jessie was staring at him, he held out the shower gel to her and she walked in naked, she was aroused, her nipples where rock hard, she shivered as she opened the glass shower door, the steam rushed passed her, she closed the door and took the shower gel from him, both of their breathing got faster, she poured it into her hands and dropped the bottle, rubbed her hands together and stepped forward then ran her hands down his chest and circled his nipples, he bent down to kiss her and she stepped back, he smiled at her and she stepped closer again and continued down his body with her hands covered in gel, she did not take her eyes off of him she grasped him and he said her name he bent to kiss her again and she stepped back again . He was rock hard and fully aroused. She stepped closer until his thick hard shaft touched her tummy, he still did not move but his breathing was getting heavy, she slid her hands up his neck and stood on tip toe her hard nipples pressed against his chest and his shaft slid down so the tip of his thick shaft just slid in-between her legs. He was shaking, he growled her name slowly, he was breathing faster now, she licked his ear and nibbled the bottom of it.

Then she whispered into his ear softly and made a little

noise of wanting just to make him even harder and told him, this is just to give you something to remind you of me tonight, just so you remember your mine and then kissed, him she licked his bottom lip and slid her tongue over his, pressing her body gently to his, just so his shaft rested at her hot wet silky nub, and she made another little noise, he was shaking and hard, she licked his nipple and stood back. Remember your mine and we will finish this on our honeymoon. She turned and put a swing in her hips as she stepped out of the shower and walked away. He did not say a word he just watched her. He had to turn the shower on cold otherwise he would have grabbed her and driven himself into her fully and hard. He was not going to sleep tonight, and she was goanna pay.

When he came out of the shower and walked into the living room, with his button up jeans on and a black tight t shirt that made his muscle bulge, she was stood by the table with a stretch back dress on with his heels and no under wear. It was low-cut at the front of the dress, it touched every part of her and she had make-up on, she looked like a hot ad for sex and he was rock hard again. He growled out and crossed the room, picked her up and sat her on the table, he parted her legs and stood between them, her dress rose up, he grabbed her hair gently and kissed her hard she pushed herself forward, he was not winning this one she thought and she wrapped her legs around him and kissed him back She let her legs drop and then laid herself back against the table an touched her self between her legs and called his name. He was ripping his clothing off, she was not getting away with this, he wanted her now, he would make her beg and call his name.

There was a knock at the door, Marcus said let them knock and undid his belt. she closed her legs slowly making a little noise, he thought he was going to come before he got his jeans off, his phone was ringing, shit he said, Jess please honey don't do this to me. She wiggled to the end of the table and said I'm sorry; he could tell she did not mean it. She was teasing him and enjoying it too much.

Marcus could here Kirk at the door laughing and saying, if you don't let me in or you don't come out, I am coming in to get you. Go way Marcus shouted and took a step back from Jessie, he wanted her so fucking much he let his jeans drop to the floor. Go have fun with the boys! I'm coming Jessie shouted out to Kirk while looking into Marcus's eyes, she then slid off the table and turned around and pushed her bum back into Marcus's hips, she could feel his rock-hard shaft threw his boxer shorts. Jessie turned around and giggled and said you go play with the boys and I will play with the girls and slid her hand in her dress at the front and touched her breast, her head dropped back and Marcus just grabbed her and kissed her hard and fast, she stepped back and ran to the door laughing.

Marcus picked up his jeans and did them back up as Jessie let Kirk in. Well, he said looking at Marcus, come on you it's your stag night. Jessie was giggling and stood behind Kirk saying Kirk protect me, Marcus wants to carry me off. Kirk could see what she had done to Marcus, what it is to be young and in love. Come on old man Kirk said, she's all yours tomorrow.

Marcus laughed "old man" can't you give me five more minutes? No, said Jessie laughing, he has to go now.

Marcus picked up his t shirt, put it back on and walked to the door not taking his eyes of Jessie the whole time. I will see you tomorrow my wife. Marcus just walked out of the apartment with vengeance in his eyes, Kirk held the door open for Amanda and Robert to get Jessie.

Jessie looked like an angel in her wedding dress, made of ivory silk with the thinnest straps, it showed the shape of her breasts and hips and went to the floor, it had a slit from the floor to just below her hip on one side with ivory lace up ribbon hi heels. She wore the diamonds Xander had given her. She looked so pure, her skin glowed and her eyes sparked. Everyone looked proud to do their part and the wedding ceremony went off like clockwork, they exchanged two thin gold bands, that went on next to their Jerusalem rings. On the way out of the register's office it was like someone flashing a thousand lights there where photographers everywhere with TV vans. Jessie froze she was sun blind from the flashing lights.

Marcus swept her up and carried her to the car followed by the bodyguards, who got in the front and in the other cars, leaving Jessie and Marcus in each other's arms in the back of the wedding car? Now wife your mine for the next ten whole minutes till we get back to the brotherhood reception hall. The next time we will be together and alone will be on board ship in about seven whole hours' time and I will be taking you over and over and over in that dress on that boat, make no mistake! I had wet dreams about you last night, that's when I could sleep and I had lots to drink and still could not fine peace, all I kept thinking about was making love to you over and over, and when you touched yourself. So now we have eight minutes I want you now Jessie. She wiggled off his lap and said can they see us.
  No, Marcus said so she sat on the opposite seat and opened her legs, put one of her hi heels each side of Marcus, she

slid her hand up the leg pulling her dress aside and slid her hand in she slid her fingers between her legs and touched herself, she was wet, she wanted him he looked so Horney and sexy in the back suite.

He licked his lips and she pushed her head back, her nipples pushed the fabric of her dress, he unbuttoned his jacket and went to lean across to grab her legs but she was to quick and put her one foot with her hi heels on to his chest to keep him at bay. She rubbed herself again and looked him in the eyes she was breathing fast, she pulled the front of her dress down so he could see one of her breasts, when she touched it she bucked and called his name she really had to push her leg to keep him back, she rubber herself between her legs again and then she came, thrashing her head and arching her back, Marcus she gasped out. Her leg went week, he pulled her legs apart and pushed her dress up, he licked and sucked her everywhere between her legs, then sucked her nipples, the car slowed to a stop. Shit, Marcus said, he locked the doors and had to pull himself off of her. They tried to straighten up their clothing but, in the end, he pulled her on to his lap and put his jacket around Jessie, her nipples where still hard as he was.

He unlocked the door and carried her inside and straight to the ladies room, took his jacket and his shirt off and undid his belt without taking his eyes from her, he turned her around to face the mirror and slid her dress off, grabbed her hips and entered her fully and hard, she cried out his name, he grabbed her breasts but could not hold on, hot tight muscles were still contracting around him and her hot liquid was sliding over his shaft, Oh, Jess honey I can't, last he entered her again and called out her name and bucked, hard and fast into her up to his hilt . He slumped against her panting hard whilst kissing her back. After a few minutes

Marcus came out and said to Christine and Kirk and a few others she will not be long morning sickness he said.
A big smile swept across Kirks face for he knew it was a blatant lie, just seeing the feeling of victory rolling off of him.

We should give them a few minutes and let the others know Kirk said, and steered Christine away. Marcus went back in to see if Jessie was presentable now. Jessie was stood in the wedding line up to their great their guests. After a few minutes of standing and greeting their guests Jessie could feel the baby getting very hot inside her as she could sense all the other immortals. Jessie could hear the baby babbling very fast, she was too excited. She needs Xander and Phillip. She stepped back and bumped into Robert, he put his arm around her for support, Marcus ,Robert said and Marcus turned and looked alarmed, Jessie! he went to pick her up, no, she said, he gave her a second, By now there was a little crowd of people around her, she put her hand on her tummy and said out loud I'm ok, I need Xander, I am here is the she ok. Yes, Jessie replied, she is too excited, she can sense all the others. Please talk to her and calm her. Can we sit, I need Phillip close to me he shields her from a lot of their senses, Of course.

James stopped everyone from coming in and they sat Jessie down at the head table, let them wait Xander said, she is more important. Xander placed his hand on her belly while security surrounded them giving them privacy. Marcus sat the other side of Jessie and put his hand on top of Xander, he could hear her asking lots and trying to talk fast, he said be clam little one, be at ease.

Daddy she said, yes darling Marcus said out loud not talking quietly like Xander to her, she giggled just like

Jessie had and he smiled, a red glow came from Jessie's tummy and she stared to settle as Phillip was getting close. She will not be at rest for long. She sleeps when she feels Marcus around to give us time to be together, but there must be a lot of power in the room, I can't believe how strong she is.

I am ok now, I probably got too excited about the wedding she looked at Marcus who went red, we will change the seating arrangements, Xander clicked his fingers and it was done. Xander and Phillip were one side and Marcus and Christine the other with Kirk. Xander, Jessie said it's just us and the brotherhood here isn't it, yes, why what bothers you child, well I don't want someone bumping into me, and the baby talking to them or her glowing again that's the first time she's done it and I don't want someone freaking out. No, it is us and the entire brother hood and not just here all around the world has heard about our heavenly visit, no one will freak, they will not mind waiting they will understand about anything that may happen, they all pledged their life to save yours and your little one now. So, no more worrying, ok, Jessie said and Xander clicked his fingers again and James started to let the guest in. After the greetings and speech's, it was time for their first dance. Marcus took Jessie in his arms and danced very slowly to her favorite song, he kissed her slowly and gently and Jessie never felt so loved and happy. Their growing baby felt warm Marcus could feel the love and warmth.

He could stay there with her forever and not move. When the music stopped, they did not notice, the DJ played their song again, everyone was cheering and whistling, when the song ended again everyone clapped and Marcus broke their kiss, stepped back, bowed and took Jessie back to her seat. Then everyone filled the dance floor. Jessie turned to Xander and said would you come with us on our honey moon as I have invited Aunty Chris and Phillip and well you are our family to we all need family time and she would not like having you far away from her she shares a strong bond to you and asks for you when she wakes up because she sleeps when Marcus near and the second he is not she wake's the little madam. I was hoping she would play that card. Yes, he said, thank you my dear and patted her hand. She does worry me, why Xander said, well Jessie said if she is this strong at now how strong she will be where she is born, very interesting but I was thinking the same I think we will have to wait and see. Yes, Jessie said we don't have a choice.

What are you two whispering about Kirk said? Our little one Jessie said. Yes, Kirk said if she is anything like you my dear, she wills break many men's hearts all over the place you know. Yes, Jessie laugh. Are you feeling up to a dance Jessie because your husband dances with my loved one? Jessie turned to see Marcus dancing with her aunt? Well we can't have that now can we, lets level up the score shall we. Marcus was thanking Christine, because if she had not called him that day, he would never had met Jessie. When he looked up to see Kirk and Jessie laughing their heads off while dancing, he smiled but a pang of jealousy shot through him, her smiles were for him and so was her laughter, she looked so beautiful.

So, every time Marcus and Christine got close to change partners they moved away. Kirk held Jessie closer as Jessie turned and smiled at Marcus, he then gave up, he knew they were playing with him and he gave a big white bright smile, laughed and shook his head, pointing at is heart and took Christine back for Phillip to dance with her.

Do you think my life would be worth living if I let one of the waiting men dance with you? No, Jessie said he can only take so much teasing and he is very protective? Yes, your right and I like my head where it is. Just then Jessie's baby woke up, as Kirk's hand was on her back holding her to him and the little girl whispered to Kirk, "grandpa" Kirk stopped and looked down, Jessie said quick keep moving or Marcus will be over here and my fun will end, if you talk to her in your head she can hear you. Hello little one why do you awaken, danger grandpa you passed danger with mummy, what do you mean danger, there was a man who does bad things he burns people and he wants to hurt mummy, he was near to us but he is not near us now.

Kirk looked at the people he danced passed he could not pick up on anything. Are you sure little one, yes grandpa? If we go pass the man again can you tell me which one without hurting mummy or being scared, yes, she said I will try. Are you ok with that Jessie? We need to find him, Jessie replied. Why did you not sense danger earlier little one, I was with daddy and Uncle Phillip they make me sleep. Yes, Jessie said that's right she tried to say something earlier. Kirk said, right are you ready little one. yes grandpa. He smiled he like that "grandpa" he felt love and calm wash over him. Danger grandpa, Kirk looked at a group of four men and slowed their dancing more danger grandpa, she was shouting mummy's in danger, danger and Kirk moved away but Jessie's tummy lit up with a red glow. Kirk stopped and drew his sword and stood in front of Jessie, the little light had now covered Jessie and the people dancing around them stopped and moved away.

Marcus was stood with his heart in his mouth he was over the table and jumped down onto the dance floor. Kirk's hand was on Jessie's belly and the baby was telling him that there was a man in front her that hurt mummies, mummy and daddy. He burned them; the baby was so worried he was going to hurt her mummy. Marcus stood to the side of Kirk saying what is it my friend? Jessie's light had now got bigger, brighter and she was now a blue color. The little one is very frightened for Jessie's life she is protecting Jessie with her light. The little one said that one of these men killed Peter and Leah he burned them to death. Jessie's blue light now covered Marcus and Kirk, the little one is trying to protect us.

Phillip was now near Jessie and could touch the babies light, he could also hear the little one without touching Jessie. Phillip erupted in total light, stronger and brighter. Xander felt her fear and drew close to Phillip, and Phillip said stay back do not approach, Xander stood still all the bodyguards had moved in behind Xander and Jessie and security had closed in. Phillips light covered them all. Can you show me little one? Kirk said out loud, a little red light like a torch shone out from Jessie's belly and touched a man? He jumped back and pulled a gun out and a white light shone around Jessie, Phillip moved in front of Jessie and her little light stopped. Phillip gripped Marcus by the shoulder and said my sister needs her husband and your daughter needs a farther. Marcus let Phillip pull him back slowly behind him and in front of Jessie.

You killed my parents now I kill you, a bright white light with a blue flame shot out of Phillip and burned the man's eyes out, a flash of light filled the hall and a shot rang out, Kirk moved and the light stopped, the man's head had been severed from his body and was laying on the floor.

Kirk was slummed over Phillips body, Christine started to scream and run towards both of them. Marcus was there lifting Kirk off of Phillip. Phillip was ok just drained, but Kirk had been shot in the chest, Jessie ran over and was at Kirk's side, leaning over his body. She held his hand to her belly, her baby was calling "grandpa", I am here little one but not for long, no, she said. Mummy give him some blood, Jessie said Marcus give me your gold knife.

He produced the gold knife with the diamond on it, the one he had cut her finger with and she cut the palm of her hand, it was now dripping with blood. Ok what now darling Jessie said. Jessie let her blood drip in on the hole on Kirk's chest and put some in his mouth. He needs a bit of your light mummy, how do I get it Jessie said, Grandpa Xander, Jessie called Xander over to them, he knelt beside her, and she held out his hand and cut his hand, now the little one said hold yours to his and then put one hand on grandpa Kirk and one hand on me and I will do it for you mummy. She did as her daughter asked, she put hers and Xander's hands on her belly.

Robert grabbed Christine and said stay back. Then a pure white light shone out from Jessie's eyes and mouth and she bent down and kissed Kirk on the mouth and the light shot out throw the hole in his chest until it closed. Jessie slumped over Kirks body, she was weak, she tried to get up but could not, Marcus picked Jessie up and held her to him, Xander was helping pick Kirk up and Robert let Christine go. Peter was helping Phillip up and Christine cuddled him to her and was kissing him. Kirk laughed and said I am the one that's been shot where's my kisses and hugs woman. Oh, you come here and she flung herself at Kirk, saying you old fool. They were all stood around, Jessie and Marcus as he was on his knees holding Jessie to him.

Is all ok Xander said, yes Kirk replied is Jessie and the little one ok? she saved us all and found a traitor in our mists. Jessie said she has stopped talking I can't hear her and she hugged her husband to her for comfort. The security team had removed the body and when Marcus lifted Jessie up all the brothers of the knight went down on their knees in homage to Jessie and her daughter, what do you want to do Marcus said we can stay and finish the reception or we can go it's up to you honey? Can we stay I know it's horrible but our daughter needs to draw power from them to make her strong? Ok we stay, Xander I need you to sit next to Jessie give her a cuddle, your granddaughter needs to draw on your strength again, yes, he said Marcus went and spoke to Christine, Kirk and Phillip, and they all agreed to stay to help the little one needs to get her strength back.

Xander spoke to James and he told the DJ to play some soothing music. Christine went over and hugged and kissed Jessie and said thank you darling, then she hugged Marcus and kissed him on his cheek. Everyone took their seats. Soon people where dancing. Jessie thanked Xander, I need to use the ladies, please excuse me, Robert stepped forward and he and Amanda accompanied her to the ladies. Essie came back with a big smile and said should we cut the cake husband; I love you.

Marcus told her how he loved her to; she smiled at Marcus and said I am not talking to you. Marcus beamed a big smile and touched her belly, Xander and Kirk where on their feet watching intently. Marcus said daddy 's here darling daddy loves you honey. "Daddy" a little sleepy voice said I love you. Daddy loves you to honey and she felt warm in Jessie's belly as she went to sleep.

Marcus hugged Jessie to him and kissed her. Xander and Kirk both felt relief flow throw them as did James. Jessie and Marcus cut their wedding cake and enjoyed another slow dance, a glass of campaign then gathered their family and went to their cars, to go to the yacht.

Marcus kissed his wife deeply in the car and said to her don't forget your mine the second we get on the boat and in our room. I am going to take you with no interruptions from anyone. He moaned her name softly and Jessie started to unbutton his shirt and kiss her way down his chest, by the time she wanted to take off his shirt the car was slowing to stop. He put her on the opposite seat and did all of his buttons back up she said remember earlier and she put her leg up to his chest and he growled at her and said I have forgotten nothing not even you on the table yesterday. He got out first and then she got out, he took her in his arms and carried her on board and straight to the cabin, he locked the door.

Now your mine he said he laid her on the bed, he stood back looking at her and she shivered with anticipation and bit her lip softly, he unbuttoned his jacket and looked at her he had fire in his eyes and wanted possession. He watched her as he unbuttoned his shirt and she crossed her leg and sat up, he unbuttoned the last button and dropped it on the floor. Jessie laid flat back on the bed and uncrossed her legs and started to touched herself. Marcus stood over her and looked at her while he undid his belt and unzipped his trousers and Jessie closed her eyes and touched her breasts with her other hand. Jessie look at me, she opened her eyes and he knew she was not far off of releases, he pushed her legs wide open and entered her, she came right there and then and he dove into her over and over, she was crying out his name she was his he felt her tighten her muscles around him she was going to come again and as she did he filler her fully with his hot seed. He slid sideways; he did not want her to take his weight because of the baby. He pulled her to him, she was still dressed and had her shoes on, he still had his trousers on but did not care. They fell asleep.

An hour later he woke up he wanted her again and he was rock hard. He got off the bed and finished undressing himself and untied Jessie shoes, took them off and got back on the bed, he woke her up, she smiled up at him. Are you sure you're awake because I need to take you again honey? She reached up and kissed him, he turned her on her side facing away from him and put his hand up her dress and pulled it over her hips, he entered her from behind fully and he made slow hard love to her, he could not last long she was so hot then they drifted off to sleep together with him still in her.

The sun was coming through the curtains and the gently swaying of the boat woke Jessie up, the clock said 7.30am she stretched her body feeling stiff and found this woke Marcus up, he was getting hard her muscles contracted around him tight as he was still inside her from last night and it was very erotic. Marcus moaned her name gently and kissed her neck and back, he slid his hand up and over her breasts and said good morning wife, she pushed her self-back further on to him wanting him now, but he withdrew slightly and said I remember what you did to me in the shower and on the table and if my memory serves me right in the car as well, now it's my turn he said and withdrew a bit more Jessie made a wanting little groan.

Marcus pulled himself slowly and fully out of her and rolled Jessie on to her back and straddled her he pushed both of her hands above her head and held them there with one of his bag hands and he kissed her lightly. He teased her with his mouth and still holding her hands he licked and sucked one breast slowly at a time. Her body was shaking and she was wriggling and calling his name, he moved down her body kissing her still holding both of her hands together, he moved his other hand down and slid his finger between her legs, she was hot wet and ready. She groaned his name out loud with lust and with need in her voice. He pushed his legs in between hers and spread her legs open and slid his hot thick hard shaft, into her. She was now gasping his name. He went to kiss her and lifted his head, she tried to push her head up to meet his kiss but he was too strong and held her hands back against the bed. Marcus please, she gasped, he slowly lifted his body and withdrew from her and touched her hot wet silky bud with the tip of his shaft and she called out again, begging for him to take her, he slid himself forward and the tip of his shaft was just on the entrance to her body.

She was trying to push her body on to his. Marcus please I am begging you please don't stop. He slid himself into her and she bucked and gasped with pleasure. He then withdrew from her and said now were even and let go of her and rolled of the bed, very quickly so she could not jump on him and he walked off to find the bathroom, he was still very hard but very smug. He didn't look back because he would have given in and taken her again. Jessie hurt from wanting him, this was not over this was war.

When Marcus came out of the shower, he was still smiling, a bit too much for Jessie's liking but she smiled back and walked past him to the shower. When they were ready, they went out onto the deck, they were at sea and the sun was shining there was an assortment of food all laid out and Xander was sat at the table reading a paper, Jessie was on

the cover again and on every single one for the past few days. The headline "billionaire weds teenager".
Christine and Kirk were sat with Xander. Good morning you two love birds Xander said, how are you both today. Hungry Jessie replied. That's good Christine said, where is Phillip? Jessie asked, Kirk said I have already checked on him and he is fine he is still asleep, and how are you feeling after yesterday Kirk. I am as good as new and he winked at Christine who went red, and the little one Kirk asked, she is still asleep but she knows when Xander is near and all she wants to do is talk is to him.

Marcus pulled Jessie's chair out so she could sit down and he got her some breakfast, she said Thank you husband you do take care of my every need and looked at him. He said thank you my wife and smiled back at her. After breakfast Jessie asked where they were going, Xander informed her that the first stop will be the French Riviera. We should reach there about 11am, we will spend a day or two there and go on from there, you will be able to go shopping and sightseeing. We have all been invited to a dinner dance tonight with the French ambassador; he is an old friend of mine. Jessie thought that sounded great.

Later in the day Jessie was talking to Christine while the men planned there the trip and were briefing the body guards. Jessie's baby started talking, she was asking for Xander and asked how grandpa Kirk was she sounded worried. What's wrong Jessie dear, Christine asked? She wants her two grandpas she feels them near and wants their attentions while she's awake. Why can't I hear her Jessie? Because you're not immortal, but I think you might be able to when she is born or it might stop.

Ok, Jessie said out loud, what is it Jessie, Christine asked.

She's like her father she can't wait.
Amanda can you contact Xander and tell him the little one is asking for him and Kirk, yes, of course, one second Jessie, Amanda opened her phone and spoke quickly, they are on their way thank you, Amanda and with that Amanda stepped back next to Kevin. Within a few seconds the men appeared they were all smiles. Xander said how is she today? She's asking for you and Kirk she likes her two grandpas' attention, just like her farther. Marcus looked at her and gave her a grin. Xander sat one side and Christine moved so Kirk could sit the other side. Marcus said I am not sure if I like this situation, I don't get to talk to my daughter and I don't get to sit next to my wife and I am not sure about people putting their hands on my wife. Jessie laughed; would you deny your daughter time with her grandpas! I am going to talk to my brother in law if I am not wanted here, he then winked at Jessie and left.

After a good twenty minutes of the baby talking the ears off of Xander and Kirk and she was happy that they were ok she asked for her daddy, he had just come back from talking to Phillip. Xander remarked, just in time she wants her daddy. She's just like her mother in that way and Jessie just glared at him, the two men moved away so he could be with his wife and child, she sounded sleepy again "Daddy I love you", and his heart melted again, he said "daddy loves you to honey", is that my name Daddy? for now, he said me and mummy have to give you a name, daddy mummy has a name she likes, what it darling is and Marcus looked at Jessie. Jessie could do nothing. Leah the baby said. Well I like that name too Marcus said do you like it.

Yes, yes, I do and she felt hot in Jessie's tummy, she whispered "I love you Daddy" and she was silent, Jessie said, she gone to sleep for today she talked herself out, you should have told me you were thinking about names. Well I am not sure what you like, but I was thinking about my mum that's where she got the name from because she felt the love I have for that name. Marcus nodded and said Leah it is then and Jessie grabbed his face and kissed him and someone said we are about to dock sir. Jessie broke the kiss. Are we ready for shopping ladies Xander said let's go and spend some money?

After hours of shopping for clothing, shoes, under ware and maternity clothes, Jessie was not going to keep her shape for much longer and had to buy a few things bigger. Jessie and Christine when into a perfume shop where the woman behind the counter with the low top on with her big chest was trying her charms on Marcus and Jessie did not like it, a pang of jealousy ran through her and to make matters worse Marcus was lapping it up. The shop assistant sprayed some sent on her chest and lent forward for Marcus to smell, Marcus could see Jessie's face in the mirror and new that, one she was watching him and two she was not happy. He declined the woman's offer not that he would look twice at her, he said sorry but it's not up to my wife's standards.

But she had done her job and made Jessie jealous, as he had been all day watching men pander and flock to her. It confirmed that she was his and Jessie was about to stake her clam on him, he had no desire to upset her or make her stressed, but he wanted to know he came first and he did, he knew she was going to make him pay and he just turned and smiled at Jessie.

Marcus walked over to her and marched her out of the shop before Jessie could confront the assistant, she turned on her heels and left the shop but Jessie turned and gave the woman one last glair as she was being pulled along. So, Jessie said if that's what you want then you're welcome to it, you're married to me and you flirt with that pig, it did not take you long.

Jessie pulled her arm out of his grip. Marcus just smiled he knew he was defiantly in for in later, he loved Jessie's passion and spirit he loved being married she was his and he would never even look at another woman she was more than a match for him he was the luckiest man on earth, he just smiled. Xander and Christine went into a baby shop as Kirk was now escorting Jessie, since the perfume shop, Marcus walked behind with Phillip. Marcus said it's you and me kid I have been demoted and Phillip laugh, you're a better man than me Phillip said I would hate to be in your shoes tonight, even I am scared to get on the wrong side of my sister, look Phillip said there's a pub let's have a quick drink while you are already in the dog house, then I can blame you to. I dare you Phillip said, come on then she will be in there a good half an hour Marcus said but you're on your own if we get caught.

Kirk and Jessie where looking at evening dresses when Kirk spotted one, look at this black velvet one Jessie, it was made for you wow, shall I try it on? yes, Kirk said and the assistant got the dress and Amanda went with her to try in on. When Jessie came out there were a few loud whistles from men in the shop with their wives and a few from the single men. Robert went over and stood next to Jessie.

Well Kirk said, your husband won't know what's hit him, not only will he be drawling all over you but he will not want any man near you, Jessie turned around, Kirk whistled the black dress was completely back less and where the back did start in was in a v shape just on the top of her bum cheeks and met just at the start of the gap at the top of her bum, the front was a halter neck that had a v down between her breasts and to her navel and the dress went down to the floor with a slit up the front.

What do you think Robert, he said I think you had better go and put some clothes on, you look like a movie star? Do you think this is ok for tonight then Kirk, oh yes that will defiantly get him going? Jessie turned and walked back in to get changed. Robert said "thanks Kirk, my jobs hard enough already, he is going to freak when he sees her in that", I know. Jessie also brought matching shoes and wrap. When she came out everyone was outside laughing. Are we ready to go back to the ship Marcus said yes, let's go said Jessie as she and Kirk walked arm and arm? Marcus said would you like to take my arm young lady. But before Jessie could answer Kirk said no its ok old man you will need all your arms for latter believe me and just waved his hand in the air and kept strolling with Jessie back to their cars.

Jessie went in to have her shower and locked the door behind her she was going to make him beg big time, he was not going to see her naked or in the shower, he was not going to make love to her before they went out tonight. Let's just see how he reacts to her having a bit of male attention. Not that she wanted any other man she only wanted him.

Marcus went to unpack everything they had brought but Jessie had already done it, he could hear the water running and decided enough was enough; he had tortured her enough for one day and had to give her what she had wanted from him all day and what he had needed as well. But she had locked the bathroom door, so she had not forgiven him, he smiled and used the guest bathroom, when he came out looking and smelling sexy, he looked like a model, Jessie had to swallow a gasp, you look good was all she could manage. He asked her what are you hiding under your wrap? an evening dress, well he said at least it covers you and reaches the floor.

Yes, darling she said, and well you look beautiful from what I can see. When she walked the split at the front of the dress opened and he could see her legs, wow he said what have you got on, my wife. There is nothing under this dress, are you ready husband, yes, I am let's get going.
When they all arrived at the embassy the reception was under way. The ambassador and his wife introduce Xander and his party to their guests and the people Jessie and Marcus were to sit next to at the ambassadors table, they were the ambassadors son Andre and his wife Maria who was also pregnant as well but her bump was just starting to show, Jessie had noticed that her breasts where bigger today, they were shown to their seats and just before Jessie sat down she removed her wrap turned around just so Marcus could get the full effect and stretched slightly and handed it to Amanda, who took it, she turned back around to find ever pair of male eyes on her .

She didn't look at Marcus she just sat down and smiled. Marcus was struck dumb and could not move he just gazed like a school boy with his mouth open and eyes out. He thought he was going to come there and then and Jessie breasts looked bigger.
She looked all woman and not the girl who virtue he had taken, he could hardly control himself he wanted to take

her now. She then smiled up at him, her dark eyes sparkled like the diamonds she wore, but they could not hold a candle to her eyes, no wonder she did not show him her dress it did not even cover her bottom you could see that she did not have any under ware on and it barely covered her breasts, you could see her navel, and she smelled like an angle, you could see nearly all of her legs as well. She took a small sip of her campaign and said are you all right darling? All he could do was smile, well he was not excepting that, she had him and that was just fine with him. He looked around the room when he sat down, and men were staring.

The evening went on and after their meal and drinks the music started, a few woman were dancing and Maria said would you like to have a little warm up dance with me Jessie as my husband is very jealous and possessive and will not let any man dance with me, yes I would love to dance, Robert thought ah shit here we go, as he stepped forward to pull her chair back. Jessie walked slowly and put a little swing in her hips she knew that would drive him crazy and made sure she made the most of it. Maria stepped forward and took Jessie's hand and led her to the dance floor, they held hands and danced slowly together. Andre moved over one space and said without taking his eyes from their two woman and said to Marcus you're a very lucky gifted man to possess such a beautiful and very rare woman. Yes, I am Marcus replied, be careful the vultures are starting to circle my friend; it seems our two pregnant wives give a very erotic picture dancing together. I am going to claim my wife before someone else try's. I am with you my friend I would kill any man that even tries to touch my wife, we are rightfully possessive aren't we. Marcus gave him a look to say he meant every word.

Jessie and Maria where laughing and giggling and

comparing notes about their husbands and changes in their bodies from pregnancy, they were holding each other quite close and had not noticed the large audience of men gathering on the edge of the dance floor. But had noticed that Marcus and Andre were moving towards them. I think you two ladies have thrilled your audience enough for one day poor saps Marcus said as he stood behind her and wrapped a protective arm around her and kissed her neck as a show of ownership of her. Andre move Maria away to dance together.

Marcus stopped kissing her and looked down the back of her dress he could see her bum cheeks. He turned her around and pulled her closely to him he looked down at her, god she was so beautiful he looked down her dress and growled in her ear as he started to breath heavy he said Jessie your killing me honey and kissed her with need, pulled her to him crushing her breasts against his chest he ran his hands down her back and her nipples went hard against his chest, he felt it and it just made him even harder he thought he was going to lose control and take her then and there. He stood back from her gasping, and danced slowly at arm's length to calm himself and regain control but that was not happening.

Are you ok honey Jessie said or do you think you over did it in the pub this afternoon or this morning, I think perhaps you over did it then because you could not make love to me? Perhaps Kirk is right, he said something about your old age damaging your vigor perhaps it is you age because you were encouraging that old hag in the perfume shop, Phillip he said, no Jessie said, Kirk he said, no she said, then who Marcus said, Xander saw you and Phillip coming out of the pub and Leah got it out of him in the car when she woke up, you were in the second car, he did not turn you in she read his mind and I heard.

Now he felt guilty no wonder Phillip shunned him in the car on the way here, he had an ear bashing from Christine for him going into the pub. Oh this was his payback, and he had upset her and let her down. I love you, and I want only you, and you drive me crazy my wife and I will never want another Jess, please forgive me. Before Jessie could reply a man tapped him on his shoulder and said may I have this dance, Marcus looked at Jessie like he would die if she said she yes it would kill him to watch another man hold her. She could not do it, Jessie shook her head, and Marcus said my pregnant wife has no wish to dance with you and he led Jessie back to her seat, where Xander asked her to dance with him and she did, two men asked Xander if they could dance with Jessie but she refused. Xander returned her to her husband, Kirk asked if he could dance with Jessie, and Marcus said only if you're up to it old man, Kirk grinned, yes, of course Jessie said and Kirk danced with her for four songs and then returned her to Marcus, he said go slow old man you had better rest I wouldn't want you to pull a muscle at your age, would we, Jessie you are to kind to the elderly.

The nights not over yet Kirk said and winked at Jessie she danced with her brother, and he thanked her for turning him in to Christine, Phillip said I was worried you were going to give me an ear bashing to. Jessie looked up at Marcus to see he was talking to Andre and a very good looking man at the table, when her brother took her back the man could not take his eyes off of Jessie, Andre introduced the man to Jessie as Pierre his younger brother, he kissed her hand and looked into her eyes and said would you give me the pleasure of a dance Jessie, yes, I would like to give that pleasure, he took her arm and she did not look back because she could not.

Marcus's face because she knew he would be furious. Marcus felt a pain in his gut, he was not pleased that Andre's brother had asked his wife to dance, he had just met the guy and he was trying to move in on his wife, he clicked his fingers at Robert and Amanda. Jessie kept him at a distance to keep it respectable but he had other ideas and pulled Jessie closer. Amanda walked up to Jessie and said can I have this dance and Amanda did not wait for a response, she just grabbed him and danced away from her, Robert took her hand and danced with her, he said you are going to be the death of me if you keep this up, Marcus is going to skin me alive, a man tried to ask her to dance and Robert said if you want to keep your hand mate take it off of my shoulder now and go away .

Robert then led her back to Marcus who was waiting with her wrap, Andre said that was done very nicely and very quick my friend? Yes, it was, Marcus said I like you and your farther I would not want my killing your brother to come between us, good night Maria and Jessie kissed her on the cheek and wished her well with the baby. They said their good nights and he and Jessie left, Marcus did not speak to her in the car, it was not her fault men were drawn to her and she had not encouraged anyone, but enjoyed telling Pierce, she would pleasure him with a dance had just made him snap just the word was too much. She was his. He walked behind her watching her bum as she walked back to their cabin, she opened the door and slid off her wrap, he slammed the door and Jessie stood back against the bed, she looked frightened, this is what it would feel like if another man took her, he felt sick and could not even think it, she looked frightened and scared. Please don't look at me like that Jessie.

When you look like that men will want you, as I want you now Jessie, do you want me to take you like that, it hurt him to say it. She shook her head and said no. he lowered his voice and said I love you honey, you drive me crazy I just have to look at you and I want you all to myself, she smiled and he stepped forward, she said you drive me crazy to, that's good to know he smiled at her and the tension eased in the room.

He moved slow and unbuttoned his jacket and she watched him intently, he knew she loved this bit, he undid his tie, she licked her lips and he could see that her nipples went hard. He slid his jacket off, but left his tie where it was, he unbuttoned his shirt and left in open so she could see his body, she loved that she licked her lips again and made a little noise. Her eyes where shinning at him again. He loved that, seeing her want him it made him even harder.

She took a step closer to him, he did not move he just took a deep breath, she was not looking at his face now she was looking at his body he tried to control his breathing but he couldn't manage it. His breath was getting faster the closer she came to him she was biting her lip, then she looked up at him and she reached out with her hand and touched the muscles on his stomach, he gasped her name she pushed him back against the door and ran her hands up the inside of his shirt and gently bit his nipple then licked it and gently sucked it she kissed his neck and he whispered her name, she licked his bottom lip and bit it gently she then kissed his neck and bit him and sucked his neck hard, he knew she was marking him with love bites, but let her have her way she was marking her territory on him.

Then she slid her hands down his chest and stomach, bent

down on her knees and un did his belt she licked the skin above his belt and drove him crazy, he was gasping and saying her name, he looked down he could see down the front and back of her dress, she was unzipping his trousers she pulled his shaft out and enclosed her mouth around his shaft and sucked it while she looked up at him, he could not hold on and filled her mouth he grabbed her hair and was trusting into her mouth, she swallowed everything and sucked him again, gasping her name she stood and left him to recover, she went to the sink and brushed her teeth.

While she bent over the sink to take a mouth full of water, he came up behind her, his hands ran down her back and over her bum she looked up into the mirror and turned the water off and dabbed her mouth with a towel. He still had his clothing on and the look on his face told her that he was not finished with her yet, he had let her have her way and take him now he wanted her.

He looked into her eyes and excitement shivered threw her he pulled her hips back and she stood back slowly, his eyes on her eyes in the mirror, both of his hands ran up her back and over her breasts, he pulled her dress aside of her breasts, exposing them he just looked at her hard pink nipples her breasts looked fuller and bigger, she closed her eyes and rested her head back against his chest he kissed her neck and slid one hand over her breast and held her neck with the other while he sucked it and bit her neck marking her in return .

He loved doing that, his hand slid from her breast to her abdomen to where his child lay asleep growing inside her, he took a slow deep breath, he was hard again, his hand slid lower into the slit at the front of her dress and he slid his fingers in there and found she was hot and wet, he slid his finger inside her and she gasped and bucked against him, he withdrew his finger slowly and did it again, she arched her back and called out his name, he withdrew his hand and turned her around and kissed her slowly, licked her nipples and sucked and ran his thumbs over them, he lifted her up and wrapped her legs around him pushing her dress aside he laid her back and held her hips and back with one strong hand and ran his other hand over her breast then held her hips with both of his hands and entered her, feeling her mussels and flesh stretch to make way for him.

She bucked against him and said his name, her breast rose up as she arched her back and he thrust harder but he wanted more of her. He withdrew and she cried out no, don't stop please no, not again please. He soothed her saying were going to the bed it's ok honey I won't stop, I promise, she let go with her legs but could not stand so he lifted her up kissing her, he laid he down on the edge of the bed and she wiggle herself and turned over he lifted her dress out of the way and ran his hands over her bum and held her hips and pulled her to him and entering her fully, feeling her flesh give way to him filling her with his shaft, she flung her head back as she arched, he made her moan out load in a sharp gasp as she grabbed the sheets to steady herself . She moaned again when he withdrew and thrust into her again, she was so tight he groaned out, he thrust faster and harder, deeper into her pulling her hips harder and harder he was calling her name taking her over and over the sweat stared to drip off of him, sweat had gathered in a tiny pool in the middle of her back, she was moaning loudly for him not to stop she was panting.

He felt her tighten up even more, he found it hard to thrust they were both shaking and she cried out his name and threw her head back, she came over him she was still convulsing, he thrusted again and she lost it calling out and pushing herself back on him again and again, he could not hold on, he filled her, he could not stop pulsating in her and they both fell on to the bed trying to regain their breath.

He just pulled the sheet over them to cover them both and they drifted off to sleep.When they woke up, they were still dressed and their clothing was tangled. Jessie could see the huge love bite on Marcus's neck she went red, she did not think she had been that rampant she looked down his body she had bitten him just above his navel and he still looked like a male pin up with that shirt wrapped around him. Do you like what you see Jess, yes, she said, I do very much I love you she said and she kissed him good morning. Its ten past ten you know, so what he said he looked at her taking her in, she could not get up because her dress was wrapped around him and he had no intention of moving, so she wiggled out of her dress and went into the shower leaving him looking at her from the bed.

When she looked into the mirror, she could see the love bite Marcus had given her, it was twice as big as the she had given him. it went from below her ear at the side of her neck to half way down her neck and round to the front you could see he had done it from behind her and every one would know how he had taken her, no wonder he looked smug, everyone would know what they had been doing, it made her Horney to know he wanted to possesses her all the time, he had laid claim for all to see like she had done. She showered and dressed and left her hair down. She put some black and red French Lace under ware on, a red baggy t shirt, a black stretchy skirt and black flat shoes on. She felt good and looked good, pregnancy agreed with her, her skin had a natural glow or was it all the lovemaking with Marcus that had that effect on her.

Marcus had come out of the bathroom with jeans and a v neck t shirt to show off his love bite, he knew she would be blushing all day every time she looked at him and it felt good, he heard Jessie talking to someone in the bathroom, he asked who are you taking to honey? I will be out in a second, Marcus went over to her bathroom and she opened the door. She smiled at him and he said who you are taking to. Well she said who do you think I was taking to and looked down at her belly, he smiled and put his hand on her belly. "Daddy" a little excited voice said and Marcus melted at the sound of her little voice.

Leah, daddy loves you honey. I know daddy where's grandpa, he is not far honey, Daddy what's underwear? why honey, well mummy was thinking about her underwear and I wanted to speak to grandpa and she told me I was not to talk about underwear to anyone, he then looked at Jessie who looked down at him with a disapproving look. Well honey I think mummy is right it's something big girls think about and when you're old enough say in 30- or 40-years mummy will talk to you then about it, ok honey, and mummy's thoughts are hers, you are never to tell anyone what mummy is thinking sweetheart ok, its private honey. Daddy what's private, it means you do not tell anyone, ok Leah, yes daddy I love you daddy and daddy loves you to honey, in a fed-up voice she asked if she could speak to grandpa, yes darling, oh goodie she said.

Marcus stood and said sorry Jess, I was trying to tell her not to tell grandpa about my underwear when you called to me. Yeah, I got that, and you look beautiful today darling, as do you Jessie, he could see his mark on her neck and said do you like my love bite my wife gave it to me and smiled at her. Let's go and see grandpa so we can have breakfast. Everyone on deck was waiting for them, they had been up hours and had breakfast but the table was still all laid out for them. Can I sit next to grandpa and grandpa on the sofa so I can talk to them? Eat while she talks their ears off, yes of course sweetheart, he nodded to the butlers and they placed a small table in front of Jessie with tea and toast and fruit. They all saw the bite on Marcus's neck and they all looked at Jessie's neck. Kirk said, what has he done to you child it's barbaric and winked at her.

When she finished, she said to Xander quietly you said there is a doctor a board, yes, what is it he sounded alarmed, Kirk and James felt his alarm as did Marcus and Phillip. I am fine Jessie said I just wanted a chat with the doctor that's all. Right away Xander said he lifted his hand and James stepped forward. Please take Jessie to the doctor immediately. Yes, replied James and led her away. What is it Xander, Marcus asked, Xander said Jessie requested to speak to the doctor, perhaps you're being overly vigorous with her, Xander reached out and touched Marcus on his neck where Jessie had bitten him?

That would be my guess, but what does an old man of my age know of love, lust and desire in this day and age. Kirk went to say something and Marcus said don't even say it and sat down next to Phillip, who said you grassed me up cheers mate, Marcus told him it was Xander who saw us coming out of the pub and Leah got it out of him in the car on the way back, she told Jessie and Christine, sorry mate we have to be more careful and they both laughed, caught out by a baby how sad is that! When Jessie went into the medical room, doctor Adams was there, Jessie smiled at her, doctor Adams said what can I do for you Jessie? James closed the door and left the two women to talk. Jessie said my breasts hurt a lot and have got a lot bigger, I have had a lot of sex I cannot seem to stay away from my husband. Anything else? she looked at Jessie neck, and said tell your husband not to do that again while you're pregnant. Jessie went red, ok I will. Well since you know about me, do you know that my baby speaks to me, no the doctor said I did not but that's not as unusual as it sounds, she also speaks to my family, Oh, that's not normal, does she want to speak to me, no, Jessie said she's gone back to sleep.

Ok, do you mind if I examine you Jessie? I will also give you an ultrasound, as well, can you do that here Jessie was surprised! Would you like your husband present for the scan? Yes, please she said. Doctor Adams checked Jessie over and listened to her heart she pulled the screen across for Jessie to put her clothing on and get ready for the scan, the doctor opened the door and said to James could you ask Jessie's husband to come down as he is needed, also I wish to speak to Xander could he wait outside until I am finished with Jessie. James nodded and opened his phone.

Marcus ran to the medical room and Xander was behind him. James knocked the door and Marcus went in, close the door please the doctor said, please come and sit, don't look worried your wife if fine and we are just going to look at your daughter, she did the scan and printed off some picture and said there is something, she's fine your both in perfect health, what is it Marcus said. Well you know you don't have a normal pregnancy, you daughter is starting to grow at an increased rate so for every one day she is now growing two if she increase at the same rate each day she will arrive quicker and even sooner, Jessie in now nearly four mouths she will start to show more by tomorrow and at the increased rate she could have the baby within two weeks and without taking a biopsy of her tissue cells I can't give you a date and I can't tell you if she will develop enough to survive. Tears started too rolled down Jessie's face she now felt scared for her baby, will a biopsy hurt her Jessie asked, the doctor, there is a risk of miscarriage with the procedure.

Then no, I am not having it done Jessie said. That's fine Jessie you don't have to have anything done, but I will still need to take your blood if that's ok? The doctor turned to get a needle and a bright red glow shone out of Jessie and surrounded her and this time it had a purple haze around it. Ok, the doctor said which one of you is doing that. Jessie said Leah she thinks you have upset me and that you want to hurt us, she's trying to protect us, Jessie, Dr Adams said that is taking a lot of energy from the pair of you; you must rest more and eat a lot more. The doctor touched the haze and it gave her a shock. Dam, Jessie you need to be able to calm her. I need Phillip and Xander, Jessie informed the doctor. Marcus stood to try and touch the haze and he got a shock to; shit she packs a punch. Marcus went to the door everyone was in the hall and Marcus called to Phillip and Xander. They both walked in and James closes the door behind them. What is it, is all ok Xander asked?

Wow she's better than me Phillip said seeing the light coming from his sister. Well she is trying to protect Jessie from the doctor Marcus said, Leah thinks the doctor is going to hurt Jessie, the scan woke her up and she was not a happy bunny because Jessie was upset. The doctor needs blood and she not playing ball. Xander walked over and touched the light and it stung him. she is getting stronger, yes, I can see that Marcus said how do we get her to turn it off so the doctor can get the blood.
Let me try said Phillip, he walked over and the red light did not affect him he touched Jessie's belly and little white

sparks shot out of Phillip's eyes and Jessie's and the purple haze went, the red light faded out and she went back to sleep. The white sparks stopped coming out of them and Phillip said wow, you really upset her, what did you do. Nothing Jessie said she felt my fear for her life while she was asleep, bless her I scared her it's my fault.

Please do not be angry with her, is it safe for me to take blood now the doctor asked, yes, Phillip said, I will stay if it's ok with you doc. Yes, please and thank you Phillip the doctor drew the blood quickly, Phillip moved away from Jessie. You can get dressed now Jessie we have finished for now thank you. The doctor asked if she could I speak to Xander and Marcus outside. All three of them left the room and went into the doctor's office and she closed the door. Xander I need one of your trusted men to take me to the mainland now immediately with this blood sample, the brother hood has a full medical facility in every country don't they, I know they have built them up over very long-life times. Yes, Xander said why, I will need to test Jessie's blood and I don't want other doctors knowing what is happening to Jessie you will have to destroy all the equipment I use there after I have tested her blood without question, I need one no two of your men to carry out my orders and I don't want any problems with the facility.

That baby will be hear in about two weeks which means, one the baby might die, two it might kill Jessie, three if both are ok then I will have to sedate Jessie which brings a whole range of risks to life with it unless you can subdue that baby, because if Jessie runs in to problems giving birth then that baby is not going to let you anywhere near her and

I have just examined Jessie she will start showing by tomorrow and at that rate of growth will require a lot of energy, food and rest, it will also take its toll on her body, stretching that quickly, mentally it will affect her in some ways, what a body normally takes 9 months to build up to Jessie is going through in under three weeks. I suggest that she is not left unaccompanied at any time and does not go anywhere that you are not near a brotherhood medical hospital, you need to put them all on alert and tell them to have a big room ready just in case you have any more visitors, you need baby things at the ready, also there is something else, are you ok Marcus with me speaking about your wife in front of you grandfather, yes Marcus said what is it.

Well it's the baby's size that bothers me I think we know it's not going to come out the usual way, Jessie is not big enough to accommodate the baby, but you never know! It looks like a cesarian will be necessary but again it's a combination of all the dangers we have touched on and please talk to Jessie and the baby get them to understand that we are here to help and the birth will be difficult, again it's how baby will cope if we put her life support to sleep and then cut her life support open to take her out, you have two weeks gentlemen.

Xander said I will come with you, with James and Victor are you ready doctor? yes, I have to wrap the blood then we can go, we will use the helicopter and I will phone from there. Marcus you must prepare her family, let them know all the risks and what is happening.

When Jessie is ready talk to her and Leah about everything and buy whatever you will need, we will continue this trip to give her time to rest. I am ready the doctor said then let's go.

Marcus helped Jessie back on the boat after baby shopping

all afternoon Marcus said I think Christine and Kirk were more excited than us, when it comes to buying baby stuff, I never knew Kirk could be like that, he seemed very happy I felt it. Yes, Jessie said I did notice. I need a nap I am totally wiped, it's nice on the deck I might take a nap on that big sun bed. Can you carry me; I don't think I can make it. Marcus picked her up and carried her to the sun bed and laid her down she was asleep, flat out bless her, he took her shoes off and covered her, he sat on the big sofa next to her. He just watched her sleep.

After an hour Christine took him a cup of coffee and sat next to him, she gave him a cuddle, are you ok Marcus? she is everything to me and in two weeks I might not have her with me and its rips my insides out. I would give my life for her he said, wouldn't any of us Christine replied, you have made her so happy and fulfilled her, she shines like a star when she is with you Marcus. She hugged him and asked, do you want me to sit with her so you have a bit of time? No, I am fine thank you Mum ,can you tell what she was like as a child, well she was bossy poor Phillip he did everything she asked he was so protective well that you know, she used to make him go out the front and push her dolly's pram up and down with her.

Just in case one of the other girls or boys wanted to pick her dolly's up. He is very close to her. Yes, Marcus said that I do know, she is so like Peter, Christine said, yes, she is. There is something mum, he said, name it, do you think that you and Dad meaning Kirk, could organize some takeout food for her and get some family board games for tonight please she would love that. Yes, yes, she would, Christine kissed his cheek and left him with Jessie.

When Jessie woke up Marcus was cuddling her hand on her belly which was bigger, she could feel. He kissed her and said I love you Jessie, I love you two Marcus and kissed him back. How long have I been asleep she said, about four hours baby? Xander is due back we should get ready for dinner, do we have to go out tonight she asked, no honey hopefully mum and dad have organized something for us. Ok, Mum and Dad what's going on? Marcus kissed her and said we are a family and with our baby coming soon I don't want any confusion they are like parents to us both so why should they not have the same name privilege, its honor's them and their place in our lives. Yes, your right Jessie said.

While Jessie and Phillip were having their showers, they could hear the helicopter land and knew Xander was back, the phone by the bed rang and Jessie picked it up "hello" it was Robert to say dinner was ready, ok, thank you Robert and she put the phone down. Marcus was ready in jeans and a black v neck t shirt. He took her breath away; I am a very lucky woman. Well yes, you are he said smiling, you look lovely to in that dress. You can see my bump now, see she turned sideways and you could see her bump. Your breasts are bigger, trust you to notice. Well it's a bit hard not to in that long stretchy dress. Come on he said you will love dinner. They went onto the deck and fairy lights where everywhere and soft background music was playing, everyone was already sat down.

I am starving what are we having? They all stood while the ladies sat, then the men sat. and the butler brought half of the take away menu out and laid it on the table in front of her and her face lit up, she had a bit of very thing and a few sips of Champaign, Marcus felt love and affection for everyone at the table and it flowed over everyone.

It felt right they were a family and Jessie had brought them all together, after desert they sat around and chatted until

Christine said I have family games or cards and no cheating please. After hours of playing cards they had gone from single players to buddy teams Marcus and Christine, Phillip and Kirk, Jessie and Xander.

Jessie and Xander where winning as not only had they won a whole jar of sweets from the other players they had won IOU favors from them all and £22.75 cash and a tie .Marcus said you two have wiped us all out, all I have left is my t shirt on my back, well Jessie said take it off then, you can put up or shut up, let's see the goods and everyone laughed, he was not enjoying loosing every hand to the pair of them, they were cheating but he did not know how, he said I will see you for that, stood up and took his t shirt off and put it on the table, Jessie whistled at him and could not stop looking at him, Xander said stop distracting my partner please, what about you Dad, your quiet Jessie said, yes, he said you two have wiped us all out, you are defiantly using some kind of system, sorry unlike your husband I wish to keep my dignity, we fold . What you got husband?

Marcus laid down his cards in triumph, sorry Xander said it's not enough, Jessie take our winnings and Jessie stood to pick their winnings up, Christine said you two have been too lucky. Yes, well Xander said bad losers do say things like that; come on Jessie let us split our spoils. What do you want to keep Jessie said to Xander? If I may I would like the sweets, then I will take the I O U favors the cash, the tie and t shirt, ok Xander said well-done Partner and keep your spoils for next time. Yes, she said victorious with a big smile and her eyes shining. I bid you all a good night and Xander picked up his sweets and kissed Jessie good night and went to his cabin.

I feel like I have been robbed by my own sister, Phillip you played well, dad said and patted Kirk on the shoulder and went, Marcus said come on wife lets go. Yes, she said and put his t shirt on. Good night, dad and mum kissed them both. Marcus picked her up and carried her back to their cabin, he set her down, Jessie put her spoils down and took Marcus's t shirt off, put it in the draw and closed it. Oh, right it's like that then is it, you're learning very quickly my wife, yes, she said. Jessie was taking the site of her husband in without a top on, she loved it, he was so beautiful. He could see the fire in her eyes and the hunger for him. She licked her lips and he smiled, and he said I am all yours my wife, come and take what you want from me, you have had the clothes off my back, with that she went into the bathroom and closed the door, he could hear her humming quite happily, that worried him what was she planning now, he took his jeans off and got into bed and put the bedside lights on.

Jessie came out of the bathroom with a silk dressing gown on and her long dark brushed hair, ,she had put his favorite perfume on she pulled back the bedcovers her side and untied her silk dressing gown and let it slip to the floor, she looked like a porn star she had on a black silk body suit that she had brought before her breasts got bigger, now it looked tight and it made her breasts look even bigger, she had lip gloss on to. She smiled at him and got into bed and pulled the cover over her then leaned over to switch her bed side lamp off, as she did so she said I would not take anything from my husband that he would not willing give. Good night darling thanks for the t shirt and laid back down to go to sleep.

Hell, no woman, he climbed on top of her and put her light on and said you fleeced me of my sweets and £2.75 and my t shirt and two I o u's. and I offer you to have your own way with me and you shun me, what's going on Jessie, nothing husband you were drawling all over my body not two minutes ago he said, I was not, in an innocent voice she was teasing him, he would play along he said I think Xander is a bad influence on you, the doctor thinks you should not bite me again while I am pregnant, oh, she was on top form. I feel quite used now he said, you where undressing me with your eyes and ogling me like I was naked and you come out of the bath room looking like a porn star and get in bed, now you've had your wicked way with me with your eyes, he laid back in the bed and pulled the covers up to his chin and turned. She giggled and turned the light off and laid there in the dark waiting for him to make his move, but she could not lie still. She kept giggling like a little girl and he could not resist her, are you laughing at me he said because you will give a man a complex.

He started to sound frustrated so she slid over the bed under the cover and straddled him, he was not playing he just laid there and ignored her, so she leaned over and turned his bedside lamp on and sat back on him, he closed his eyes and tried not to smile. She slid off him and got out of bed, opened her bedside draw, took his t shirt out and the tie, closed the draw and marched back around to his side of the bed and threw his t shirt on the floor and said you're a bad looser are you happy now. He did not answer her, he put his hands behind his head and laid there. Ok she said you asked for it, she pulled the covers off him and straddled him sitting on his chest and she tied his hands to the bed post, he did not resist in fact he smiled, still with his eyes closed.

He wanted to tell her that her knots would not hold a kitten let alone a grown man, but he did not want to upset her she was trying so hard and putting all of her effort into it. He was having a lot of fun but tried not to show it, there she said what your goanna do now, you are at my mercy. He nearly laughed she sounded so triumphant. He knew with one hard pull and the tie would be off, so he decided to lay back and take one for all mankind. She wiggled down his body and pulled his pants off and wiggled back up, she leant forward she kissed him and nibbled his ear and bit it gently, she let out a little noise, that got his attention he slowly started to breath heavy she licked his nipples and sucked them and kissed her way down his body, by the time she got to his navel his body had betrayed him he was fully aroused.

She looked up to find he was watching her intently she licked her lips and let out a little growl, she took him in her mouth and sucked hard a few times she then sucked his balls, he was calling her name out. She wiggled back up him and sat up a few inches from his shaft looking at him she slowly pulled her straps down to her nipples, which were hard, bigger and darker. She slid her bum back until his shaft met her black silk body suit, and leaned forward so he could see her breasts down her top, she sucked his nipples and pushed her self-back against his shaft, her body suit stopped him from entering her and he gasped out her name she flung her head back and gasped uuuhhhh Marcus, she wiggled herself and the body suite moved enough for his shaft to rub against her very hot very wet bud between her legs, he was breathing very hard and fast, oh, Marcus she pushed back gently and rubber herself against him. She flung her head back again he wanted her now hard and fast. She rubbed her bud against him again and then pushed back so the tip of his shaft just entered her.

She slid down his shaft gently, he was filling her with his shaft; she was so tight he called out her name and she just sat there and touched her breasts, he was trying to buck hard under her.

Oh, Jessie please, please honey, then lifted herself slowly off him, she was kneeling over his shaft and touched herself, threw her head back and called his name out. Her body suit slid off her and he went crazy. He was so turned on he ripped his hands down and grabbed her, pulled up his body and held her above him while he sucked her breasts and kissed her hard, he then laid her on top of him and grabbed her bum. God, he needed her like air its self, he rolled her on to her back but he could not open her legs her body suit was wrapped around her knees so in one swift movement he ripped it in half, all of his mussels flexed and she said hurry Marcus. He entered her hard and fast and she came and that just pushed him over the edge he took her over and over with hot fast deep need. He could not take his eyes from her; Hot Pulsing pleasure claimed her again. She was scratching his back trying to hold on while he took her, he would never get this image of her out of his head so full of pleasure and lust want and need. He never ever dreamed it could ever be like this, this was another first for him. He filled her with his hot seed and could only slump over her gasping for breath. When he could just about recover enough to move, he did, he did not want her taking his full wait. They fell fast asleep while drawing breath together.

It was 10.39 am when she awoke with Marcus watching her. he leaned over gently and kissed her and made love to her slowly there were no need for words. At 11.45 am they went up on deck where everybody was getting ready for lunch. Jessie was definitely showing more today. She had one of Marcus's t shirts on as it hung off her with some leggings and sandals, she felt very much at peace. They all sat down for lunch enjoying the day, where are we sailing to now? Jessie said to Xander, we will be docking in Spain later today, the little one is not awake yet Xander asked, no, Jessie said she grows quicker when I am asleep but I did not get much sleep last night, and she still grows which is why I think she still sleeps

.
The men spent the afternoon fishing off the back of the yacht while Jessie and Christine spent some time on the top deck under the sun shade on the big round sun bed, planning what Jessie needed to buy, like bigger bras, they looked threw some magazines and were cuddled up and both fell asleep with the sway of the boat. About 4 .30 pm the men were putting away their rods when Marcus's phone rang, it was Robert, yes, Marcus said, you better come up to the top deck and be quiet you need to see this, ok I am coming now, he closed his phone and took his shoes off and ran up to the top deck, Robert was stood at the top of the stairs and looked down at Marcus and waved him up, when Marcus reached the top deck he could see Jessie and Christine cuddled up together and a bright white circle of light covered them, what happened Marcus said, well they fell asleep, I was stood here and the butler came up and moved closer to them to collect their glasses and a red beam of light shot out of Jessie and hit the butler, it knocked him backwards and stunned him, when he stood up and withdrew, the red light stopped and that white light covered them both, then I called you.

I think the baby is protecting her while she sleeps, she does not like being woken up. Xander, Phillip and Kirk where at the bottom of the stairs and Marcus waved them up and put his finger on his lips as he looked at them. Robert repeated to them what he had just told Marcus. I don't think we should wake them, but Leah will need to draw on our strength Xander said, yes, I agree Marcus said. They look like angels don't they said Phillip. Yes, Kirk said very precious angels. Marcus went to move closer and the light stated to turn red. She wants the girls to have their sleep, let's not upset her and stepped back, wise choice Xander said.

They all sat on the deck watching the women sleep, the light returned to white and about ten minutes later the light faded and Jessie woke up. Marcus wanted to hold her but thought he would give her time to fully wake up as he wanted Leah to settle, Christine woke at Jessie movement. What are you all doing sat down there Jessie said? Well Leah would not let us sit on the sofa and watch her protect you while you both slept and she gave the butler a sting as well because he got to close when you were asleep, she sensed him and he must have startled her that's all. Is he alright, I believe so Marcus said? How do you feel after your nap? Really good and hungry, me to Christine said. When Jessie stood you could see her bump had grown out a few inches.

The Yacht docked in Spain and they all got off for a bit of shopping and a meal. Jessie brought her bits to fit her for a few days and Marcus felt love wash over him when he held Jessie's hand, and the others felt it flow from him, never in all of his life time had he ever felt like this with anyone, he had waited all of his life for her and now he could not speak he just strolled hand in hand, absorbing it all, peace.

They all stopped near the quay for their evening meal then went back on board. Xander asked if anyone would like a re match at cards and a chance to get their belongings back, yes, Jessie said with excitement, ok everyone agreed. Everyone went to get there betting spoils. Xander said to Marcus could I have a moment and Marcus nodded at Amanda to go with Jessie, what is it Xander?

I have received a communication today from our brothers in Italy they are asking for us to attend an evening dinner dance that they are giving in Jessie's honor, this will be one of the biggest gathering of knights and brothers for nearly a thousand years, word does travel fast Marcus said, yes, and some are travailing a great distance to get to Italy. Will Jessie or Phillip be in any danger? No, I think they can bring forth the messenger that protects them and I don't think any of the brotherhood would disrespect fathers gift, but we will take a fully armed security team with us just in case someone may wish her harm or try to kidnap her, I have spoken to Victor and he has told a second security team to fly out from England and be ready for tomorrow night, but I think most just want to see her for themselves to know father has sent her should be enough.

You must remember, she must do what father has sent her to do at some point, she must get used to meeting them, but her other power is very unexpected and uncontrollable at the moment given her condition. So, we must take steps and be ready for anything. Thank you for letting me know Marcus said, later if you get a chance speak to Phillip on his own and let him know so he can be ready.

Everyone re took their seats and once again they played in their pairs and Jessie and Xander where fleecing everyone.

Marcus said how are you two doing it? Phillip said I feel hot when we play and I felt hot the last time we played, he looked at Jessie and said is she awake Jessie; tell me you're not using my niece to cheat. Marcus reached over and touched Jessie's little baby bump and he could hear his daughter giggling, he said with a big smile on his face Leah can you tell daddy have you been helping grandpa and mummy to win. Yes, daddy she said its fun, mummy likes it. I bet she does honey, I love you daddy, and I love you to darling. Are you happy that I helped mummy? Yes, darling I am. He took his hand off Jessie and said shame on the pair of you. I only went along with it to please Leah said Xander. Jessie laughed, I could not help it, she felt hot and each time one of you picked up a card she could see it in her mind and showed me and grandpa, she thought it was great. Don't blame the baby said Phillip.

Next time we play don't use the baby because I will know. I'm having a drink and going to bed, good night Phillip said Xander, I will join you, yes, Christine said it late let's all go to bed. Kirk said goodnight, Jessie kissed them both on the cheek and then she and Marcus went back to their cabin. Well my wife you tied me up for being a bad looser it's only fair that I return the favor for cheating don't you think, that is a just punishment for you my wife. Jessie smiled and went into the bathroom and changed. Marcus could hear her giggling and wondered what she was up to now as she had a habit of surprising him. When she came out she looked like an angle she had on a white short see throw lace slip her hair surrounded her and she had a hit of a tan on her, he could see her swollen breasts and her nipples were erect and dark under the lace, he could see between her legs and the light behind her gave a very erotic picture, she had that perfume on that drove him crazy and her baby bump definitely grew when she slept there was no doubt that she was pregnant with his child, he growled at her and said in a soft voice jess honey your killing me, how can I tie you up when you look and smell like that.

Dam, he dropped the tie that he had ready and walked over to her slowly, Jessie started to breath faster he could see her excitement build as he approached her and could see her chest rise and fall quicker, her eyes where shinning and her body started to shake. His heaven was here on earth with him now, she was so beautiful he took her hand and kissed her wedding ring and then he kissed her gently on the mouth, he knelt down and slid his hand up her legs, lifted the lace and licked her slowly and gently between her legs, she came instantly in his mouth, she cried out his name as her legs turned to jelly. Marcus had to support her until he stood, he lifter her up on to him, she wrapped her legs around him and braced her between him and the wall and then he lowered her down on to this think hot shaft and took her many times over and over until his legs could bear no more, he then took her to the bed and laid down pulling her on top of him, she rode him, they were both covered in sweat and could not get enough of each other, she was making so many little noises it drove him on, she flung her head back and came again and he filled her with his hot seed, he was shaking and calling her name.

When Marcus a woke the next morning, it was 9.45 am and Jessie was not in bed and had not been for a while as her side of the bed was cold and he could not feel her presence in the cabin. He lifted the phone next to the bed and dialed the top deck, Robert answered. Marcus said tell me that Jessie is with you! Robert smiled and said yes, she is and she's been here having breakfast with the rest of your family for the last hour. Ok, Marcus said he sounded relived and put the phone down.

When he arrived on the deck after his shower, looking

every inch the male model, he walked over and kissed Jessie on the mouth before greeting everyone. Kirk smiled and said your age is showing when your wife has to leave you in bed to sleep, Marcus grinned at him, and said yes, it is old man, make the most of it because when that baby gets here you won't know what a lay in looks like. Yes, Marcus said another female just like her mum to keep me from sleep and he smiled and winked at Jessie who's face turned red. Marcus had breakfast while Xander, Kirk and Phillip all took their turn and spoke to Leah, who loved the men in her life. Jessie had gotten bigger since last night there was no doubt about that, fact, it was probably hunger that made her get up. Marcus thought he would get a fridge in their room stacked with goodies for her.

Victor approached the table and said please forgive my intrusion but just to let you know that we are a few miles from docking and Joshua's team arrived last night and have advised us to wait off shore until this evening to give them time to arrange everything sir, Yes, Xander said Joshua's knows what he is doing and he will contact Paul's team on board later to update them sir, very well. The phone next to Robert rang again and he said very well I will let her know and put the phone down, he walked over to Jessie and said the doctor would like you to go for a checkup scan after breakfast. Very well Jessie said. What's up Marcus said to Jessie, nothing the doctor wants to give me a checkup scan to make sure everything is ok. Jessie giggled and then said out loud, no honey she is not going to hurt us and you must not sting her again she is looking after us, so just relax.

Phillip asked, do you want me to come with you and Marcus? Jessie looked at Marcus, he nodded and she said yes, just in case. Jessie had her scan and the doctor said you're just over four and a half months pregnant now and everything looks ok, the baby cooperated well done. I would like to try and scan you every other day until mid-next week then we will have to do a daily scan. Any problems and I mean at the first sign even a twinge then you come to see me Jessie. Yes, Dr Adams. I have a question Jessie said, sure fire a way, would it be ok to swim in the sea, sure light exercise is very good for you, but make sure someone is with you ok, you will need to rest more to. Thanks Jessie said, and Dr Adams gave her, a copy of her scan, thank you Marcus said to the doctor and they all left she went back to the cabin to change and put a peach bikini on with shorts and a sun top. They went back on deck everyone was waiting for news of the scan and Jessie showed everyone the scan picture.

Xander said if you ladies would excuse us men, we are going to talk over the arrangements for this evening's dinner dance. Oh, good I love dressing up, I can't wait and she flashed a big smile at Marcus. We are going to sun bathe but later can we have a swim in the sea. Yes, darling Marcus kissed her again and the men left and all the body guards left apart from James, he went with them to the top deck so they could lay in the sun, after an hour and half Marcus and Kirk appeared with their Speedos swimming shorts on and they both cut a very fine male model figures, the two woman could not take their eyes off them.

They all went to the back of the boat where the men had been fishing the day before and they took a bit off the boat and put a diving board down and steps into the sea. Marcus was the first off, the diving board he looked so sexy in the water Jessie wanted him. He swam back and waited by the steps to help Jessie down. His jaw dropped open when he saw Jessie take her shorts and top off to see a tiny peach bikini, she barley had on and even with the baby showing she looked like a goddess and he went hard. It was a good job they were already in the water.

Christine pushed Kirk in and then jumped off the board into the water, splashing him, they all played and splashed in the water. After a little while Kirk got out and got a towel, he helped Christine out of the water and wrapped her in it and then said lunch in one hour to Marcus and carried Christine off.

Jessie was just watching Marcus wave to Kirk; she could not believe she was married to him he was so sexy and he looked even more so in the water with the sun shining on him. Marcus turned in the water to see Jessie's eyes full of desire and fever, she was just floating closer to him and could see her see her nipples threw her wet bikini, he shouted to one of the bodyguards "leave us" and they all withdrew, leaving them totally alone in the water. Marcus ran his hand threw his hair and water ran down his face, Jessie was drawn to him, he was watching her intently, he swam towards the steps and held on and put his hand out to Jessie, she took his hand and he pulled him to her.

They just stared at each other without saying a word, he

held Jessie to him and she took her bikini off and threw it onto the boat. She then curled her arm around Marcus's neck and kissed him with need, she let go of him and ducked under the water and took his Speedos off and threw them on the deck, she then wrapped her arm around his neck again and wrapped her legs around him, braced her feet on the steps of the boat behind him and pulled herself up on to his body, she slid straight down on to him then let go of him with her arms and held the steps behind him. He said her name over and over. She took him slowly and deeply many times without words just the need to feel him inside her, until they were both satisfied. He helped her out of the water wrapping both of them in towels and carried her back to their cabin where they showered and changed, now very hungry for their lunch.

After everyone had their lunch, Xander asked Phillip to accompany him to his cabin as he had a gift for him and everyone else went back on the top deck to sunbathe, Jessie had a sleep cuddled up in her husband's safe and loving arms. When Phillip arrived at Xander's cabin, Victor and James were there as well as Peters bodyguard. Xander said I have this and he picked up a sword and a dagger and a little gold knife like Marcus had, and gave it to him and said, I am not forgetting that you to are a guardian, these are for your protection even though you have your own bodyguard, I had them made before we left and I would like you to keep them on your person all the time. Peter will show you how to wear them under your clothing, ok. Thank you said Phillip and gave Xander a hug. James did not know what to make of it, Xander just smiled. Phillip gathered his objects and returned to his cabin with Peter.

When Jessie woke up, she stood up and stretched Marcus could see that her baby bump had grown, she now looked about four to five months pregnant and her breasts had grown a little to, her hips looked a tiny bit wider and fuller. The boat was docking Jessie and Marcus could see from the top that there where at least 20 black cars with tinted windows in parked near to the quay side and the police had cornered off an area around the quay side where they would be docking. In the distance you could see reporters and TV crews just outside the dock. Come Jessie let's get ready for this evening and they went to their cabin.

When she came out of the bathroom, she had to look twice Marcus had a black dinner suit on and his short hair was swept back, he'd had a shave and that after shave! She whistled out loud and he smiled at her. Jessie had hi heeled lace up ribbon cream sandals on and a cream baby doll evening dress, that came to her ankles with thin straps and her bump showed. Her hair was twisted up with little ringlets hanging down and she wore the diamonds Xander had given her. She looked like a fairy; she was so beautiful. Well I am going to have trouble with you tonight my wife, no dancing with anyone apart from family.
Ok, yes, she said and rolled her eyes at him, she had that perfume on he loved. He pinched her bum on the way to the upper deck. Everyone was ready and waiting to go, all the men had evening suits on even the bodyguards and Christine had a dress that Kirk had brought her, a black long evening dress and she had her hair up to. Wow sis you really are getting bigger by the day said Phillip and everyone looked at Jessie's baby bump that was pushing out threw her dress. Yes, Marcus said and ran his hand over it and he smiled that sexy smile that Jessie loved.

Victor said Xander you will go in the second black limo with Jessie, Phillip and Marcus and I will go with James,

Amanda and Robert in the first, Christine and Kirk you will go in the third with Peter and Kevin and an extra member of the security team will go in the front with the driver and the remaining cars will have the rest of the first security team and Joshua's team is in place ready at the brother hood of the knight castle. Right let's load the cars up and go. Everyone filled their cars as they pulled up alongside of the dock. They had the police escort all the way to the castle gate where the police stopped, they waited outside of the walls. Then the gate closed behind them. Xander said Jessie, we will all go in together and we will be shown in to the banquet hall, you will sit on a seat like a thrown and I will be sat one side and Marcus will be sat the other, Phillip will be sat next to Marcus and so on ok.

There will be a man called Tobias he is the elder here in Italy as I am in England, he will be sat next to me and there will be a lot of the brother hood here tonight and all wanting to meet you. The second it becomes too much let me know and we will stop anyone approaching you, they have been warned that you may need room if Leah wakes up so don't worry if she makes her presence felt, all you will have to do is just shake hands but mainly they will just want to kiss your wedding ring. The car stopped under a canopy so nobody could take pictures, Xander got out and was immediately greeted by Tobias, there was a man stood behind him which was one of his bodyguards. Then Marcus got out, he then helped Jessie out of the car and Phillip followed her. Xander introduced everyone even though the brotherhood all knew each other, it was done for Jessie's benefit.

He took her hand and looked at her ring and kissed it and nodded and said I am your servant Mrs Dewdney, this is her brother Phillip Bagbie, and Tobias shook his hand, by then Christine and Kirk had arrived and were being introduced. Then with all of their security they entered the castle and went into a giant hall.

Jessie could hear lots of voices in another room joining on to the hall and looked at Xander, he told her, we will get you settled and then they will be allowed in. Everyone took their seats, all of them were sat on a thrown with Jessie's one in the middle and her thrown was slightly back from everyone else's by a few inches and all the bodyguards where stood close. Tobias nodded and the doors opened, the people came in, in pairs and in a line the voices fell silent and the band played soft music. The first two men approached and one man stood by Tobias and bowed to him and then nodded at Xander, he then stood forward and knelt on one knee, Jessie put her hand out, he eyed her ring knowing what it was and he kissed it, he then looked at Jessie she could tell that he wanted her, he smiled at her and stood and nodded at her and then shook Marcus's hand, the next man came up, after half an hour Jessie needed a break, before the next man could get to Xander, Jessie stood, her bodyguards stepped forward and stepped in front of her, Marcus stood and was at Jessie's side, what is it darling?

Jessie turned to Marcus, I need to walk about my legs are going numb with the baby and I need the loo, more now every day. Where is it? Victor stepped forward and said let me escort you Jessie, she took his arm and her bodyguards went with them. Tobias's men stopped the people from entering, Marcus said to Xander, Jessie will need to eat soon don't forget she is nearly five months pregnant now, that's enough they can admire her from afar, very well Marcus your right.

Xander spoke to Tobias. When Jessie retuned, everyone was standing, Jessie said to Marcus what's happening now. We are going to the other end of the hall where the others we have met are seated and we will sit at the head table, they will then let everyone else in and we will eat. Thank god Jessie said I am starving.

They all took their seats and the rest of the people came in and were being seated when Jessie picked up her bread roll and broke off a bit and ate it, now her mouth was dry she took a sip of her water and after a few minutes Jessie felt funny, she felt sick and Leah felt hot, Jessie leaned over to Marcus and said what is that smell its making me feel sick. I smell nothing what kind of smell, he asked, she said I don't know like violet water, can't you smell it not so bad by you she then leaned towards Xander, she could smell it more but where was it coming from.

Xander picked up his water and Jessie new it was Xander's water, Jessie grabbed Xander's arm, he leaned over and said what is it child? don't drink that Xander, can't you smell it, it's making me feel sick there is something wrong with it, please don't drink it, have mine, please take it away, or I will be sick. Very well Xander said and just said Victors name softly and he appeared at Xander's side. Xander said there's something wrong with my water have it checked immediately the smell is making Jessie unwell.

Yes, master and Victor took the glass of water.

After a few seconds Jessie said that's better and had a bit more of her bread roll. Xander said do you smell anything else Jessie, no, sorry it was just the water I smelt it more when you picked it up, sorry Xander, don't be silly child you did the right thing.

Everyone enjoyed their meal and desert, Jessie felt better after something to eat. Victor appeared at Xander's side and whispered into his ear, Xander said "thank you" and stepped back, Jessie could see Victor talking to James. Is everything ok Jessie said to Xander yes, of course my child and it seems that I am in your dept as there was something wrong with my water, thank you Jessie and Xander kissed her hand. Jessie noticed that Victor also spoke to Kirk as well.

The first dance was about to start and Jessie said to her husband would you mind if I dance with Xander for the first dance, no not at all. Xander smiled and said it would be my honor. Every male in the room was on his feet when Jessie stood and walked to the dance floor with Xander, they danced slowly around the floor Jessie said Leah is waking up because I am so close to you, good she does not want to miss out on all this fun, she feels very hot so I am not sure what she will do as she can feel the power rolling around the room.

Just then a bright white glow surrounded her belly, and Jessie said I told you, now she is showing off, I think she's trying to release the heat from all their power. Good, Xander said, now everyone can see what they've come so far to see and it proves to them that you are the guardian of light. One of Xander's security team closed in all around the edge of the dance floor and people had left their tables and were stood around to see the light coming from Jessie bump.

Jessie could see Marcus talking to Kirk, Phillip and Victor they all looked worried. Jessie said to Xander perhaps I should dance with Tobias he is our host, yes, your right but only if you're up to it, they stopped dancing and walked back to the table. Marcus was the first to her. Is everything ok honey. Yes, Jessie said, she's just very hot there's a lot of power and she was just trying to get rid of it.

Phillip came over and put a protective arm around her and said I can help if you want, thank you but no, let them all see that's what they come for but stay close brother and she kissed him on the check. Tobias was talking to Xander and raised his hand and the music stopped and he stepped forwards and said please everyone be seated and give our guest some room, if you wish to dance then please do so. Tobias came over to Jessie he was looking at the light coming from her, she said you're in no danger if she did not like you, you would know it, very well, would you give me the pleasure of this dance, she looked at Marcus who nodded and the she took Tobias arm and they danced slowly around, all eyes were on them, Tobias's bodyguard felt unease and James touched his shoulder and said be at ease brother, Xander could feel the calming coming from James and turned to see what he was doing. Kirk and Christine danced and then joined in when there danced had finished. Tobias said thank you and returned her to Marcus. Marcus kissed Jessie on the mouth and pulled her to him, now it's my turn wife and Jessie's light stopped and they danced. Tobias asked Xander why the light had stopped. Because the baby sleeps that's all, Xander thought Tobias need to know.

Marcus brought Jessie back to the table for a rest and after a while Kirk said loudly, daughter would you dance with me while mum dance's with Marcus, yes, come on then dad, Tobias looked at Kirk as if he had just told a secret and Xander just sat back and was taking everything in. They danced, Jessie was smiling and giggling like a little girl and then Jessie said you done it now, what Kirk said as he slowed their dancing and he heard Leah saying love you grandpa, he nodded at Jessie, Kirk could feel the love rolling from her and he felt hot inside and a beam of light shot out of Jessie, bright blue and a flame surrounded Jessie and Kirk, sorry Jessie said that's me she has built up a lot of love and power from the room and it's kind of over flowed, I could not keep it in she went red in the face and Kirk laughed, don't worry daughter every man including your husband will be jealous. Marcus and Phillip where approaching, see, Kirk said, your knights await.

I keep getting you told off Jessie said to Kirk, I love getting into trouble but don't tell them, he winked at Jessie who smiled back. Ok you two what's going on Marcus said, you're a bad influence on my wife old man, everyone was looking because of the flame light. Phillip said come on sis let me help, Marcus and Kirk walked back to their seats and Jessie and Phillip danced but with the power coming from all the immortals in the room it made their power together very strong and Jessie's light got bigger not smaller and went blue and the flame now stood about ten feet tall and out about eight feet, everyone stood back, white sparks of light now came from Jessie eyes.

The first man that kissed Jessie ring came forward, Jessie had known he had wanted her and now she could feel he wanted to touch her, kiss her and he wanted to take her, as he got close to her the light, a red haze shone around her the man reached his hand out, the light threw the man clear back across the dance floor and everyone went silent. Phillip was now soothing her and using his power to help Jessie, the red light went and the flame got smaller and smaller and Phillip felt Jessie slump against him, he lifted her into his arms.

Marcus approached and everyone was watching to see if the red light was going to come back and hit Marcus, it did not. Marcus said is she ok, yes Phillip said there was too much power in the room and Leah took too much, it overflowed from Jessie and what about the red light is she in danger. No, Phillip said, but that man tried to influence Jessie with his power, he wanted to mate with her and she did not like his advance, so it was not Leah with the red light? No, it was Jessie protecting her and it was a lot of power in that she will need Xander to recover. Ok thank you brother and Phillip placed his sister into her husband's waiting arms.

The white light was still coming from Jessie and Marcus carried her back to the table. Xander, Jessie needs you to recover, I need you to hold her and hug her, is it not Leah? no, Marcus said I will tell you later. Xander clicked his finger and the security team closed in around them so no one could see, are you sitting comfortably yes, Xander replied and Marcus kissed Jessie and laid her down in Xander's arms. Xander held her to him and James felt the need to touch Xander's shoulder because he could feel love and feeling from Xander. Be at ease brother all is well Xander said.

Marcus turned and moved away he headed towards the man that tried to touch his wife, Kirk, Phillip, Tobias and their bodyguards were hot on his heels, they could feel the anger and rage coming from Marcus, was going to rip the flesh from his body and chop him in to bits. He was in the men's room recovering from his shock, he stood when Marcus entered the room, Marcus could tell that he was about the same age, Marcus said you are not a man of honor and you tried to bond with my pregnant wife, the man just smiled, Marcus punched him in the face as hard as he could and blood splattered everywhere as he broke his noise, Marcus hit him again and the man was out for the count on the floor. Kirk and Victor tried to hold Marcus back as he drew his sword. Phillip touched Marcus and said think of Jessie and Leah they would not want you to do this, I am her protector and I am a guardian, Leah cannot read all my thoughts she can only see a small glimpse I don't want her to see this, if you pleases my brother and Marcus took a deep breath and dropped his sword and kicked the man for good measure and left the room. Kirk picked his sword up and followed Marcus.

Tobias said it is the death penalty to touch a female guardian, after what happened to the last one. Good Phillip said as, he let his rage out light flashed from his mouth and eyes and a red flame like fire shot out and covered the man on the floor, Victor stood back with Tobias, when Phillip had finished there was nothing but a pile of ash where the man had been. It took Phillip a few seconds to gather himself and Victor helped Phillip to stand, Peter then entered the small room and took hold of Phillip and said thank you, but please leave us. Victor Sheppard everyone outside and closed the door, he left security there while he walked Tobias back to his seat.

Tobias said, I am so sorry, please convey my deepest apologies to all of your family. It has been dealt with now but yes, I will pass it along, thank you, and shook his hand.

When Victor returned to Xander, Marcus had his wife in his arms and was holding her to him, is she ok Victor asked, yes, Marcus replied she is asleep now. Victor informed them that it had been delt with and nodded at Marcus who nodded back. Where is Phillip Xander asked? Victor touched Xander's shoulder, he is with Peter. When Phillip returned a few minutes later Marcus said let's go we are done here for today.

Amanda stepped forward and gathered Jessie's gift and purse and then formed a line to say goodbye and to shake hands with Tobias and his family before they left, security surrounded Jessie and Marcus as they left first with a nod to Tobias. Robert stepped forward and Marcus laid Jessie in his arms so he could then get a blanket from the car and covered Jessie with it. Robert passed her back to him inside of the car and Marcus hugged her to him and kissed her on the head.

When they arrived back at the boat Robert took Jessie gently from him so Marcus could get out of the car and then handed her straight back to him, he took her back to their cabin and laid her on the bed he undressed her and gazed at her, she was beautiful, each time he saw her naked he was in awe of her. He covered her with the bedcover, had a shower and got in bed naked next to Jessie, pulled her to him and cuddle her. There was pain still within him, she must have been frightened and worried to use a lot of power like that in public, to keep that man from her and to fend him off.

Jessie moved she put her hand out she was dreaming calling for him, he soothed her and touched her face and said I am here honey don't worry it's all ok and he kissed her neck. She turned over and faced him, she was shaking and looked scared, he sat up in the bed and put two pillows behind him and pulled Jessie in to his lap and cuddled her to him, pulled the blanket over them both and drifted off to sleep.

Marcus woke up he could hear a little sound he listened and could hear it again, he looked down at Jessie who he was still hugging and it was not her, he realized that it was the sound of his daughter sleeping soundly, like a sound crossed between snoring and contentment. He felt love and joy spread over him, he was the luckiest man alive. He put his hand on Jessie's tummy to get a better reception, so to speak, he could hear Leah he was sure she was snoring and then he heard her yawn a little baby yawn and tears spilled from his eyes. She murmured I love you too daddy in a little sleepy voice and went back to sleep.

Jessie woke up and Marcus hugger her to him, he had tears in his eyes and Jessie smiled and touched his face and said I love you my husband what is it? He said I love you and I would die without you and kissed her Jessie asked him to help her sit up. He smiled and lifted her up and Jessie knelt on her knees and stretched, Leah had grown lots and Marcus looked and said Jessie you must be at least six and a half months pregnant, she looked down and said oh god, it must have been all that power last night. Yes, Marcus said I was just cuddling you and I could her snoring inside you, Jessie smiled she gets that from you. I don't snore, oh yes you do after we make love and you are fully satisfied you snore. Shall we try it now and see he said with a big smile on his face. I am the size of an elephant how could you want me, come here and I will show you, he rolled her over gently on her side and pulled her hips back and pushed her back forward gently so her bun was pushed out towards him and he entered her slowly and gently and fully, he cupped her heavy breast and kissed her back, while taking her slowly.

It felt so good Jessie could not get enough of him, she was pushing herself back onto him, harder and faster Marcus, please I need you and he slowed his pace to tease her but it just turned her on more panting and making little whimpering noises, she came bucking back against him her hot liquid covered his shaft and he filled her with his hot seed. When they eventually got out of bed, they showered and Jessie said after breakfast I think we had better get a scan as I am so big now just to check, yes, I think that very wise, he picked up the phone by the bed and spoke to the doctor who agreed.

Marcus helped Jessie dress she had to put her bigger maturity stretch leggings on and one of the maturity v neck t shirts she had brought the other day. I will need bigger clothing by tonight or tomorrow, this is the biggest I have I didn't think I would need it till next week, she informed Marcus. Don't worry honey we will get anything you need today. It took them a few minutes to get on to the deck for breakfast as Jessie was waddling along and took shorter steps because of the baby. When they got their doctor, Adams was talking to Xander and Christine. Good morning everyone it was 10.45 am. I am starving but no one seemed to notice that Jessie had spoken they were all looking at her baby bump. The doctor stood when the men stood and said to Jessie, I will see you soon and can you make sure that the baby is awake and please tell her you're having a scan, Jessie smiled and nodded.

Today Jessie choose not to sit next to Xander or Kirk she wanted to sit next to Christine, the two grandpas looked a little put out as Jessie hugged Christine and sat down with her. Marcus sat with the men to give the woman some time together. Xander said Victor has filled me in on everything that happened and I have had a full account from Joshua. but just to update you, he said the smell that Jessie could smell did in fact come from my water it was poisoned. It must have been her pregnancy or a gift you do not yet know about, little is known of what powers a female guardian has, but she saved my life. I thought everything was tested Marcus exclaimed, it was Xander replied, not only by Tobias's team but Joshua's team as well. It must have been put in by someone who was in the hall before Jessie went to the ladies because once she met them, they roamed around until being seated. I watched all the events from last night and I am sure none of it was Tobias's doing. Xander then asked Marcus, what are you planning for today, well Marcus said we'll we are having a scan after breakfast and I will plan more after her scan.

After breakfast Christine, Phillip and Marcus went to the medical room where the doctor was waiting. She asked Christine and Phillip if they could wait outside for a few minutes, while she checked Jessie over. The doctor closed the door and asked, how do you feel Jessie? Fat she said she grew a lot last night. Yes, I can see that. Marcus helped Jessie off with her top and the doctor checked her over, ok Jessie everything looks ok I need to scan you heart, what for Marcus said. Well Dr Adams said she has grown a lot in the last few days and I need to check that it's not putting any strain on Jessie's heart. She did the scan on Jessie's heart which took twenty minutes, by this time Xander and Kirk were pacing the floor in the waiting room like expectant fathers.

The doctor informed them that everything looked fine, Jessie let's check your baby, does she know I am going to scan you? Yes, Jessie said running a hand over her round belly. Ok then would you like your mum with you as well, Jessie looked at Marcus and said we have little time as a family I would hate to rob you of this time, nonsense Marcus said we are all a family.

Dr Adams told Marcus to go and get the others and please ask them to be quiet. Marcus did and the little room was suddenly filled with bodies. The doctor did the scan and printed some pictures for them and said to Jessie do you want to hear your little girl's heartbeat? Yes, she said and squeezed Marcus's hand. Is she ready, I am not sure what this will sound like to her but she is in no danger! Ok Jessie said and the doctor put a round end on the scanner, turned a dial on the machine and everyone could hear Leah's heart banging like a little fast drum. Tears welled up in everyone's eyes and then like a like voice on the radio everyone heard Leah say grandma. Christine said I heard that all right and Kirk hugged her. Don't ask me how she did that Jessie said, you could hear her little giggle before she yawed and then she fell silent. The doctor turned the machine off and asked if everyone could go back into the waiting room and I will be in to talk to you all, I would like to speak to Jessie and Marcus.

Marcus helped Jessie wipe her belly off and helped her off the table. What is it doc.? A few thing's all good but you might not like one on them, one she will be hear within the next day or so and not a week if she continues to grow at this rate and second you need to eat more, a lot more Jessie you need more rest and sleep, no more sex until after the birth if you can help it. Will it hurt the baby Marcus asked, No, Dr Adams said, it uses a lot of energy up and Jessie needs every bit of energy she can get. Ok, he replied, what about the birth where do you want your baby to be born because if it's in England then you need to be sailing back today but then you might not have time, you need to be near a brotherhood medical hospital this ship is not the right place. You need to talk that over now with the others because we have to be ready and I need a sample of breast milk so I can test it. I will make a list of anything you will need and give it you or Xander, I will put a breast pump on there and a few bottles, right shall we talk to the others?

They all went into the little waiting room and the doctor talked things over with them all, it was agreed that Leah would be born where they were, which gave the doctor time to get their medical facility ready and get everything ready for Jessie and the baby.

When they had all gone back on deck, the doctor motioned to Xander and he followed her back into her room and closed the door. What is it doctor, well she said I would advise that by tomorrow we all have to move into the brotherhoods apartment because you will not be able to move her if she goes into labor here? She wrote a list out while she spoke to Xander and said I will need this for Jessie by tonight and I will need you and your men close to me and Jessie at that medial facility, you need time to get equipment in that they don't already have, so I really need to be there asap. Pack your things doctor we will go today, Xander said, let me sort them all out upstairs first and we will go and make all our arrangements.

After a few minutes Xander appeared on deck and asked what the order of the day was to Marcus. Well, mum, dad, me and jess are going to get jess some more maternity clothing, good, and as the baby will arrive here I will contact Tobias and we all will be moved in to the brother Castle or apartments by the medical facility today, I know you have brought lots for the baby but you need more as she will be born here you will need a cot, bedding, carry cot, baby alarm, nappies, cream, blankets, night lights, creams, pushchair the hole nine years and I am paying! I know you will have it all at home but we need it here .Have lunch out to and I will call you with more details, if Jessie needs to sleep take her to the castle they have a suite there ready for her just in case and Phillip you must stay close to your sister, have a good day, Tobias has sent ten of his most trusted men to protect you today and you will have your bodyguards and some of our men, you will also have a police escort so no reporters or news van. See you soon, he hugged and kissed Jessie, she said hold on, someone wants to say hello, Xander touched her tummy and Leah said grandpa I love you and giggled he felt love wash over him and James again felt it, grandpa love's you to be good for mummy little one. I will grandpa.

Their day was spent in a crowd of security, shops and a fleet of cars, by four o'clock Jessie had fallen asleep in the car, on the way back to the brotherhood castle, after buying everything that was needed from cream to a car seat and pushchair, she also had ice cream, it made her full and content. Marcus put his hand on Jessie's belly as he was holding her to him in the car and could hear Leah lightly snoring and smiled, what is it Kirk said, Leah is snoring, little baby snoring listen! Kirk reached out his hand and touched her tummy and could hear snoring, and said that is the sweetest sound, he withdrew his hand and cuddled Christine and kissed her cheek. Phillip said I wondered what that was, I can hear her now if I am close, I don't need to be touching her or her light.

As they pulled into the castle the police stopped at the giant gates and the cars pulled in under the enclosed canopy, Phillip got out and walked around and took Jessie from Marcus so he could get out of the car.
Christine and Kirk followed. Marcus did not take Jessie from Phillip but instead stood in front of them, what is it

Phillip asked, I don't know Marcus said I can sense something but I am not sure what, a red light like a giant flame shot out of Phillip and it covered all three of them, the bodyguards all took one step back to give him room. Kirk said what is it Marcus and drew his sword, I don't know something I sensed, something I am not sure it's gone now.

Kirk told the bodyguards to be alert, he opened his phone and called Victor and asked where he was, Victor replied in the castle with everyone, we have been waiting your return. What is it Brother, Victor we are outside, Marcus is uneasy he senses something, is all well within? Yes, Victor said but wait, it is not like Marcus to raise a false alarm he has perfect senses; we are on are way and he closed his phone.

Marcus took his jacket off and covered Jessie with it, he then turned to Phillip and asked, how long can you keep the protective shield up for? It depends I think maybe half an hour, maybe more. That's good to know. Just then Victor, Xander, Tobias and James came out with a few other brotherhood members. Phillip withdrew the shield from Marcus and kept it around him and Jessie. What is it Marcus? Xander asked I don't know I sensed something or someone, something did not feel right, Tobias's team is hear with Joshua's team and the place is being searched twice a day, while we are here, is Jessie ok? Yes, Marcus said, she's asleep and Phillip is protecting her. Yes, Xander said I can see.

Be at ease son and Xander touched his shoulder. Marcus said ok let's get Jessie in, she needs to rest, will she be up to a celebration party this evening, here, to honor her, as this event will go down in our history as a holy place, where Leah will be born and the brother hood here and Tobias feels very honored, no one here has ill feeling come.

Kirk put his sword away and took Christine's hand. Ok, but give Phillip plenty of room to take Jessie in, he will not put the shield down until she is in our room safe. He nodded and Tobias said clear the way and everyone stood back, Marcus followed Victor to their new room and Phillip followed behind with Jessie, Kirk and Christine. The entire second floor had been set up for them, Christine and Kirk were one side of Jessie and Marcus, Phillip the other side and Xander was next to Phillip. Victor opened their door it was a big suite, table chairs and sofa a master bedroom and an on-suite bathroom, the other bedroom had been turned into a nursery. Phillip laid Jessie on the bed and his light faded, he whispered to Marcus, catch you later and Marcus shook his hand and said thank you my brother.

Phillip went to his room. Marcus covered Jessie and closed the door. He went into their little living room, Xander and the others were there. Jessie is fine, mum are you ok? Yes, Christine said, dad take mum back to your room and get her a hot drink, I am sorry I did not mean to worry you, don't be silly Christine said, you were looking out for Jessie and she gave him a hug. Kirk took her hand and they went to their room. Robert and Amanda went to stand outside the door but Marcus told them to stay in the room with them, from now on Tobias's men can stand outside the door, Amanda go in with Jessie please, there is a seat by the window in there, she nodded and went and Robert stood inside by the door.

Do you think you are on edge because you worry for your wife and daughter, I don't know Marcus said? Victor said to Marcus, do not doubt yourself Marcus you have expert skills, I think it is us that need to be vigilant my brother. Yes, Tobias replied, I know of your skill and have heard many stores of you over your life time, I think that Victor is right and if you think Jessie will come to any harm or is not up to it, as even I can see the miracle has grown more since yesterday. No, she would love a celebration we will be glad and thank you for allowing us to visit and for giving my family a place to stay at this very special time. Tobias fell on to one knee and said you honor us and kissed Marcus's ring. He then stood I will see you tonight at 7 pm, bowed and then left. Let Marcus rest and everyone left leaving Robert and Marcus alone.

Marcus went into the bedroom and nodded at Amanda who left the room and closed the door. Marcus undressed and pulled the covers back and undressed Jessie, she was completely naked and he gazed at her, it was the vision of her he first had of her on the night he took her virginity, her breasts full of milk and her belly full and round with his child she was so beautiful, he got in the bed and covered them both and spooned her. Holding her to him. He kissed her neck and went to sleep.

He woke up, to Jessie stroking his hair and face, she smiled at him with desire in her eyes and said, you are so handsome and you're my husband I can't believe how lucky I am, then kissed him slowly and ran her hand down his chest, she stopped at his navel and put her hand on his hip and drew circles in his skin on his hip with her finger. He ran his hand over her breast, kissed her back and she made a little sound off need, he gently rubbed her breast a bit harder. Jessie slid her hand down his hip and grasped his hot shaft, he kissed her hard and fast, she then slid her hand down his shaft pulling him back in her hand, he bucked into her hand and she tightened her grip. He broke their kiss and gasped out her name please, I can't the doctor said no sex until after the baby and look how much you have grown in your sleep. Jessie let go of Marcus and said don't you want me because I am fat. Little tears welled up in her eyes.

Oh no, honey I want you I love you and how could I not want you when you carry our child, it's just that you know what the doctor said and she scares me and I am already in her bad books. He wiped the tears in her eyes and hugged her, he kissed her head and said it's six now we have a party in your honor tonight. It starts in one hour, let's get ready.

After Marcus helped her shower and dress, he got ready, she put her wedding gift from him on, the ruby earrings and necklace and pined her hair up, put her make up on and the perfume that Marcus liked. Her dress was a blood red princess dress with think straps and showed a lot of her now ample cleavage and had a v down the back, the dress went to the floor and matched her jewelry, she could have passed for a supermodel apart from the fact she was now nearly seven months pregnant, she did not take a wrap or bag with her. Marcus whistled when he came out of the bathroom dressed in the black trousers suit with the white shirt Jessie loved to see him in and he smelt divine. Wow Jessie, pregnancy becomes you, your dark hair and eyes really make you stand out in that dress you look stunning and growled at her. She smiled and said let's go.

He took her hand and Robert opened the door; they all went downstairs. As they approached the ballroom, they could hear the party music playing, Xander, Tobias and their security were all stood outside while their guests where inside. Where is mum, dad and Phillip Jessie asked, they are already inside dancing Xander said, should have guest laughed Marcus. Are we ready? Tobias asked? Yes, Marcus and Jessie replied, then let's go in. Xander and Tobias went in followed by their bodyguards and then Jessie and Marcus followed with their bodyguards and security.

There must have been three hundred people, men and women half that of yesterday and at the end of the room there was a red carpeted roped off area full of security and table and chairs for their party. To the right side of the room there was a bar and a few doors that must have been rooms and at the end where they came in were a DJ and a buffet. They had waiters in their area. What would you like to drink Jessie, Tobias asked, can I have some champagne and a glass of fruit juice please? He clicked his fingers and the waiter walked off and came back within a minute with her order, another waiter took Marcus's order.

The DJ played a requests and Marcus said come on then you and took Jessie by the hand and led her to the dance floor, he looked in her eyes and smiled, Jessie said, I love the old songs and Marcus smiled back at her and laughed. When the song ended, they walked back to their seats. Kirk asked if Jessie was up for a dance! Oh yes, she said, the question is Marcus, he looked at her and his eyes sparkled. Kirk led her to the dance floor and twirled her around slowly she loved it. Marcus could not take his eyes from her she was enchanting and he wanted her. When the song ended Kirk returned her breathless and smiling and she had fire in her eyes, it took his breath away to see her like that and knew he had been wrong to refuse her in bed earlier. Jessie felt full of happiness it was just like a party, no one was staring, it felt normal and everyone was smiling and enjoying it.

While Jessie was having a rest with Kirk and Xander, Marcus danced with Christine, she could see them dancing and having a good time. Phillip was dancing with a woman, who was a bit taller than Jessie, had blonde hair, was thin and very pretty, about 35 years old and had nothing on under that wafer-thin black dress, suddenly she let go of him and tapped Christine's shoulder, said something to Christine and Christine let go of Marcus turned and danced with Phillip. Marcus did not look very happy but still took the woman in his arms and danced with her, Xander and Kirk could both feel Jessie's mood change instantly.

She said to them, I can't dance with other men but he can dance in front of me with another woman! Be calm Jessie, Kirk said I don't think all is at it seems. When the song changed Marcus continued to dance and Phillip and Christine came back. What's going on? Jessie asked Christine, what did that woman say to you. Oh, don't worry darling, No, tell me. Christine looked at Kirk and Xander and said, she said would I like to dance with my son so she could take a dance with her old lover. What Jessie said and stood up. As she stood up, she could see Marcus ushering the woman into one of the rooms at the side of the hall. Oh, hell no, Jessie said and went to walk over the dance floor when Xander stood in front of her and said shall we wait and see what Marcus has to say before you do something rash my dear. Jessie's red fame shot out of her and covered her instantly, she told Xander, I love you, I have no wish to hurt you so please don't make me do it for Leah's sake, very well as you wish, he bowed and stood aside.

Jessie marched over to the door Marcus had gone into, to find Victor stood outside. Please move aside Victor, he looked at her not sure what she was going to do if he did not. From over Jessie's shoulder Xander said, do as she asks. When Jessie opened the door, Marcus was stood holding the naked woman by both of her arms and the woman's head had fallen back like he had just kissed her, her dress was at her feet. Jessie just gasped, tears filled her eyes she felt like she been stabbed in the heart, Marcus looked shocked and looked at Jessie and then at the woman in front of him and immediately let go of her and said in a shaky voice, Jessie honey this is not what you think it is, nothing is going on. Jessie just stood in shook, tears rolled down her face and she put her hand on her very big baby bump and gasped again. Marcus took a step towards Jessie and she hissed, don't you even think about touching me after you had your hands on her and a red haze shone out around Jessie. She tried to take off her wedding ring, but she was shaking so much. No, Jessie please honey don't I am begging you.

She ripped the ring off her hand and threw it at him and said we are no longer married then ripped her necklace from her neck and threw that at him as well, I am no longer yours I hate you; I want nothing from you, go to hell. Jessie ran from the room crying her eyes out and holding her baby bump. Phillip and Marcus ran after Jessie, Marcus shouted to Phillip can you subdue her. Jessie stopped running she just wanted to die she put her hand on the wall for support and to catch her breath and could hear Phillip and Marcus behind her, she knew she could not out run them so she took a deep breath and let her pain and anger out, her red flame turned black and both men stopped, Phillip went to approach her but the force kept him back, he tried his white light but it could not get through the black flame that was protecting Jessie. Phillip said, I don't know what the hell that is or what she is doing but it's definitely Jessie and not Leah, if it was Leah, I could get threw but Jessie is doing that and its very, very strong. What the hell is going on what happened in that room? Phillip asked Marcus, I don't know I have been set up. Jessie can you hear me honey are you both ok, please honey speak to me. Just then Christine and Kirk came round the corner followed by their bodyguards. Phillip started to feel Jessie's pain and said everyone stand back and bright red raging flames shot out from Phillip, he said sorry its being close to Jessie, please everyone move back more, give her room all that energy is draining her and the baby Phillip said.

Kirk, Christine said, you come with we and we will take Jessie with us to our room for tonight and give her time to calm down and then you can help her heal and give Leah some of that energy back. Is that all right with you Kirk said to Marcus? He was about to say no when Xander put his hand on his shoulder and Xander said yes that's a very good idea, we do not want to push her any further, its weather Jessie is agreeable to that Kirk said. Jessie, Christine said as she approached the black flames. Jessie please be careful don't hurt mum and dad they only want to help said Phillip. After a second or two the flames turned red and every one could now see that Jessie was slumped over on her knees holding onto the wall, her light then died, Jessie did not move and Kirk said Jessie its dad I mean you no harm I am going to pick you up sweetheart, mums here, she did not move or turn. Kirk knelt beside her and picked her up and carried her while she cried her heart out and held on to him, Christine followed them with Robert and Amanda in tow.

Phillip and Xander had to hold Marcus back, he was so upset he could see the state of Jessie and it broke his heart.

Marcus started to shake with rage and James stepped forward to protect Xander, Marcus said I am going to kill her, where is she? Victor has taken care of her she will be held and interviewed, be at ease you are no good to your wife and child in this state, Xander said. I have done nothing I have been set up, well it looked pretty convincing to me. Thanks, Xander you're not helping. No, Xander said let's all go have a drink and calm down then we can all go to my suite and discus what happened, what Jessie saw then perhaps we can find a way out of this mess, come on Jessie is in good hands she safe, do not add more to her distress tonight, come now and they all went to the bar.

Kirk could here Leah crying and sobbing while he carried Jessie, who was doing the same, Leah had seen everything that Jessie had and he could tell Jessie was trying to hide the pain inside from her but she was in no state to do it, a tearful little voice was saying mummy does daddy not love us anymore is it because of me that daddy does not love us mummy I am sorry. She sounded so confused; Jessie was so upset she could not answer. Kirk could now feel the full force of Jessie's pain as he was carrying her and tears began to roll down his face, never in his life had he felt this kind of pain he wanted to be sick and blank out the pain that was coming from inside Jessie. They went into their suit and Christine opened the bedroom door and pulled the covers back, Kirk laid Jessie on the bed, she stopped crying and did not move.

Kirk stood back, just then Christine said oh my god, Kirk you have blood all down your trousers and arm. It's not me and they both looked at Jessie her dress was red as blood and they could not tell, then Christine touched Jessie's lower back and blood dripped from her hand. Oh my god Kirk said we have no time, he picked Jessie back up; she was unconscious and not moving or responding. Kirk ran from the room Robert and Amanda said what's going on and Christine raised her hand with Jessie blood on it all she said was it's the baby. Amanda grabbed Christine who was stood still in shock and said come on Robert. Amanda said for him to go and tell Marcus and Xander, don't tell him that down the phone, go and Robert ran.

Kirk ran into the medical room which had been one floor below the castle and three floors below their room. He called out and doctor Adams appeared, what is it? she just froze for a second when she saw Kirk dripping with blood and Jessie in his arms. Where? he said, she pointed to a hospital bed behind the door in the large room. Kirk laid her on it, What happened? the doctor said, she and Marcus had a fight and she got upset and black light came out of her which her brother could not get through and when the light went she was slumped on the floor, I picked her up and took her to our room she was bleeding the baby was distressed and crying but she stopped talking upstairs so I don't know. Jessie can you talk to me, Jessie its doctor Adams. She looked pale the doctor listened to her heart and said get me that scanning machine just push the whole thing over here now. Christine was at the door with Amanda who then said perhaps we should not watch, wait till the doctor is finished, let's let Kirk assist the doctor, come on and Amanda closed the door and hugged Christine.

The whole ball room fell into silence when Robert burst into the room, he looked around to see everyone stood at the bar. Marcus instantly new that something was wrong and fear filled him. Robert said quick Jessie is bleeding, it's the baby, Kirk has taken her to the medical room. They dropped their drinks and ran downstairs to the medical room. When they got there, they saw Christine crying and Amanda cuddling her and blood that had dripped from Jessie's body across the floor, where is Kirk? Marcus said. He is assisting the doctor as there was no one else Amanda informed him, Marcus went to open the door and Amanda said no, don't go in there Marcus you don't want to see her like that. Xander agreed, she's right son the doctor will come out when she has news, let her do her job, I know your hurting but Jessie must come first think of her, come now lets us wait.

Kirk moved the big machine to where the doctor wanted it, right while I get this ready, I need you to open that top draw and there are three bags of different colored fluid, the doctor gave him orders while she worked. Kirk put everything the doctor had asked for on a tray and held it out to her while she worked at setting up a drip for Jessie, when that was done the doctor said I need you to cut in half or cut a hole and get that dress off of her, so I can get to the baby. Kirk just ripped the marital in half making a hole, right go and wash your hands, I need your help with this. The doctor asked Jessie, can you hear me, it's ok no one is going to hurt you we are just scanning your baby and Leah if you can hear me, I am not going to hurt you or mummy. Kirk returned and she said, I need to put that gel all over the baby now. she handed him the gel and she scanned Jessie's tummy and said "shit" she handed Kirk the scanner and said put this on the end. The doctor turned dials and put switches on and put a BP cuff around Jessie's arm.

She then put the scanner back on Jessie and they listened to a faint little heartbeat. Kirk behind me there is some numbers in green, what are they saying? Kirk looked over and said 89, ok, we have to get the baby out now. Go and get the others, tell them to be quiet. Kirk ran to the door and opened it, Marcus stood up and Kirk slapped him right across the face as hard as he could, Marcus stumbled back into Xander.

The doctor wishes to speak to you all now and be very quiet and let her speak. He turned around and ran back to help the doctor not giving Marcus a second glance, everyone was stunned but went in. They all stopped behind the scan machine Jessie looked dead.

The doctor looked up and said, right Jessie needs an operation to stem the flow of blood but we can't do that because the baby is in the way and in sever distress, she has to come out now otherwise you are going to lose them both. I know some of your customs are different, Marcus you will need to sign some paper work, Tobias you need to get another doctor, a surgeon, a pediatric doctor and at least three nurses, I know when I spoke to you to day you said you had that under control. Tobias opened his phone and spoke into it, as she told them what she needed. Tremendous stress did not help this situation as soon as the team arrives, we should have the baby out pretty quick and then we will operate on Jessie that should take about an hour maybe two. I need Amanda to help me undress Jessie and get her ready and I need two of you to put that privacy screen up and put it at least half way across the room, I need Phillip and Marcus to be sat there but if you can't handle that then say now as you cannot interrupted us as we work.

I need you to wash up and take your shirts off. What Marcus said? Your shirt off, why Marcus said, well usually the mother is awake and the baby needs to bond with a parent and draw hormones from you and they do that by skin to skin, mum is best but dad will have to do now. He nodded, I will come and get you when we are ready for you. You do not need to sit there the whole time, I might need Phillip to subdue the baby if she comes around the doctor informed them, Marcus said if she comes around what the hell does that mean? like I said she was in a very distressed state and her heart rate is dropping, she was crying as well.

The baby and Jessie are both unresponsive, she has used a lot of power and energy up, I have not given her any drugs yet, to give the baby a better chance and I need to know from you Marcus if and only if we can only save one which one do you want us to save or do you want me to make that choice at the time to which ever one has the better odds of surviving, it might not come to that but I need to know before we start. Xander stepped forwarded seeing Marcus's face was too much for him and said you decide doctor. Ok then the screen please, let's get ready.

They moved the screen and Amanda helped the doctor get Jessie ready, the doctors came in, the nurses were getting all the baby stuff out ready and they wheeled a little baby life support machine and incubator in. Everyone waited outside and no one spoke a word. After twenty minutes went by Phillip said what's taking them so long, they should have her out by now, still no one said a word. Phillip asked Kirk why did you hit Marcus earlier? I do not apologies for it I meant it Kirk said, he eyed Marcus and Xander said, at ease brother, that is easy for you to say, never in all of my life time have I felt such pain come from a human being and the longer I held Jessie the more I felt it, I wanted to be sick and I wanted to be rid of it. I have stabbed people to death and killed hundreds if not thousands of men in battle and felt each and every ones pain but even if you put all that pain together it would not come close to what that child was feeling and then to hear a tiny baby cry and try and take the blame for what he did. You are lucky you still draw breath in front of me!

So now you know a little of what Jessie felt and that baby was breaking her heart, Jessie tried to shield her from it but she was awake and she saw and heard everything Jessie did and that just about killed Jessie inside. Yes, Xander said and now I understand and I am very sorry you felt some of Jessie's pain, I had forgotten that her feelings are felt by us all and affect us as well, I miss judged you brother and ask your forgiveness as anyone carrying Jessie would have felt it including me and Kirk nodded at Xander, all I can say is I am so very sorry.

But I was set up said Marcus, but Xander said we must see it from poor Jessie's view, one you danced with another woman in front of her, and two the woman told Christine and Phillip in front of you that she was your ex-lover and then Jessie saw you go of your own fee will into a room with that woman. Marcus asked, why didn't you not try and stop Jessie, well we did, not only did she protect herself quite rightly but she threatened me and Victor with her light, when she opened that door you were holding a naked ex-lover which, it did look like you had just kissed. Now can you see things from her shoes? I think you're lucky she didn't incinerate you because if I was her, I would have done. Shit! it does look so bad Marcus said.

Just then the door opened and doctor Adams came out said how does the baby get her power or energy from Jessie, how does she charge her batteries quick? she draws power from the elders Marcus said naming Xander, Kirk and Phillip, right then I will need everyone you have just said and you, take your tops off and wash your hands, now hurry the doctor said we are about to take her out. After a minute all the men were sat down in a line, they could hear the machines all beeping and Jessie's breathing machine. They were all beeping fast and the doctor said, she's out. A nurse and doctor walked past them to the babies' side that had been set up and the nurse said, she's not breathing, her heart rate had dropped just before they got her out. The doctor worked on the baby; all the men had tears rolling down their faces. They put tubes in her mouth and attached wires everywhere and then the doctor said, I got a faint heartbeat. Which one of you is dad? I am, Marcus stood, good bring your chair over here and sit there in front of that machine. The doctor put Leah still with all her wires and tubes attached on to Marcus's chest, he cried tears of joy, after a few minutes the nurse put a cover over Marcus and Leah to keep her warm, she was so tiny, love poured out of him and the others felt it.

After ten minutes the doctor said she needs her energy now, that's my job exclaimed Xander and the nurse lifted Leah from Marcus. Xander stood, she then wrapped Leah up in another blanket and Xander sat, the nurse put Leah on his chest and Phillip came up behind Xander, his white light surrounded all three of them, sorry it's too hard I am drawn to her I could not be from her, I know Xander said. Jessie's machine stopped and made a screaming noise. "Shit" one of the doctors said, come on Jessie don't do this to me now come on honey breath, ok, start CPR, the doctor said that was giving out orders.

Marcus and Kirk just looked at each other, Marcus went to push the screen back and Kirk grabbed him, no Marcus stand back let then help her, let them do their job they can't do that if you're in their way. Just then Jessie's machine started to beep again. Ok let's get this finished and then we can close, shouted the doctor. When Phillip had finished helping Xander boost Leah's power and the doctors had finished their operation and were about to close, Phillip said, do not sew my sister up, I will heel her, she will not be happy with big scares, you can do that can you Phillip doctor Adams said. Yes, I can, but I need Kirk and Marcus also which means Leah will need Tobias power to. Ok, Marcus said and pulled out his phone, Tobias came in and washed up and took over from Xander so he could rest. Doctor move your team back please, said Phillip, she nodded and her team all moved away.

I need your knife again Marcus, he pulled his gold knife with the diamond on the end out and gave it to Phillip, he cut his, Kirk and Marcus's finger and let the blood drip down on to Jessie's belly, then Phillip stood at Jessie's head with Marcus and Kirk stood each side of the bed. Phillip said I need you both to put one hand on Jessie's belly and one hand on her shoulders, keep your hands where they are and I will do the rest. They did as he asked, a white and blue light shout out of Phillip and out of his mouth and eyes and he put one hand on top of Kirks hand and one hand on Marcus's hand and light passed through their hands, Phillip kissed Jessie on the mouth, he was pushing light down into her belly closing the hole, light was beaming out of the hole in her belly until it closed and then he kissed Jessie and his light stopped, he slumped forward and Marcus and Kirk grabbed him, a red light shone out from Jessie's belly and covered her.

They managed to drag Phillip out of the way. The doctor asked, how long will that last. I don't know a little while until she has recovered. Her body is doing that Marcus said, it's protecting her while she sleeps, ok replied the doctor, but don't take Phillip anywhere in case we need him, he nodded and helped put Phillip onto a chair to recover. The nurse said she, the baby has to go into the incubator now and took Leah from Tobias, checked all of her wires and placed her in the incubator. Kirk said hold on and went and got Christine so she could have a quick kiss and cuddle before they closed it. When Christine had finished with Leah, she said I want to see Jessie, please tell me how she is. Everyone turned to doctor Adams who said, well they are both really lucky to be here it was touch and go for a little while for both of them, Leah will have to stay here for a few days maybe a week or even two, again that depends on lots of different things and her rate of progress, but I might need Phillip in a minute as I need to take milk form Jessie as Leah is going to need a feed soon and I have not tested her milk yet, it should be ok and at the moment.

Jessie is covered in her protective light, her operation went ok we repaired the damage, I will check her over again fully when she comes around but I don't know when that will be. Thank you doctor I will be back in a few hours, but if there's any change then please inform me at once, doctor I have one more question for you, will she be in that terrible state when she wakes up? Good question, I don't know what state she will wake up in, whatever her state she will panic because she no longer carries her baby and loss, as she will not have that connection to her, she had a lot to adjust to in these last few weeks and no time to take it all in, so yes that and the trauma of last night she will need time. Christine turned to Marcus and said I pray to god that you did not do what I saw when Jessie went into that room.

I heard everything out there but I need to see evidence as Jessie will, I love you both, this will rip our family apart and that I could never forgive you for not even for Leah's sake, because it will destroy her life without both parents living together as a family, like Jessie, she lost her parents 18 years ago now you might have condemned your daughter to that same fate and may god forgive you because if that ever happens I will never be able to. Then she turned and left.

Kirk move to followed her and Marcus held his hand out and said thank you for all of your help you saved Jessie's life and Leah's, what can I do to thank you? Kirk shook his hand and looked at Leah then back to Marcus and said, fix this mess. Marcus, doctor Adams said, go and get some sleep there is nothing that can be done for many hours if there is the smallest change I will alert you, Phillip stood up and doctor Adams said oh no you cannot go anywhere you will have to stay we will get you a bed, I need you, I have to get milk from Jessie for Leah so you will have to drop her shield so I can get some. Great, thanks doc. Marcus shook Phillips hand, thank you for everything you have done my brother, it's my honor and then the doctor took him behind the screen. Marcus shook Tobias's hand, thank you for helping my daughter, I am very honored to be even asked, I will see you in the morning and I will do all I can to vindicate you Marcus good night. Come, Xander said let us rest and be ready for whatever tomorrow brings us. Marcus looked at his daughter and said I swear I will put this right and left with Xander.

Marcus heard his phone ring and woke up it was 8.40am; he opened his phone, yes. Sir it is James, Xander wishes you to come to his room at once, Ok I am getting up now and closed his phone. Marcus went to Xander's room with his dressing gown on and bare feet. James was stood at the door waiting for him, what is it Marcus said as he entered, he saw Joshua, Victor, and Tobias, now I am worried. Please sit down we have very good news and evidence that will clear your name, what, how tell me. Better still Joshua said I can show you. Joshua turned to the TV and pressed the remote control and we have sound to, it's all thanks to Jessie, yes Xander said when Jessie found that my water in my glass had been tampered with, we did not know who and how so Joshua insisted on CCTV in every room while we were here.

Look, the DVD showed Marcus ushering the woman into the room and saying you're crazy what's wrong with you telling my wife's family that you are my ex-lover, you're not, you are a psycho I turned you down flat so what game are you playing, who sent you just then the woman's head turned as she could hear Jessie shouting at Victor outside of the room and the woman pulled her dress off and gabbed Marcus who was pushing her off him when Jessie burst in, oh thank god Marcus said.

I love you and jumped up and kissed Joshua on the check. I have I few copies so don't worry, and Victor said I have a confession she was paid and sent by Crispin he paid her £1000.00 and we traced her phone log to that house in Winchester in England. Can you give me two copies of the DVD now, yeah sure Joshua said here? Thanks, he then ran from the room and went to Christine and Kirk's room. He knocked their door loudly. Kirk answered and said is Jessie ok? I don't know Marcus said, I have something to show you both, get the TV quick, I have fixed this mess.
Is Jessie ok? Christine called; I don't know Marcus is not making much senses. Kirk put the TV on and Marcus

pushed the DVD in and said watch this, he pressed play and they all watched the DVD. Oh, thank god Christine said and hugged Marcus. Yes, Kirk said but how are you going to get Jessie to listen let alone get her to watch a DVD and there is Leah, I will put that right to, I think she will be the easy one, Let's hope so Kirk said.

Marcus ran from the room leaving them a DVD, showered and dressed and went to see Jessie and Leah with flowers and a teddy. Marcus walked in to see Leah's machine had been moved and Phillip was asleep on a bed where the machine had been, just then doctor Adams walked in, where is Leah, Marcus said, don't worry she is with her mum, Jessie is feeding her they are bonding so I left them alone together for a few minutes, Jessie woke up about two hours ago, she was frantic so we moved Leah closer to her and she settled.

You can go around but do not upset them. Yeah sure doc. Marcus walked slowly and could hear Jessie cooing over Leah and love washed over him, it was coming from Jessie, he thought he would never feel that again, he stepped around the corner, Jessie was topless her hair was down and tangled around her she was holding Leah to her breast and Leah was feeding, in fact she sounded like she was guzzling it down, he did not move he was in Orr. She was so beautiful seeing her feed their child for the first time and Jessie looked so happy and beautiful, she could not take her eyes from Leah and did not notice his presence, his heart filled with love and happiness, he took another step forward he was drawn to her he had to be near them both. Jessie grabbed the cover and covered herself and Leah, he had spoiled the moment.

Sorry he said I just wanted to see how your both doing, we're fine, now go get out of my site you disgust me, I will make arrangements for you to see Leah as much as you want, now leave, she could not look at him. Leah started to cry and Marcus remembered what Kirk has said about her crying when he carried Jessie, that was the picture in his head and it hurt so much. Ok, he said but I am coming back when Leah is asleep and withdrew.

Phillip was awake and sat on the bed is she still mad, yeah and I can't blame her for what she thought she saw I would be gutted if I was her but come into the office, I have proof. They went into the office and watched the DVD and Phillip said Joshua saved your ass and your family. Yes, I know but how do I get Jessie to listen to me let alone watch the DVD? After twenty minutes the nurse came in and took Leah from Jessie, changed her and changed her tubes and then put her back into her incubator, Leah went off to sleep and the nurse helped Jessie put her bra on and a button-down bed top. I will be back in a bit with a hot drink and some food you need to eat Jessie for Leah and to keep your strength up, she pulled the screen back and Marcus could see Jessie sat up in bed, he went back over and stood next to her bed and said in a soft voice, Jessie honey please for Leah's sake please just hear me out and then I will leave you alone and I will never bother you again ever.

She did not say anything, Jessie I understand your reaction yesterday and if I was you I would have done the same thing if not more and that shows me how much you love me and I love you and will always love you and our daughter, the distress you both felt yesterday was down to me, but it was unintentional I did not do what you think I did and it looked very bad even I must admit that, so I take full responsibility for that and in time I hope you can forgive me the pain you felt, it was inflicted deliberately by the man who followed you and mum, I have a lot of evidence that clears my name and as for the pain that Leah felt I cannot imagine how you and she must have felt and I promise I will make it up to you both, I was set up, we were set up and I love you both so much. The nurse came in with Jessie's cup of tea and tray of food. Jessie drank her tea and pushed the tray away. Jessie please eat something if not for you for Leah, she still refused to look at him.

Tears started to roll down her cheeks, please don't honey, I love you and this is killing me, no it's killing us, you are my wife and I am your husband and we are her parents and that will never change I promise you. You are feeling this pain because I failed to protect you and nothing has ever hurt me more than the pain, I saw in you last night it ripped my guts out, like you did to me Jessie said you killed me in there, go to hell and leave me alone. She turned away from him, he could see she was still hurting he just wanted to make it all stop. Ok, but I am not giving up I will not lose my family!

He put her flowers on the end of the bed and put Leah's little teddy on top of her incubator, looked at her then left. Christine and Kirk were waiting outside with Xander and Phillip. Would she not listen Kirk said, no and she is refusing to eat which means she won't be able to feed Leah? Right one of you go and get a TV and a DVD player, take it in and leave us girls to talk ordered Christine. Phillip did as was asked. Christine went in, Jessie I love you with all of my heart and I could have killed him yesterday in fact Kirk slapped Marcus across the face so hard, but Jessie look at me. Jessie turned back over and sat up, if you don't eat that food then I am going to ram it down your throat so help me god I will, you will not take this out on your child, now eat and I will talk and then we have a DVD to watch.

Christine told her everything that she saw, heard, what she saw on the DVD and what she had said to Marcus and what the men did to save their lives, how devastated Marcus had been and the only thing he was guilty of was stupidly taking that woman into a room to protect you. Jessie finished her breakfast, right Christine said now let's watch. She played the DVD twice and they have a confession, everything Marcus has said is the truth sweet heart, I know that vision of that woman will be stuck in your head but you can clearly see it was not of his doing, he understands on what you walked in on even he admitted that it looked so bad and that hurt you but it's killing him and Kirk it killed him to hear little Leah crying and that's why he hit Marcus.

So now I am going to take this tray out and send your husband in and by the time he comes and gets us I want to see you back together and wearing your wedding ring and feeding that baby or there will be trouble. She took her hair brush out of her hand bag and handed it to Jessie, brush your hair and undo a button or two and I will go get him ok! She kissed her on the cheek and left. Christine went back outside and gave the tray to Xander and said to Marcus right she has listened to me; she has eaten all her food and has seen the DVD twice and is now brushing her hair. It's now down to you, so get in there and make up, I will keep everyone out.

We will wait I want to see my family all together. Marcus kissed her and went in, he walked over to Jessie's bedside, she looked at him, she was not crying that was head way and she had not told him to go yet so this was good. Jessie he said, I love you and I am so, so, sorry please try and find a way to forgive me, seeing me in that position will take some getting over I understand that but would you could you please put your wedding ring back on, you are mine and I am yours you are my wife and I am your husband and I could never want another, ever please believe that I want us to be a family again in every sense of the word. He pulled her ring out of his pocket and held it out to her in the palm of his hand, she took it, he said please let me put it back onto where it belongs. She gave him the ring and he put it back on her finger and kissed her ring. Thank you he said and looked at her, Leah made a little noise; she knows your here she can sense you.

Has she spoken to you yet? No, Jessie shook her head I can feel her; she has not spoken one word since what happened yesterday, she wants you to pick her up, do I need to get the nurse back in to get her out? No, open the side door and lift her out but make sure none of her tubes get stuck. Ok Marcus said and went to walk away, where are you going, Marcus turned and winked with a big smile on his face and said I remember what the doctor said hands and chest, he washed and dried his hand and then walked back to her bed and faced Jessie, took his t shirt off slowly and threw it on the bed next to Jessie, her face went pink and she could not take her eyes off him and that was another good sign he could tell she wanted him.

He turned and picked Leah up and held her, Jessie was staring what is it Marcus said, nothing, it's the first time I have seen you hold her. I wish I could have seen you hold her for the first time, you did when you came in this morning the nurse had just come in, picked her up and gave her to me then helped her attached to me and I started to feed her and you came in. Leah made another little noise and Marcus held her closer, Leah tried to suckle on Marcus and Jessie laughed, what is she doing he said Jessie laughed again and said she is trying to feed she is getting hungry again, oh, he said and lifted her off his chest, both of his nipples went hard and Jessie was looking at him.
Ok, what do I do now? Just put her back for a minute and give me a hand. Leah cried out the second Marcus put her

down. Marcus did not know who to go to, Jessie said she is ok she just wants your attention and she wants to be near you it's a guilt trip. It works very well he said.

He walked back over to Jessie she was unbuttoning her top and he couldn't take his eyes off her. She could not get the top off and he helped with that then she said I can't undo my bra because my boobs are too big and get in the way, so, he leaned over her shoulder she could feel his breath on her neck he was so close to her he undid her bra, his breathing got faster he slid the straps off her and then he had to stop for a second and pull himself together. Jessie knew she would have to take her bra off in front of Marcus to feed Leah and as he stood up her bra slid down, Jessie pulled it out of the way and he could feel the want and need in him rise, he stepped away and picked Leah up who was now crying louder and making lots of noise. Her crying slowed when he picked her up Marcus kissed her and turned to see Jessie top less and holding her arms out to him she was a vision, her face was flushed and her eyes sparkled he was handing her to Jessie, she pulled Leah to her breast and Marcus's thumb touched Jessie's nipple, she gasped and he did as well, Leah's mouth found Jessie's nipple while both of her parents where just staring at each other.

The sound of their daughter guzzling and feeding from Jessie broke their gaze, he touched Leah's cheek and she made a little noise, he looked up and kissed Jessie gently and softly on the lips and she went bright red. Marcus did not want to move a way but Jessie had to feed Leah, he said is it ok if I get mum while your feeding Leah she wants to see you .

Yes, that's fine but could you pass me that white sheet on the side so I can cover myself and then dad can come in with Xander if he is ok with that, are you ok with that she said. He smiled again and said yes, I am. Marcus went outside with a big smile and Christine said oh thank god, we heard Leah cry and feared the worst. No, we were not quick enough to get her to her food. Jessie is feeding her now; she is covered up with a sheet so if you would like to come in and see them both. Christine did not need telling twice, Marcus held the door open and nodded to Kirk and Xander who nodded back and went in. Christine was lent over the bed and had pulled the sheet back a little bit so you could only see Leah's head on Jessie breast. God, Christine said listen to her she's enjoying that. Christine touched Leah's head and she made a sound of comfort. The men could hear her from where they stood.

Jessie, Christine said she is just like you when you were that age. Christine stood and looked over at Kirk she had tears of joy in her eyes. Dad and granddad why don't you come over I am sure that when she is finished, she would love a cuddle from all of her favorite men, they all stood around the bed looking at the newest member of their family. When she was finished Marcus stepped forward to help Jessie and said to Xander and Kirk hands and chests, they both went to wash their hands and take their shirts off and Marcus lifted Leah off Jessie. She had gone back to sleep Jessie told them, Christine said she needs winding. Jessie pulled the sheet back up to cover herself. Marcus kissed Leah again and handed her to Christine who put her on her shoulder and rubbed her back until she brought up some wind then Christine kissed her and handed her to Kirk. Leah started to make a little noise and Kirk looked up and said is she ok, Marcus laugh, she is snoring she's been fed and winded, she's very happy and loved and contented, after a good cuddle Kirk handed her to Xander.
She made a little noise and a little white light shone out of Leah and covered her. Now she is just showing off to

impress grandpa Jessie said. Save your energy little one, Xander kissed her and the white light went, she started to snore again, they all felt love flow over them and healed any pain that had been left between them.

After a week both Leah and Jessie were fit and well enough to be released from the medical facility. Marcus carried Leah up to their room and Jessie walked beside them and their bodyguards followed. Marcus was greeted by Kirk at the door as all three grandparents and uncle unpacked all the new baby stuff they had brought and got the nursery that was in their room all warm and ready for Leah. Everyone had a kiss and cuddle before they left them to it. Markus put Leah down and put the baby monitor on while Jessie expressed some milk ready for Leah's night feed that Marcus gave her, it was a tiny little bottle, that way Jessie could sleep. When they were finished Jessie said I am going for a shower, she got up and went to the bathroom and took off her clothes and stepped into the shower she loved the water on her skin, it had been the first time since that night that they had been alone together for some private time.

Marcus picked up the baby monitor and walked in to the bathroom to see Jessie, all week without her top on had driven him crazy with need but he knew she had needed some time to adjust and was going to need a lot more, but the sight of her naked and wet was just too much he did not want to push her but he needed her just some part of her for him and he needed it now, he would take anything no matter what it was. She turned to see him looking at her with fire in his eyes. She did not move or break their gaze. He put the baby monitor on the side and stripped his clothing off, he was fully aroused, Jessie knew what he wanted from her she was turned on just by the sight of him and her inside stared to throb in excitement and need for him. He opened the draw and took something out she could not see what it was he had it in his hand he entered the shower and stood for a second just looking at her.

Her nipples were hard and she was breathing deeply Jessie stepped back against the wall, he approached her slowly not taking his eyes from her he stood in front of her and just looked, she could feel the heat from his body on her nipples he was so close but he was not touching her. If she wanted him, she would have to touch him he was not going to take her, she was going to have to give herself-willing to him; he would know then that she had forgiven him. He would die if she would not it would kill him inside. Still silence from both of them, Jessie knew he was waiting for her so she stepped forward pushing her breasts against him and she curled her arms around him and drew him down to kiss her that was all he needed. He kissed her back and ran his hand over her body needing to feel all of her, he licked both of her beasts and she nearly came, he slid his hand between her legs and found she was hot wet and very ready for him she was making little noises of need it was driving him crazy, he slid his finger in her and she came, she called out his name and bucked against him and he had to stop for a second a take a few deep breaths to control himself.

He produced a condom from his hand that he had taken from the draw and put in on, he lifted Jessie up and she wrapped her legs around him he could not wait any longer and pulled her down on to him and entered her, she was so tight he came and slumped forward pushing Jessie up against the wall he held her there, he needed the wall to support them both. When they could both breathe again, he gently released her and withdrew his body from hers.
He kissed her like he had never kissed her before then wrapped them both in towels and carried her and the baby monitor back to the bedroom. They dried each other and

got in bed and he pulled her to him and held her, she had needed that just as much as he, if not more. They drifted off to sleep.

Marcus woke up and look around, Leah was not crying but it was just as if someone had spoken to him. He got up out of bed, he was still naked and went to check on Leah. She could sense him and opened her and just looked at him as his heart began to melt as he stared into to eyes that reminded him so of Jessies.

When Jessie had finished and put Leah back to bed Marcus said come wife, I am going to make love to you again and he picked Jessie up and laid her on the bed, he got a condom from the draw by the bed and put it on.

Jessie watched intently he slid himself over her and parted her legs with his and entered her with need to claim her as his, with such desire for her he drove into her over and over, she called out his name and he could not get enough she was the air he needed to breath with, he had licked and sucked every part of her and still wanted more they were both covered in hot sweat, Jessie knew she needed to calm him, his need for her was his pain coming out. So, she took a breath and held his face and said his name softly, he looked in her eyes and stopped, she said its ok honey I forgive you and I love you now roll over on to your back and let me show you.

She straddle him and slid down on to him, he gasped out her name she took him and made love to him she came on him again and he thought he was going to die, she slid off him and took the condom off and took him in her mouth and he came insanely filling her mouth with his seed and she swallowed it all down then laid next to him and he cover them over and they both fell off to sleep.

Jessie woke with a little cry from Leah she looked at the clock it said it was nearly eight am, god she had missed two feeds she must be hungry. Marcus was flat out asleep she went in and picked Leah up and said are you ok honey why didn't you cry before and a little voice said I waited as long as I could because daddy made you tired. Oh, Leah, she kissed her and held her to her breast, mummy and daddy will always have time for you please don't go hungry again, and Leah said your love filled me up and made me feel better, Jessie kissed her little hand and sat in the feeding chair, covered her and Leah with a blanket. When she finished Jessie gave her a bath and changed her and put a pretty little summer dress on her that Kirk had brought, she kissed her daughter and put her back in her cot while Jessie showered and put her own little summer dress on, a white lace thin strapped low cut hanky chef style dress, she put her hair up and applied light make up and perfume, when Jessie looked in the mirror she did not recognize herself she looked like a very beautiful woman from the movies, she put her sandals on and picked Leah up and her baby bag, the clock said 9.15 am, leaving Marcus to sleep as he too must have been so upset and stressed and with his love making he had needed to calm down since that night and the worry of Leah and the release last night had all taken its toll emotionally.

When Jessie opened the door to leave Robert and Amanda where waiting, Jessie said to Robert I want someone here while Marcus is asleep please, I don't like leaving him and I want one of Joshua's men to do it, who do I need to speak to, to get that done now. I will do it now, Robert opened his phone and relayed everything Jessie had said and before Robert could close his phone there was a man walking towards them. Amanda let the man approach he was dressed in a dark suit and dressed like them, Amanda said Jessie this is Eli he will watch over Marcus for you. Good, he is not to be disturbed he needs to sleep and thank you Eli. Where do I go for breakfast on this lovely day? Amanda said everyone is on the sun balcony, ok let's go there.

When Jessie appeared, everyone stood up and bowed to her, Jessie walked over and kissed Xander, Kirk, Christine and Phillip then Jessie handed Leah to Xander and said she would like to talk to grandpa and everyone looked, with an excited voice she told them how Leah had spoken to Marcus and her last night. Little one Xander said I have missed our chats and sat down with her. Is everything ok, Kirk said where is your husband? I think he is worn out, Kirk smiled, say no more, Jessie blushed, not like that, well maybe a little I just think the past few weeks have taken their toll on him so I let him sleep in and I asked for one of Joshua's men to watch over him, it did not feel right to leave him unprotected while he slept. Good, I think you two need a night alone together away from us, me and mum would gladly look after Leah, don't feel you have to wait for time away to ask we would have her anytime, thank you dad and she kissed him on the cheek, come and have breakfast with us, please sit.

> The butler came and took Jessie's order. Jessie took some sun cream out of her baby bag and a little sun hat and said dad can you help Xander with this she

needs to have cream on and a hat It's getting hot and gave him the cream and hat. After a couple of minutes of giggling and saying hold that Christine took control and had it done in seconds, they all finished breakfast and Jessie said its nearly ten I have to feed Leah again, Phillip reluctantly handed Leah over as all he had done with her was laugh and giggle for the last ten minutes, she said mum can you pass me that little blanket out and the men stood to leave, no, Jessie said please stay she turned her chair way from them a little bit and the bodyguards all turned the other way to give her some privacy, Amanda and Robert stood to the other side of Jessie's chair so they could see any one that approached and Christine put the blanket around Leah and Jessie, she fed her daughter sat in the sun and looking out over the castle and town below and everyone could hear Leah guzzling Jessie's milk back.

Xander exclaimed by god she's like her dad she likes her drink and everyone laughed.

It was nearly 10.25am when Tobias appeared on the balcony with a man, they walked towards Xander, Robert and Amanda moved and stood in front of Jessie everyone stood and the two men bowed to Xander. Tobias introduced him and said this is an envoy from the brotherhood in east his name is Adele. They have heard that the guardian has arrived and they wish to meet her or know that it's true, a wish to know when the ceremonies of light will start. Jessie finished feeding Leah and asked Christine to take Leah and wind her while she made herself respectable again. Xander shook the man's hand and said yes, it is true and yes, she is hear now, please sit and wait she is seeing to her baby.

A butler brought them a drink while they all waited. Christine returned with Leah over her shoulder and sat next to Kirk and again all the men stood and then sat again. Phillip stood up and stood in front of Leah and Christine and no one said a thing accept Adele whispered to Tobias and said, what's his problem so Phillip could hear him, is he the baby's father? No, Tobias he is the other guardian and is very protective over his sister and her baby so don't do anything and do not attempt to go near her unless she invites you to or he will increase you where you stand, I have seen it myself very close up and first hand, as you know it is the death penalty to even touch her let alone be stupid enough to try and influence her to mate, ok good to know Adele said. Jessie stood and moved her chair back and all the bodyguards took their original positions.

Jessie took Leah from Christine, Xander and all the men stood up and Xander introduced Adele to her, she did not move from where she stood, Xander could tell that Leah was talking to Jessie and Jessie took a step back and a giant red flame shot out from her, covering her and Leah. Kirk drew his sword and stood in front of her, Phillip took a step towards Adele. Xander asked Jessie, what alerts you? He is not who he says he is and a white flame shot out of Phillip and surround Christine, Xander and Kirk. Satisfied now Xander said to Adele, yes, Adele said I have no wish to distress her she is everything you said and much more and I used my power but I have no wish to burn to death, a red haze filled Jessie's flame and

Tobias said, that's are queue to leave, come brother and with that Tobias and Adele left. Jessie's flame went white and then went, Phillip's flame went to. Kirk put away his sword. Phillip said what's going on Xander? Jessie walked up behind Phillip and put her hand on his shoulder and said it was a test brother. Yes, it was and you both passed. But why? They want us to perform a ceremony as they feel my presence more since I had Leah, Jessie told him. Very good Jessie, Xander said, how did you know he was not who he said he was, because I felt he had more power than even you Xander, he desired me, you keep him away from me and Leah or I will not be responsible for my actions. Very well Jessie he will be told. Come let's all have a drink in the shade as it's hot.

It had just gone 10.40am when Xander went inside to talk to Tobias and Adele or whoever he was. Jessie said dad could I take you up on that offer tonight for you and mum to have Leah, I will have all of her bottles ready for her and you could have her in our room because the nursery and everything's there or I can move her cot, if you have plans, but before she could finish he said we can't wait that's fine, wait till we tell mum when her and Phillip can stop wrestling each other to hold Leah. She giggled, Kirk said where are you going to go, I don't know Jessie said but he needs a break I thought about the boat or dinner and dance or a show and a night at a hotel, what do you think he would like? Well how about you and me go out and arrange it and we will be back by lunch time, mum and Phillip can have more time to fight over Leah as that's what they are enjoying. She smiled and said thank you, do you need to feed Leah again? No, she had two feeds in her bag, great let's tell them then go. Jessie took his hand and Christine and Phillip where overjoyed that they could have Leah.

As Jessie and Kirk walked through the castle holding hands, they walked through the great hall where Xander and at least ten other men were sat around on sofas by the giant fireplace talking, Jessie's red light instantly came out of her and covered her and Kirk and she slowed her pace. Kirk tighten his grip and said be at ease child they mean you no harm and her flame went white and then flicked. Its ok Kirk said no one will approach you and her flame went. They went to walk pass Xander and the men and they all stood, Xander held his hand out to her and she looked at the other men, Kirk said its ok, Jessie and she let go of his hand and gave Xander a hug and kiss on the cheek, that caught the attention of a few of the men among them, at least one new Kirk. She could sense it.

We are going out to arrange a surprise for Marcus, mum and Phillip have Leah we won't be long. Ok darling take any of the cars Xander said. Jessie took Kirks hand again and smiled, come on dad. Just to make sure they all understood his importance to her. Kirk knew why she had said it and felt honored. Where are we going? well there are things we need first Kirk said. Adele asked Xander is Kirk her father? No, he is not her biological father that was Peter Bagbie, Kirk is her stepfather so to speak, interesting she shares a very strong bond with him. Yes, Xander replied and she would kill anyone without a second thought to protect her family she has many powers and she gets stronger by the day, she has given him blood and she saved his life, I for one thought him dead he had a massive hole straight through him and she healed him in seconds and that little display was nothing believe me, that was a warning to keep back, she used your power to do it. I notice she shielded him as well, how far can she go. A distance was all Xander said. And her child Adele said, I would kill anyone who would even wish ill feeling to her or my family, she and I send you all a warning she sensed you wanted her said Xander. She is bonded to Marcus and they share a child she wants you to keep away from her and her child. She will do her duty to us and that is it, if you or any one was to approach her or her child then they will die, do I make myself clear on this matter? Yes, they all said, good then let us continue.

Marcus touched the bed where Jessie had been did he dream she was in his bed again and Leah, there was not a sound he looked at the clock and it said 12.04 pm he had slept all night and all the morning, he was sure he had made love to Jessie, where was everyone and why had no one woken him up. Did he just dream she had forgiven him? He could sense there was someone outside of his door and he opened the door to see Eli, what is wrong brother, is all ok and where is my wife and child? Be at ease Marcus your wife requested that someone be here and that you were not to be disturbed while you slept, she did not want you unprotected while you slept. She and your daughter are well, I believe she had breakfast with the family and now they're about to have lunch soon. Thank you, Eli, Marcus went back in and showered, so last night had not been a dream he had made love to Jessie and she had forgiven him. He showered and put his black jeans on and a white v neck t-shirt and his after shave the one he knew Jessie loved. He went in search of his family, Jessie had been back about ten minutes and everyone had gathered around to start lunch when Robert stepped forward and whispered in Jessie's ear that Marcus was up and Eli said that Marcus was not sure of what was happening, he had showered and was on his way down, thank you Robert.

Kirk heard all that was said because he was sat next to Jessie feeding Leah, and said I think your right he does need a break he will love tonight. Just then Marcus appeared and ran over to Jessie who stood to great him he lifted her up and kissed her, put her down and said to Kirk every time I see you; you have one of my women in your arms old man, come on hand her over. Kirk stood and handed Leah over, she did not make a sound when Kirk took the bottle out of her mouth to hand her to her dad. Marcus gave her a cuddle and kissed her and said daddy loves you and daddy has missed you and mummy and finished feeding Leah. Marcus gave her to Christine to wind while he ate. He could not take his eyes from Jessie she looked so beautiful he wanted her more than his food. Christine gave Leah back to Jessie and Jessie cuddled her until Leah fell fast asleep.

I think she has had far too much sun and fresh air for one day I am going to take her and put her down and express some milk. Let me carry her said

Marcus, Jessie smiled and handed her over to him, she stared to snore, told you just like her farther and they went back to their room. While Marcus put Leah down, she expressed enough milk to last Leah for some time. Marcus had to force himself to wait till Jessie has finished with Leah's milk he wanted her now. When Jessie had finished she stood up and put the milk in the little fridge and Marcus came up behind her, held her hips gently and she stood up and said yes what do you want husband, she turned around and his eyes were on fire you my wife I want you now and he lifted her up and took her to their bed, Jessie said no, and he stopped.

She said I am saving myself for tonight husband but I can see to your immediate needs. So she wiggled and he stood her up, no I need to take you I need to be inside of you Jessie, please honey I am begging you, she put a finger on his lips and then she kissed him and wrapped herself around him he pulled his t shirt of and she kissed his chest and licked his nipples and sucked them gently, he was panting hard and fast saying her name she knelt down and looked up at him, he undid his belt without taking his eyes from hers he did not have any under ware on and his shaft fell out of his jeans, he was so hard Jessie took him in her mouth and grabbed his balls, Marcus was breathing so hard he grabbed her hair and he bucked hard against Jessie and came in her mouth, hard and fast and so much Jessie had to swallow twice. He tried to gain control quickly. After a few seconds he let go of Jessie.

She got up and went to the bathroom to clean up, she left him to recover. When she came back in his jeans were done up and he was picking his t shirt up, he said I am sorry honey you're so beautiful I just needed you the second I saw you. Are you ok? she smiled I am fine don't worry? Marcus went to the bathroom to freshen up, there was a knock at the door it was mum and dad eager to take over from them till tomorrow. Come in please Marcus won't be a second. When Marcus came out of the bathroom, he saw Jessie going through Leah's routine, what is this? Marcus asked. Come husband tonight your mine I have planned a surprise for you, she kissed him and he kissed her back. Kirk said you are not there yet. Jessie broke their kiss, she hugged mum and dad, thanked them both and took Marcus by the hand and took him to a waiting car.

Where are we going and what are have you done you little minks. After everything we have been through these last few weeks, I have arranged for me and you to have some time alone together. They dove to a private six-star resort some of Joshua's team were there. Their car pulled up to a private glass bungalow and it had its own private pool. They went in, there where flowers everywhere and the glass doors where open, they could hear waves on the shore line as they had their own little private beach. Now, she said while pouring him a large brandy and coke you can rest or we can have a little swim and then I am going to give you a full body massage, then we will have a little dinner dance tonight at the club house if you want or we can order in and then bedtime, she smiled at him and gave him his drink and told him to sit, he did as she asked, she went off into another room and came back with a tiny black bikini on and he nearly choked on his drink.

I will see you in the pool and she ran out of the room before he could grab her, he followed her to the pool and finished his drink, watched her dive into the pool her hair spread out like a giant fan and then she stood at the other end of pool dripping wet, that bikini just did things to him. He put his glass on a chair and stripped naked he asked Jessie where are the condoms? there are none I want you inside me I need to feel you. Jessie knew he was going to take her there and then and he did not disappoint her.

When he had finished, he carried her to the bed and she had a sleep for an hour while he held her to him. When she woke, she told him to take a hot shower and she was going to give him a massage, he invited her into the shower to wash his back, she declined because he would take her in there as well. When he came out he looked better in himself and looked like a god his muscles looked like they were bulging and he had a small towel warped around him, now that was all for her benefit she had a fold up massage table up and lit candles everywhere, she was going all out for him so he would try and control himself more but she was going to have her hands all over him, she gave him another drink and he took it and said thank you jess.

She had changed to, she had on what looked like a little very short white outfit that did not button all the way up because of her chest, he wondered if she had under ware on. He finished his drink and said what way would you like me jess? on your back please she turned and dipped her hands in warm water and oil and turned back, he did as he was asked, she was expecting him to have taken his towel off to be naughty but he did not she knew his was trying to be good.

She lowered the table a bit and stood at his head and leaned over his face and ran warm oil over him from his shoulders to the middle of his tummy as she could not reach all the way down, he went hard immediately she continued to do all the top half she could feel him relax, until she touched the top of his leg just where the little towel that was now just covering his massive hard on was and he whispered, Jessie softly, he then put his hand up her little dress to find she was not wearing anything oh honey please. She moved forward out of his reach and continued, he said I can't turn over and looked down his body, sorry I was being very good it's you, Jessie wiped her hand and lowered the table again and took his towel off, she looked at him and he growled at her, she climbed on top of him and straddled him, both of his hands came up under her dress to touch her, she was wet and ready her skin felt soft he grabbed her hips and pulled her down on to him and her head fell back, she rocked forward and they both gasped out, she leaned forward to kiss him and he squeezed her breast and she pushed her self-back on him, he said her name she took him slowly and fully.

When they both got out of the shower Jessie went into another room to dress, he found his black suit laid out for him he knew she loved him in that and he smiled and put it on for her.

He came out of his room he looked at her and stopped dead, he did not think it was possible to want to fuck someone so much, she had a dress on, no you could not call that a dress it did not have any sides it was one piece of white silk at the front and one piece of silk on the back that came to her knees and a gold rope around her neck that held it together and a thin gold rope tide loosely around her waist with high heeled gold tie up sandals, her hair was tied up with think gold thread and you could see lots of her body and you could see that she did not have underwear on, there was not room for it.

She had thick black eye liner on with gold lip gloss, her eyes sparkled. He was gasping for breath, she went over to him and slapped him on his back what is it honey Jessie asked, you Marcus said you're trying to kill me you're not leaving this room with that on, no one else is going to see you like that. Jessie smiled and said don't be silly they will all be too busy looking at the sexiest man in the world on my arm, Jessie you look like a queen. Come on I am starving. Do you have a coat or wrap? she smiled again and said no, they walked to the car and Marcus was sure he could here Robert saying to Amanda oh shit she trying to get me killed? They got out at the club house and walked in, their security was there in place and they had a table in a roped off area everyone looked at Jessie and Marcus. There was Champaign on ice and a club photographer took their picture Jessie had Champaign, Marcus made lots of complements to her they danced together and no one had the balls to ask Jessie to dance she was out of their league and the amount of testosterone Marcus was giving off the air was thick with it.

She was his there was no doubt to anyone in that room. He felt he was 100% pure male and very protective over her. He felt like his old self but nothing had changed since the second he clapped eyes on her, all he wanted to do was make love to her. She was driving him crazy with desire and need, he had taken so much already she made him feel that way she had wanted him in the same way and he felt it every time she touched him and that turned him on like a burning flame and looking the way she did when she got dressed up just made him hunger more for her. They had their meal and a few more drinks the photographer gave Robert their photo and he gave it to Jessie, Robert said there are no other copies and Marcus nodded at him, Robert stood back in line. Jessie thought they looked like loved up movie stars. It is us Jessie; I know I did not think I looked that pretty. Oh, Jessie you look like a goddess and you smell like angles and everyman desires you. Oh, Marcus she touched his face and kissed him she had fever in her eyes when he broke their kiss and he knew it was time to leave and give her fully what she now wanted from him, he would deny her nothing.

They left the club house hand in hand and got into their waiting car and Jessie said I love you and kissed him, again her nipples were pushing against the silk and he went to slide his hand up her dress, the car stopped they were back already. He got out of the car and held his hand out and they walked hand in hand into their bungalow the windows had been closed and the curtains drawn. Marcus let go of her hand to lock the door, he watched her walk to the bedroom and followed her in silence, she stood beside the bed he took her in his arms and kissed her hard and slow, he touched her everywhere he ran his hands up under her dress, he thought she had come she was so wet. He just said softly oh honey, he knelt down and licked her she came then, he took her weight as her legs gave out and he placed her on the bed and then stood back, she said strip slowly he did as she commanded, she started to touch herself and lick her lips her eyes were on fire and tiny white sparks shot out from her eyes, he could take no more he pushed her back on the bed parted her legs and entered her they both came instantly. When he could talk, he said Jessie honey I am your salve I love you. He laid next to her and they fell asleep.

Jessie woke up at just before 4 am and looked at Marcus he smelt so good she wanted him again so she slowly took her shoes off and the belt of her dress and eased him onto his back and straddled him, he was hard and she eased herself on to him and make a noise of fulfillment and need and rocked gently forward, Marcus woke instantly he thought he was dreaming, Jess honey he could hardly breathe she took his breath away he let her take what she needed from him they were both covered in sweat and tears of happiness and fulfillment rolled down her cheeks while she took him, he tried so hard not to come but when she came all down his shaft she soaking him he could hold back no more he held her hips tight and pulled her down and he filled her with his hot seed and gasped out her name . He pulled her down on him and held her to him.

When they woke it was 10am they showered and had breakfast on the balcony and after breakfast they went for a walk along the beach together arms around each other like the lovers they were. When they returned everything had been packed up and Jessie said we have to go back for Leah. I know and he kissed her and said thank you for doing this for me, for us I love you. They got back into the car and went back to the castle. They arrived back just before 1pm Marcus looked and felt great they found their family just finishing lunch, Christine stood with Leah and Jessie took her daughter into her arms and kissed and cuddled her, a bright white bubble burst out of Jessie and covered her and Leah and everyone felt a love burst over them it felt very powerful, Jessie realized what she did and went red in the face and said sorry, the bubble got smaller and then went. Marcus pulled his wife and child into his arms I want more of the love sharing and everyone watching had a big smile on their faces. This is good to see Xander said. Was she ok mum? yes, she was a little angel, she gets that from her mum Marcus said? and kissed Jessie and touched Leah.

They were cooing over their baby when Kirk said that's it, I can't take it no more I am making this official woman, Kirk kneeled at Christine's feet and said "will you do the honor of becoming my wife as soon as possible" and produced a massive diamond that Jessie had help pick yesterday when they were out. Christine looked shocked and said yes, I will, Kirk stood and he slid the ring on, it fitted like a glove and he took her in his arms and kissed her. Good, he said it's all arranged for the day after tomorrow. Jessie and Phillip helped, you can blame your granddaughter she wanted to know if we are a family and if so, why you and I had different names, I told her it was my fault and I would put that right straight away. So, Jessie if you could take mum out and get her a dress or we can have them come here! Marcus, I need a best man, Phillip could you give mum away? another big smile burst across his face, oh yes and Xander could you do the very special duty of accompanying your granddaughter as her mum will be busy as bridesmaid. Tobias and the brotherhood are going to do the castle up and arrange for someone to come in and do the ceremonies, the reception is here as well so it will be totally secure and nobody will have to travel.

Ladies you are having your night tonight so we men can look after Leah and us men tomorrow night then the wedding. So, who is looking after Leah while the girls go out, I am Marcus said? Do you have enough milk till I get back as we will have to go now? Yes, we have two more bottles, good that will give us enough time lets go mum. Jessie handed Leah to Marcus and kissed them both, no more passing around she needs to be put down in her cot, yes mum Marcus said and kissed her again. Kirk released Christine from their kiss.

Xander spoke to James and he pulled his phone out and spoke to someone and closed his phone. When they got to the car Victor said I am to accompany you ladies, please allow me and he opened the car door for Christine and Jessie, Victor sat in the back with Amanda and Robert, Kevin got into the front and they had a police escort. They went to the best bridal shop and Christine tried a few dresses on and while she was doing that Jessie found Leah little dress and tights, it reminded her of her wedding dress trip. Then Christine came out with a white strapless dress that went to her knee and showed her tan off as she was a thin short woman with big boobs. Wow you look about twenty in that as she whistled and said that's the one you look like a model, do you like it then Jessie, yes, she replied and dad will love it he won't be able to keep his hands off you. Victor was sat on a sofa taking in the two women, he had to come to love them both it felt strange to him but new, it was Jessie's power and feelings that affect the men in the brotherhood she could not help it. Something caught his eye in the giant mirror by the window, a man sat in the café opposite.

Victor knew he was an immortal he sensed it; the gathering was not for another week. Perhaps he was just having coffee, but he could not take that chance with Jessie, there could be more he had not seen, so he slowly opened his phone and spoke to Joshua and asked him to send a team just in case. After Christine got all of her bits, they got Jessie a dress. Jessie, Christine said, oh honey you look so beautiful it was a simple white dress with tiny think gold thread straps you look like a goddess, oh mum you sound like Marcus, but you know what's missing, another bridesmaid and she turned and looked at Amanda and raised her eye brows, oh no Amanda said oh yes Jessie asked for another dress the same as hers for Amanda and they got little white silk flowers for their hair and white silk shoes to match. Kevin took the dress out and put them into the boot of the car while Jessie paid and then the woman walked back to the car.

Victor noticed that the man was definitely watching Jessie like a hawk. They all got into the car and left and went back to the castle. Victor knew that the man had been subdued after Jessie had left buy Joshua's team because Kirk and Marcus met them at the car, they must have been alerted and were eager to check on their woman. The man knew he would be held and interviewed. Victor got out of the car and eyed the pair and just shook his head slightly, they knew the woman had known nothing of the man.

Marcus pulled Jessie to him and kissed her, she broke their kiss and said where is Leah. Grandpa is with her he is reading her stores. Oh, good. Jessie turned to see Kirk was still kissing Christine and Amanda made a noise like she had something to say, Marcus looked at her, oh yes Jessie said we needed another bridesmaid so I hope you don't mine but I roped Amanda in and got her a dress, she will need the night off to come with us as we all have out fits for that to and I got one for doctor Adams to, he smiled that's ok. Come, let's get ready to have an early dinner we have been busy little bees and did the bar up in the ball room for your hen party tonight. Oh, good do we get male strippers? Marcus looked at her and knew she was teasing him; did you not get enough last night wife and Jessie went red. Jessie put her hand on Marcus's mouth to stop him saying anything else.

They all went back to their room to get ready for dinner. They all met and had dinner together and the woman went back to Jessie's room and put their very small and tight fitting naughty school girls out fits on with a loose tie and with lace top stocking that finished before their tiny skirts started, Christine has a red sash that said bride to be on it, they put their hair up and had bits of ribbon in it, their little white shirts did not do all the way up, just to underneath the bra and it showed a lot of chest, they applied loads of make up on and black hi heeled shoes and perfume. When the four women came down, they passed through the giant hall, where all of the men were sat around the giant fire place, they were sat with about twenty other men and Jessie could see Marcus stand and give Leah to Xander, all the other men stood as their wife's were attending the hen night. Marcus wiped his hand over his mouth like he was thirsty, he was drawling and said Jessie come here honey, she smiled at him, no take care of Leah, he started to walk towards Jessie, Phillip grabbed his arm and said sorry mate woman only.

Marcus just stared after her and said honey can't you spare ten minutes for your husband, ok five. Oh Jessie please come back I swear two minutes oh come on I will beg and got down on his knees, the woman's laughter filled the room, I will be here waiting for you when you're finished in there, she winked at him and blew him a kiss he caught it and then the men laughed at him. Dam did you see that dad? yes, where is your dignity; I don't have any when my wife looks like that, the other men agreed. As they all sat around telling stories Xander said to Marcus can I get Leah ready for bed and put her down. I would like to do that if that's ok with you, yeah sure, she would love it, Marcus took her from Xander so he could get up, he cuddled and kissed his daughter, and said why don't you have her in your room tonight and keep her till the morning as me and Jessie might be up all night, Xander looked at him and smiled, Jessie has put loads of her milk into bottles in the fridge in Leah's room and take her mosses basket, baby monitor and her changing bag and you know where we are if there's a problem.

You be good for grandpa, miss and Leah giggled softly and said I will, I love you daddy and daddy loves you to honey, he kissed her again and handed her over to Xander for safe keeping and said See you in the morning, then sat back down. When the girls went in there were at least twenty to thirty other women that they had met before. There were fairy lights everywhere, a DJ and white and pink flowers and petals and pink balloons. After a few drink's the woman danced and told jokes and swapped stories about their men.

Marcus was like a caged tiger he could hear the woman screaming out with laughter, laughing their heads off every few minutes and wondered what the hell was going on, are you sure there are no men in there with then because there having lots of fun and there's lots of giggling. Kirk said your worse than me come sit down be at ease son and gave him a little drink to calm him. There are no men in there, let the woman have their fun and release they deserve it. Yes, I know that but did you see what they nearly had on and the men burst out laughing at him again. God, he hoped she had under ware on and he hope she was not going to be too drunk as he was going to take her many times till, he had his fill of her the second they were alone.

Another roar of screaming laughter broke off with clapping and whistling. That was it he pulled his phone out and ordered Joshua to come to him immediately. That's low said Kirk. Joshua appeared with a big smile on his face knowing full well what Marcus was going to ask him. No, Joshua said there are no men in there and all the other doors are locked and that door there is the only way in and out and no you can't see the CCTV as I am under orders from Xander and your wife it was to be turned off in there tonight. But if there is anything else, I can help you with? Sorry. You're going to have to wait till they come out good night and Joshua left the room, the man laughed at him again, you get ten out of ten for effort old man Kirk said. Jessie's got your number, yes, she learns from you all far too quickly and it appears I have been out witted by my 18-year-old wife yet again. Visions of Jessie doing all kinds of thing in that room was driving him mad. At 11.30 the door opened and he was on his feet and at the door trying to look inside the room but Kirk and Phillip were there and had to drag him back, he could feel the heat come out of the room and he could smell her perfume, four woman came out all drunk and holding each other up and laughing their heads off. Their husbands had been as quick as he to claim their wives and took their wives back to their rooms. A few minutes later the door opened again and seven women staggered out laughing,

Marcus was so desperate to find out what the woman where doing in there, what do the you think the woman are laughing about what's so funny. Kirk said it has been my experience in the past that I have found that when woman get together they are worse than men and only talk about sex and men's body's and say thing's that they don't say to men in general and the amount of sex you and Jessie have, she must have lots to say. What my Jessie is taking about having sex with me. Yes, as is Christine and every other woman is doing the same, they swap stories and they try things out on you that other woman suggested that's how they learn how to please their men.

Shit, I didn't know that. Just then Christine and Jessie came out of the door screaming with laughter and tears rolling down their faces, Marcus was there calming his wife and the other men cheered, Marcus put his arm around her and she kissed him and lead her off, Kirk put his arm around Christine and lead her away back to their room.

When they got back inside their room Jessie pushed Marcus up against the wall and pulled him down for an urgent kiss, he ran his hands up her legs and grabbed her bum she had a tiny thong on and he lifted her up, she wrapped her legs around him, oh Jessie honey he whispered in her ear you're not too drunk are you because I need to know you know what you're doing and she whispered into his ear I know what I am doing now shut up and take me. He ran his thumb under her thong, she was hot and very wet, oh Jessie honey I can't last long he pulled her tiny thong aside and entered her, she pushed herself-hard down on to him and said his name and she came down him and he came throbbing into her.

He just held her and she kissed him hard and with fever she wanted more and continued kissing him he moved to the bed and laid her down then ripped the front of the shirt open and sucked her nipples, she started to tremble and he pulled her up the bed and spread her legs wide apart and tore the little tong off her, he licked her and kissed her between her legs and she came again, fucking hell Jessie your so fucking Horney and he pulled her back down the bed and turned her over, she knelt up and he pushed her little skirt up and ran his hand over her bum, gripped her hips, she groaned his name out and he entered her, she rocked back against him making more noise and he took her hard and pushed himself deep into her, she was screaming yes, and gripped the sheet to steady herself, he pulled her back onto him as he pushed so deep inside of her, faster and faster she was moaning don't stop she loved what he was doing to her and he fucked her harder and lost control he could not stop himself he was pushing himself into her harder and harder and then she came again, it was so hot and all of her muscles contacted around him he held her hips and came into her so fast and hard she called out again.

He slumped forwards on to her unable to hold himself up, after a minute he rolled sideways and pulled her into him their clothing was soaking wet form sweat they were both panting very fast trying to regain their breath. They fell asleep like that. When Jessie woke, she had a banging headache and there was no doubt that Marcus had taken her big time. She hurt inside and out. She was alone in bed it was 9.30 am she knew he had gone for Leah and would be at breakfast she pulled herself out of bed and staggered to the loo and then showered. She put a sun dress on and didn't look to bad considering her night she took some pain killers and went for breakfast, she noticed that Amanda was not on duty that did not surprise her, Eli was with Robert, she went to the sun balcony there were lot of people, it was not so private, they had come for the wedding. We are over here and Eli led Jessie to her family the men all stood and bowed and then sat back down, Marcus went to her and kissed her and whispered, was she ok? Jessie knew what he meant, I had two pain killers but I am fine I am hungry, he kissed her she took Leah from him and gave her a kiss and a cuddled, mummy loves you.

Xander told her that Leah had been no trouble. Where is Phillip? no one answered, Marcus could feel concern coming from her, its ok Jessie he is fine he has female company. Who? now we never kiss and tell Marcus said. oh, ok, where is mum, she is still asleep I am surprised you are up and about. I needed to see Leah I missed you both and I wanted to check that Tobias has everything done for the wedding. It's all done. Jessie looked around, what it is asked Marcus, I can feel that Adele is near, how do you know Adele? he looked at Xander and said tell me you did not when Leah was here with her and he stood up, how could you have been stupid anything could have happened and you put Leah in harm's way. Marcus was very angry Tobias and Adele approached and Xander stood and said Adele is the King, I don't care how many titles he has if he come near my wife and child again, I will end his very long existence You should have told me Xander. Jessie stood and Marcus took her arm and left, they walked around Tobias and Adele without a second look.

I could kill Xander for what he has done you maybe the guardian of light but first you are my wife, he had no right. What is it, why are you so upset she asked Marcus, when they were back in their room? Marcus slammed the door and that made Jessie jump and Leah cried, Jessie took her in the other room and closed the door she gave her cuddles and fed and changed her. Jessie put her down for asleep and went out and closed the door. I am sorry I did not mean to frighten you or Leah. Is she ok? She was a bit frightening but she's ok now she's asleep. Shit, he said. Jessie went over to the sofa and took both of Marcus's hands and said now calmly tell me what is wrong, and tell me everything, I did not know there is a king I nearly burnt to death a king. What! Marcus said, we will get to that, now start talking?

Ok but I need you to answer me a question first. Ok she said what is it? Well last night Jessie you were so god dam Horney did you feel his power or influence or sense him at all last night. No, why, so last night was just me, yes why, look Marcus l love you and only you and I want need and desire only you and when I am near you I feel your influence it's like a drug to me, I just want you, now last night I could not turn it off I sensed you sat out there and I sensed your mood and desire for me and that affected me all night, to the point I just needed you to take me anywhere.

I don't think of anyone else and I don't feel anyone or want anyone the way I want you.

The second someone is trying to influence me or use their power, my body senses it, that's all it does, not make me want them, it just makes me want to put my shield up. Now does that answer your questions enough? Yes, thank you and I am sorry I had to ask. Ok, now tell me why you needed to know. I will but first tell me how you met Adele. Jessie told him that she was feeding Leah and she felt a power present someone with more power than Xander, this man and Tobias approached Xander so I gave Leah to mum and I heard Tobias say he was just an envoy come to see Xander. I felt his instant desire for me, which made me feel sick I was then worried for Leah so I picked her back up, as she is drawn to power and my red light shone out, dad jumped up and drew out his sword and Phillip was there in front of us, them someone asked what the problem was, and all I said was he is not who he says he is then a red haze covered me. Tobias and the man left and Xander asked me how I knew that he was not who he said he was, I told him he had more power than him and I told Xander to tell him to stay away from Leah or I will not be accountable for my actions, then nothing till today.

Leah was close and I could feel him approaching me, I had already told Xander that Adele needed to keep his distance that I don't fancy him and I am not drawn to him but Leah is drawn to power Marcus, my worry is for how it will affect her and that's it. Thank you and that's good to know. Adele is our king there is only one but Xander is our Knight and holy man so to speak Xander could have been King but after seeing the messenger and seeing the other guardian he chose to keep faith in our father and let Adele be king. We are very rich because we have built our wealth over thousands of years and life time and we are very experienced at everything because of our long life but as king Adele was given power by us, but power has other benefits, woman are drawn to him, like we are drawn to you. But if you were drawn to him and he asked to touch you would be powerless to say no and I could do nothing if he influenced you, you would desire him and want him and he would take you and if you said yes, he as king has the right to make you his.

God, I feel sick just thinking about it. Right, because Xander must have had great confidence in me to test me without you there and I would be more distracted with Leah there. He must have known I would pass. Well, he took a big risk with my family and now I cannot trust him. Look what could have happened if you failed the test Jessie, he would have you in his bed now, but I am not he does not affect me in any way I just sense his presents more as I do any elder, as I said my only worry was Leah and now you. He has been warned to stay away and if he ever touched Leah, I would kill him myself- Jessie said. We must show him we are united and that he does not worry you. He must know why you are rightful angry at him, Xander and Tobias, yes Marcus said, and you said your peace to Xander. So let's leave it at that and try and get a long Xander must be upset with himself by seeing your reaction but he loves, you and our daughter, yes, I know and that's what made me so angry and that's my fault because I was angry you felt it and that just made things worse, so I am sorry to. Marcus kissed her and said your right come let's get Leah and let's go and get you something to eat.

Jessie got Leah who was fast asleep and wrapped her in a blanket, Marcus got her changing bag and they went back downstairs. Most of the other guests had gone but Xander, Adele and Tobias were all now sat in the shade talking and mum and dad were sat down with Phillip and doctor Adams who Jessie realized had spent the night with her brother. Kirk and Phillip stood to great Jessie, and Jessie handed Leah to Kirk. Doctor Adams just said hello. Is that food? I am starving, and a butler came over and took Jessie's order. Jessie asked Christine, how you feeling after last night? Christine just looked at her, oh, that good. Phillip said are you ready for tonight dad, yes, I am Phillip. Good about seven down at the bar then. And the big day is tomorrow. Don't forget your staying at dads tonight as mum is with me and Amanda is staying to. What, Marcus said I am not going to be with you tonight, oh hell no, way? Phillip, dad is with you, Amanda and mum in our room with Leah and I am going to be in bed with you, in mum and dads' room and that's it ok, me and you are together. There is nothing on this earth that is keeping you from my bed. Oh, I like it, he so masterful Jessie said. She winked at him, Kirk told Marcus, Xander wants you to go to him. Be nice Jessie said? Marcus kissed Jessie and Leah and went over to see what Xander wanted.

Marcus sat down, Xander said you know Adele! Marcus nodded, Xander said, you have every right be angry at me it was not Adele's doing but mine, we had to be sure she was strong enough, after having Leah, and she had him pegged at 25 yards. I asked Adele to test her, believe me he did not want to, I made him test her we have to have the ceremony of light soon and I need to know that she is up to it I would not have let anything happen please believe me. Jessie needs to be strong enough to fend off all and he was that test. Jessie is not bothered about that. Leah is drawn to power, you could have hurt her and that is what Jessie is very angry at, as am I, she is a baby and she is just protecting our child as am I. Now I cannot trust you, you did that, you lost my trust, when you put Leah at risk. I know, I did not see that, I see what I have done, I am so sorry, I would never put her at risk. But you have already. Adele said.

Marcus please know that it was not my wish or intention to cause up set and distress to Jessie or your child you are a family unit and I have no wish to come between a man and his family, no matter how beautiful the woman, not when you share a child together, but I would admit I would give everything to have her, as any man would and I do envy you with everything I have, I would trade it all to be you now, you have a very good looking goddess for a wife that only has eyes for you and a gifted most beautiful child, these are things that no rich man could ever buy; you don't know how very lucky you are my friend. If I thought I could get her to look at me the way she looks at you, now I am being very honest I would try with everything I had, but she could not and would not ever look at me or any other man the way she looks at you. Her desire for you is so strong, never in all of my life time have I ever felt anything so strong and powerful. I can feel it coming off her now, do you not feel it. Yes, I do replied Marcus. Please tell me you're secret. Never, but in truth he did not know himself. Ok Adele said I will do everything I can to avoid being near to them, I have no wish to hurt anyone let alone an innocent baby, please forgive me, he stood and held out his hand and Marcus shook it. Now, I have to get back to my family, he nodded at Tobias and Xander and went back to Jessie and kissed her and Leah.

He wants you, he admitted it but has said he would not try anything, be on your guard, he said he was sorry of any distress and would try and avoid Leah. Well-done and you did not kill anyone Jessie said, now what would you like to do this afternoon? He smiled at her and she said we have tonight for that but if you're up to it she whispered into his ear I need some new underwear as you keep ripping it off me and I am running out fast. I am up for that only if I get to choose something for you. Ok, make it sexy and I will wear it tonight. He picked Jessie up and kissed her, wait, Leah oh yes Marcus said. Kirk handed her back; do you think you will be well enough tonight to look after Leah mum. Oh yes Jessie. Ok see you all later, buy and she kissed them both, nodded at her brother then left.

Marcus was like a little boy in a sweet shop, poor Robert and Eli were stood outside of the ladies under ware shop. Marcus wanted to buy everything. Jessie said, we are going soon choose something, she got some lace thongs he loves them on her, she brought some little tight dresses and a few little things and three little dress up dresses together with a pair of hand cuffs.

She made sure he did not see half of what she brought and he chose a fine see threw white edge with fine lace teddy top that had tiny ties at the front and a thick lace with a tiny bit of the see threw material thong, he paid and they left the shop with four bags and one big smile on his face. They went back to their room and Marcus got ready for the stag night and Jessie put a few things into a bag for her night with Marcus, she tried on the little set Marcus had chosen and looked into the mirror and turned around to see herself from the back when Marcus came in, he stopped and looked at her and looked at the clock and said Jessie come here in a very male voice, she smiled, no it is for tonight when you get back I was just trying it on and she turned around and when she looked at him he had his hand his hand his mouth biting it.

You're not doing that to me again come here, no, Jessie laughed and tried to run around the bed but he was to quick and he grabbed her and threw her on the bed, she tried to get a way but he was on top of her using his wait on her and all that wiggling just turned him on more. Ok she said I give in and he rolled over and pulled her on top of him he ran his hands over her and she wanted him, he could not untie the little tie in the middle that held the top together because his hands were too big. Jessie told him, if you can untie it without ripping it from me, I will take you with my mouth, oh, Jessie honey. She rocked herself against his trousers and she could feel he was fully hard and ready, that distracted him. He was making little frustration sounds and she did it again, he growled at her she touched her breasts through the thin fabric, he ripped it in two and pulled her down to him he sucked her breasts, there was a knock at the door, not again I don't believe this, I want you now Jessie, I know she said but I have a backup treat for you tonight. I promise you will love it. Ok, I am coming he shouted, not yet she said tonight and rolled off him, he just looked at her bum he knew it would look like that on her when he brought it dam.

Jessie came back with a dressing gown on and he picked her up, she wrapped her legs around him and he walked to the door with her warped around him, tonight I promise, she said and last night just so you know you drove me crazy, she slid down him and let him go. The door knocked again, it was Kirk and Phillip, now what has she done to you come on you need a big drink. With that Amanda and Christine turned up with chocolates and a DVD, the boys said good bye and left. When the men got to the bar Xander, Adele, Tobias, Victor and half of the other bodyguards and some of Tobias's men and a few of Adele's men were all drinking and talking, Adele shook Marcus's hand Adele said you are the luckiest man in the world my friend and Marcus winked, I know, by the time they left the bar it was 11.45.pm and they all huddle together and where staggering back to their rooms laughing and joking. Marcus helped Kirk take Phillip who was out of it back to his room where Kirk said he would look after him.

Marcus had been looking forward to this moment all night she had been on his mind and when he went into Kirks room and locked the door Jessie was stood there, in a tiny bad cop girl, dark blue uniform dress that barley buttoned up to her breasts that where swashed together, it was short like it just covered her bum cheeks, she had a pair of hand cuffs in her hand and a pair of hi heels on. As she turned and walked into the bedroom, he could just see the bottom of the bum cheeks, she walked away from him and the light from the bedroom shone through her legs. Yep the luckiest man in the world he thought and went in after Jessie and closed the door.

- Jessie showered and woke Marcus up, he tried to enticer her back to bed again but she was not having any of it she left Marcus and went and got ready with the girls. They were all ready and the last thing Jessie had to do was feed and dress Leah. Victor came and escorted the woman down to the great hall. Xander was stood there ready to take Leah. You all look so beautiful and Leah has a matching dress.
- Phillip took Christine's arm and Jessie and Amanda walked down the aisle behind her then took her flowers. Jessie looked at Kirk and then she could not take her eyes from Markus, he looked like a god in a shrine, back suit and the crisp white shirt, she thought about the way he had taken her last night, he glanced at her and smiled, her face went red, she looked back to Kirk and Christine and then Kirk kissed his wife and lead her up the aisle. Marcus claimed his wife and kissed her and Phillip took Amanda's hand and followed everyone, they all went outside and had wedding photos taken. Christine threw her bouquet and doctor Adams caught it.

Marcus congratulated them both and pulled a box from his pocket, mum this is from us all and gave her the box, Phillip came and stood by her, she opened the box and looked in, it was a thick solid gold bracelet with the words mum inscribed on it in big scroll letters, it said with love from all of your family Jessie, Phillip, Marcus, Dad, Leah and Xander. Oh, thank you and tears rolled down her face, she kissed and cuddled each one of them and then he produced another box and gave it to Kirk, this is a wedding gift for you, he opened it and he had a matching men's solid gold band with the words Dad inscribed on it with love from all of your family and all their names on it. Kirk had tears in his eyes and hugged and kissed all of them. Christine said I know I am only 42 but I have something to tell you, she looked at Kirk and said, I am pregnant I found out yesterday. Phillip slapped Kirk across the back, welcome to the family in more ways than one then pulled Christine to him and kissed. Marcus hugged Kirk, congratulations to you both another one to our number, you and the doctor next Phillip! Congratulation mum you deserve this, a brother or sister. What is this? Xander said, a double celebration my wife is expecting.

That was quick exclaimed Xander, Jessie laughed and said not as quick as Leah, well that's super sperm for you said Marcus and everyone burst out laughing. Jessie's white light exploded over all of her family, everyone looked.

Adele, Tobias and the other elders all looked on Adele said to Tobias she is very powerful even more so then I. Yes, Tobias said she has a reed to start the ceremony soon. The word has been sent those wishing to see father must come here, now more than ever she must be protected, yes, I agree her mate is very protective more so than the brother, and he would kill you without a second glance regardless of who you are, this I have seen. Oh, I fully believe that and expect that, because any man that possessed such a woman would have to fight to the death for her as would I, gladly Adele said and he must be something very special for her to want him so much.

As no woman has ever resisted and passed the test, was he her first do you know? Yes, I believe from what Xander has told me she was pure and innocent and just of age, she chose him and drew his spark from him at their first meeting. So, it is true love then after all, that makes me even more jealous as I have never felt true love, look at me a king and all the wealth in the world, I am immortal, I have power and none of it could get her to love me. What will you do? Tobias asked, Adele said, one, I wish to live, two, I wish to see the little one grow and I am a man of honor and her mate has been honest with me as Xander has been. I could do nothing as she is stronger than I but like all the brotherhood here I am drawn to her and I will do everything in my power to protect our little family. I can feel the love and power from here, I can feel her feeling. Yes, Tobias said everyone and all the bodyguards report that they all have felt the feeling, she affects us greatly. Yes, and that should be a warning to us, why has she been sent now and what is about fall upon us all.

I have also spoken to Victor; Crispin is loose in England and tried to kidnap her. He must be found, I want him alive, I want to know how he knew about her, and as for that woman he sent, that little stunt nearly killed them both as she would not live without him and that is another reason not to try anything said Adele. You know about the messengers don't you, yes, is it true? all of it, then I would not anger father she must be left with her family, come let us enjoy the celebration we will talk more with Xander when he does not have Leah.

After all the picture they all went inside to take their seats for the speeches and while they were doing that Jessie took Leah in the next room that had been laid out with all the bit's for Jessie to feed and change Leah's nappy. She was contented and put her into her pram to stretch out and sleep. They had their meal and Jessie said to Marcus and dad, Adele will asked me to dance, I feel he has accepted thing's, I will dance with him only if you agree and are happy for me to do so, he does not worry or affect me my worry was and is for Leah, she is drawn to power and I don't know what that could do to her and dad must dance with me after as I might need to release some energy and it looks more natural and fun if I am laughing with dad, is that ok with you both? I feel that would go a long way with the other's here, but it's up to you two. Kirk looked at Marcus I think you have a very wise wife, Marcus said only if your 100% Jessie, I am. he knows I am stronger but I sense a change in him a step back so to speak. Ok then but only if he asks. This change's nothing, he is not to go near to Leah I will not and could not control myself if his power hurt her; I would kill him. They all agreed and took their seats and Jessie put the pram next to her and Marcus.

They all watched while mum and dad danced around the floor. Phillip danced with Christine as did Xander and Victor. While she had a rest, Marcus danced with his wife and Christine looked after Leah. When the song ended and

Marcus finished dancing with Jessie, Adele approached slowly walking across the floor to them and every one stopped talking, Adele bowed to them and said, could I have this dance please, Marcus looked at Jessie, she nodded and Marcus handed his wife's hand to Adele and left the dance floor he could not look back. Jessie smiled and Adele knew everyone was watching, he danced with a space between them as a mark of respect, he did not attempt to look her in the eyes nor did he pull her to him.

Mrs. Dewdney may I speak with you. Jessie nodded. You must know I mean you and your family no harm I am just like the rest of my kind who are drawn to you, I would like personally to apologize for my part in Xander's test it was not my intention to cause any upset or harm, please forgive me but it was necessary and I cannot refuse Xander I may be king but he is our holy man, I have lots of respect for your husband and hope that in time we can become friends as our paths will cross a lot and I will do my utmost to keep my power and influence away and under control when you and your child are in my presence, thank you for hearing me out and thank you for dancing with me I am very honored. The dance ended he stopped and said thank you again Mrs. Dewdney and took her hand and kissed her wedding ring for all to see he then bowed to her. Jessie said thank you, Kirk was there, and Adele handed her to Kirk may I, yes, she said and they danced. As soon as they were away from him Kirk asked, are you ok Jessie? yes, I am fine he was a gentleman and apologized for any miss understandings and offered friendship.

Did he now! we all saw him be a gentleman. Kirk whirled her about and was laughing and joking with her and her white light shone out, that's you and Marcus now knows that was you. You made me do it and you're in trouble again, she said to Kirk as Marcus is coming and they both tried to look serious. You too are very bad actors, the pair of you always do this, your worse than children when your together now stop it said Marcus. They both burst out laughing. Amanda was coming to calm you dad, we are in big trouble now, and Marcus laughed with them. Amanda took Kirk off and Marcus pulled his wife to him and claimed her, he kissed her and pulled her to him tightly, a few people whistled, she whispered to him that she had the thong on from the set he brought her and nothing else and talk about Horney, she said the way you took me last night it was I all I could think about this morning and the way you look now I just want you, all of you inside of me, I am so wet, she kissed him harder and said you are driving me crazy you look like a male pin up. He ran his hand down her back and gently squeezed her bum and pulled her close. He could feel her heat build more within her and he slowed their kiss and said, soon honey, soon I promise, I need you to. He slowed their dance and it took them a few minutes to calm their desire for each other. He led her back to their table. Xander said it's a good job your married that was some show, Jessie went red and noticed that the doctor and her brother were looking loved up on the dance floor.

Jessie hugged and kissed mum and dad again and the rest of the evening went off great. Jessie danced with her husband once more and he knew she could no longer wait, her need, desire and hot fever filled her eyes and her body felt hot to the touch and the way she was kissing him and touching he could tell she was trying to hold on. He broke their fever filled kiss and said gently, let's get Leah and I will make love to you all night my lover.
He walked her back to get Leah, who was asleep and lightly snoring. She picked her daughter up and Marcus could not wait and picked Jessie up with Leah in her arms, he turned to Kirk and Christine and Kirk could feel the

need they had for one another and just nodded and took his family back to their room, where he kept his promise and made love to his wife all night long giving her everything that he was with all of his body in every way. Nobody left their room till the next afternoon.

Marcus had left Jessie in the shower and wrapped a towel around himself and got Leah ready, by the time he had done that Jessie was ready and he went and changed, they went out onto the sun balcony in search of their family, by the look of it they were the last ones up. Everybody turned to look at them and they all seemed to know what they had been doing all night. Jessie did not care Marcus was her husband. Kirk and Christine got up to meet them and kissed them both and they had their meal together. When Victor and Tobias went and sat down with Xander and Adele, Jessie felt a very warm strange feeling coming from the pair of them, Jessie got up and looked at them and sniffed in their direction, Adele said what's wrong with Jessie why is she looking at you two, what have you been doing. Marcus stood, what is it jess? I don't know but I am going to find out. Mum can you have Leah a second, I will not be long.

She walked to Xander's table without taking her eyes from them, all the men stood and Jessie said to Xander, Leah has been asking for you, can you please tell me where you two have been and what is that smell and where is coming from, as I could smell it from over there can you not smell that? They all looked at her. Xander said tell her now she has excellent sense of smell, are we in danger Jessie. No. but I need to find that smell.
We have been interviewing a prisoner he refuses to eat drink or sleep and will not talk he had been watching Jessie the other day, he could have been following her but Victor spotted him. He is immortal and has shown nonaggression

or ill will. Take me to him now please. What is it Jessie, Xander said? I don't know I just need to meet him. Why? Adele asked and she turned to look at Adele, because that smell is from no immortal it is a message for me. No one spoke they all looked at each other Xander stood and looked at Marcus, ok but we all go in with her. James, Marcus give me your sword and he looked to Xander who nodded, Marcus waved to Phillip. What is it Phillip said, we don't know Jessie can smell something can you smell it? No. Ok stay with Leah and be ready for anything.

Tobias led the way, Victor said I am sure he is immortal as am I Tobias said. They took Jessie down to the room where the man was being held. They opened the door and all the men went in first. The man did not move nor did he look scared. But when Jessie entered the room he stood slowly, Marcus drew James's sword and the man looked at him and spoke he simply said be at ease I mean you or your mate no harm. He knelt down at Jessie's feet. It is ok she said to Marcus he means it. You are not immortal, are you? Stand, she said to him. He took her hand and kissed her ring. You carry father's light with in you and your child. Yes, how do you know this Jessie said. The same way you know I am not immortal.

Victor went to talk and Jessie raised her hand and silenced him you need to see the day light don't you, please come and she took his hand, Jessie told Marcus its ok please trust me I think know what he is and he is about to show us. She took him to the great hall and let go of his hand, he looked like a lost child.

Victor I need you to stop anyone from coming into the hall Jessie said, yes, he pulled his phone out and spoke into it. It is done he said. Right Jessie stood back a few steps and said please give him lots of room and all stand behind me please Xander asked her, are you sure about this Jessie? Yes, and looked at the man, he smiled at her, Jessie could tell that none of the men behind her liked what was going on one bit. I am going to touch you with my light and you will feel better, I want you to show yourself to us, but I am for you the man said, Marcus just hissed. They will need to know what you are and they will understand. Jessie can you just not tell us, no, she said you must all see and you will all understand. But how do you know what he is and we don't, she did not answer.

Right she said, please no one move this will not hurt you and a giant white flame shot out of Jessie and covered her and she covered him with it, a massive white blinding light filled the room and it felt like a powerful gust of wind and the noise was like birds flying. Jessie stopped her light and the bright light dimmed but shone around the man who was again knelt at Jessie's feet with a giant pair of wings each wing was longer and wider than a tall man and now he was also naked and very male. He was an angel he reached out touched Jessie's hand, he kissed her ring and stood, he had grown taller by about two feet. Jessie's face went red she had never seen a naked man in the flesh apart from Marcus, the angel smiled at Marcus as Jessie turned away. The angles light shone out again and he changed back to his original form, he had his clothing back on. The Angel Spoke again and said please forgive me, I did not mean to offend you and Jessie turned back to face him. Are you the angel the messenger told me and my daughter about? Yes, I am for you and Marcus hissed again.

What is your name Jessie asked? I cannot tell you my holly name it is forbidden but my human form is Archie. Xander asked Jessie may I speak to Archie, yes of course let me introduce you, this is Xander, I know Archie said you feel love for him and the massager told me about him. Archie stepped forward and shook Xander's hand, Xander felt peace and this is my husband Marcus, Archie looked Marcus up and down and then looked at Jessie and back to Marcus and smiled, he held his hand out to Marcus who did not shake his hand, Archie said we will talk later and this is Adele he is, Jessie chose her words carefully, ruler of the brother hood on earth. Archie said its ok to call him a king, Jessie smiled he understood she did not wish to offend him and he shook Adele's hand, You have made a wise choice make sure you stick to it or you will answer to me, that's if you still can draw breath when her mate is finished with you, Archie eyed Adele. This is Tobias, of course he said and shook his hand and James he shook his hand to. He nodded at the other bodyguards. Xander you have a question Archie said, yes why have you been sent here to Jessie? She is from father; she has felt deep pain. It was not of her doing and this is not what father wishes, father loves her she is his light and her power draws you to her, there are men that wish her harm and I am here to full fill father's wishes and what is that Xander asked. I cannot tell you; I am for Jessie but if you wish to know anything else, I would be happy to talk to you all but you must know this no one else must know I am here unless Jessie wishes it to be so. May I meet your child now asked Marcus, I mean her no harm, the messenger has spoken about her and she holds fathers' gift, as do you and you shared it with your mate and child? Father has felt your love for her and that pleases him. Marcus nodded as he looked to Jessie. Marcus then took Jessie hand and went back to their child followed by the other men.

Phillip stood with Kirk as they approached, Christine was cooing over Leah, everyone I would like you to meet Archie this is my brother Phillip. Archie bowed to him and shook his hand, Phillip gazed at him and knew what he was and looked at Jessie who nodded and this man is Kirk, he is a father to me and grandfather to Leah my child, I call him dad. I am very honored to meet you Jessie has a lot of love for you and wishes you protection. This is Christine, you call her mother and she is with child, Archie fell to his knees and kissed Christine's hand I am honored to be in your presence. Christine gave Leah to Jessie and Archie stood, Jessie said and this is my child would you like to hold her? I have no to wish to up set your mate he is very anxious and your child feels it but she knows who I am she is gifted, when your mate is ready then I will, he nodded to Marcus who was not feeling any better about Archie.

If you will forgive me Jessie I have to talk to the elders and then perhaps me and your mate can have a drink at the bar and have a very much needed talk, I will come to you if you should need me for anything, he looked at Marcus, smiled and went with Xander and the other's back to their table. He is a lovely man exclaimed Christine and how did he know about my baby, he is gifted mum in lots of ways, Marcus gave her a disproving look and said may I tell dad about your friend? Yes, she gave him a kiss and said I am only yours, she looked him in the eyes and said I love only you, he kissed her with love. Good she slapped his bum and said I think you should have a drink with dad and then one with Archie.

Kirk kissed her and Leah and they went off to the bar together. Jessie spotted Phillip slopping off with Dr Adams. Well it's just us girls, Jessie fed Leah and sensed Archie watching her and taking her feelings in, the two woman chatted until Marcus and Kirk came back and Leah gave a little cry in frustration, what is it Marcus said she wants Xander, mummy is sorry I did ask earlier, Marcus turned to get Xander, Archie was escorting Xander to Jessie's table. "Little one" Leah cried again, oh come to grandpa, Jessie handed her to Xander, she was quiet instantly, come Marcus lets have that drink and get to know each other better. Jessie eyed the pair of them and said play nicely boys. Kirk informed Jessie, mum and I are off out for a meal and show, that's lovely have a great time I love you both and Jessie got up and kissed them, they then left leaving her alone with Xander to talk.

Xander said, Jessie, the massager appeared, now an angle and father sent you, what is it Xander? well its more something Adele said, What! well you should be asking your friend Archie why do we need so much protection, what is coming our way, we need to know to be prepared, we need to make plans Jessie. I cannot lose Marcus I have lost my son and his wife to war already. I have lived to long I no longer wish to feel pain and loss Jessie. I knew it was too good to be true. What is Jessie? my luck she said?

Marcus order a brandy and coke and looked at Archie, I will have the same, come on spit it out Marcus what do you want to know, I know that Jessie would not want me to lie to you and she wants me to tell you everything. They took their drinks and sat down. Ok Marcus said tell me what you mean when you say I am hers. I will do everything and anything that she commands me to do; does that include you having sex with my wife?

Archie smiled I could be anything to and for her but I could not be you, as you my friend are free will and true love I am not permit to interfere as that is fathers gift to all humans, you are married so again I am not permitted and I know where this is going, Archie told Marcus, if you falter as her husband or bring her such pain and upset as father has felt and if it was Jessie's wish I would have to give myself to her fully to comfort her, that's why farther changed my body to look like yours .

But before you say anything know this, as I have seen Jessie's sole, she has never lied to you about anything and never would she has never desired or wanted another and I know she never would, her sole shines like no other when you make love to her she is truly innocent in this world, and no one not even an angel could turn her head from you, that desire inside of her is what you have given to her by the way you touch and want her and the many different ways you take her, that is what you do to her, your gift to her and no one on this earth possesses that. It is a pure gift of love and your love turned into your child, a true gift of love and bonding and that is why you both desire each other so much. So, you see I do not possess your gift, so she could never feel that way for another man or angle, I have watched the way you make love to her it is very intense. You watch me make love to my wife? It was fathers wish that I should know what to do if you ever falter as a husband. Be at ease Marcus we have no wish to draw attention to us now do we.

Marcus lifted his glass and the barman took two more drinks over to them. I know you love your wife and are passionate about that and you are right to protect her from other men and would give your life for her, there is no greater love, make no mistake, but the thought of life without you would kill her and nearly did and that father does not want that. So, provided you do not stray or get killed then I cannot and would not make love to Jessie, so you have nothing to worry about do you! Now do you feel better. No, you are a backup of me, but it has eased my mind that you cannot make love to my wife while I am alive but I am still not happy. Good then that is out of the way. Marcus took a swig of his drink and said now I know why I can't keep my hands of her, I now can understand why you feel love and fear and why you are so protective because if I were a man then I would be as proactive as you are, so no more watching us Marcus said. No, but know this Marcus there will be times I will need to be in my true form in front of Jessie and I can never be far from her, if she is upset with you then I must comfort her that is my purpose and like you I would kill anyone, who would mean her harm or try to take her against her will or use their will on her and that includes you.

What about my daughter, she is innocent and pure and a gift, as you once said to Jessie the same applies to her? Marcus said you have been paying attention. Yes, I have. Ok I can except fathers will but I don't have to like it or you and one more thing the naked angel thing, yes! Archie said, don't you have a loin cloth or something to cover yourself. Yes I felt her unease and shyness, she has never seen another man naked, but like I have been telling you the body that she saw was a copy of yours angles don't have genitals as a rule, like I told you father changed me, I am what you would call a virgin and yes I will cover myself, I have no wish to make her feel uncomfortable in my presence, but she needed to know what I looked like. Think of me as a back husband in case of emergencies with no sex. I have learned lots from you. Ok, we covered no more peeping, we have Archie said and the question you have yet to ask is, yes, I feel her every need and you fulfill her fully in every way, not that you need me to tell you that but I merely confirm that for you. Ok, could you tell me why my daughter grew so quickly, well she would have died if not, for the messenger that father sent needs to be here before.

Before what Archie? if Jessie is in any danger then you tell me now. I cannot it is forbidden. Husband number two my ass if you want that status and felt anything for Jessie you would tell me. I feel everything that you do for Jessie and every desire and pain, remember I have to I don't get a choice like you. Ok, Marcus said I am sorry for that remark, so you have my back number two, yes, he said as long as you do not falter as a husband to Jessie, I am surprised you let that dog Adele still breath Archie said. Yes, I have considered it, I was unaware that he was here, till Jessie brought that to my attention. We should go back Jessie is starting to worry Archie said, ok let's go and find her, she is where we left her with Xander.

They went back to find Xander holding Leah, she was sound asleep and snoring lightly, Jessie stood and held her arms out to Marcus who pulled her to him and kissed her, then let her go so she could pick Leah up from Xander, she asked Archie. would you like to hold Leah now, Archie looked at Marcus and Marcus nodded, she placed Leah in his arms and he felt love roll off the angel and felt sadness for him as Marcus new all the love was for Leah and him and not love for Archie, Marcus understood that and why father had sent an angel because no man could bear that pain and want to live and Archie just looked at Marcus because he knew the truth . Right, mum and dad are out tonight, Xander is playing cards with the elders and Phillip has gone somewhere with Dr Adam, so that leaves us four.

Yes, we have to find you a room and some clothing. Anything you have will fit me perfectly Archie said and you have a sofa in your other room in your suite and it's very comfortable. Jessie looked at Marcus and he said trust me it's better you don't know.

Here take Leah and let's go, they said good bye to Xander and went back to their room. Jessie put Leah in her cot and went for a shower, Marcus said we will go out for dinner, so you can shower when Jessie has finished and here is a suit, shirt, some pants and socks. She likes it when you wear that black suit and white shirt, it drive's her to distraction you know said Archie. Yes, I know, if you're not going to where it can I? No Archie you bloody cannot. Ok but you must find me something as she is nearly finished, Archie you want to make Jessie happy right, no Marcus that's your job now, you know what I mean, yes I do and I know what you're going to ask me, the black dress she wore on her hen night and don't ask again he said. Thanks number two I think I will wear my black suit tonight after all, here is an old one. Jessie came out with her bathrobe on and went into her dressing room and closed the door. Marcus said hurry up and shower and no peeping at any time, I know we have been over that. Go then.

When Archie had finished Marcus ran into the shower and was out in record time put his suit and aftershave on and went into the living room, Jessie came out he was right, she looked amazing, she took Leah out and put her in the pram and Marcus pushed her. Archie followed, when they passed though the great hall Xander was just getting ready to play cards and said I will gladly look after the little one and keep her this night till tomorrow, Leah let out a little cry and Jessie picked her up, did you and grandpa arrange this, you're not going to help grandpa cheat are you madam and Leah giggled and said I want to stay with grandpa .
Ok but no late nights. Jessie and Marcus kissed Leah and laid her down in her pram and gave James her bag. Jessie told Xander to keep her away from Adele do you understand me, yes, he is playing cards with us, well you

make him sit the other end and only you and James get to pick her up. Good night and she kissed Xander on the cheek and whispered into his ear, cuddle her while you play cards, she loves it and fleece Adele of every penny. Then left.
Where are we going to Jessie said, I know you like dinner and a dance and there's one at the hill top 5-star hotel tonight, I love to dance with you husband, yes, I know but it will be slow dances in that dress you nearly have on my wife. Do you remember the last time I wore it and her eyes sparkled at him? yes, I do, knowing full well that the angel that was sat next to him did as well? Marcus could do nothing with the angel sat next to them and that made him more frustrated. Jessie asked, Archie how old are you if you don't mind me asking, put it this way Marcus is a child compared to me and he smiled. Jessie tried not to laugh as Marcus gave him a dirty look, they arrived and went in and were seated in a corner booth near to the dance floor, Jessie excused herself, they stood and she went to the ladies with her bodyguards.

Marcus asked Archie, how long you have been watching us? Father sent me the second she chose you and drew your spark. Ok so when did he change you Archie? the second you touched her, when you went to London in your bedroom the first time before you took her innocents, and no I did not watch, then father said it was forbidden it was her moment. Marcus was relived. Every man in here desires her you know, and yet she is un a where of it and even she thinks I am here to protected Leah, she wants you and has since the second she saw what you had on, I could be sat here naked and she would not even notice.
Marcus smiled at him and noticed Jessie walking back, she was looking at only him her eyes were sparkling and she looked like hot sex, he wanted her more. Please calm down Marcus I feel your heat and I feel Jessie's excitement

anything could happen, have your drink and pull yourself together. Marcus through his drink back but could not take his eyes from her, he was trying not to think because he knew Archie could read his mind. They stood and Jessie sat down and said is everything ok, Marcus could not speak, yes Archie said we are admiring your wedding ring and your beauty, as all the other men in the room are. Oh, her face went red, Jessie had her drink and Marcus ordered more drinks, they had their food then Archie said I must leave you two to finish your evening, Jessie needs to be alone with you. I will go back and take the sofa goodnight and left.

When Archie was outside he stepped into shadows and changed in to his angel form, as he could be a man no more the need that flowed from Jessie was affecting him so much he wanted to take her and Marcus did not help, why had father given the ability to feel everything, he felt better as he flew through the sky with his wings fully extended, he was only supposed to act if Marcus ever faltered, but he then knew this was his price to be in human form and to be so close to her was not so easy. Marcus thought Archie looked fluster when he left but he was happy that he had gone. Marcus danced with Jessie and after one dance he said we have to go jess, she understood, his eyes were full of hot fever and need, they left and got into the car to go back to the castle.

The second they were alone she, straddled him and kissed him deeply, she ran her hands down his shirt and ripped it open and said take me now please Marcus I can't wait, she pulled her dress off, she was naked, she sucked his nipples, he lifted her up and placed her on the opposite seat and undid his trousers, she could not take her eyes from him, hurry and he pulled her legs apart and pulled her to him, she came calling out his name and he filled her saying oh

Jessie honey. He pulled himself from her and locked the door so they could adjust their clothing.

The car had already stopped, come my wife we will finish this in our room. When he got out of the car, he lifted Jessie up and pulled her to him and took her back to their room, but he had to walk through the giant hall to get there. Xander and the others turned to see him carrying Jessie, he did not look at any of them, he was looking into her eyes and they all could feel sex and heat roll off them, no one said a word, Xander just looked at Adele as he could feel envy coming from him.

Marcus locked their bedroom door and laid Jessie on the bed and took his jacket from her, she turned over and he ran his hands over her feeling a deep need to take her, she was his. He was rock hard and entered her, oh honey he whispered, she was so wet and tight she threw her head back and called his name, he had to stop and take a deep breath, she whimpered, and growled out with deep need and said I am begging you please Marcus don't stop, she pushed herself back on to him and he fucked her so hard and fast he cried out with deep need for her. They climaxed together and the wild animal passion left them, Marcus took her again slowly and gently and lovingly, the sun was just rising in the sky when there need to have each other had left them and peace and sleep found them.

Jessie hurt everywhere and opened her eyes, Marcus was standing by the bed watching her, he had just got out of the shower, and a big smile shot across his face, good morning beautiful, Jessie asked him how his legs worked,
he gave a light laugh and said I love you; I love you too. Jessie noticed that he had love bites down his neck lots of them, oh my god I am so sorry I don't remember doing that, I just remembered I didn't want you to stop, that's

nothing he turned around and he had deep red scratches all down his back. Oh, please forgive me I never meant to. He laughed, don't be silly they are my trophy marks from you I am very proud that you gave them to me; you defiantly marked your territory last night, you drove me crazy with lust last night Jessie and I did what you asked of me and what was that she said.

You asked me to bite you when I was taking you from behind and now, I am hard again from just thinking about it. What! she jumped out of bed and went to the mirror and held her hair up. Sorry I could not help myself you were driving me crazy jess. The noise you made when I did it just made me want to fuck you more, he took his towel off and kissed her neck and slid his hands around to her breasts, squeezed them and the memory of last night shot through Jessie and Marcus entered her, he took her again with all the heat of last night.

When Jessie had finished in the shower she looked into the mirror her love bites were under her jaw, by her ear, down the side of her neck and on the back of her shoulder, you could tell that he was behind her when he had done them, he wanted everyone to know that he had taken her many times. When Marcus went into the other room Archie was not there, it was midday and they went in search of their daughter, everyone had gathered on the sun balcony for lunch and there were lots of people there. When they arrived at their table Leah gave a little cry, Jessie picked her straight up from Xander and kissed her, she wants mummy to feed her, she got the blanket out, Kirk said please Jessie sit next to mum.
Kirk turned her chair away from everyone and put it next to Christine and the bodyguards stood in front of her so no one could see what she was doing.

Marcus sat next to Xander and Archie and then Phillip and Dr Adams arrived, Marcus knew they had been doing the same thing as them. Kirk joined them while the woman talked and Jessie fed Leah. Xander said it is barbaric what you have done to that child's neck again, can you not control yourself; you should be ashamed of yourself. Marcus replied, no I can't she drives me crazy. Yes, I can see she likes to mark her territory on you and claim you as hers Kirk said taking Marcus side. Quite Marcus said proudly and they are not my only trophy marks, he beamed a big smile. You are quiet Archie what's up, I am listening to the sound of love and satisfaction coming from your child, and the men stopped taking and they could hear Leah suckling and guzzling her mother's milk and making a tiny little noise of contentment.

Love touched all of their hearts. She loves it when Jessie feeds her, there's just something about a woman feeding her child, yes Archie said its unconditional love and bonding. Something Jessie not only shares with her child but also her mate which is a rare thing in this world. Marcus could tell that the angle was not himself and looked at Archie and said we need to find you a room. Yes, Archie said the other side of the castle please or near the roof so I can fly at night. Marcus understood an opened his phone spoke into it. Victor and Tobias walked out and Marcus said find our friend a room far away from mine or the apartment on the roof I think will better serve his needs, and buy him some clothing he is my size. Archie nodded at Marcus, thank you and he went with Tobias and Victor. When Jessie finished feeding Leah, she gave her to Marcus to wind, she wants her daddy, she kissed Leah and then Marcus then Jessie had lunch. Well Jessie said Leah told me you won every game last night Xander. Yes, it was very interesting, I think they knew that the little one was helping me and where gentlemanly about it. We could all do something as a family this afternoon, like go to the beach and play, Phillip agreed that it was a great idea, we'll take a picnic and a beach ball and some games we should all play beach rounders. Yes, I think that's a good idea Xander said. We will need shade for mum and Leah, Jessie said and could some of the bodyguards play to make the teams up as Tobias has his security and the Joshua team, what do you think James? asked Xander, it will work James said. Oh good, Jessie threw herself at James and kissed him on the cheek. He did not know what to do.

Call yourself a bodyguard, kisses are my job Kirk said and tried to sound hurt. Everyone laughed. Jessie told all of their bodyguards to go and get changed into swim and beach wear, you have one hour and we will all meet up on the beach by the steps. They all went to change. When Jessie came out of her changing room Marcus just looked, Jessie had a one peace bathing suit on it was red and hi cut at the front and low cut at the back, her hair was up and everyone could see his love bites on her body, she was all woman and he whistled, she gave him a spin and he had forgotten about the love bites down one side of her back. He was going to tell her but he had gotten lost in her when he took her again this morning. He did not say anything apart from, you are putting on shorts and a t shirt with that, yes, and came back with a little tiny pair of cut off jean shorts, you could just see the bottom of her bum cheeks and a flash went through his mind of the bad cop girl outfit from the other night. He had to go to the bathroom and close the door or he would have taken her again. Jessie found a little white t shirt and put that on along with her beach shoes and got two towels and a little towel for Leah just in case and some sun cream. Marcus came out of the bathroom with shorts and a t shirt on and Jessie said do you have your black Speedo's on under there. I am not telling you otherwise we will never get to the beach. Marcus carried Leah in her mosses basket and Jessie carried their bags.

Everything was ready for them on the beach and some of the brother hood were there just relaxing and swimming. A giant gazebo and tables and chairs had been put in place for them. A big rug was on the floor which Christine was sat on with her one peace swimsuit on. If you're going to sit mum would you be ok to watch Leah? Yes, of course sweetheart, put her basket on the floor next to me you don't have to ask, I know it's just I feel I leave her a lot. Don't be silly come here, Jessie knelt down and kissed and hugged Christine. Xander came down with a few of the elders and Archie who Marcus noticed looked better. Ok Xander said let's choose teams.

Phillip suggested grandpa X team verse grandpa Kirk team. Kirk said I am up for it if you are but we get one guardian each so there's no cheating. Ok Kirk said I pick Jessie and Xander said I will have Phillip; Kirk then chose Archie and Xander chose Marcus. then I choose Victor said Kirk, and Xander chose James, I choose Amanda, then I will take Kevin and Peter, ok Kirk said I take Robert and Adele and you can have Tobias. We will bat first and you can field Xander said. Then let's get this show on the road Kirk said, two-minute team talk then we start. They all huddled together, chose fielding positions and who was bowling and discussed team tack ticks and who to watch. They were off, Adele was near to Jessie and was looking at her love bites on her neck and smiled, Archie moved closer to Adele and when the ball came their way Archie made sure he jumped for the ball and landed on Adele, Marcus laughed because he knew why he had done it and said way to go Archie. Xander said to Marcus, do not cheer for the other team its degrading. That angel just did not like Adele, Marcus liked Archie more. Xander's team only had one batter left in James, Jessie was hot and took her t shirt off it distracted James and he got caught out. Xander said that is out right cheating, oh sorry Jessie said a bit sheepishly, let them take it again dad sorry James I did not mean to distract you.

Archie looked at Marcus who was going red and then he looked at Jessie's back and a big smile broke out across Archie's face, are you ok Jessie? She turned her head and the ball whizzed past her head and Archie was quick as Adele was throwing himself towards Jessie to catch the ball and would have landed on top of her but Archie changed to his angel's form and swooped her up into the sky and Adele landed on his front in the sand. Marcus was clapping his hands and cheering for Archie. He covered Jessie with one of his wings and landed back onto the sand next to Kirk and whispered to Jessie I could not see that dog jump on you. Thank you Archie and she kissed him on the cheek, he knelt down on one knee in the sand in front of her and spread his wings, bent his head and said the honor is mine, he took her hand and kissed her ring and then stood and changed back to his human form and said well-done Adele there out. Kirk suggested they had a break for half an hour and we will change to bating then. They all had refreshment and Jessie cuddle Leah and Marcus. Archie had a chat with Marcus who said, I was worried about you; I know I could tell, but you're ok now right Marcus said. Yes, I am ok now.

Nice distraction when Adele was going to jump on top of Jessie and claim it would have been an accident, yes replied Archie, he saw her love bites and wished it was he that taken her from behind and that he had done that to her, he just wanted to feel her skin he is lucky I did not peel his off, he jumped before the ball moved so I knew what he was planning to do I could not see that dog touch her, so I could not help it I changed, no hard feelings Archie said. No, your joking, you were protecting my wife and that's ok with me and her and patted him on the back.

Last night Archie said I don't know how you do it, I had to go she wanted you so much it was hard in my human form to feel both of you like that, I went outside and changed and now I have the room on the roof it will give me distance from you both but if needed, could be near her in seconds. They went back to bat; we need ten to win Kirk said and Marcus was bowling. He took his t shirt off and everyone could see what Jessie had done to him, she went red in the face, he had the biggest smile on his. Amanda and Victor did well they got five between them, Adele had got one which took them to eight so Archie needed to get two or they had to get one each.

Archie hit the ball so hard that everyone ran home which meant Jessie had to hit this and run all the way around to get home, she said be nice husband and he smiled at her and said right everyone stand right back and be ready, oh Marcus, I have to honey you're on their team. Her team were calling her name and cheering so Jessie turned a bit and wiggled her bum at him, he stop dead as he saw the bottom of her little bum cheeks and he thought of that bad cop girl outfit again, Jessie said if you drop the ball I have a nurse's out fit to match my cop girl one and I will put it on tonight just for you. Xander exclaimed, that not fair we don't use back mail, please stop that at once, Jessie looked at Marcus and licked her lips and wiggled her bum. Marcus was lost he threw the ball gently and Jessie hit it towards Marcus who make no attempt to even move he just watched

Jessie as she ran around to get home and win.

He then bent down and picked the ball up, no one said a word as Kirks team cheered as they all would have done the same thing. Marcus went over and picked Jessie up and carried her to the sea and threw her in, she screamed with pleasure and tried to push him in but could not, but he relented and let her push him, she jumped on him, he said do you really have another little outfit, yes I do and I will keep my promise. He growled and pulled her on top of him and everyone was looking at them. Everyone is watching come on you let's get our daughter, she got up and gave him a hand up out of the water, he put his arm around her and they waked back to the gazebo together like the lovers they were, and her team congratulated her for their win. That was very well-done Kirk said I like your tack ticks. Xander just shook his head at Marcus, and said you are to easily brought. It was worth it and more and looked at Adele. Come my wife lest us get ready for dinner tonight in the great hall as it marks the beginning of the ceremonies for tomorrow, best clothes tonight.

Phillip and everyone went to get ready for their big event. Jessie fed and changed Leah who was tired out while Marcus was in the shower and then she got ready. Marcus had a jet-black suit on, black shinny shoes, a bright white shirt and black bow tie with his hair swept back he looked better than James bond. Jessie had on a long dark green fine silk halter neck dress that looked like it was touching her body, when she moved it out lined every inch of her body and went all the way to the floor, it was back less and her hair was pushed up, there were little curls everywhere,
she had make-up on and black hi heels, her skin looked wet but it was oil and she smelt like heaven. Marcus put his fist to his mouth and bit his fist. He just turned and picked Leah up and put her in her pram and got her bag and said Robert

would you and Amanda take Leah down we shall be down soon and gave Leah to them and closed the door. Jessie was stood behind him, he turned and looked at her and said I am your slave, you look a queen. I want you now I cannot last till later. Jessie smiled and went in to her dressing room, he followed her, she opened her closet door and pulled out a little nurse's out fit and said it comes with stockings, now you can take me now in any way you want, as I want you just as much or you can wait till later and I will take you in every way possible, but not both.

Now look at me and tell me what you want as we will be late to dinner. He said fuck jess what are you doing to me honey, I can't choose he was hard as rock; they were running out of time so she said I will use the handcuffs again tonight if you want! They went down to the hall together hand in hand, everyone fell silent when they walked in and all the men in their dark evening suits knelt on one knee as they walked to their seats. Jessie whispered to Marcus what are they all doing. They are paying homage to you. Jessie noticed that the ladies had an assortment of designer evening dresses on and they all just watched in wonder. Jessie could see that there were little fairy lights everywhere and flowers the sent was beautiful and all the tables had been set out around the edge and a dance floor had been put in the middle, every table had been dressed with fine white linen and red napkins and the chairs had red covers with gold and silk bows and what looked like gold cutlery and goblets made of gold, little name cards set out neatly and every tables had a center peace in red and gold flowers.

The giant chandeliers had candles burning on them. It was like an enchanted fairy tale. They of course sat at the head table, it was a long table that looked like something an old-fashioned king used, it was dressed like all the other tables and every one was sat in a long line looking out at the other tables. They were the last to arrive.

Xander and Tobias sat with Adele on one end with Dr Adams and Phillip then Jessie and Marcus, Archie, mum and dad and Victor and Leah fast asleep in her push chair by mum and dad. When Jessie took her seat, the men stood and seated their woman and then sat. The King, Adele banged a little wooden hammer on the table and started the evening with a speech about the brother hood and what they had done over the years and their history and ended with thanks to everyone and Tobias for holding this historical holy event. Then Xander stood and gave a speech about the guardians and the ceremonies of light and gave a prayer. Tobias then stood and gave a speech and thanked everyone and then the Kind banged his hammer, he raised a toast to Jessie and everyone stood apart from her and raised their glasses and said "to Jessie our guardian" and they drank their drinks and sat back down. The king banged his hammer again and the band started to play and the food came out.

Jessie noticed that every time her glass was empty someone filled it and that Archie was drinking more than anyone, the rest of the men had been putting it away like there was no tomorrow. Jessie realized that for some people in this room there was no tomorrow as they were going back to meet their father via her. She felt like it was a wake before the funeral. Archie asked Jessie if she was feeling ok and Marcus asked, what is it jess? Oh, nothing my mind was just wondering that's all. We are to have the first dance it will be slow, shall we? Yes, why not. Marcus led her to the dance floor and they danced slowly and close Marcus whispered to her, I love you Jessie you look so beautiful. I love you to, you look so handsome I can't believe I am this lucky. Marcus noticed she covered some of her love bites with makeup to the ones down her back, he smiled as he had proudly made sure that everyone could see his. He could see that Jessie went red every time she looked as his and that made him smile more. There dance ended and they returned to their seat but on the way back Jessie noticed Royce and a few people she remembered from England; he must have flown over to witness the ceremonies. Marcus said you will be expected to dance with one or two people if you're up to it and if you wish to as they think I am keeping you from them. He looked at Adele and Tobias, but it is death to touch you without your consent, do I have to wait for them to ask me or can I choose someone she asked. He looked at Jessie and said it is a great honor to be chosen, and I have never heard of it before, who do you wish to choose?

He asked with a frown on his face and even Archie looked interested, well what do I have to do, Archie said just go and ask, shut up Archie I want to know who my wife wants to dance with, its someone you know, she then stood up and walked over to Royce's table, his table had all men sat at it and they all looked very official, they all stood up when Jessie stopped at their table. Jessie knew they all desired her apart from Royce who felt fear and knew it had come from Marcus. Royce, she said, please excuse me gentlemen but Royce would you please do me the honor of dancing with me, Jessie could tell all the men where dumb struck and envious.

He looked so shocked he nodded his head and took her hand and kissed her ring, the honor is mine please and he led her to the dance floor and looked at her, he didn't know where to put his hands, Jessie smiled and said shoulder and hand, he did as she said and they danced around the dance floor, every pair of eyes were on them and there were whispers everywhere around the room.

Archie, said Marcus why did she choose him? Because Marcus he is about the only other person in this room she knows, she is playing it safe and she likes him, he is one of ours so to speak. When there dance had finished Jessie said can you take me back to my seat please, of course, when he took her back to her seat Marcus stood up and Jessie kissed Royce on the cheek so everyone could see, he took her hand and kissed her ring and said thank you Mrs. Dewdney, Marcus shook his hand and he went back to his seat where he was bombarded with looks and questions. You choose well my wife, Archie asked if he could dance with Jessie, Marcus eyed him and Archie beamed a big smile at him and raised his eye brows, Jessie laughed and said come on then you, I will be watching you carefully, remarked Marcus smiling at Archie. Jessie and Archie danced around the floor and Jessie looked very comfortable and at ease with him they looked like they fitted together, Marcus remembered what Archie had said, that he had a copy of his body, he did not know what to make of that but he knew it was not jealousy. When Archie returned her back to Marcus Jessie had another drink and she said come on dad you know I love getting you into trouble. Marcus laughed and said come on mum are you ready to dance with the best-looking man here and they all went to the dance floor. Phillip and the doctor got up and danced as well.

As usual Jessie and Kirk where laughing and giggling, before they knew it the power and love in the room had built up and flooded from her in a massive white light, every one gasped and looked, oops Jessie said do you think that everyone is looking at us? Kirk looked around, well let's say their getting their money's worth. Good. They danced two songs together and her flame burned out, I'd better take you back, ok she sounded like a little child, he was spoiling her fun. He smiled at her and said come on you, you will get me shot. They returned back to the table and Marcus said its always you dad leading my wife astray. Jessie had another drink and was feeling a bit tipsy but felt good, she asked for fruit juice as she would need to feed Leah again soon. Jessie spoke to Dr Adams and Phillip.

Archie was talking to Marcus, that dog will ask Jessie to dance soon, can I not just kill him and be done with it, me and you both Marcus replied, do you know Archie you're really starting to grow on me. I can feel him drooling from here Marcus. Feel free anytime to change form can't you smite him or something nasty like that. No, not unless he tries to influence her with his power, and the second he tried he we would be dust. You really don't like him do you Archie. No, I don't, he is a dog. Listen Archie said your child is awake. Is she, she is not crying? Marcus got up and went to the pram.
That was good timing she just opened her eyes Christine informed him, Marcus smiled and picked her up and said Leah daddy loves you. Jessie went over, come on you she said let's get you fed. I will take her and he walked with Jessie carrying his daughter to the room that had been set aside for her, they went in and Marcus locked the door and just stood there looking intently at Jessie her nipples went hard and he licked his lips, Jessie was turned on by the way he was looking at her and the pulse between her legs got faster.
Jessie knew he wanted to see her naked so she put her hands behind her neck slowly and un clipped her dress, it fell to the floor and Marcus ran his eyes over every inch of her, he noticed that Jessie had shaven herself, he growled

with need and desire and Jessie stepped forwards and took Leah from him, gently brushed a kiss across his mouth and stepped back, kissed Leah and held her to her breast. He couldn't take his eyes from her, Leah was sucking. Marcus did not say a word he just took his jacket off and un did his tie, he could tell Jessie was fully aroused, he took his tie and shirt off and walked around behind Jessie, put his arms around her and just and held her and Leah. When she finished feeding and laid Leah down in the little cot Marcus turned Jessie around and licked every inch of her body an she came fast, he lifted Jessie up and laid her back onto the side and did not take his eyes from her, he parted her legs and took her, fully thrusting deep into her and slowly she could not control herself and gave herself fully to him gasping his name as she was taken with ecstasy. He wanted more of her, heat rose up in him and he filled her with his hot seed and slumped on to her gasping her name, I love you my wife.

Xander said to Christine they have been a while was everything ok with Leah when she woke up as I saw Marcus carry her to her room. Yes, I think so. Archie said taking another drink, I would not go in there if I were you, they will be out when they're ready any way Marcus has locked the door. Never in all my years, what is wrong with him. Kirk giggled, are you blind he is married to the second-best looking woman in the whole word and if you were his age and you were married to her you would be in there as would any man in here. Phillip over heard what Xander had said, way to go sis. Christine said Phillip really! Come on Archie said let's all have another drink and celebrate true love.

Xander asked Archie, what is your purpose here angle? I am hers. Yes, but why? Just then Adele and Tobias came over and Archie hissed a warning at Adele and the two men stepped back. Be at ease brother Xander said to Archie they mean you or her no harm. Archie hissed again and eyed Adele, he maybe a brother from father but I see in his heart. With that Marcus and Jessie came out of the baby's room, Marcus carried Leah holding her to him while she slept with his other arm around Jessie and her bright white flame covered them both, it was overflowing love and sex, satisfaction filled the room and everyone one in the room felt it. What is going on Marcus asked, nothing Christine replied, everyone was just making sure that little Leah was ok that's all.

It was too much for Archie in his human form with both of them together so close to him, the love he liked, it was the overpowering power of their very intense love making and need they had for each other, it was ok in the other room but not now the sent was so fresh it was like he had just taken her, he had to hold her to protect her now, father had linked his body to Marcus so tightly that he felt everything now . Archie looked at Marcus and said I am so sorry I cannot and Marcus understood, he stepped back and changed so quickly it knocked Adele and Tobias over. As Archie changed to his angle form a gust of wind covered every one and a bright white light shone out, he grew to about 8 feet tall and stretched his massive wings, flew up and circled the hall. The whole hall went quiet; they were all in Orr of the Angle.

He felt better and did not feel the human power as much, but felt the love, he needed to hold Jessie and swooped down and stood in front of Marcus and Jessie, he knelt in front of her and she held her hand out and he kissed her ring an as he stood he wrapped his wings around Jessie, Marcus and Leah and pulled them to him and totally enclosed them, tight within his wings and a bright light shone out from the angle, it went through the castle like a beacon to heaven. Archie lifted them all and flew out from the castle back to their bedroom window and placed them on the floor. You need to be here with your wife make love again or I will he said, I can feel the heat rising within her again, and this is her moment. Marcus knew no one would be watching and waiting. I must go I will smooth things over with the others, as he turned to leave Jessie kissed his cheek and touched his cheek and he left in a gust of wind.

Marcus laid Leah down and took his wife 's hand and knelt before her, kissed her ring and said I am yours and they made love together till the sun touched the sky. They were up and ready and going outside to breakfast they could feel the excitement in the air. Xander and the men stood, Jessie kissed Xander, Christine and Kirk. Archie walked over to Jessie as she was handing Leah over to Kirk for a cuddle, she is very happy to day and very fulfilled, Yes replied Kirk and she is not the only one is she and winked at her. He sat back down next to Christine. Good morning Archie she said and kissed him on the cheek. Good morning Jessie he kissed the ring on her hand and stared into her eyes and smiled at her. Please sit and have your breakfast. We were going to have a quick chat to Xander first about today said Marcus, No, she must come first they can wait let her eat she is hungry please. Archie said to Jessie I need to talk to my number one and took Marcus off, what is it Archie what wrong with you it's a big day for Jessie, more reason to let her eat he said, he looked at Marcus, I want to know something but you cannot tell Jessie because I have just found out. Is it to do with Jessie? Well, yes and no Archie said, I was not allowed to watch it was her moment with you and father felt your love and if you had not made love last night then I would have had to. Spit it out will you Marcus said. Remember you cannot tell her or anyone else swear it on your life. I swear it. I only tell you in my human form as I have so much inside me, father said it was hard for humans and if I where you I would want to know. She is with your child. Marcus had to gasp to take in what he had just told him. You awakened such love and desire in her, but be warned do not tell her. Why Archie? I only tell you as her husband and the child's father. Will the child grow like Leah? No Archie said and turned his face away, Jessie want's you go now. The angle looked sad as he walked away from him.

He smiled lovingly at his wife she carried a new life inside her his child no wonder Archie had been so insistent she rest and have her breakfast and a big grin broke out across his face. What are you up to with Archie you look so happy what is it? Oh, nothing he wanted to know if we were both ok after last night. Come and have some of this before I eat it all. No, it's yours, after last night you need to keep your energy up. Marcus had some coffee and toast. Stay with mum and dad and I will sort things out with Xander and Phillip. Is Jessie not going to listen asked Xander, No, leave her to rest, she knows what to do you don't need to drill her. Is everything ok? Yes, sorry Xander it's just everyone seems to want a piece of my wife. I understand go back spend the rest of the morning with her; she looks full of life and so beautiful today married life aggress with her. Yes, it does he said and went back to the rest of his family. The doctor and Christine where going to look after Leah till after the ceremony, everything was set Jessie took a big breath and said I am ready.
Remember we will be right here waiting for you ok so don't worry just stand with Phillip and your light will do the rest no one will touch you. We cannot go in as it is there time to go back to father and not ours. Good luck

Xander said to Jessie, Tobias and Adele went with Victor and wished her well, Kirk gave her a hug and she kissed his cheek, Marcus kissed her and they went into another room and the giant doors were locked from the outside there must have been at least five hundred men in loin cloths on and nothing else, Jessie sat on a giant thrown and Phillip stood about six feet in front of her. In front of her there was only candle light. The men where calm not wanting to frighten her, Jessie thought of Marcus and Leah and a giant flame shot out of her and hit Phillip, he project her light out like a giant window and thunder sounded out around the room, the men walked slowly one by one into the light it took what felt like forever but it had only been about half an hour and as the last man went through Jessie stopped her light and tried to stand, she fell on the floor. Phillip turned to pick her up and a blast sent him across the room and darkness claimed them both. Marcus was pacing the floor, Xander said stop it you're like an expectant farther. Marcus stopped and gave a light laugh and looked at Kirk, grandpa you will be a dad soon, our little family has grown.

A massive explosion rocked then castle, the door blew off its hinges and dust filled the room. The whole room was stunned for a few seconds. Marcus sat up and pushed rubble of himself and Kirk, who had a gash on his head and was bleeding, he checked himself he had a few cuts but was ok, Victor's arm was trapped under the door that had landed on him and Tobias was giving Adele CPR. Marcus went over to help Tobias assistance and breathed for him while Tobias pumped her chest. Kirk got to his feet Marcus shouted, help Jessie and Phillip and climbed over the rubble, staggered into the hallway or what was left of it. Amanda and Peter were dead and the door to the great hall was gone and so was the great hall. Rubble and smoke blocked his way there were two maybe three other body's in the hall way Kirk went back into the room, Xander was calling for help he said I am ok I just can't get up, Kirk found him under some rubble James had thrown himself on top of him, Kirk pulled the rubble off James then rolled James off Xander, James was dead, he had given his life to save Xander's. Kirk help Xander up and all of their phones started to ring, Xander was barking orders down the phone.

Joshua's security team were the first to get to them they brought a medic who managed to bring Adele round and were now sitting him up and giving him oxygen, they could here sirens, and all of Joshua's team lifted the door from Victor, it did not look good for him. They patched Kirks head and said he needed stitches, we need to find my wife, son, daughter, granddaughter and Dr Adams now he said. Kirk could hear Marcus frantically calling for Jessie and Phillip. Kirk, Tobias and some of Joshua's men who were with them tried to get in the hall to search for Jessie and Phillip but could not get in. Tobias was shouting down his phone, get the bloody lifting gear in hear now. They had to pull Marcus back as it was unsafe, it took six men to drag him a way. They managed to calm him down. Where is that fucking angel Archie he was shouting. Archie had been crying on the roof he was powerless to stop anything, it was forbidden by father he couldn't interfere in what men did, this was their destiny. As soon as the explosion happened, he swooped down to cover Christine, Leah and Dr Adams but he felt too much pain from Jessie, that was not supposed to happen he changed back to his human form.

The floor had collapsed and they fell about twenty feet he wrapped himself around Leah and Christine and tried to hold on to Dr Adams as they fell. They were all alive Dr Adams was alive but was unconscious and Archie knew she had a broken leg by the way she lay, he did move her and he could not change his form because there was not room, they were trapped. Christine was ok but crying with shock and fear and Leah was screaming her head off. Archie said to Christine you and your unborn child are fine I need you to calm yourself and Leah your safe here with me, they will find us soon. Archie was himself trapped; his shoulder had been impaled as he had his arm out to hold on to the Dr Adams. Kevin died from the blast trying to cover Christine, there were a few of Tobias's men and Adele's men that had been blown to bits along with everyone else that had been out on the balcony.

Four hours had passed since the blast and all the other members from the brother hood that had gathered for the ceremonies had helped and pulled all of their very rich and wealthy resources and were doing everything to clean up and take the bodies out and search for survivors. The brotherhood in other countries and been put on alert and elders from other countries where coming to help and offer their assistance and many more of the Kings men were coming. A command center had been set up outside the castle but still within its grounds by the North side as it has been unaffected, giant cranes and lifting gear were bought in. The police closed all roads around the castle to allow emergency vehicles to go in and out. Adele walked in to the command tent after discharging himself from hospital, to see dirty bleeding shattered men who had not taken a break, eaten or even had a drink and had done everything to save his life and that of the members of the brotherhood. By the look of it they had not found any of their loved ones.

Right one at a time bring me up to speed then I as your king order all of you to go to the next tent and get cleaned up, get medical treatment, have some food and a drink and rest for a little because when we find the rest of our family and loved ones you will need to be in a fit state for them, you will be not 10 feet from here so you will not miss anything and the second I know anything you will know.

When Adele spoke to Marcus, he said I am in your dept, you helped save my life thank you my brother we will find them, now go. Marcus sat bolt upright and looked at his watch it was ten past ten at night be at ease Kirk said there is no news. Did you just speck to me before when I drifted off? No why, he then remembered when Leah had spoken to him when he was asleep. Leah is calling me. He ran outside it was so light, flood lights were on everywhere. Shit, he ran into the control room where Tobias, Xander and Adele were talking. He said get on the radio and tell everyone in the area where mum and Leah were last seen and turn there lights off now, tell them to watch out for a red or white little glow of light or listen for a baby crying as Leah was trying to call me.

Adele barked the orders down the radio, we have fifty men searching each floor in that area now they can get in there. After a few minutes a voice said I can see a little tiny white light it's not very bright its right down at the bottom of the collapsed area, hold on he said I can hear a baby its faint but there looks like there's a woman's body down there she's face down and looks dead, you're going to need a lifting team back around here, now I cannot see the baby just the light. Kirk held his chest oh please let it not be Christine. Marcus said tell him to stay where he is and do not move and to stay on the radio, put the lights on, I am going there now. Wait, Xander shouted but he had gone followed closely by Kirk.
They were there before the lifting gear, where Marcus shouted to the man who stood two floors above him, there and shone his light on the hole where the two floors had been.

The little light has just stopped "Leah" Marcus screamed daddy's here can you hear daddy; can you cry for daddy Leah and then his heart jumped he could hear a tiny little cry. That was it, no Marcus, Kirk said they could be trapped under the rubble you might kill them or yourself you must wait. Kirk took the radio from Marcus and said Leah is alive we need that lifting gear now where is it? It's coming as are we Adele said, bring a medical team with you. The lifting gear had been moved around to them and the rescue man climbed down on a rope and attached straps to the rubble and lifted it out of the hole, the rescue man was on the radio again and said I need a medic down here now and a cutting crew there is a lot of blood everywhere and someone has been impaled and no sign of the baby yet. Marcus went over and picked a harness up and put it on. What are you doing it is not safe, exclaimed Xander?

I don't care my daughter is down there and he climbed down with the medic. He panicked when he saw all the blood everywhere. The medic asked Marcus to help lift her up, then we will turn her over and put her straight into the rescue basket, then I will assess her. As soon as they turned her over, he could see it was Dr Adams, is she alive the medic checked her breathing and said just she needs surgery on her leg to save it, let's get her ready for them to pull her up. Marcus worked with him and told the other man with the radio to tell Xander that its Dr Adams and tell him that she's alive but needs urgent surgery and she's coming up now.

Archie could hear them trying to get Dr Adams out and knew they would be out soon, but he had lost so much blood he did not know if he could make it. Leah had survived by drawing his power which he had very little of now as she needed feeding and was very week now. Christine was week but had just passed out as it was very cold. The cutting crew where cutting a metal pole off someone but they could not get there to see because there was still rubble to be cleared, they needed to take the pole out first. When that was done they cleared the rubble, Marcus knew and could see it was Archie, he was face down and from his position it looked like he had tried to protected the doctor which is how he got in paled but he looked like he was protecting something under him, he still had some of the pole going through his body.

Marcus asked the medic is he alive and is he going to make it? Its touch and go he is barely alive, I don't know how the poor bugger has held on for so long. Get him off that pole now and be careful my daughter might be under there. Marcus took the radio and spoke to Xander, we found Archie it looks like he tried to protect the doctor that's how he got impaled, remember he must be treated here he cannot got to a hospital, it looks like he might not make it he has held on a long time in a lot of pain to protect something or someone. They lifted Archie up and put him on a rescue basket and the medic said he was on the baby and a woman, oh my god Leah, mum. No, the medic said they could have injuries slowly, slowly you could do more damage. Marcus spoke into the radio again, they found mum and Leah, there not moving Archie was protecting them.

The Medic was working on Leah, is she alive? Quiet, I can't hear a heartbeat. Everyone went quiet, Marcus had

tears in his eyes and his heart was in his mouth, Christine still had not moved. There's a beat, she needs fluid now, get me a drip Pac out of my red bag and pass me that little yellow box and tape. Marcus did as he asked. Marcus said get on that radio and get some blankets down here now, right the medic said to Marcus hold this bag up right above her head and the medic put a little needle into Leah's leg and taped it down to her tiny leg she did not even cry, she is exhausted poor little thing you're lucky you found her when you did but she is not out of the woods yet. Tell them that Leah is coming up next and needs one of Grandpas special hugs, said Marcus. The man on the radio relayed the message.
The medic wrapped her in a blanket and Marcus gave her a quick kiss and hug and one of the rescue workers pulled up the strapped to him. Be careful this woman is pregnant Marcus informed them, ok, they checked her over. She needs fluid, she is cold and has hypothermia, pass me anther drip Pac, that yellow box. tape and that blanket, she will be ok then Marcus said. Far from it she's in shock, cold and she could die. We need to get her out of here now, tell them to blue light her to hospital ASAP and tell them she's pregnant said the medic. They lifted the last rescue basket up and then pulled the rest of them out.

Marcus saw Adele, where is Leah, she went to hospital with Xander and Kirk has just gone with Christine. I want bodyguards sent there with them and security all over that place now, it has been done, ok, where is Archie? They have taken him down to the bit of the medical unit here that is still in use, Marcus you have been in that hole just over four hours you must rest.
I need you, I have a job you won't like it, but first I need Tobias and anyone else that is here that is over two and a half thousand years old, the older the better and I want them with Archie, now make that happen and I want a list

of the dead and the missing and who is alive, do we have a list of the brothers that were in the hall just in case they did not get through, come on lets go now that angle needs to live and send that lifting gear back around to the hall, I want my wife and her brother found now. What is this job for me Adele said, Tobias is holding a woman she was sent by Crispin, I was set up she got me on my own and ripped her dress off just before my wife came in the room and she tried to grab me? We have a confession but it's not enough she must know more, I thought as she liked to take her clothing off, that's your field but that bitch had some balls to come here from England, do whatever and I mean whatever you need to get answers for all we know she could have planted the bombs and more. Do you need her alive Adele said? No just make sure she has no more information than burn the body.

Marcus made his way to what was left of the medical faculty where there were doctors trying to help Archie. Marcus asked, what the update was, a doctor stepped forwards and said I am Dr Sullivan this man or being needs blood but we can't get a match, we have a drip with fluid and pain killers, but he needs blood now, right Marcus said he has the same blood as I do so get a needle doc. Are you sure, it could kill him if your wrong? I am 100% sure. Right we do not have much time, so sit next to his bed and roll up your shirt we will pump it straight into him, two pints for now and then we will see. Has he said anything yet? No, the doctor said and then worked on Marcus.

The elders started to arrive Marcus said I need you all to be holding his hand or stand very close to the bed he needs to draw energy from you all, he is the only one that can lead us to the guardians, my wife and her brother and we are running out of time, it has now been just over twelve hours since the explosions. He knew the longer it took the less chance of finding survivors alive.

Adele picked up his shirt wiped the sweat and blood off of his face and then wiped his shaft with it, as it had been many years since he had raped a woman and with some force and enjoyed it. In this day and age, women are giving themselves too willingly and it had been nearly a thousand years since he had torched a woman but he always got results, sometimes he missed the old days. He had slit her throat after he raped her the third time. And threw the shirt on the floor next to her still bleeding body, he said burn the bitch and send me a copy of the disk I am going for a shower and did his trousers up and left the room.

It was 6.30 am when Adele went into the command tent asked Robert for a full update on the people in the hospital. The death toll was now rising after they had found another seventeen body's and they found only two others' alive, the lifting gear had nearly finished at the far end of the hall but not sign of Jessie and Phillip. More of Xander's people from England had arrived. They are worried about their holy leader and his family thought Adele, it did not look good at all for Adele or Tobias as Xander and his family had been under there protection when the attack had happened and they had failed to protect the guardians, heads would roll as the elders would want answers, where is Marcus now, still with Archie in the medical facility.

When can the searchers get into the hall? In about half an hour's time? Ok Adele said make sure we get full up dates from every one of our units and team and I want this place checked for bombs again, I want more men at that hospital and I want our people treated by the best doctor's money can buy. No more fuck ups. I want everyone else searching for the missing, I am going to the medical facility, call me the second there is any news.

Adele arrived at 6.45 am to find Marcus asleep in a chair next to Archie with what looked like two drips in his arm, one was going from Marcus to Archie and the other looked like fluid. Adele stopped the doctor and asked what's wrong with Marcus? He was very upset about his wife and distressed, he gave Archie two pints of blood so I gave him fluid as he has not eaten or had a drink for a long time. I am surprised he let you do that; he didn't I gave him a sedative his body needed rest. He has been out for about three and a half hours he will come round in about an hour or so.

Shit doc I would not like to be you if he finds out what you did and how is Archie? Well he had surgery on his shoulder and we gave him Marcus's blood that's what saved him, he has absorbed lots of power from the elders that has helped him lots to. Ok thanks doctor and Adele left and went to the site by the hall to see if he could move things along When he arrive everyone was quiet and no was moving and no work was being done. What's going on Tobias? Adele demanded. One of the rescue team thought they heard a cry for help so they have had to stop until they locate whoever it is. Where is Marcus? Tobias said he had nearly finished giving blood to Archie when I left.

Adele smiled and said the doctor sedated him without his consent. Silly man I would not like to cross Marcus. Yes, he rivals even me. How long do you think till they get to whoever it is an hour maybe two what's the time now? Tobias asked. 7 am whoever is alive has done well but it doesn't look good for anyone we have not found yet. Who do we think it is? Well Tobias said there should be nobody in this part of the hall unless all the brothers did not make it through and in that case, you will be looking at a massive death toll, but if that were the case, we would have found some more body's here by now.

Xander had not left Leah's side all night he was so worried about her and he was feeling loss for James and the rest of his people and for the pain his family were now feeling. He was eased by Joshua's presence, he had not left his side and watched out for all of his family. There where hi ranking officials from the government in Italy there at the hospital getting everything they needed and more security from the brother hood had now taken over the wards, the A and E department and the car park. The doctor they hand flow in form another hospital by helicopter last night had seen to Leah all night had just come in again and said to Xander your granddaughter is ready to come off the oxygen now and the drip's, you will be able to hold her soon but she will need special baby milk until her mother can feed her again and the sooner that can happen the better.

So, she is fit and well and no permanent damage then! oh no, but she needs her mother, but granddad will do for now, are you ready and Leah gave her first tiny little cry of frustration. The doctor took all the tubes off her and wrapped her up and put her into Xander's waiting arms. He had tears in his eyes, he cuddled her and kissed her and he felt relief and love, Leah's little tiny voice said grandpa I love you and the tears rolled down his face as he told her, grandpa loves you to. Where is mummy and daddy? All Xander could say was daddy is helping mummy and they both love you little one. Where is grandma? She is in the next room little one, she has not woken up yet. She then wanted Christine and Kirk so Xander went to Christine 's room.

Kirk stood as he had been sat next to Christine all night and asked, any news yet? Xander shock his head. Kirk smiled and held his hands out to Leah, Xander handed her to Kirk who kissed and cuddled her and asked how she was. Fully recovered she needs Jessie. Grandpa a little voice said, yes Leah I love you. He kissed her and Xander asked how Christine and the baby were. The doctor said she needs to come around soon as her body could close down, due to shock and the cold, we could lose them both. Leah said grandpa I can help grandma. Are you well enough little one? What is it? Xander asked, she wants to help Christine, what do you think? Kirk asked Xander. Leah gave a little cry of frustration. Xander nodded and Kirk placed her beside Christine on the bed, then put Christine's arm around her to hold her.

A little white light came out of Leah's chest and covered them both, her little white light went red and the men stepped back to let her heal Christine. Xander asked Joshua to stop anyone from coming in, Joshua opened his phone and spoke, security surrounded the room in minutes, keeping even the doctors at bay, they were there just over half an hour and Leah's light went red then stopped. Kirk picked her up, kissed her little cheek and said thank you little one. I love you to grandpa. He handed her to Xander to get some power back. Ok Joshua let the doctor in, as Joshua spoke into his phone Christine started to move and come around Kirk picked her hand up and kissed it, saying it's all right love I am hear take it easy your safe you're in hospital, we will check on the other's and come back. Thank you both, Xander nodded and left with Leah.

Next was Victor he was still out of it after his surgery he had lost his arm and broken a few bone's but would mend. They then went to see Dr Adams she was ok after her surgery; they saved her leg but it would take some time to heal. Xander took Leah back to her room, he fed and changed her. Xander told Joshua, I want all of Leah's and our people's medical records, blood test, X rays and everything else taken care of and sent back to England. It is already being taken care of Joshua informed him.

Marcus woke up to Archie looking at him, Marcus couldn't remember going to sleep, how are you Archie and where is the doctor? I am fine thanks to you; you saved my life and the doctor said he would be back to take all the tubes out in a minute. Thank you for saving Leah, Christine and Dr Adams but Jessie and Phillip are still missing, why did you not save Jessie Archie, I have to know, I need to know please. It was Jessie's wish that I saved Leah, it was one of her last thoughts before the darkness and pain took her, and her very last thought was of you, I cannot say any more about your child it is forbidden, I now see differently in my human form. Archie are you well enough to change and find Jessie, please? Yes, I am good! The doctor came back in and Marcus gave him a look, the doctor just took the tubes out and said its good you two are awake, Marcus replied, it's good for you we are leaving. Come on Archie. Marcus pulled his shirt sleeve back down and Archie got dressed.

They went to where the hall used to be. Can you sense her Archie? No, not even her thoughts I will have to change, ok hold on get Jessie first, do you think you could find Phillip also, please? I will do my best. Adele and Tobias saw

Marcus and Archie stood the other of the hall. What do you think there up to? Tobias asked Adele. I think that Marcus got the angel better to find his wife, like I said clever very clever. Archie changed form and flew up into the sky he circled the hall, he sensed something and swooped down near to where the searchers were, he hovered then lifted a giant stone and found Phillip he slid his giant wing under him, picked him up and dropped the stone. Archie then flew over to the first aid tent and laid him on the ground, Marcus ran over as did Adele and Tobias. Archie circled again and hovered over another giant bit of rubble and lifted it, he scooped the body up and laid it on the floor next to Phillip, who medics where working on already.

Robert, Marcus exclaimed, medics were over the pair of them. Archie flew over the hall again, swooped down and moved a piece of the outside wall that had fallen into the hall, Marcus felt pain in his chest and bent over to catch his breath, Marcus knew Archie had found her. Archie bent down and picked Jessie's body up, he held her in his arm and the angel screamed out in pain. It was painful to hear. He wrapped his wings around her, a bright white light shone out from the middle of his wings where he held Jessie, he landed on the floor next to Marcus. Tobias and Adele went over to help. Archie let out a very loud warning hiss and they both stopped where they were, held their hands up and took a step back. Archie said you gave that dog breath to live and looked at Marcus. Let me see Jessie and the Angle lifted one wing to see Jessie she looked dead. No, Marcus screamed and went to take Jessie from him but Archie refused. Tobias stepped back, what's wrong Archie?

Archie give me my wife, I know its very pain full and heart breaking for you because I feel it to but if you don't give me my wife now, I swear I will cut your wings from your body where you stand, on her life I will. Archie opened his wings to their full extent and stood up tall and held Jessie out to him, she has a deep cut on her head and she was bleeding, and the baby? Marcus asked. Archie just looked at the floor and shook his head. But you said no more pain, Jessie has had enough. She does not know she's with baby remember! Marcus took her to the ambulance and laid her down. Phillip and Robert where taken in the other ambulance. Adele said continue the search then got in a car with Tobias and went to the hospital on the way he called Joshua to let them know that Jessie and Phillip had been found and were on the way to hospital now, there condition was unknown.

Joshua asked Xander if he could speak to him alone, Eli please take Leah to see her grandparents in the next room Xander said, when Eli took Leah out of the room Joshua informed Xander that they had found Phillip and Jessie and that they were on their way, their condition is unknown at this time. Thank you, Joshua, I want all of our men here outside all of their rooms, 1 want everyone's stuff packed up and shipped home. I want a female doctor and nurses on hand for Jessie now as Marcus will not let her be treated by a man. I want one of our men inside the room with Phillip, at all times, is Simon and Levi here with their teams yet? Yes, who is the female that's replacing Amanda? It's Morgan. Make sure she is with Jessie when Marcus is not, is she fully up to speed Xander said. Yes, we had a group meeting today and are all kept up dated. Good, when everyone is fit enough to travel then we will go home, make sure everything is in place for our return. Your knights are ready and their teams are already in place sir.

The A & E buzzer sounder to alert everybody that an ambulance had arrived, let us see what is going on.
Jessie's ambulance came in first they wheeled her out of the back of the ambulance, she had a neck collar on and a

head brace, the female doctor and nurses took her to trauma room one and Marcus went in without looking at anyone, his face looked void. Xander went in after him. The doctor asked is there any possibility that your wife could be pregnant as she is bleeding, Yes, she is pregnant or was. I think she is having a miscarriage. Please don't tell her if she comes around, but I want to know ASAP and no female exams, give her a full body scan. The doctor looked at Xander who nodded and said come let us leave Marcus, let the doctor help Jessie. Marcus this is Morgan she will take over Amanda's position. Where is my daughter and how is she? take me to her now!

She is fine there is nothing wrong with her, she is with Christine and Kirk. Please don't go in to see her in this state and Jessie is pregnant is that something you want Leah to know, if she is losing the baby do you want Leah to know that to. She will ask Jessie about it. She's been asking for you both and she helped heal Christine and her baby Xander informed Marcus. Kirk had come out of Christine's room he, had known something when Eli had taken Leah in and not Xander. He had just heard Xander say that Jessie was not only pregnant again but her baby was dying. Did I just hear right Marcus, is that true? Kirk felt terrible, Jessie was losing their child while his lived after everything they had been through. Yes, Jessie is out of it and does not know, just keep this between us, she could not cope with this, please don't tell her I am asking you both not to tell her or anyone, she has a very bad head injury and they have Phillip in the next room, he is bad as to is Robert, Archie found them all. Now we have to wait and pray for our family and friends.

Leah is tired out come and holds her she is too tired to read your thoughts and mum would like to know you have found the rest of her children.

Marcus walked in; Christine could see the state of him. Oh Marcus she said sitting up with Leah asleep in her arms, hear take your daughter and Marcus took her, sat down and cried his heart out while he hugged and kissed his daughter in his arms, he felt so lost without Jessie and now she has just lost their second child because of someone else, when he found out who had done this, they would pay with their lives as had his child. Kirk told, Christine they have found Jessie, Phillip and Robert, they are here and getting medical help. Marcus asked Xander, can you or dad hold Leah? If she was strong enough to help mum, she could help Phillip. Why not Jessie? Christine said and the men looked at each other, Phillip will have to heal Jessie it would be too much for Leah, why is Jessie badly hurt asked Christine. No, Kirk said don't worry love. I am going to check on Phillip it will be about two hours for Jessie's scan to be complete. How is everyone else first? Xander filled him in and then he went off to see Robert and Phillip and left Leah with Xander.

When he went into the hall Joshua was talking to Simon, Marcus said you're a site for sore eyes my friend and shook Simons hand, Joshua's phone was ringing. Is there a problem Joshua? Marcus said. One sec Joshua said to Marcus. Yes, Joshua was saying down the phone, no its Xander's orders, they will be kept up dated, it is Xander's wish that his family get their treatment, then he will have time for others, they must come first, ok thank you and closed his phone. Joshua turned to Marcus, Tobias and Adele are outside, they are not happy because no one is allowed in here, they were trying to throw their wait around. Who is communicating that to them now?

Marcus asked. Levi is communicating that to the pair of them Joshua said with a smile. They won't get any change out of Levi and they won't intimidated him, Tobias knows him from old and he will calm Adele. Come Simon let us see how Phillip is doing. They went into Phillip's room, how is he doctor, he has a fractured skull and a swelling from bleeding in the brain, we need to operate to drain the blood and he has a few broken ribs due to the blast's in pack. He will ok though after the surgery asked Marcus.

Well its about 50/50 at the moment and the longer we wait the less his odds, we need a signature so we can operate, I am his brother in law, his mum is here but she is a patient, ok the doctor said you will do. There was knocking at the door it was Joshua he said Levi has Archie outside and he said that it was ok for him to come in and you would know why. Yes, send him in here, Doctor can you give us a few minutes please a relative would like to see Phillip before you operate. Ok but only a few minutes. Archie walked in and Marcus said Simon leave us and make sure no one comes back in here not even the doctor. Simon nodded and left the room. Archie looked at Marcus and then at Phillip, he is in a bad way; can anything be done for him. Cut the crap Archie you knew this was going to happen you could have saved Jessie from this and why tell me about the baby when you knew this was going to happen, angel my ass, if you felt a dam thing for Jessie because you are hers, then you would heal both of them, what is going on? Be a man or angle or whatever you call yourself, just tell me what the fuck is going on. Archie looked at Marcus and said I am a man on earth and an angel when need and when I am with father, I am his. I sit between the two worlds that is all, I am not allowed to interfere.

But you did Archie, you love her the same as I do with everything I am and with everything that you are, we are the same, father made you like me for her and you fulfilled her wish and saved our daughter and for that I thank you.

Jessie and Phillip did their bit and sent our brothers' home. Now I know father cannot be seen to tip the scales in our word with free will and all that but he made you like me and I would do anything and everything to help them, you see father made you like me so you could do the things he cannot. Now if Jessie had known about the baby, she would have wanted you to do everything to save our unborn child. Archie just continued to eye Marcus. I know there's something more going on and I cannot worry about that now, if Jessie was awake, she would heal her brother but she is not awake and cannot ask you because our baby is dying no thanks to you. So, I am asking for her, heal her brother please. I have helped you; you ask to much of me Archie said. No, the cost of my child is too much! what do you think would happen to you on this earth if she wanted nothing more to do with you Archie because you let our child die, and then refused to save her brother's life.

I think she would kill you herself. Archie hissed at Marcus, look just heal Phillip, and he will heal Jessie. Look Archie why did you come here if you did not want to help, did you want to see my pain our pain because I bet you are felling it to, is it killing you inside like it's killing me? Yes, Archie said the more time I spend in human form the more I have feelings. Archie then said step back, thank you Marcus said, and stepped back while Archie changed his form. Blinding bright white light filled the room and Archie lent over Phillip and cover him with his wings, after a few seconds Archie stood up and changed back. Marcus said are you alright Archie? Yes. And Phillip? Marcus asked. He is fully healed and will wake soon; can I see Jessie please? Yes, soon they are scanning her they should finish in about an hour, after the doctor has finished, we will go in. Thank you, Archie said and left the room.
Phillip woke up and Marcus said take it easy how do you feel now? Like a train hit me, where is Jessie? Take it easy

she' in the next room, can you tell me what happened in there? Phillip sat up slowly and said well we had just finished the last man went through. Jessie fell to the floor and there was a loud noise, I got pulled backward and that's all I remember, till I woke up just, now. Ok rest for a bit, the doctor will come in and check you over again. Is the doctor, Sarah? No, she was hurt, she broke her leg and had to have surgery, but she is ok now, she is recovering don't worry and Marcus left and sent the doctor back in to check him over and sent Simon back in.

Archie was stood outside of Jessie's room talking to Eli and Xander. Marcus said thanks to Archie, Phillip is well and awake and all of the brothers went through the window before the blast. That's good Xander said, he can go in and see Kirk and Christine and Leah. No news of Jessie yet? no Xander said, but it shouldn't be long. Ok, can you update Tobias as they don't need to look for any more bodies in the hall. Jessie's door came open and the doctor asked to speak to Jessie's husband. Marcus stepped forward and said come on Archie you can come in with me. The doctor closed the door behind them. I am very sorry but your wife has had a miscarriage but with rest and time she will recover, there are no problems in that area everything has come away, she has a bad concussion and will have some very bad swelling on her face and head and I will have to stitch that deep cut on her head. When can she feed our daughter Leah, Jessie's been breast feeding her maybe a week or two because of the pain killers? Can you give us a few minutes doctor, please? she nodded and left, Morgan go outside and keep everyone and the doctor out please, till I say so, thank you Marcus said. Marcus walked over and looked at Jessie and he felt hurt and pain deep within him. the cut on her head, the baby, he closed his eyes and he kissed her gently, Archie said ok, I cannot take anymore please step aside. Archie changed form and healed Jessie, when he changed back, he kissed her on her cheek. Thank you, Archie, Marcus said, can I have a little time with her please. Archie nodded and looked at Jessie and left the room.

Marcus reached over and put his hand on her abdomen where his child had been, and he said a prayer. Jessie started to move and he held her hand and whispered it's all right honey I am here and everything is ok, Marcus could hear Leah screaming her head off next door, she must sense that they were near and wanted them. That's our daughter she is missing us, I will feed her please bring her in before she screams the hospital down Jessie said to Marcus. Are you up to it jess, yes, I just ache? Marcus stepped out of the room and told Morgan, don't let anyone in there and don't go in, she's not up to finding out about Amanda just yet. When Marcus went into Christine's room everyone was stood there trying to pacify Leah and Xander said well! Marcus shook his head and looked at Xander and Kirk, Xander handed Leah to Marcus and she stopped crying just like that and he said come on you, what's all this fuss, mummies going to feed you now and he kissed her and took her to Jessie, who had taken her hospital gown off and pulled the sheet up over her chest she was sat up in bed with her arms out and Leah gave a little cry.

Marcus handed her to Jessie who kissed her and said mummy has missed you darling, come on then and pulled the sheet down and feed Leah while Marcus just watched them both. When she had finished she just held her till she went back off to sleep .Marcus said do you think you are up to traveling home today, as I think it will be safer to get back home, yes Jessie but what about Leah's passport, its already done Xander has taken care of it and don't worry about anything we will talk later and I will fill you in on everything, but for now let's gather our family.

I will take Leah if you get dressed, I'll be right outside the door. She nodded and he left the room with Leah in his arms. By now Xander was in the hall with Kirk, Phillip and Simon and more of their team. Right Jessie is getting dressed and when she is ready, we will gather everyone and leave, the only three we will have to leave who are not up to travailing are the doctor, Victor and Robert. There is no way on this earth that I am leaving without Sarah, stated Phillip. Kirk said she is Phillip mate and we will not leave her. What can we do about this Xander said? Archie, Phillip said come with me, Simon can you take us to Dr Adam's room please, and Eli can you get Victor and put him in with Robert, we will be back soon and have four, wheel chairs ready please, one of them is for mum. Then everyone is ready to go.

Eli stood outside of Dr Adam's room with the rest of Joshua's security. After a few minutes a bright white light was coming from under the door then faded, Archie came out and held the door open Phillip was carrying Dr Adams wrapped in a hospital gown and sheet he kissed her and said are you sure you're ok for this baby? She looked down at the big cast on her leg, I feel fine now, good Phillip said and kissed her again, they all walked back to where Xander was still standing and talking, Jessie was now stood with them and Kirk was pushing Christine out of her room. Phillip placed Dr Adams in a wheel chair. Right come on Archie one more stop and walked down to Roberts room. I will heal Robert and you can heal Victor. Ok let's get this done and get our family home. After a few minutes Archie carefully lifted Victor and Phillip helped Robert to stand and get to the door, Victor was placed into a wheel chair and Simon took a wheel chair over to Robert. Thank you both, Xander said to Phillip and Archie, who now were both looking tired. Ok, let's all go back to the yacht, Joshua one team will stay to make sure there no loose ends on our behalf, and then fly they home, now please be good enough to send Tobias and Adele so we may say our goodbyes before we leave.

Levi escorted them down to where everyone was stood. Marcus gave Leah to Jessie; he did not want them near her. Tobias just looked around as did Adele, Xander held his hand out and said we would all like to thank you for allowing us to stay, this place will go down in history, this is where you all brought us together and this is where Leah was born and where our first ceremony of light has taken place. For that and all of your help we thank you, but now we are returning home, one of my most trusted teams will stay to help, I must take my family home they will all need time to recover they must come first, but make no mistake whoever did this will pay.
All the men shook hands, Archie stood in front of Jessie and would not let Adele or Tobias approach her, they nodded from where they were stood and she nodded back .The person who did this to us all will be found Adele said, good buy my brothers and thank you they filled there fleet of cars and went to the port and boarded there yacht, the rest of the security that could not fit on the ship went by plane to get things ready for when they arrived in a few days. When everyone was on board and everything was stowed, they cast off and headed for home.

Jessie got Leah fed and sorted out and put her back down for a sleep. Marcus said come on Jess let's sit down and talk about what has happen and who we have lost, he told her everything except the bit about the baby, he held her while she cried at the loss of life and her friends and for Amanda. We both need time to take on what has happened and time to heal honey, I love you, he then kissed her gently on the lips and went for a shower. She sat there her life had just flow by so quick, so much had happened to her

in such a short time, she needed to take stock of her life.
She watched Marcus come out of the shower with a towel wrapped around his hips. he looked so good and smelt like he always did magnificent, she looked at herself and thought she better make an effort. Is everything ok honey you look a little lost. I am still taking everything in, I will be fine I am going for a shower and she kissed him on his cheek on the way by. Marcus wanted to die in side, he felt he was grieving for his child and could not tell Jessie and he could not bring himself to make love to her even though they were a lone. It would be a problem if she needed him to console her over Amanda's death. She was fully healed but he needed that time. He looked at Leah god what would he be feeling now if he had lost her or Jessie, he felt so fucked up. He needed to pull himself together for them.

He dressed for dinner and poured himself a very strong brandy and coke and drank it down. When Jessie came out of her dressing room she had on white trousers and a black soft off the shoulder jumper, her hair was up and she had soft make-up on, he could smell her from where he was sitting. Jessie could see he had made an effort he had a grey suit on with a dark shirt and no tie, he had a few buttons open and she could also see that he had already had a drink, he must have needed it, she would not make any demands on him as he had lost friends, he just needs a bit of male time and probably needs to get drunk, as that's how men deal with things. You look beautiful Jess she smiled at him and said so do you my husband. She put Leah in to her mosses basket and covered her with a blanket. Marcus stood, I will carry her Jess, thank you Marcus and then handed the basket with Leah in to him.

They went up on deck and took their places for dinner the other two decks were also being used for sleeping and living quarters for the extra men and security team they had taken and sent for. Marcus ordered a few more drinks with dinner as did a few of the men, Jessie had noticed that Dr Adams had taken the cast off her leg and was now part of her family. Jessie also noticed that Marcus hardly touched his dinner, so, when everyone had finished Jessie said I find myself in need of female company and chit chat. Xander took her lead and said yes, come gentlemen lets go to the bar and leave the ladies to it, the men stood and kissed their loved ones and went to the bar. The woman spoke about what had happened and the people they lost, about some of the good times to and what they all were looking forward to, the start of their new lives when they get back home. Dr Adam's said please call me Sarah as we are like family now.

What about an engagement party for Phillip and you Sarah, as we need lots of good family news? Jessie fed Leah and gave her to Sarah for a cuddle, mum is going to have a baby soon and that will be another family event and winked at Sarah. Well I am washed out I think we had better go to bed and leave the men to it; I think they all need some male bonding time together. Yes, I agree Christine said, good night girls and went back to her cabin after she kissed them all. Jessie gave Sarah a hug and put Leah back in to her basket and took her back to her room, bathed and changed her and put her down. Jessie had another shower and got changed in to a long white silk night dress and went to bed leaving Marcus's bed side light on and went to sleep.

Archie did not say a thing all night he just stood at the bar with the men and paced Marcus drink for drink, he could feel his pain in side and also the pain that his feelings where giving off, as could Xander and the rest of the men that stood anywhere near him. Apart from Phillip, who knew there was something up but did not know what and as for Kirk his heart went out to Marcus, but all he could do was just be there for him.

Phillip had to call it a night about 11 o'clock. It was nearly one o'clock by the time Marcus had his fill of drink there was only Kirk left with him. He felt safe enough to hug Kirk and cry his heart out, Kirk understood and did not say a word apart from, its ok son. Kirk helped him back to his cabin, Jessie woke up when Morgan knocked the door and Jessie got out of bed and helped Kirk get Marcus on to the bed, Kirk helped Jessie to get Marcus's clothing off. Thank you, Jessie for bringing him back and looking after him, he needed a bit of male bonding time, thanks dad. She kissed him on the cheek and gave him a hug, goodnight and he left her with Marcus.

It was ten thirty in the morning when Marcus woke to the smell of coffee by the bed. The last thing he remembered was being at the bar, he did not remember anything not even how he got back to the cabin or how he got undressed and Jessie oh, god he could have done anything to her including making love to her, he had been a mess, she could have needed him and he would have taken her and did he protected her if he did, he needed to know what happened and Leah he had not heard her cry and who had left the coffee. Just then Jessie came out of the bathroom with two pain killers and put them next to his coffee, oh thank god, he reached out and took her hand and said sit, I need to talk to you, she did as he asked and he sat up in bed and took a sip of the coffee. Jessie, I need to ask you, how did I get back from the bar last night? Dad brought you back, it was after one. Who undressed me and got me in to bed? Dad put you on the bed and we undressed you. Did we have sex, please tell me that I did not, not like that?

Oh no, we, never. Oh, thank god, I am sorry for the state of me last night I can only apologize, don't, Jessie said I love you, now drink your coffee and have a shower and then come and have something to eat, while I save Xander and

Archie from a million questions from our daughter. She kissed him and went back on deck.

Two weeks had passed since they all returned home and settled into their new home at Chilwoth in Southampton. There days had been filled with everything from paper work to the funerals of those they had lost and meeting all of the security and members of the brotherhood, as well as everyday life. It had been over two weeks since Marcus had made love to Jessie, he was keeping her at arm's length, he had avoided being around her when she dressed, undressed and showered, she had understood after everything that happened he had needed time, they both did but now they need to be close, a full complete family in every way.
Archie also had a new home with them, he stayed in the guest bedroom in Phillip's part of the house until the room over the new garages was complete, as Archie liked to have room to fly in and out of his room from time to time and that meant lots of room. He was offered room at Xander's, who had now taken up his residence just up the road from them in Chilwoth. Archie was also offered a home at the brother hood hall but refused, he had also all other offers, as far as he was concerned, he was where he needed to be.

Victor was in the brother hood medical facility, even though he had healing help from Archie and Phillip he still had a long way to go and was being helped by Dr Adams, who had not only taken up full residence at the medical facility but was now their permanent doctor. She was fully healed herself. Robert had recovered to and was now head of Jessie's personal security.

Jessie had arranged for mum and dad to have Leah that

night so she and Marcus could have some husband and wife time together. Jessie booked an appointment at a beauty salon and had her hair cut short but not to shot there was just enough to put her hair, she had a fringe cut in to, she looked very sophisticated when the hair dresser had finished, next she had her nails done, her eye brows shaped and they applied make up to her, Jessie no longer resemble that 18 year old school girl or the model look she had archived in Italy, she now looked like a very desirable young woman. When they had finished Jessie turned to Morgan and Robert, what do you think? Robert just whistled and said my job with you is hard enough already, without you drawing more attention to yourself. Morgan thought said she looked like a new woman, Jessie missed Amanda, she would have said he won't be able to keep his hands off you or something more forward. Jessie thanked the staff and Robert paid, they left the salon, it was nearly five thirty pm

. They got home just before Marcus did. Jessie was in her changing room while Marcus was in the shower so he had not seen her transformation. Jessie put on the sexiest under ware she could find, black bra and thong with stocking and suspenders and a little above the knee skirt with a lace up front blouse that was red and black with black hi heels and load of Marcus's favorite perfume that he loved on her, she put the jewelry he had given her for a wedding gift on and went downstairs to say goodnight to Leah.

After that she went back into the hall where Archie was stood, he looked very sexy, in his black dinner suit. He looked like Marcus, more and more lately. Wow look at you, he gave a very loud wolf whistle, picked her up and spun her around as Marcus was coming down the stairs, he slowly put her down and kissed her on the cheek near her mouth so that Marcus could see. Are you going to introduce me to your friend Archie? Jessie turned around to look at Marcus. Don't you know your own wife anymore Archie said to Marcus, he just looked, he could not believe it was her, you look amazing. Archie put his arm around her and pulled her to him, yes, she does! You are holding my wife and you just kissed her! Jessie said he kissed me on my cheek, Marcus eyed Archie who just looked at Marcus right back and said your faltering Marcus, with a big smile on his face. Archie kissed her again on the cheek whilst still looking at Marcus and let her go.

Robert opened the front door for them to leave for dinner and Jessie went to the car, Archie caught hold of Marcus's arm, remember my purposes, I am your number two so to speak and I will do what you obviously cannot do, you had time and you have not even told your wife how beautiful she is or the amazing effort she has made for you or us, it depends on you, remember if I take her she will think it is you and I made an effort just in case, he smiled. Watch your step Angel and Marcus pulled his arm back and went out to the car, slamming the front door behind him leaving Archie in the hallway alone. Jessie noticed that Marcus didn't look very happy in the car he was cross. Jessie didn't say anything she just crossed her legs and looked out of the window, that seemed to grab his attention as he was sat opposite her. He could just see the seam of the her stockings and looked more closely at what she had on, he liked it, the car was full of her perfume she had made lots of effort for him and she had her wedding gift on, and her hair looked beautiful, he had been neglecting her she was beautiful in every way and he wanted her. He had been selfish, he leaned across the car and took her hand and kissed her wedding ring, please forgive me, she smiled at him with longing and need in her eyes.

Again, he had been wrong to deny her for so long. He moved across and sat next to her, took her face in his hands and kissed her fully, she responded fully, she touched his face and ran her hand down under his jacket and down his shirt, she wanted him, she pressed herself against him, he ran a hand down her back and over her hip and down her leg, she started to breath faster and tremble, she made that little noise that drove him crazy. He kissed her neck and she kissed his and whispered, please Marcus. He ran his hand up under her skirt and uncrossed her legs then ran his hand up the inside of her leg, he touched her thong it was so wet, he rubbed his thumb against her and she cried out with pure need, he slid his finger under her thong and across her hot wet bud and she gasped out his name, he laid her down and the car pulled in to the hotel. Marcus looked down at her and kissed her softly, I am so sorry honey we will have to finish this later. He pulled her up gently her face was red; she could not talk she could only manage a small nod.

He opened the car door and helped her out and he pulled her to him as they walked in to the hotel. They were escorted to their table, everyone in the room looked at them they were both beautiful and good-looking people. They had champaign with their meal, no desert and left before the dancing started and went to their suite for the night. As soon as the door closed Marcus picked his wife up and took her to the bedroom where he put her down by the bed, he looked into her eyes and kissed her passionately, she slid his jacket off and unbuttoned his shirt and ran her hands down the inside of his shirt pulling it apart she needed to touch him, she kissed his chest and sucked his nipples. He ran his hand down her back and up under her blouse, up the front until he found her bra and pushed it up over her breasts and ran his hands over her breasts, squeezing them.

She flung her head back and was gasping his name, he wanted her breasts in his mouth and removed his hands but could not unlace her top, so he gripped it tight and ripped it in two and took her breast into his mouth sucking, licking, kissing with desire, he ran his hand down her back and squeezed her bum, he pulled her skirt up and grabbed her bum and pulled her harder against him, she was calling his name pleading for him to take her, he slid his hand between her legs and slid his finger into her and she gasped and had to grab him for support, oh Jessie he turned her round and bent her over the end of the bed and undid his trousers and pulled a condom over himself, he pulled her little thong out of the way and entered her fully, he felt rock hard inside her, and she was so tight and wet he gasped her name and thrust so hard forward taking her up to his hilt and slowly withdrew, she screamed out, oh yes Marcus don't stop oh please and he did it again, she came over him and that just made him go faster he held her hip tight as her pushed himself into her over and over, taking her with his own need, she came again and he could not hold on and came to. He slumped forward on to her and then moved sideways so he was spooning her.

After an hour he stirred and kissed her back and neck and then he kissed down her back and hips, she was making her little noises of pleasure so her turned her on to her back and pulled her skirt and thong off, leaving her stocking's and suspenders on and kissed her legs, he licked between them, she came while he licked her, she grasped him. I need you now please and he reached for another condom and parted her legs and slid into her, he called her name she was moving under him and he pushed himself forward she wanted more faster, faster, I need you Marcus please, his rhythm got faster and faster, she was touching him and pulling him to her and kissing him, he could not last and filled the condom with his release . He kissed her face to calm her and held her to him, whispering words of love to her, they drifted off wrapped around each other.

It was near dawn when Marcus could her hear whimpering and talking to him, she was dreaming by the sound of it, he touched her face and called her name and kissed her lips, her eyes opened, she had little tears in her eyes, he kissed them away. She slid over and straddled him and pushed herself back on to him so quick he wasn't expecting it and did not have time to reach for another condom.
The heat and tightness of her body felt so good against his shaft, he grabbed her hips and pulled her down on to him hard, oh honey he gasped out and she ran her hand down his body, he was even harder and he let her take him with all that she had in her for him.

He could feel her hot liquid pour over him and he thrust into her pulling her down and filling her with hot seed. She fell against him, both cover in hot sweat and gasping for breath. She felt complete again.

After breakfast in their room and a shower together, they dressed and Marcus gave her his white shirt while he put his jacket on as her top was in two bits, she had no top to ware back. Robert did not say a word when Marcus helped his wife into the car, he tried not to smile but it was hard not to, Marcus said inside the car, you look very becoming in my shirt Jessie, you might have to ware that again later and he growled at her. Kirk was drinking his coffee and looking out of the kitchen door when they came home and he just smiled, it was quite obvious what they had been doing, and it was good to see them so happy, his family was whole again. Hey dad got a cup for me Jessie said, sure he poured her a cup of coffee and handed it to her and he held up a cup to Marcus who nodded. How was Leah? She's been a little angle no problem, mum is just changing her now.

He handed Marcus a cup of coffee with a big smile and did not say anything about their clothing, they must have had a bloody good night. Just then Christine came in with Leah, Jessie put her cup down and picked Leah up and kissed and hugged her, oh darling mummy has missed you and held her in his arms, Christine just looked at Marcus and Jessie she was going to say something but looked at Kirk and closed her mouth and smiled at Kirk, he winked at her. He held his arm out and Christine slid into it and kissed him on the cheek.

Archie came into the kitchen singing "love is in the air" good morning everyone and poured himself a cup of coffee, how is every one on this fine day. Good Jessie replied, very good and kissed Marcus. What is this Phillip asked, a family meeting or what, is there enough coffee for two more in that pot? Sarah came into the kitchen behind Phillip and smiled at everyone; Phillip looked at Jessie and Marcus, wild night then sis? Phillip really, said Christine. Archie poured them both coffee and handed it to them, yeah it was really wild. Christine looked at Jessie, well really Jessie and everyone laughed.

Five months had passed since there return from Italy it was now mid-December, and everyone had settled into their everyday routine, Jessie and Phillip had there nineteenth birthday at home with their family, Christine's pregnancy was going well, Xander was busy organizing Leah's baptism for the day before Christmas eve and the next light ceremony with Victor, which was to be held between Christmas and the new year as Xander was planning a big family Christmas and a big new year's eve party. Phillip spent all his time between Xander and the brother hood and Sarah. Marcus spent most of his time investigating and trying to follow up leads from the explosion from Tobias and Adele, and trying to find Crispin and the brotherhood and been reshaped due to the losses in Italy and all new security protocols and surveillances stepped up. Archie had moved in above the garages and spent most days with Jessie and Leah, he never seemed to be far away from her, Xander even built him an attic room at his estate just up the road and Jessie's time was taken up by Leah who was still growing at a slightly increased rate, she was now the size of a one year old, her knowledge was also increasing as well, Jessie was worried about the long term effect that it would have on her but for now she would put everything on hold and enjoy their first Christmas together with her larger, new family.

Jessie went into the kitchen to find Kirk laying the table for tea, can I help with that dad, sure Jessie you can and he handed her the cutlery, eyeing her, is everything ok Jessie? you know you can tell me anything, if I can help I will. I'm fine, I was just wondering when you and mum were planning to put the Christmas tree and decorations up, I love Christmas and this will be our first together and I wanted to help. I am just eager, for Christmas shopping and the lights and family time with a bit of fun and games, I don't see why we have to miss out on any of that just because we are older. Well I agree with you sweetheart why should we, how about we start by all of us going out tomorrow and getting a tree and some decorations and light's and then coming back and we can all put them up together, how does that sound? Yes, brilliant and her eyes lit up like a child's and a big smile beamed across her face, she threw herself at Kirk for a hug and his heart filled with love and comfort, just as Marcus walked in the door.

He looked at the pair of them. What is it with you if it's not my wife it's my daughter! Your husband is home, where is my hug. Jessie kissed Kirk on the check, thanks dad and let go of him and hugged Marcus, she gave him a deep kiss, I'll get mum and

Leah for tea and left the kitchen. What is that all about? Being a family Kirk replied and you are taking tomorrow off and spending time with your family, we are going shopping for a family Christmas tree and to do all the thing's a normal family does together.

Marcus smiled and held his hands up, I surrender. Good now finish laying the table while I get dinner out of the oven. The next morning, they were all down at the kitchen having breakfast together, planning what they were going to buy first and that the last thing they would buy is the tree. There was an air of excitement, mainly coming from Jessie but everyone felt it. Archie and Xander said they would have Leah for the day as she enjoyed questioning them all day and loved the power that she drew from them, even before Leah was born, she had shared a very strong bond with Xander and of course all the cuddle's and attention that he gave her every second they were together. Jessie gave her one last kiss and handed her to Archie, any problems call me ok! then handed him her changing bag and bottles for the day to take to Xander's with him. Archie kissed Jessie on the cheek, she will be safe with us, go and have a good day.

Marcus always watched everything that Archie did or said around Jessie, he was never sure of his real motives and he felt that he would be a fool to trust him 100%. Archie looked at Marcus, she is in safe hands be at ease brother, we will see you all late and left with a nod. Marcus pulled Jessie to him and kissed her, right come on you let's go, are you ready mum and dad? Marcus turned to see that Phillip was still kissing Sarah, when you're ready Phillip. He stopped kissing Sarah, we are ready, I meant ready for shopping and Sarah went red in the face.

Christine said, come on you lot or we will never get out the door; I don't know where you all get it from, you my dear, said Kirk. They all left the house and got into their cars with their drivers and security. They all went into town and brought lights and decorations and had lunch out together. They were all enjoying their family time together, they stopped off on the way back home to buy one of the biggest trees Jessie had ever seen. Marcus was watching Jessie, she looked like a child in a sweetshop when they choose the tree, he did not fight the urge, he pulled her to him and kissed her deeply.

Archie looked up from his game of chess with Xander, she's just woken up. Xander stood and went to her crib and said little one come to grandpa, she gave a tiny little cry and smiled, he picked her up and gave her a cuddle and kiss. Would you like your bottle little one? No grandpa, I want to talk to you. He smiled at her, what questions do you have now child? I want to tell you something grandpa, it's a secret. Yes, child what is it? I want you to help me grandpa, is everything ok do you need your mother little one? Archie stood up, is everything ok? I don't need mommy, I need you grandpa, I am ok thankyou Archie. Xander said I am not sure what she is asking of me, be calm. Tell me little one I am listening. Do you remember when the angles came, and what he said to you? yes Xander said, he told me that I was your protector, I would lay down my life your you darling. I want you to know I must change soon grandpa; I will need you close to me.

Why what do you mean you must change, try and remember what else the angle told you, I need you to find me a mate grandpa a man with power like you grandpa, he must be for me only, but he must be near to me grandpa. This is fathers wish grandpa. I see how long do I have little one before you change. Soon by the end of this year grandpa, you are having a gathering soon, father said mummy was helping him. Yes, little one, mummy is helping father get some of his children home. And mummy said that your friends are coming for a party.

You could choose someone then grandpa. Yes, little one, I will have to tell mummy about this, we could not keep this from her or daddy. Ok grand pa, can I have my bottle now please, yes, little one, he kissed her cheek and passed her to Archie, I will just heat her milk. As soon as Xander left the room Archie told Joshua to call Marcus, tell him and Jessie they need to come and get Leah when they are ready as I want to talk to them urgently about her, tell them that she is well and not to be alarmed.

Jessie had just put the angel on top of the tree and Kirk had just switched the lights on when Marcus's phone rang, Jessie just knew it was about Leah. Is she ok, Jessie said when Marcus closed his phone, yes, but change of plan Archie will not be bringing Leah back, Xander would like us to go and get her as he would like to talk to us that all? See you in a bit mum and dad, come wife let's get our child. Paul opened the car door for Marcus and Jessie to step out of the car, Xander's front door was opened by a butler who let them in, Xander also came and greeted them. What's up Xander. Jessie looked at Xander's face. Be at ease, everyone and everything is fine. I need to talk to you both now without anyone overhearing us that's all. Come, Leah is fine Archie is giving her a bottle. Xander lead them to his Library, please sit, when they were all seated Xander said please wait until I have finished speaking before you say anything. I put Leah down for a nap and when she woke up she told me that father had spoken to her in her dream and told her that she will change soon, when I asked her when she would change she said before the end of this year, but she never said why she would change or into what, but that's not all, she asked me to find her a mate, like me someone with power and that he would have to be near to her. She asked me to remember what the angles had said to me when they visited Jessie.

I told her that I would have to tell you two, she did not want to speak of it, she just wanted her milk, she did say that when we have the gathering, I should choose someone then and then I called you. Jessie and Marcus could not speak they were dumb struck. While you two take that in let me point out a few things. One we should keep this to ourselves until we learn more, two it only gives us, just fewer than three weeks or less, three I don't know how fast or even what she will change into or what powers she will possess or how strong she will be. This is being done for a reason, but as for the reason, I have no idea, but I think we should be ready for anything and whatever she turns into she wants or will need a mate and it is to be an older man, I don't think it is for sex but for her to draw power as you do, but to what end and that means she could change into a young or older woman or an angel, I just don't know. But the most important question is who do we pick and what do we tell him, whoever he must be prepared. I will lose my little girl and we have not had any real time with her, Jessie let out a gasp and Marcus took her hand, don't worry no matter what she will always be our little girl. Ok, I want a bodyguard for her starting tomorrow, someone who knows her, but is not wrapped around her little finger, someone who can see danger and is not blinded by love for her, Victor, Jessie said. Would he do it, I know following a baby about and spending time with her is not a man's thing, but it will be mostly for when she changes.

Yes, Xander said very wise. Do you think he would do it? Of course he would and as for a mate Jessie said, don't choose one, get a few, I will have to leave the vetting to you and Marcus, but know this, nobody and I mean nobody, will even approach my daughter for any reason and I mean any reason, until I see for myself what she changes into, I want to see if she is old enough to choose for herself. It could be just the fact that she is drawn to the power that the brother hood has, it just could be that she may not know what she wants, she may just think she needs more power when she changes. Remember she is a baby; I know she has power and knowledge but I am her mother and I will kill the first person to abuse my trust in any way and I don't care who that is. Are we clear? Yes, replied Xander, this means we will have to bring our plans forward a bit that's all.

Marcus you're very quiet! we will talk later Xander. I am still taking everything in, come on Jessie let's get Leah home I think we both need to talk to her. Xander, we leave you to start making arrangements, and thank you for having her today, no problem anytime. They all stood, Jessie was the first out of the door, Archie had felt her distress and was walking down the hall to her with Leah, she if fine Jessie look see for yourself. Leah let out a little cry for Jessie to pick her up and she did, she held her to her and gave her a kiss and cuddled her. Thank you, Archie, she leaned forward over Leah and kissed Archie on the cheek. Archie gave Marcus Leah's changing bag. Thanks' Archie. Jessie asked him if he was going back with them. No, I am going to stay and chat to Xander for a bit but I will be home later if you need me, I will know it. He smiled and winked at her. Come on wife lets go Phillip and dad will have tea done. Bye and thank you Xander, Jessie leaned forward over Leah and kissed Xander on the cheek and they left.

The house looked lovely when they returned, they had put even more dec's up around the house, it looked like something from a movie and tea was just being set out onto the table. Jessie was in Christmas heaven once again and put the shock revelation about what Leah had said to Xander, away in a room at the back of her mind till she was a lone with Marcus and Leah later. Now was family time, they enjoyed music fun and games till bed time, Jessie went up to have a bath and took Leah with her, she would talk to her more when she was in the bath with Leah a bit of mother and child bonding time. After Jessie had spoken to Leah, Marcus came and took Leah to get her ready for bed and Jessie had a little time to herself. Leah said in a sleepy voice don't be sad daddy I love you and everything with be ok and Leah drifted off to sleep while Marcus was still putting her sleep suit on, he kissed her and laid her down in her cot and turned the baby monitor on. He went for a shower and let everything run through his head, there was nothing he could do, he just had to protect his family as best as he could, he could tell that Jessie was upset, he had felt her protectiveness come out as did Archie; he made a note to have a chat to Archie on his own.

- He knew Xander would be grilling him even now. He turned off the shower and dried himself off, he walked by Leah's room to find Jessie with a little nighty on looking down at Leah. He went in, come on Jess, let her sleep she's going to need all of her rest soon as we will.
- Jessie turned and walked towards Marcus and she let her tears flow and worry roll down her face, Marcus held her and comforted her in his own satisfying way that she loved.
- Xander was having breakfast with Victor and Joshua and talking over the security plans for Leah for the next few weeks, with lots of people coming for the next ceremonies of light and a few extra people for Leah to choose. With the Christmas and New Year's party they needed to be on top of everything and they also talked about the answers' they still hadn't got yet, the woman that had set Marcus up, also the explosion in Italy and there was still the issue of Xander's drink that had been tampered with and the man that had killed Peter and Leah Bagbie,

they only found him out thanks to Leah. Which meant someone had killed Peter and Leah Bagbie and the 53 other Guest's that night at the hotel fire, 19 years ago and the death toll in Italy. The death toll was mounting up. We are missing something said Xander, we need to go back at least 20 years check our register and get a list of visitors and get the list from the brotherhood party at the hotel that night, any lists of anyone who knew our plans and anyone close to Peter and Leah. Marcus sensed something at the castle in Italy he sensed danger.

I think we have over looked lots of things, we should trust ourselves more instead of leaving everything to modern technology and I want every brother accounted for. Everyone! Victor stated, yes start with our registers and books and once that is done, I want everyone on that list accounted for and spoken too, make sure we have missed no one. Even the brother's that live or travel alone, then contact all brotherhood halls in every country and get them to do the same and get them to send us their information and we will put it all on to one main dater base. I know we have something like that all ready as do many other countries, but I want every brother drawing breath, on that dater base and any information about them including medical records, children and wives, death's and rebirths as well, we could only be talking about twenty to twenty-five thousand men may be less. We have the list of the 500 men that went back to father so we can account for them. Joseph Bird is our record keeper and Archivist he has an assistant already, get him two more and anything he requires to get this done.

Also, the Angel he plays a part in all of this, to what

end I do not know yet. It plays on my mind that something nasty is coming our way; father would not send so much protection for no reason and on the other side to that there is Jessie and her power, her unknown potential and gifts. There is Leah and her power and gifts and why father has made Leah grow so quick, there must be a reason and Phillip's powers. Yes, it makes you think and gone are the days of fighting back to back in a battle with swords said Victor. What kind of war would we have in this day and age and who would be our father's enemy? Are we even at war now, are they cutting our numbers and more brothers are going back to father soon so our numbers will be even less or has our time come to an end, will father even need any of us anymore? Ok enough doom and gloom Joshua. Yes, Xander said, Victor you will still hold your post for now and until things have settled, you're with Leah and you're happy with that? Yes, replied Victor. It was Jessie's idea, she asked for you. Well she has good taste, smiled Victor. Joshua, I hear your to be God Farther along with Phillip and Dr Adams will be her godmother. Yes, that's 3 days from now, then Christmas Eve some of the brothers will be here by then then the family gathering on Christmas day, we have the rest down in the palace.

Very good you may both go thank you, they both stood and nodded at Xander and both left. Jessie woke up to a hi pitched scream and giggling and the sound of her little girl saying Mummy, Daddy. Marcus sat up; did she just speak out loud? Yes, she did. They both got out of bed and went to Leah's room she was stood up in her cot with her arms up and out waiting for them to pick her up with a big smile on her face, her eyes shining and pink cheeks, she had grown a lot since yesterday. Daddy, she was stamping her little feet in excitement, mummy. She let out another hi pitched scream. There was a knock on their bedroom door, I will go said Jessie. Marcus was smiling and talking to Leah he picked her up from her cot when Jessie walked back in with Kirk. Grandpa, she spoke out loud and screamed again, she tried to wriggle out of Marcus hands to lean over to get to Kirk, well I never, I heard a little scream and thought I would come to make sure all was ok and it was you little one, she giggled and Marcus passed her to him.

Leah put her tiny arms around Kirks neck and gave him a hug. She started to wiggle again and let of another hi pitched scream and said mummy come here! you little rascal Jessie said. Leah tried to throw herself at Jessie in excitement but Kirk had a good grip, you little monkey, he kissed her on the cheek and passed her to Jessie. Leah screamed again, be calm Leah and held her to her and kissed her cheek, then Leah's little body relaxed and Leah whispered into Jessie ear I love you mummy but Kirk and Marcus could hear her. Well you certainly found your voice today madam, Kirk said. Just then Kirks phone rang, he opened it and said thank you and closed his phone. Victor is here, he looked at Marcus. Jessie explained, that is my doing, he is to be with Leah for a little while maybe a few weeks. Ok, what's going on? asked Kirk. Phillip called up; Victor is here. Marcus went to go out, can you take Leah and cut the feet of that sleep suit it's too tight. It will have to do till I get her something bigger. Ok, Jessie passed Leah back to Marcus. He and Leah went to greet Victor. What is it Jessie, what's going on that you two could not tell me! Dad we only found out yesterday when we went to pick Leah up from Xander, she told him to find her a mate because she is going to change in the next few weeks and I asked Xander for a bodyguard, someone who is not wrapped around her little finger and someone who could see danger because we or I don't know how fast she will grow or the age she could reach, I could go out and come back and she could be 25, I don't know, if she changed quick I need someone there some one older to help her and knows what to expect. It was a shock to me and we were going to tell you today but as you can see Leah and Victor beat us to it. I did not want to worry you. Yes, she is growing quickly again and it's so worrying darling, come let's have a cup of tea and let us see what Victor makes of her new voice.

Marcus went into the kitchen and Leah stopped giggling, she hugged Marcus tightly, and Phillip exclaimed, my god Leah what are they feeding you? he put his hands out to her and she giggled and let off another hi scream, uncle Phillip and everyone just looked at her, she stared to wriggle again, Marcus handed her to Phillip who willing took her. Victor, thank you for coming. Victor looked between Marcus and Phillip not only has she grown but she has found her voice to. Leah said daddy is going to cut off my feet, Phillip and Victor looked at Marcus

. Yes, I am you little Madam, mum pass me the scissors from the draw please. Marcus could feel Victors unease, don't worry I am cutting the feet off her sleep suit it's too tight, she grew so much last night and we don't have anything bigger, till later. Victor felt better and Christine passed Marcus the scissors. Hold her really tightly Phillip, Sarah would you hold her leg while I cut the foot of, I don't want to cut her. Be still Leah said Phillip, she did not move. Marcus was very quick and finished in seconds. Right all done and kissed Leah's little feet. she screamed again as Jessie and Kirk walked into the kitchen. Leah beamed a smile at Jessie. Christine held her hands out to Leah, be careful Leah, nanny has a little baby inside her said Phillip. I know, will he be like you Uncle Phillip? What do you mean by that Leah, Kirk asked, will he look like Uncle Phillip and will he have light inside him like Uncle Phillip? I think grandpa is asking how you know it is a boy Leah and not a girl like me and your mummy, Christine said. Because, I know nanny has a little boy growing inside her like I grew inside of you mummy, and uncle Archie told me nanny has a little boy inside her so he knows as well. Leah hugged Christine, I love you nanny and gave Christine a kiss.

It's a boy Kirk said, he had to wipe a small tear from his eye and hugged Leah and Christine. After breakfast Phillip said he would look after Leah while Jessie and Marcus went out and brought her bigger clothing, some extra clothing in a few bigger size's just in case she grew more again in the night and nappies. It gave them a chance to do a bit of Christmas shopping while they were out together, Jessie brought a silk wrap and a silk dress to fit a three to four-year-old for the christening in a few days. If the dress does not fit then we will wrap her in the silk wrap with a baby grow under it, it will have to do.

When they got back about lunch time everyone looked frazzled and warn out. Leah was sat up in a high chair eating spaghetti on toast with child size cutlery and a bottle of tea with Victor. Just in time Kirk said she has worn everyone out, she's been running around with Phillip and Sarah and then had a story with mum and Victor gave her a bottle of tea while I made her lunch and now, she is quiet and feeding herself. Leah turned and looked up at her mummy and daddy and gave them a big smile with sauce stuck to her face and then turned back to finish her dinner. God Marcus, Jessie said she just like you. Marcus smiled at Jessie, no Jessie she's just like you, she's so good looking, she thinks that smile will get her anything. Yes, that's true, but the only thing it's getting her is a wash and a nap then some new clothing. Leah said I have finished grandpa, ok, finish your tea then I will get you down. Leah picked up her bottle of tea and guzzled it down, put her bottle down and Kirk lifted her out of the hi chair, she ran to Marcus, he bent down and picked her up, come on you let's get you cleaned up, he was so amazed by her. Mum get the camera first please and get some pictures, Jessie said. Victor told them that Kirk had offered him a room there for a few weeks and asked it if would be ok. Yes, that's not a problem Victor and thank you for doing this, you don't have to be around her all day every day it's just mainly when we are out and when she it at Xander's and as soon as the brotherhood start arriving, then it will be 24/7 Jessie informed him.

The day before Christmas had come around quickly and it was the day of Leah's Christening. It was held at the brotherhood of the knight hall and everything went well, Jessie felt her family was complete and tried to put her worries about Leah away and just enjoy this time and take it all in and store all of the memory's at least she would have some photos. They all celebrated at the brotherhood hall with cake and a few drinks. Are you ready for tomorrow night? Xander asked Marcus, yes everything is ready and wrapped up for father Christmas to come and leave his gifts? I think I am more excited than Leah. Yes, I can see that you're looking forward to it. Do not wear Leah out to much before you all come over for lunch as I have been wrapping all week and have lots of gifts for after lunch.

- Eli came in and whispered to Joshua, who just nodded, Eli nodded to Xander and left. Jessie knew someone had arrived and this is what Eli had said to Joshua, he did not use the phone because Leah would have questioned him, so they were more aware of Leah and her understanding of things, very clever Jessie thought to herself. She had been more aware of every one's movements especially since the bombing. The brotherhood Elders had arrived, she could feel them. Archie had felt her unease and moved next to her and looked at Marcus.
- Marcus had been watching Jessie and understood that Archie had picked up on whatever Jessie was giving off and asked Xander, who has just arrived? I see like your wife you miss nothing. No, Archie gave it away, Jessie must have felt uneasy and Archie moved to protect her, look Phillip is at ease. Yes, I see that and you still have not answered my question, who is here?

Marcus said. Some of the elders they have been placed in the furthest room's from us and they have all been warned not to approach Jessie or Leah, if anyone were to find themselves even in the same room or hallway, then they have been told to withdraw this is Leah's home but they have come early to help and decide the best choice for a mate for Leah. Just a few of the elders and a bodyguard each will be here, also for security purposes due to their hi statues, the rest of the brothers will be placed at the brotherhood apartments here and elsewhere. Are we having Christmas lunch with them? Marcus did not sound to happy, be at ease son, we aren't, it is our family time together. Marcus suddenly felt better, he was sure it was coming from Joshua, but still he felt at ease. Leah came running over with her hands up screaming Grandpa, Xander bent and picked her up and she threw her little arms around his neck and kissed him, then she put her hand's out and touched Joshua's face and said that feels nice. Marcus could see that Jessie was not happy, she had felt that Leah had picked up on Joshua's influence and Xander new it to. Joshua stopped using his influence at once and stepped back he was taken back that she could pick up on it. We have to go home now Leah said as she turned to see Jessie walking across the room towards them. Come on you that's enough for one day, say good bye to Grandpa Leah. Leah gave Xander another hug and kiss and Xander gave her to Jessie as even he could feel her unease. Thank you for today Xander, Jessie kissed him on the cheek. Kirk helped Christine up, Phillip and Sarah were ready, everyone said their thanks and good buys and Marcus said I will be back later when Leah is in bed. Xander nodded. Archie already had his arm around Jessie and Leah as they were walking out of the door, Marcus did not like it but he understood.

When everyone went Joshua said, I am very sorry Xander, I knew Jessie could feel us as I know Leah could but I did not know she could feel my influence, I was calming Marcus pleases forgive me. It is no one's fault, Leah is drawn to power and feels us, I think this is a part of her growing, now we know she feels our influence we know not to use it around her, Jessie will not have like that, Leah felt it but she will understand.

When Marcus retuned later Xander welcomed him and asked where Archie was, he is refusing to be away from Jessie. Is she still upset then, no, sometimes he just has the need to be near her and comfort her that's all? When he thinks she is settled he will come? Come let's have an evening drink with the others. When Marcus went into the study, he had found that Xander had made more room, the big table had gone and there were now four sofas around the fire place. Marcus knew everyone sat in there but it had been many years since he had seen some of them and only months since he had seen Adele and Tobias. The men's bodyguards were all seated against the walls on single chairs. Xander introduced everyone to Marcus, you know Adele and Tobias of course, he nodded at them and this is Akim from Saudi Arabia. Yes, I remember your name means" whom god exalts" if I remember rightly, Akim nodded at Marcus, and this is Elfie form Norway, and your name means "immortal" does it not? Marcus asked, he nodded and smiled at Marcus.

This is Alexi from Moscow, "helper of man" Marcus said. Very good said Alexi with a nod, your memory is perfect Marcus. It is. Please sit Xander said and let us discuss what has brought us together, I have brought every one up to speed with everything about the guardians of light, your marriage and your daughter, Adele and Tobias covered the ceremonies of light in Italy and the booming, and we have spoken about security issues and now we need to choose a mate for Leah. Marcus explained, I can tell you all know that you may all select a person each, then we can talk about each one, I will speak to my wife, it will be down to her and then it will be down to Leah to choose, if Jessie thinks she is ready and of age then she can choose for herself and if Jessie think she is not! What will happen then Adele said. It will be down to Jessie, but we will have to wait and see, first the amount of change in Leah, it could be that when she changes that she does not want a mate anything could happen, but no matter what she will always have a very close bond to Xander, she will never be far from him, so her mate if she has one, he will have to live here with us. You make all speak to the other elders who are not here or are coming for the ceremony of light, but whoever we choose he must be here before the New Year.

There was a knock at the door and Eli said, sir Archie is here, very well show him in, Xander stood up. Adele and Tobias stood up to and the others were not sure who Archie was but he must be someone with a lot of power to make Adele stand up so they took Adele's lead and stood. Archie came in, gentlemen he said and stood next to Marcus.

Marcus knew that he could not tell the rest of them who Archie was so unless Archie was going to say anything Marcus would not, he knew Adele and Tobias were also sworn to Archie's secret, and the others would just think he was an immortal anyway. Xander introduced Archie and informed them that, he has a very strong bond to Jessie, as I have to Leah and introduced everyone to Archie then said please everyone sit.

It was just after midnight when Archie whispered to Marcus, go Jessie she needs you. Xander noticed Archie's movement and said, I think we had better call it a night gentleman. Yes, I must go, good night, Marcus stood up and hugged Xander and left.
Marcus went back home and checked on Leah, she was sound asleep and then walked into their bedroom to find Jessie with the blanket on the floor and she sheet twisted around her, her little night dress had worked its way up, she was naked apart for the bits of her that were covered with the sheet. He went hard he wanted her, she must have been dreaming or having a nightmare. So he stripped off his clothing and tried to unwind the sheet from her as best as he could, then slid an arm underneath her back and lifted her gently, her hair slid back and hung from her head he could not help himself and kissed her gently on the mouth and took her night dress off, laid her back down and got into bed next to her and pulled her to him. He touched her face and said Jessie honey. he ran his hand down her, Jessie opened her eye and looked at him, I was having a bad dream and then I was flying with you and you kissed me, it ok, I am here, are you sure your awake honey as I need you, yes.

He slid on top of her and kissed her passionately and touched her everywhere with his mouth, kissing her, licking, sucking, tasting her and then he wanted to be inside her so badly he nearly cried, he rested himself between her legs and pushed himself into her, he cried out with need, she was so tight he could feel her flesh making room for him and pushed harder and called out her name. She could feel his hard shaft throbbing inside of her, he felt so big she gasped and had to hold onto him, his rhythm built, all the little noises she was making just pushed his need on harder and faster until they were both covered in sweat, he could not take his eyes from her, he kissed her over and over touching her feeling her, she was intoxicating him, her release was explosive and pulsated through her body in hot waves of pleasure, she was bucking against him calling out his name, he gripped her hips and his hot full release filled her. He collapsed on top of her gasping for air. It was a good few minutes before he could move and take his weight off her. The sheet was soaked with their sweat. Marcus could not talk he just pulled her to him and went to sleep.

After Marcus had left, Xander had said goodnight and left the rest of the men talking with Archie. Adele asked, how is the little one Archie? She has grown to the size of a two-year-old child already. She walks, talks, runs and screams, eats and drinks like her father. Tobias laughed, does Leah look like Jessie or Marcus more now? She still looks like Jessie, more and more every day. Akim stated, we are at a disadvantage to the king and Tobias as we have yet to meet Jessie and her child. Yes, Elfie agreed, would she agree to meet us. I to would like to meet her Alexi said but I take on board what Xander has said about how protective she is over her child.

Not forgetting how protective the rest of her family rightfully is over her and her child said Adele, Tobias agreed, we have seen it firsthand no man would live or get a second chance believe me. You would not live to tell the tale if you got anywhere near to Jessie, let a loan her child, as we have seen firsthand. This is true Adele said. What of the story's Elfie asked of the messenger's? It is all true Tobias said and her brother Phillip? Yes, it's all true.

Akim gave a little laugh and what of my old friend Kirk. Adele told him that Tobias and himself had seen firsthand that he share's a very strong bond with Jessie, she protects him, she gave him blood and she gave him life when he had a hole straight through him even Xander thought him dead, she saved him, she call's him dad, and Leah even call's him grandpa.

He is her stepfather and is married to her Aunt that brought her up, as her mother and father died in a fire when she was a baby. Well I never thought I would see Kirk married; his wife Christine is pregnant. Well I never Akim said and what part do you play in this Adele? Have you used your influence on Jessie yet? Adele just looked at him and Tobias said yes, he did to test her at Xander's request, and what happened, have you bed her yet?

Archie stood up and hissed at Elfie. Elfie's bodyguard had moved and stood by Elfie's side and other bodyguards stood up.

He meant no harm Archie he just wanted to know if she was taken by my influence that's all and No, she was not, and she let us know that she was not happy about it. Now Adele said to Elfie, tell your bodyguard to sit down. Elfie looked at the others, Tobias and Adele you obviously know more than we do. Tobias said Archie I am going to stand up and Archie eyed him and nodded. Tobias said to Elfie just do as Adele asks, we have no wish to end this night on a bad note now do we! Tobias stood in front of Elfie's bodyguard. Elfie looked at Adele who had not moved. Elfie spoke a few quick words in Norwegian and the bodyguard withdrew and sat back down, Adele said sit and the other bodyguards did the same. There, no one meant any harm or disrespect to Jessie they just knew of Adele's reputation that is all. Tobias nodded to Archie, and Archie nodded back and left the room, he went upstairs to the roof and changed form and flew home. Alexi said what was that about Tobias, Adele, what you are not telling us? Adele said there are lots of small stuff in between but know this, do not cross that man ever, that is all we are permitted to say and do not ever provoke him, You, are lucky you still draw breath Elfie as is your bodyguard. Jessie has more than one protector that is all, if she chooses to tell you then fine, but we cannot. We are not holding things back from you but we are bound that is all.

My bodyguard would have killed him in a second Elfie said, No, in that second, he could have killed all of us you fool and remember not only our we on Xander's territory, we are guests in his home, and we are speaking about his family. He does not have to include any of us in this so know your place all of you. We played host to him and we let him down, our enemy tried to kill us and other members of the brotherhood. Father calls us all once again, be that to go home or to fight for our kin our families as knights. That is what our holy man is doing now, so show your age and your manors. We are all brothers, remember our purpose and if you cannot then you will not live very long around here. Believe me, take on what I and Adele, and all of what Xander has said and has warned you all about. Good night, Tobias then nodded to Adele then left. I think Tobias has covered everything, good night gentlemen and they all stood and nodded to Adele and he went to his room. What do you make of all that? Alexi asked Akim, I think we should do as he says, he is right and I too am taking my leave, so goodnight and with a nod to them both he left the room.

Kirk got up and looked at his pregnant wife asleep and thought of his family and his son growing. He felt at peace. He found himself looking forward to the next few days, he found that he was now just as excited as Jessie had been. He showered and went to the kitchen; he was normally the first person in there in the morning. But today Archie was up and ready, he had laid the table ready for breakfast and made coffee and switched all the Christmas lights on and had soft Christmas music on low on the radio, it was only 7.30 am. Good morning Archie and what has you awake at this hour? Good morning to you Kirk, I found that I could not sleep. Why what upsets you Archie? Kirk did not like the fact that the angle had been worried.

Normally nothing and no one bothered him. Is there something I should know Archie, is Jessie safe are we safe? I don't know yet, that was all he said before Christine came in to the kitchen and Archie eyed Kirk and Kirk and Archie both put big smiles on their faces and greeted Christine. You can feel the excitement in the air, is Jessie or Marcus not up yet? No, Archie said they will not wake up until Leah does. Ok husband do we have everything ready for tonight and is the camera on charge ready, and have we brought everyone a gift for tomorrow? Yes, my wife today we will meet a few of Xander's guests and then family fun games and a Christmas film "the night before Christmas" and chocolate then bed till Santa comes. That's just for Jessie, Leah will need a lot more attention.

By 9 am everyone in the house was up and ready and had their breakfast. Marcus could feel Kirk's influence on him slightly, and Kirk said I better take the rubbish out. Let me give you a hand old man and went outside with him. What's up, forgot to get mum something? No Kirk said, Marcus could see Kirk looked upset, what is it? The angel, when I came down this morning he was already in the kitchen, he told me that he could not sleep because he was worried, that alarmed me, then when I asked if Jessie and us were safe he said he did not know and he looked really worried, I could not press him anymore because mum came in. You are right to tell me, it must be something bad to worry him. What's on for today Marcus asked, Kirk went over what he had told Christine. The only danger we could be in or from is from Xander's guests. We will not take Christine or Leah over, but we will take Phillip, Marcus said. Do you think Archie would stay with the woman replied Kirk, I am not sure it depends if Jessie was in danger, he would not leave them?

Ok the sooner the better Marcus said, call Xander tell him what you told me, tell him we are coming now and tell him it will be a quick visit for today. I will speak to everyone now and I will send Victor out for an update. Ok Marcus said as he walked in the back door, we have a little change of plan because its Christmas eve we want as much family time as we can, Victor can you finish helping dad, Victor knew something was wrong and went outside. So, dad, Phillip and myself will take Jessie across to meet Xander's friends and Archie, could you stay with mum, Leah and Sarah, and get some games out for when we get back. Could you do that, to put Jessie's mind at rest while we visit with Xander? Archie knew what he was asking and Archie knew that is what Jessie would want. Yes, I can do that, it's my turn with the lovely women. Archie winked at Jessie and she kissed his check and said thank you.

Right, let's go. Kirk came in from the back with Victor, that's fine! Marcus called out, Morgan, Robert, Jessie looked at Marcus, well its Christmas and Xander's guests should see your bodyguards and get to know them. Get ready the pair of you, we are going to Xander's. After everyone kissed mum and Leah they got into their cars and went over to Xander's to meet his guests.

Levi greeted them at the door and took them to the main living room where Xander was stood by the fire place, talking to five men and there were a few men against the far end of the room bodyguard's Jessie thought. Jessie knew Tobias and Adele. Jessie didn't go any further into the room. Kirk approached and hugged Akim, he was pleased to see his old friend, and then greeted the others, then Kirk introduced Phillip to everyone. Marcus was stood next to Jessie holding her hand and Robert and Morgan were right behind them. Jessie turned her head to Robert and Morgan, don't get to close to me, they knew what that meant. Are you alright Jessie, yes, she told Marcus, but I don't want to hurt anyone unintentionally, just in case? You do not have to go near them if you don't want to. No, it's ok, I can feel their power and it would be different in a hall more room that's all. No one will hurt you Jessie, we are all hear.

Ok, she said and Marcus lead her over to them. Jessie kissed Xander and gave him a hug and held her hand out to Tobias, he kissed her wedding ring, hello again Jessie, it's good to see you in better health my dear, and you. Adele moved slowly and stood next to Tobias, Jessie held her hand out to him, it is good to see you again Jessie, you look absolutely beautiful and kissed her wedding ring. Elfie could not wait his turn and stepped passed Akim and Alexi towards Jessie, the moment freighted her she was not expecting it, her red light came on instantly and covered her, Marcus, Kirk, Phillip and Xander. Tobias pushed him back way from Jessie and Elfie's bodyguard moved to protect him but that meant standing closer to Jessie and a purple haze shot out of her and hit the bodyguard, Tobias and Elfie throwing them all back against the wall, away from Jessie. Adele shouted, no one else bloody move. He is a victim of his own stupidity.

Marcus touched Jessie's arm, its ok honey. Her purple haze and her red light went white. Sorry, Jessie said to Xander, he made me jump, I was not expecting it and I could not stop myself, I am so sorry, poor Tobias, Phillip help Tobias please Jessie said. Phillip went over, his white light covered his body, he touched Tobias on the head and he woke up. Phillip smiled down at him and turned his light off and helped Tobias to stand up. I am so sorry Tobias, I never meant to hurt you are you ok, please forgive me. There is nothing to forgive. Jessie went red in the face. Phillip took his place behind Jessie. Adele told the bodyguards by the wall, pick them up and put them on the sofas for now. They did as Adele told them and then they went back to their place's. Please forgive Elfie, Adele said he is from Norway you know, it's the Saxon blood in him. Are you up to meeting the rest of our party asked Xander? Yes. Xander moved closer to Jessie to reassure her, this Xander said is Alexi he is from Russia, Moscow, Jessie held out her hand, he took it slowly and kissed her ring, I am much honored to meet you

Mrs. Dewdney, then let go of her hand and stepped back. This is Akim from Saudi Arabia, Jessie held out her hand and Akim took her hand, kissed her wedding ring.

Mrs. Dewdney it is a great honor to meet you and let her hand go and stepped back. Jessie stepped back and held Marcus's hand, Xander asked Jessie how is the little one today? Victor is giving her a cup of tea in her bottle as we speak, she is looking forward to tomorrow, so be ready for a million question and lots of hi pitched screaming. I will be ready and with that Kirk said we must get back, Marcus agreed, it was good to see you all again. Kirk hugged Akim and shook the other men's hands, Jessie kissed Xander and Tobias on the cheek and said I am so sorry, she nodded to Adele and then nodded at everyone else and left with her family and went back home. Xander offered the men a drink. Tobias enquired, how long will Elfie be out for, he will wake up soon with a very bad head ache. Idiot, he was warned. Yes, and if Jessie had her child with her, they both would be dead and maybe even Tobias to.

Tobias said I won't make that mistake again; he is on his own. Akim said she is very young and very beautiful. She is Xander agreed.

Why did her brother not move to protector her, because that light is also a shield, nothing can get through it, she has more power than he and he does not need to move to incinerate you, he could do it from where he stood, so don't ever underestimate my or her warnings again any of you. Alexi asked, what of this Archie, where is he in all of this? Like I said he has a very strong bond with Jessie. I know you said last night Alexi, but I know every one of us, but I don't know him. Adele tried to break the questions and said Elfie was stupid enough to upset Archie last night and Tobias stepped in and saved his ass then as well. I see Xander said, what did he do to upset Archie? He wanted to know if I had bedded her and Archie hissed at Elfie, I see, he is lucky to still be drawing breath today then.

That is what Tobias told him last night. Alexi said you have not answered my question. All will become clear in time my friend. Ah look Elfie is coming around. What happen Elfie said, I feel like I have been hit by a train, good Adele told him, perhaps now you have learnt you lesson you idiot, you could have got Tobias killed and your bodyguard and you frightened Jessie. My head Elfie said, Eli took him a brandy and two pain killers. Elfie sat up, why is my bodyguard still out? because Adele said trying not to lose his temper, he like Tobias took the brunt of Jessie's little anger stick. Then why is Tobias ok? He is ok because Jessie saw fit to help poor Tobias. Phillip healed him instantly and you are so lucky you did not upset her more because if she had her child with her, we would be sweeping your ashes up now. You give Xander an apologue right now for your actions or I will end you now, you have brought shame to us by your deed. Xander, please, I am so sorry, please make him stop shouting at me, my head.

Jessie and her family had a wonderful day playing games and telling stores of Christmas pass and watching Christmas films with everyone snuggled up together. Leah was starting to close her eyes; I think you better tell her story before bed said Jessie. Kirk read the night before Christmas to everyone and by the time he had finished Leah was out like a light in Jessie arms. Bless her said Christine said. She is going to want her presents from Santa the second she wakes up you know that right! Yes, Marcus said she's like her mother, she can't wait for anything. I am going to put her to bed, I will be back in a bit. Jessie put Leah to bed and brought her baby monitor down. Marcus went out of the room and came back with a massive sack of gifts and put them under the tree. Have you ever heard of the word overkill Marcus? Kirk laughed, that's nothing and went and came back with another massive sac of toys and gifts. Oh, my word, dad what have you done.

Well they are not all for Leah, there are a few for everyone else as well. Now I don't feel so bad and Phillip went out of the room and came back with another sac of gifts. Oh lord, Christine exclaimed, we will be here till next Christmas opening that lot. After a cup of tea for the woman and a few drinks for the men, everyone went to up to bed.

Marcus had a wash and went back into the bedroom to

find Jessie laid on the bed with a see-through Santa's naught little helper out fit on. It had red fur on the tiny skirt, a top and a pair of red high heels, Marcus smiled and said can I open my gift now? Yes, anything for Santa. Marcus closed the door and opened his gift.

It was 11.30 am when everyone left Christine's house to go over to Xander's for Christmas dinner. Leah was giggling and screaming in excitement when Marcus took her out of her car seat, Marcus put her down and she ran to Xander with a picture she drew for him, screaming grandpa, Santa came to my house. He picked her up and cuddled her to him, she was hugging his neck, kissing him and trying to talk and show him her picture all at once, be at ease little one. Xander carried her into the living room, it had been transformed to a winter wonderland with a massive tree, gifts, the log fire, lights and decorations. Jessie could see he had gone all out, as this would be her only Christmas as a child. I think at this rate she might have to have a nap after lunch, we will see. The room was filled with people and family, Victor, Leah, Xander, Jessie, Marcus, Phillip, Sarah, Kirk, Christine, Eli, Joshua, Levi, Robert, Morgan and Archie. Leah kept every one entertained, but she was never far from Xander. They all sat down together and had their lunch and pulled cracker's and told jokes.

Leah could not eat any more and was sat on Xander's knee drinking her bottle of tea at the table, when Xander looked down she was asleep. He took the bottle out of her hand and lifted her up to cuddle her. Jessie said, I knew she would not last, where do you want me to put her down Xander, as she has out grown her crib. I could put her down in my room, if you're agreeable to that Jessie, it's not a problem. Ok, Victor would you sit with her, of course, it's not a problem. Xander carried Leah, Jessie and Victor followed him to Xander's bedroom where he laid her down, Jessie covered her and kissed her and Victor took a seat near the bed. Jessie and Xander left her there asleep with Victor keeping a watchful eye over her. They went back down and joined the others, who were all sat down on the sofas. Xander thought it was time the adults should open their gifts while the whirl wind sleeps. Kirk agreed it was a good idea. After an hour of opening gift's Jessie said I better wake her up or she will not sleep later. Its ok Robert! he looked at Marcus who nodded to him and he sat back down, Jessie went upstairs and went in to Xander's room.

Thank you, Victor. Its ok, she's been snoring. She gets that from Marcus you know! Victor smiled, Jessie pulled the cover back, come on madam, Jessie swept Leah's hair back and rubber her face, Leah woke up and smiled. Where are we, we are still at grandpa Xander's. That made her sit up and smile and giggle, Victor said it looks like she's ready for round two! Jessie picked her up, kissed her and put her down, Leah ran straight to the door and out into the hallway. Leah, no, you wait for mummy and Victor, Jessie ran after her.

Adele, Tobias and Akim where in the hallway, Leah had run to Tobias with her hand's up, he automatically picked her up without thinking, do you remember me little one, my you have grown. Yes, and hugged Tobias. Leah, Jessie shouted and the three men looked at Jessie and Victor. Archie had felt her panic and was coming up the hallway behind her, shortly followed by Marcus who had seen Archie run from the room. Alexis and Elfie could see everyone on the landing in front of them and went up to see what was going on. Adele could see what was happening and said to Tobias, put the child down and let her go back to her mother as I have no wish to die. Akim took a step back and said to Alexis and Elfie stay back give her room, don't come any closer. Jessie took a step towards Tobias and he looked at Jessie and a very upset looking Archie, Marcus stood behind Victor. I am so sorry he said she ran up to me, I meant no harm, I know Jessie said it was my fault. Adele and Akim started to back away back, down the hall giving her room.

Jessie took another step towards Tobias and Marcus stepped forward passed Archie and Victor, what happened Jessie? It was my fault, I left the bedroom door open and she ran out down the hall then ran into Tobias, if he had not been there, she might have run down to the stairs and fallen down them, I panicked that's all, I'm sorry, I did not mean to frighten or upset anyone. No harm done Tobias said. Marcus told me what you did for Leah when she was born, thank you Tobias I will not forget it. Leah turned in Tobias's hands and put her arms out to Jessie who took her, Jessie nodded to Tobias and went back downstairs. Marcus thanked Tobias and shook his hand, Tobias nodded to Marcus and said she is getting better at controlling her light! Yes, Adele agreed, you were very lucky Tobias. Jessie harbors no ill feeling to anyone she only reacts to protect herself and family and all this is new to her, she has been through lots, please keep that in mind and then Marcus left with a nod. Marcus and his family finished their Christmas with Xander and left later that evening with a worn out and very happy child. Marcus said to Jessie, I think Xander had more fun than Leah did! Yes, I think she gave him a run for his money today.

Two days later Jessie and Marcus were getting ready for the celebration of light, another party tonight Jessie thought and tomorrow Jessie and Phillip would be sending more men to meet their maker. Jessie felt like the angle of death. Victor had taken Leah over to Xander's house with Archie, as Leah would stay there, till after the ceremony tomorrow, Jessie would collect her from Xander's, it gave everyone at home a break and everyone could go to the party tonight. Leah loved to stay at grandpa's house. Marcus looked like a god as usual with his black suit on and his aftershave. Jessie had a long black halter neck silk dress on with heels, her hair was down showing her new haircut, and extra perfume because she knew her husband loved it on her. They went downstairs to the hall where everyone else was waiting and all looking very glam. They got into their cars and went to the brother hood of the night's hall in Southampton. The palace had been decorated like Tobias's castle in Italy with the same colour and finery and candle light. Jessie noticed the extra security and bodyguards. Xander, Joshua and Levi were at the top of the table with Tobias and Adele, Kirk and Christine were walking in front of them and Phillip and Sarah were behind them, as they walked up the red carpet everyone stood, as they entered the hall all eyes were on them. Jessie squeezed Marcus's hand. Its ok Jess, relax and enjoy yourself. Jessie was starting to recognize a few face's as she walked to her seat. Xander greeted her, kissed her check and hugged her, Robert pulled her chair out and she sat down as did Christine and Sarah. Then everyone sat. The elders gave their speeches as did the King. They had their meal and the music began. Xander asked Jessie for the first dance, then she danced with Marcus, while the rest of the brother hood watched, others joined them on the dance floor. Marcus danced with Christine and Sarah. While Marcus was dancing with Sarah, Jessie slid over two chairs, Kirk turned from his conversation with Akim and Christine and said, come child does your husband leave you, to dance with another women, yes, replied Jessie with a smile. Come now we can't have that, now can we? No, Jessie said with a big smile we cannot, and I need to burn a bit of energy off. Good, trouble is my middle name, come child let's see who is going to tell us off first. Kirk stood and kissed Christine on the cheek and said to Akim, I will be watching you with my wife my old friend from the dance floor. Akim just smiled, so you should. Akim nodded to Jessie, Kirk took Jessie's hand and led her to the dance floor. Akim asked Christine, what does he mean by trouble when he is dancing. Watch and you will see.

Adele and Tobias who were talking with Xander, Elfie and Alexi, also noticed Kirk take Jessie's hand and walk to the dance floor. Does she share a very strong bond with Kirk then asked Alexi? Adele answered for them, yes, she does my friend just watch and you will se., Tobias said she calls him dad and Xander told him to not be alarmed at what you will see, it will not hurt you and looked at Elfie. Every one turned to watch Kirk and Jessie dance,

Marcus smiled at them and raised an eyebrow and lead Sarah from the dance floor back to her seat next to Phillip, I see dad and sis are at it again then, it appears so. By the time the end of the first song had ended Jessie was laughing and giggling, and a great big white flame shot out of Jessie's chest and covered her and Kirk, the light turned into a very large flame people that were stood near, stood back and gave them room. Jessie knew that everyone in the hall was watching them, but didn't care, she was enjoying herself. After the third song, Kirk said we are for it now, here come's Phillip and mum to intervene. Spoilsport's. Kirk stopped dancing and Jessie hugged and kissed him on the cheek, thank you dad. No, thank you and he took Christine's hand and danced with her while Phillip danced with Jessie

.I can feel the power coming from you Jessie, her flame got bigger and taller and after a couple of minutes her flame died down and went out. Adele asked Alexi, do you feel the love peace and excitement coming from her? Yes, I can, as did Elfie, but why did her light not hurt Kirk or her brother. Tobias told them, when its white it will not hurt you but the second it changes to any other colour then run for your life, not that you will ever need telling twice. She likes you Tobias said Elfie, she did not even twitch when you picked her child up, the other day. Jessie knows I mean no harm to her or her child or family and the little one is like her mother, she can take care of herself, I share a little bond with her child that is all, but I would never be so stupid as to anger her or be perceived as a threat in any way, I have seen a fraction of the guardians full potential as has Adele and Xander, and you Elfie have felt a mere touch of a warning believe me. Is the child a guardian too then, like her mother Elfie enquired, no Xander said she is merely blessed that is all. Phillip walked Jessie back to her seat where Marcus stood and claimed his wife with a deep possessive kiss that left Jessie breathless and wanting more, what was that for? Well you had your show with dad and your brother now it's my turn. Jessie smiled and slid her arm around Marcus's neck and pulled him down for another hot kiss, when Jessie could talk, she told him, that was just encase someone was not watching the first time. Alexi and Adele agreed that Marcus was a very lucky man. Elfie looked at the jealousy in Adele's face as the music played on and the elders all spoke in their little group with Xander about Jessie and Leah. Xander's phone rang it was Victor, yes Xander said into the phone. You need to come home now its Leah, she had her bottle of tea and we put her down for her sleep, her light came on and covered her body Archie said the change has started in her and to bring Jessie and the elders at once. Ok, we are on are way.

Xander walked over to Jessie and Marcus as calm as he could but Jessie and Marcus both picked up on his anxiety. What is it Jessie said, we must go, Victor called and said Leah is covered in light, Archie said the change has started, he also asked for the elders to be there, I can only think she needs their power to draw on? Ok. Levi gathered the rest of the family and everyone made their way back to Xander's house. Tobias was in his car with the other elders who were staying at Xander house. He said to Adele, I feel like an expectant father, I wonder what or who she will changed into! You're forgetting the most important bit of all of this is, who the child will choose and who and what Jessie will allow. Yes, after all Alexi said that's what we are all hear for. That and Xander's data base, Elfie said. The child will possess lots of power and she is very gifted, I have listened to Xander and Kirk talk about the little one, she looks so much like her mother all ready and any man on earth would do and give anything to possess that child when she is grown, stated Akrim. Jessie was first out of the car, Eli greeted her at the front door, she's in Xander's room. Jessie ran up the stairs and into Xander's room, Leah was on the bed covered in red light. Archie told her that it had started under half an hour ago, Jessie looked at Victor and Archie, thank you. Marcus came in the bedroom with Xander, mum and dad are in the car and will be here soon, she needs lots of energy Jessie informed them, Marcus give me your shirt please, Marcus looked at Jessie, I am going to lay down with Leah and give her my energy, I am not doing that in this dress and shoes.

Xander told everybody to get out, let's give them some privacy. Xander closed the door behind everyone and Victor stood in front of it. Marcus just smiled as Jessie eyed him intently, he took his shirt off and handed it to Jessie, as she only had a tiny little thong on and nothing else, Jessie smiled back. You are going to have to wait till later. Jessie buttoned up the shirt, you look sexy as hell in my shirts. Jessie kissed Marcus again and he ran his hands over her body and growled. Ok, she said control yourself-husband our child needs me. Phillip will know when I have had enough and don't go far. Ok, he stepped back Jessie's light shot out of her and covered her, she lay on the bed next to Leah and cuddled her, Jessie's light covered them both. When Marcus went outside the bedroom Archie looked pale, Marcus asked Archie, do you need to be near to them? Yes, I am going to change very soon its Jessie power and need. Go in Jessie's cuddling her on the bed, Phillip will come soon. Thank you, Victor opened the door and let Archie in and closed the door again, as soon as the door closed Archie changed form and just stood and then kneeled at the end of the bed with his wings out in a protective shield each side of the bed. He felt more at ease when he did this.

Xander noticed the bright white light shining from under the door and looked at Marcus. He needs to be near her now, there is nothing we can do, why don't we go down and speak to everyone and have a drink. Victor are you ok to stand watch; nobody goes in there apart from me the doctor and Phillip. Of course. Marcus make yourself more respectable before you come down please, Xander said. I can't help it if my wife want's the shirt off my back now, can I he said with a smile. Levi went off and came back with a t shirt and handed it to Marcus. Thank you. By the time Marcus walked into the living room there were people there and everyone went quiet. Kirk said is all ok, yes dad and mum, Jessie and Leah are both fine, Jessie is giving Leah some energy, I gave jess my shirt so she could cuddle up to Leah, and Archie is in there with them so they are safe and he can help with energy, Phillip, Jessie said you will know when she has had enough, so could you and the doctor check on her, you might need to swap with her in a bit, which means dad and Xander you will need to give Jessie some energy and maybe

Tobias as well, that's if you don't mind Tobias.

Of course, any of us would be honored to help in any way we can. So it looks like it could be a long night or few days, and the only thing I also ask is that anyone going up or down the stairs please use the back stairs, as Jessie and Archie will feel your presence and I don't want them upset, Jessie will be overly protective until the change is complete and even then more so for a bit after. Akim asked, what is Archie to do with this is and why is he so trusted to be alone in the same room with the guardian, if she was mine no one would be in there, what is going on that we are to be kept in the dark about, Adele, Tobias speak! It is not for them or I to say, you will all find out soon enough, all I can say is that Archie has a purpose and right now he is fulfilling it Xander informed him. It is death to touch a guardian, Akim said, yes, yes, it is, I am glad you all remembered that, but Archie is doing nothing more than watching over her. Then why does she allow him to be so close to her and the little one asked Elfie. Phillip stood, enough, stand back now and Phillip's red light burst out of his chest and covered him, do not talk of my sister and her child like that, I am sorry Marcus but Jessie needs me I can feel her power drawing me, we must go. Marcus followed Phillip back up the stairs, Victor opened the door when he saw Phillip coming towards him.

Phillip went into the bed room and spoke to Jessie who did not respond, he could see she was getting weak. Archie, Phillip said can you lift Jessie up off the bed and give her to Marcus so I can lay down and take Jessie's place, yes but Leah has taken so much already in such a short time, the elders will help. Archie put his big white wings away and stood, then picked Jessie up, Jessie's light stopped. Phillip took his jacket, shoes and his tie of and laid down on the bed with Leah and cuddled her to him, his light covered them both. Ok, Marcus said do you want me to take her? No, she must have some of my power first. Ok but if we go down Akim and everyone is down there and I know what you said about telling people, I know Archie said but she must be away from Leah and she must come first. Come down and cuddle her and when she is better, give her up to me in front of them, no one will approach you and try to take her, we must show a united front in front of the others, ok Archie.

He nodded to Marcus, ok let's take her in the other bedroom for a second, so I can get a cover to put around her before we take her downstairs, Marcus went into the next bedroom followed by Archie who carried Jessie and a worried looking Robert, who stood outside the other bedroom, as Robert did not like being too close to Archie in his Angle form. Marcus got Archie to put Jessie down long enough to wrap Jessie up and hand her back to him. Be at ease Archie, we both want the same thing and remember Jessie's mum and dad are down there, be clam for them. Right, let me go first I will make some room for you in the far side of the living room, away from everyone. Yes, Archie said. Marcus went down, dad give me a hand with that small sofa would you, yes sure where do you want it? At the far end of the room. They lifted the small sofa up and placed it at the far end of the room away from every one and put it down, thanks' dad, please take a seat next to mum. In fact could everyone find a seat around the fire place there were four sofas there and some chair's, I am going to ask everyone no matter what happens or what they see please do not freak out, do not stand up and please do not approach them or make any sudden movements for your own safety and do not repeat to anyone what you are about to see. Marcus shouted up to Archie and he came down the stairs followed by Robert who was a good few steps back, now Archie will bring Jessie in she needs to rest and get some power ok and Archie will help her do that and for toughs of you that wanted to know about Archie, then this is your chance to see who he is.

His bright white light filled the room before he entered it carrying Jessie who looked like she was asleep, Archie looked at Adele and the other elders and let out a warning hiss to keep them back as he walked passed them, he opened his large white wings, they filled the room as he sat down, he then wrapped his wings around Jessie and his light dulled. Ok, Akim wisped, I was not expecting that, nor I Elfie said, Alexis did not say a word he just looked. After ten minutes, Archie called Marcus over, Marcus got up and went over to Archie, Archie put his wings away and handed Jessie to Marcus. Thank you, no thank you for helping them Archie. Father knows that Leah needs more help he is sending the messenger again, he will be here soon, do we need to move Leah and is anyone in danger, no do not move Leah and if everyone stay's down here then there is no danger but they will need you, Jessie and Xander. How long Archie is soon? About three maybe four minutes. Ok, no time then, let's go back up, Xander we will have heavenly guests in about three minutes please come with us now and everyone else please stay where you are.

Marcus carried Jessie back upstairs followed by Archie and Xander. What heavenly guest's does he speak of Kirk? Akim asked. The messengers from father are coming. From what I can remember of them, Sarah said they are huge and very scary, but the big one seemed to like you Kirk, you threw yourself in front of us and him defiantly new Xander. What! Elfie said, as in the messenger, as in the first messenger that took the first guardian and the very same messenger that visited Jessie when she conceived her child, I thought perhaps a little had been added for effect about the stories of our guardian. No extra, Kirk said the very same one and the same messenger remembered Xander from his first visit, and spoke to Xander on his second visit and now there third visit.

Xander truly is our holy man and Jessie is father's beloved child. Yes, Adele said he watches her and helps her with his heavenly messengers, he protects her with an overly protective Angle and blessed her with a gifted child, he has given her an immortal for a mate and has given her an extended family and a father again and true love to boot. A very tall order Tobias agreed and as Adele once pointed out what enemy are, we to face, to bring her child on and for what purpose. Thunder erupted, threw the house like an earth quake and a bright white and blue light shone out through the house. They are here Kirk said and stood up. Marcus was stood next to the bed where his daughter and brother in law lay, holding his wife, Archie was knelt down at the foot of the bed with his head bent down and Xander was stood next to Marcus when the thunder erupted, the bright white and blue light shone out and a thick white haze filled the room and there stood the two messengers with their milky white marble skin that seemed to move and their blue diamond eyes.

The smaller one stepped towards the bed and the big one nodded at Xander and smiled at Marcus, the little one did not turn but made a hissing noise and it looked like there was another being under its skin and inside it and the being inside moved when it hissed. The big one leaned over the bed and lifted Phillip up from the bed and held him and the little one and covered Leah with a blue haze, then removed her night dress and breathed light into her, he kissed her forehead and covered her with the bed sheet, then turned to the big messenger holding Phillip and touched Phillips head with his hand and light shot out of his hand and into Phillip, the big messenger looked at Archie who stood up as if the messenger had spoken to him. Archie walked around the bed and the big messenger passed Phillip to him, the big messenger looked down at Phillip as a parent would look at a sleeping child, he touched his head and then looked at Marcus and Jessie. Archie left the room with Phillip.

Outside of the room Archie said Simon and Eli come with me, Archie took Phillip into the next bedroom and laid Phillip on the bed. No, matter what no one come's in this room while he sleeps and one of you will sit with him, do not touch him and one of you will stand watch outside. Archie then left the room and went back into Xander's bedroom, he bowed down as he entered and then knelt back down. The big messenger did not even move or turn, he had taken Jessie from Marcus and laid Jessie on the bed next to Leah and was looking down at them. The little one hissed again, the big one turned around and took one giant step towards Xander who was stood back against the wall. The big one smiled at Xander and Marcus just stood still where he was, just watching everything that was going on. The big one touched Xander's head and the little one completely covered Jessie and Leah with a thick orange haze that Marcus could not see through. The big one took his hand from Xander's head and nodded at him. Marcus took a step towards the bed and the little one let out a sound like a scream and hissed at Marcus. The big one reached over and put a hand on Marcus's shoulder and Marcus looked into the bright blue eyes that shone like blue diamonds. Marcus knew that they did not want him to touch the light around Jessie and Leah but he wanted to know that they were ok as he had never seen the orange haze before.

Looking into the big one's eyes was like staring back into heaven, Marcus was in or. Archie stood up and bowed at the little one and the big one let go of Marcus and went and stood next to the little one, the little one touched Archie's head and light shot out of his hand and into Archie's head. Marcus thought it looked like an addict getting a fix. The little one let go of Archie, a clap of thunder fill the room and echoed around the house, bright white and blue light filled the room and shone out of the house. The bright white and blue haze of light faded from the room. Are you ok Xander? asked Marcus, yes! Archie you looked a bit strung out, are you ok and how long will that cover Jessie and Leah for? An hour maybe for Jessie, but Leah maybe a day or less. No one must come in here and I cannot leave or change form until Leah awakens. But there both ok? Marcus asked.

Yes, the shroud is necessary for Leah to grow quickly, it gives her the power to do that, so she does not need to drain Phillip and Jessie of their light. So why is Jessie under there, she would be ok on her own, yes, father is helping Jessie link with Leah so when Leah awakens it's not so much of a shock for her, she knows she will not be a baby or child. It's a bit like, how would you say, a talk about the birds and bees and how the female body works and how to cope as an adult female. I don't like the fact that farther keeps playing with my wife's life, and keeps changing my wife and my daughter Archie. Why is all this necessary, and why change my daughter, I don't know what to expect Leah to look like or be! Father has shortened her life and stolen her childhood years form me and jess, why Archie why? Two hours ago, we had a child, a little girl and when she wakes up, she will be a woman, how I am going to cope with that, Jessie is only 19. I know we had a little time from what Leah said to Xander, but why Leah and why now! Calm yourself Marcus Xander said, Jessie would not want you to be upset. Archie, we will be downstairs, we will be back in about half an hour, there is a guard outside the door with Robert, come Marcus, Christine and Kirk will be worried about their children. Yes, of course we won't be long Archie.

Every one stood when Marcus and Xander went into

the living room. Kirk spoke first. How are they? fine, fine Marcus replied, Phillip is having a sleep, he is fine Simon is with him as is Eli, he will wake soon, and Jessie is having a rest and cuddled in with Leah, she will be up in an hour or so and Leah is changing and will not be awake for a day or so, we don't know yet! Archie is with them both and Robert and Victor are with them, so don't worry, our visitors have gone. Mum dad when Phillip is awake would you be able to accompany him home and make sure he rests. I understand if you need to go early with mum needing her rest, I just thought you would only worry. Yes, that's fine Christine said. I will also send Morgan back home now to get Jessie some bits for her, if that's ok. Yes, of course that's fine darling and what about you? Morgan gave a nod to Marcus, and then Marcus crossed the room and cuddled Christine and put his hand on her tummy, I am fine you must look after my little brother in law in there. Christine gave him a kiss on the check, me and dad will stay until Phillip is better, but if you need us to stay, we will. Thanks mum. This must be a lot for you and Xander? Yes, it is. Joshua will cancel the ceremony of light, that was booked for tomorrow.

Would you like a bedroom to rest in or a pillow and blanket, mum? No thank you darling I am ok, for a bit. Adele asked Xander if he was alright. Yes, I need a drink that's all. Tobias gave Marcus and Xander a large brandy, please sit down for a little, all we can do now is wait. After ten minutes Joshua's phone rang. He just said thanks, ok. Joshua whispered into Xander's ear. Phillip is awake and, on his way, down, when Phillip entered the living room everyone stood up. He hugged Christine and

Kirk, I am fine, Jessie will awaken soon. That's good, Morgan will be back soon with her stuff, Marcus told him, are you up to going home to rest. No, I feel a strong pull to be here, I cannot leave.

Ok, let me check on Jessie, Xander can you make some arrangements for mum and dad to stay. Marcus left with a nod, Victor opened the door to the bedroom and Marcus went in, just in time Archie said she is waking up, please don't touch the shroud it is protecting Leah, it could damage her, wait till Jessie gets up. Jessie got up slowly and Marcus picked her up and hugged her and asked her if she was ok. Yes, I need a cup of tea, but not dressed like that, one second Marcus went outside of the bedroom to find Morgan stood there with a bag of Jessie's things. Thank you, Morgan. Marcus went back into the room and gave the bag to Jessie who went into Xander's bathroom and changed into jeans and a t shirt. Do you need anything Archie? No, but Leah will need Jessie when she awakens so don't go far. Ok. Jessie kissed Archie on the cheek, thank you Archie, I will know when she needs me, I will be in the living room and with that Jessie and Marcus went into the living room, again everyone stood, Jessie hugged Kirk and Christine and everyone stood back as her white flame came out of her and covered the four of them. Are you ok Jessie and Leah, enquired, Christine? I am fine mum and in need of a cup of tea, Leah is fine she is resting, she will not awaken for a few hours yet.

Kirk said both of you go and sit down on the little sofa and I will make the tea. Xander could you get the girls a few pillow's and some blankets. Xander nodded and Joshua opened his phone and spoke quickly into it and then he closed it again. Come on you two Marcus said let's get you sitting on the small sofa, everyone stood right back to give Jessie plenty of room. Kirk came back with two cups of tea and Phillip took the blankets and pillows from William and gave them to Jessie and Christine. Phillip moved another sofa so he was near to Jessie and Christine, also so Sarah and Kirk could sit on it and he could see everybody. Everybody, spoke softly to each other, after a little while Jessie cuddled up to Christine and fell asleep, still with her bright white light covering them. Simon moved to stand as he was sat on a chair not far from Phillip, Jessie's light turned bright red, Phillip said that was not a wise move and everyone looked up to see what had happened. Simon froze, back off very slowly, he did and Jessie's light still stayed red. Is she ok Kirk said? Yes, she will settle when she feel's safe again, don't worry dad all is well. Adele said to Xander and Tobias, she is remarkable, I thought the white light that covered her while she slept was enough. It must take a lot of power to keep that going and can attack when she is asleep or is, she alert? No, she is fast asleep and she is not using any of her power to do that, she's using our energy Xander informed him. Akim responded, that is some weapon.

Three long hours later Jessie woke up and her light went out, she stretched and stood up and touched Phillip on the shoulder, why don't you rest now brother, no, it's ok sis I can feel it will not be long. Yes, I feel it to, where is every one? Xander and Marcus made everyone go into the library, to give you and mum some peace, after you nearly zapped

Simon, he stood up quick as he was close to me and your red light came on. Is he ok? Yeah, nothing happened, he backed away. I am going for a cup of tea would you like one? No, thanks sis. With that Jessie kissed Phillip on the cheek, Robert and Morgan followed her into the kitchen. Marcus was taking to Kirk and Akim, Jessie gave Marcus a big hug and kiss, it will not be long, I can feel it, Leah will wake soon and Phillip feels it to. So, I have come for tea and toast before she wakes up. Sit down Jessie and I will make you a cup of tea and do you some toast Kirk said. Thanks' dad, she gave Kirk a hug and kiss on the cheek. Marcus said I will let Xander know, he will want to be near, I will be back in a sec and kissed Jessie again, then went to find Xander. Akim smiled at Jessie and just stood where he was watching, her and Kirk intently. Is mum awake yet Kirk asked while handing her, her tea.

No, she will sleep for a while yet, thanks for the tea. Kirk made her toast and Jessie ate it quickly, by the time she had finished Xander was in the kitchen with Marcus. Xander spoke, it is nearly time for Leah to awaken. Jessie nodded and looked at Akim. Akim said, I will give you some privacy and left the kitchen with a nod. As she cuddled Marcus, Jessie said, I would like Sarah to come up and just check her over and Phillip will need to be near, if you could be outside of the door, I would like one of our men to be with mum today, just sit with her and watch her when dad is not there because if the baby is like me and Phillip this might affect him, it might not. Also no one and I mean no one is to use their influence or calming today, as I will feel it and so will Leah, I will not be held responsible for my actions if that happens. Ok, we had better go up, it's time.

Xander spoke to Joshua, Phillip and Sarah were already at the bottom of the stairs. Jessie gripped Marcus 's hand as they went upstairs to Xander's room. Victor opened the door for them to go in. Jessie and Marcus, Phillip and Sarah went into the room while Xander and Joshua waited outside with Kirk, Robert and Morgan. Archie said, she is waking up, please don't touch Leah until the shroud is gone. Jessie nodded and Marcus and Sarah stood back while Jessie and Phillip stood right next to the bed. The shroud faded away and Archie changed back to his human form and took a step back. Jessie's bright white light shot out of her and covered her, Leah and Phillip. Leah was still wrapped in the sheet the messenger had wrapped her in, Leah moved and opened her eyes and looked at Jessie and Phillip then back to Jessie and Leah spoke her first word, Mum. Jessie climbed on the bed and hugged her daughter to her and kissed her, Marcus stepped forward and walked around the other side of the bed to get a better look at his daughter, she was the spitting image of Jessie, he could see himself in her, she looked about 16 years old she had Jessie's long dark hair and his eyes, she looked beautiful.

When Jessie let go of her Leah looked at Marcus, Dad she sounded just like Jessie, he sat on the edge of the bed and Leah jumped forward to hug her dad, Marcus held her tightly. Jessie said, Leah this is Sarah she is a doctor, do you remember her, yes, well dad, uncle Phillip and Archie are going outside now, only for a few minutes just so Dr Adams can check you over, to make sure everything is ok. Marcus kissed Leah on the head. Can I see grandpa afterwards? Yes, he is waiting outside. Marcus let go of Leah and stood up. We will be just outside the door honey Marcus said and left with Phillip and Archie. Jessie went into the bathroom to get Leah some clothes of hers that Morgan had brought over in a bag. Jessie put some under ware out, a pair of leggings, T-shirt and some wash things, after a few minutes Sarah asked Jessie to come out of the bathroom.

She is fine but I will need to check blood and urine, we can do that next week, I would estimate her physical age about 16 years. Ok, Leah why don't you go in the bathroom and get dressed, I have put some clothing out for now but we will get you some today, if we can, ok darling, yes, mum. If you don't know how to do anything then just asked me, dad or grandpa. Ok. Leah went into the bathroom with her sheet wrapped around her. Sarah said, just by taking to her I would put her mental age about 14 but that could be because she has just changed and will take some time to get used to it. She is very vulnerable. Thank you, Sarah, you may go, I wish to speak to Leah before the men come back. Sarah hugged Jessie, she's just like you and left. Leah came back into the bedroom. Leah please sit, we need to have a quick talk without any men being about. There are other men in the house, like grandpa, I know you can feel them, can't you? Yes, mum. Now I know you asked for a mate, I need you to tell me why, is it to draw power, to mate or protection because you are not old enough to mate yet and you could damage yourself. I will need to draw power from one source and if they are my mate and older it will be pure and just for me, it will be a strong source because of their age and when I am of age and married, I will mate then and not before, it is fathers wish. Ok that's fine, but if your drawn to someone you must tell me and if someone or any one tries to influence you then you tell me, dad or grandpa right away and if you feel that something is not right then you must say.

If you do like someone then say, there is no harm in that but you will know inside which one and the other thing is you know never to use your light or power outside the house or in public, that's what we have bodyguards for and you will never go anywhere without yours, do you understand me? Yes mum. Good, Jessie hugged Leah, let's get both of your grandpa's and dad to come in. Jessie opened the door, dad, Xander you may come in and meet Leah, Marcus followed them back in and closed the door behind him. Leah threw herself at Xander nearly knocking him over. Xander just cuddle her until Marcus said ok, Leah grandpa needs to breath. Leah reluctantly let go of Xander and stepped back, she then turned and said granddad and hugged Kirk, everyone was just looking at Leah. You are the image of you mother but I see your farther to, Xander told her. Yes, Kirk agreed and kissed Leah on the head, she went back to hug her dad. Leah asked where Nanny was. She is asleep down stairs Leah, Jessie told her. Are you hungry little one Kirk asked, yes granddad I would love a cup of your tea? Ok, I will go and put the kettle on and Leah let go of Marcus and went over and held Kirk's hand, she looked back at Jessie to make sure it was alright to go and Jessie nodded.

Kirk opened the door, Leah told Kirk, I am not

allowed to go anywhere without my bodyguard. Kirk introduced Leah to Victor. Victor just looked at her and nodded and they went down the stairs to the kitchen, closely followed by Victor, her mum, dad and grandpa.

Phillip had already taken Sarah and Archie down stairs to give them more privacy, they all went into the kitchen where Kirk made everyone tea. Phillip came into the kitchen, hello Leah, hello Uncle Phillip and smiled at him. What are you all doing after breakfast, asked Phillip? Jessie said we will have to take Leah out and get her new clothing that fits her, is there somewhere open today? Don't worry I will contact any shop you wish and get them to open for us. Thank you Xander. Leah finished her tea and toast. Tobias and Adele came down the hall on the way to the kitchen, from the library in search of a cup of coffee. Jessie froze and from out of nowhere Archie appeared at Jessie's side, be calm sis Phillip said. Victor moved closer to Leah. Tobias and Adele stopped in the door way when they saw everyone stood close together. Sorry Tobias said we didn't mean to intrude and they started to back way. Adele and Tobias where both staring at Leah, No, Jessie said please don't go, come in and meet our daughter. Leah did not move forward, Xander took a step closer to Leah as he could sense her unease and she took his hand. Tobias and Adele stepped forward very slowly looking between Jessie and Leah. Tobias said, Leah you have got big your just like your mother. Leah smiled at him; I remember you Tobias. This is my friend Adele, Leah nodded at him. Coffee, Kirk said, yes please. Archie told them; mum is awake now. Thank you, Archie. Jessie said. Leah let go of Xander's hand and held

Jessie's hand. Let's say hello to nanny and Jessie and Leah went off to see Christine.

None of the men moved apart from Victor and Robert. Christine could not believe her eyes when she saw Jessie and Leah walk into the living room. My god Jessie she's the spit of you, she has her father's eyes, she beautiful. Leah darling, come and give your nan a kiss, Leah gave Christine a big hug and kiss on the cheek, I love you Nan. Kirk passed Tobias and Adele a cup of coffee each. Leah is so like her mother but has your features Marcus, you must be very proud of her said Tobias. Yes, we are.

Nan were going shopping to get me some clothes, do you and granddad want to come she said with her eyes shining and a big smile on her face, oh Leah how could I say no darling, great nan I'll tell granddad and before Jessie or Victor could stop her she ran out of the room and down the hallway and straight into the kitchen, shouting granddad, everyone turned. Phillip's light automatically shot out of him and covered Leah and Kirk as she threw herself at Kirk. Kirk just grabbed her, picked her up and swung her around and put her down again, yes Leah! Oh, she said and looked at everyone, she clung to Kirk. Jessie ran into the room with her red flame around her as she felt Leah's distress. Jessie just looked at everyone and let her flame die down as she knew that Leah had given them a fright. Leah you're not in trouble but you don't run in the house and the grown up's where talking, Jessie told her. Sorry mum. You were the same as a baby. Phillip let his flame die down. Leah put her head down, I just wanted grandad to come shopping with us and nan. Yes, of course I will little one, Kirk let go of her hand and kissed her on the head.

All the noise had alerted Akim and Elfie who were now going into the kitchen. Leah ran over to Xander for protection, as she felt uneasy again. Don't worry little one no one will hurt you. Akim and Elfie just stopped and stared at Leah. Jessie announced, there is to many people in the room and it's overwhelming her, please leave at once. Adele agreed, let's all give them a bit of room and all the men and bodyguards withdrew, just leaving Jessie and her family. Xander broke the silence, how would you like it if I came shopping to, little one, that's if its ok with your mum and dad. Please, dad. How can I refuse you, said Marcus and pulled Jessie to him and kissed her. Phillip wanted to know where Leah was going to sleep that night, she not going to fit in that cot. Give me a chance Jessie said, I haven't even thought about that yet. She can have our guest bedroom till we can sort something out suggested Marcus.

We can get what every she needs today Xander said, just give me a list of what you need to be done and I will make sure it's done, as you have enough to contend with. Jessie found her day full of shopping and helping Leah choose her clothing but mainly Jessie had come to realize that Leah would and could not go to school, she had no concept of money what every she wanted she would get, she would never want for anything, and Jessie now knew why she had wanted a mate as a mate would pander to her every whim, he would protect her from the world and herself, perhaps it was just the way of all human females or just the natural way that the immortals reacted to them. Marcus knew that something was on Jessie's mind he could feel it stood next to his daughter and by how close Archie was stood next to his wife, Xander must have picked up on it, as did the other's as everyone felt uneasy. That's the coat for you Leah your father has a very good eye, after all he married your mum, stated Kirk. Jessie looked up from what she was looking at and realized that everyone was looking at her, she knew she had put them on alert and smiled. Yes, darling you look beautiful. Christine said I think she has everything now and if we have missed anything, we will make a list and come back again. Yes, Jessie agreed, I need a rest and some food. Marcus was worried about Jessie but did not want to show it in case Leah picked up on it, so he suggested to Xander, how about we go and see if Jessie's favorite restaurant is open.

Leah let go of Marcus and grabbed Xander's hand, can we grandpa? Marcus went over to Jessie to comfort her. Xander had known why Marcus had done what he did, and lead Leah away with Victor, to pay for all of her stuff. After lunch Jessie was ready to go home, nan needs to have a sleep and you need to hang up all of your new clothes and put it all away along with your shoes. Dad! can I leave you to look after Leah at home when mum has her nap, I would like Morgan to go with her and of course Victor. It will take her about two hours to hang all that stuff up, I would like to talk to Xander for a little and then we will be back, but if it's too much with mum! No, it's my pleasure to look after my granddaughter, I will guard her with my life. I know, thank you, any problems then call we will come straight back. Xander opened his phone and spoke to Joshua in the car behind, Morgan is to stay with Leah and I want extra security put on Christine's home now, thank you and closed his phone. Leah kissed Xander goodbye in the car and Marcus and Jessie got out and gave Leah a hug and told her that they would be back in a bit and Leah went happily in with Kirk and Christine.

Jessie and Marcus got back into the car and they all went back to Xander's. All three of them went into Xander's library and closed the door leaving Archie, Phillip and the bodyguards outside the door. Jessie said this is the first time since Leah woke up that we have a chance to talk, and I would like to go first. Firstly Dr Adams checked Leah over and said she's fine but I want her checked regularly, her mental age is about 14 or 15. I have spoken to Leah about a mate and she said that she does not want to have sex until she is old enough and married, but she needs someone now and when we were shopping it hit me she will never have a normal life, never go to school, never want for anything and she will always be sheltered from the world, so she needs a focus and protection from the world and herself and this is why she asked for someone older and wiser to see to that.

So, I will agree for her wish to have a mate and someone she can start to share a bond with but I want to meet them all here first, by tomorrow or the day after can that be don? Yes, it can Xander said. Ok, but I want it made absolutely Chrystal clear to all you have selected that they do not use their influence or power while we are here making her choice because I will kill the first person that did and they are all to be told she is not of age, she is to be given time to get to know him and there will be no sexual contact of any kind, because I will know. Only when she is ready, she will tell me and she will be married first. After I have seen everyone then I will bring Leah in and she can make her choice. If she does not want any of them, then we will have to rethink our choices. If she chooses someone then they will have to live here in Southampton and if they all agree to that then there will no problem from me. Marcus! he was silent for a second then said yes, I will agree but I don't have to like it and I want full control of where she goes and with whom and when and all of her affairs until she gets married. I agree to, I will go along with your wishes as you are her parents but I also must have a place in her life, stated Xander.

That goes without saying Jessie said. We will not lose her she is too tightly bound to us but it is us that will have to accept her mate, whoever that is Jessie and make him part of our family and you Xander are the head of our family, you are very wise, so I trust the people you allow near to her and in our home and the choices you will have to make. Now I am going back home as I don't want to leave her at the moment. I imagine you all have lots to talk about with the others so don't be late back husband, I will take Archie back with me and Phillip I think would like to stay with you if that's ok. Yes, Marcus said and kissed Jessie. Xander said yes please excuse me, I will gather the others we have lots to do then Xander left the room so Marcus could say goodbye to his wife in private. Phillip, please come with me Marcus will be along soon.

Joshua, gather all the elders and tell them to come to the living room now, please.

Marcus went home at ten o clock by which time Leah was sound asleep in bed and Jessie was finishing her cup of tea. It's been a long day honey, let's go to bed. We have a long day ahead of us as, all 14 candidates will all be here tomorrow morning. Jessie took Marcus 's hand and led him up the stairs to bed where they made love to each other and fell asleep holding each other tightly. It was 8.30 am when Jessie came down for breakfast, Kirk and Marcus were sat down at the table talking.

Good morning Jessie would you like some toast and tea? Yes, please dad. Kirk gave Jessie a kiss on the cheek when he got up from the table. I just woke Leah up and told her to have a shower and get dressed, she will be down in a little while. Good, Marcus kissed his wife. How is mum today Jessie asked? I told her to go back to bed as the baby kept her awake most of the night, he kept kicking her. How did Leah sleep? Like a log, where is Phillip I cannot sense him. He and Sarah are fine Marcus said, they have just left to go to Xander's to make sure all is ready for today. When Leah came down, she had her breakfast, you look just like your mother when I first met her, Marcus said. Leah had on a pair of light blue jeans, a red T-shirt and black shoes and her long dark hair hung down. Beautiful Marcus said. Oh, dad replied Leah and went and gave Marcus a hug. Right you two, are we ready to go to grandpas? Jessie had gone over everything again at home with Leah about how she would meet some men and she could pick who she wanted and if she did not like any of them, then that was fine and what to do if she liked someone.

Xander was waiting at the front door for them with Archie. Jessie gave Leah a bit of time with Xander as Leah needed it and it comforted her to ask him questions about everything and he fully indulged her in it. Once their time came to an end Jessie asked Victor, Morgan and Archie to sit with Leah while Marcus and Xander went with Jessie to meet Leah's perspective mates. Joshua opened the door to the Library and all the men inside stood up and lined up, they were all calm. Jessie noticed that Phillip was already sat in the corner of the room with Sarah. Xander introduced them all of you to Jessie and informed them that she was Leah's mother. Xander walked down the line and introduce one at a time to Jessie, no one shook her hand they all nodded. Xander told Jessie that they had all been fully briefed and of course the last four you already know, they were Tobias, Akim, Elfie and Adele. Jessie asked Marcus if he wanted to change anyone. No, he replied. Then I will get Leah. Jessie returned with Leah, the only person that had moved was Phillip he was now stood next to Xander and Marcus, Joshua closed the door behind them. No one spoke or moved. Ok Leah take your time, ok mum. Leah held Jessie's hand tightly as they walked down the line of men, looking at each one in turn.

When they finished Jessie took Leah out of the room to talk to her. Would you like more time to think about it or did you not like any of them, you don't have to choose any of them? There was one, she said I felt funny inside like butterfly's but I will need to touch him to know. Do you want to go in and show me? Leah Nodded again. Ok, then we will go back in and I will ask who you to choose and for him to hold his hand out so you can touch him, is that ok. Yes. Jessie opened the door and she and Leah went back in and walked back down the line again Leah held Jessie's hand. Leah stopped at Adele, Jessie looked at Leah and Jessie looked at Adele who did not move, Jessie said hold your hand out. Elfie who was stood the other side of Tobias broke his stand and let out an angry and frustrated shout, Jessie's red flame shot out of her instantly and went black and in that few second's Archie had changed his form and burst into the room, knocking down the door, a burst of light came out of Archie's eyes and incinerated Elfie instantly. Archie wrapped his wings around Jessie's black flame and pulled her and Leah across the room, a roaring hissings noise came from him. The men who were in line were now stood back against the wall in shock.

Phillip who had his protective flame around Xander and Marcus let his flame die down. Archie! Phillip said, calm down. Xander said, nobody moves, stay where you are please unless you wish to end up like Elfie. Marcus took a step towards Archie with his hands up. Archie do you want to take the girls to another room or would you like me to take the men away? Marcus could feel Phillip calming Archie. Take them away. Ok, they will all walk out of the room and go into the living room. Joshua ordered the men to follow him very slowly out of the room, while Xander, Phillip and Marcus stood between the men and Archie. After the last man left Archie unfolded his wings from around Jessie's black flame reluctantly. He had stopped his hissing. Phillip told them, I cannot get through her black flame and I cannot get to close or my light will come on.

No, I can't it is Jessie's defense, when she is clam it will go, she is protecting Leah. What happened there Archie? He frightened Jessie and Leah, Jessie thought he was going to attack her, I felt her fear for her and her child so I did my job. You did nothing wrong Archie and I thank you for protecting Jessie and Leah. Jessie, Phillip said I know you can hear me, its ok let go of your light no one will harm you. Jessie's light went red then white then faded. Jessie looked white and in shock, it had taken a lot out of her, Leah was tearful and frightened she was clinging to Jessie for dear life. Even Xander could not tempt Leah away from Jessie. Marcus asked Archie, can you pick them both up and take them to Xander's bedroom and I will be up in a minute with Xander and Phillip. It will give them a chance to calm down, Jessie needs to recover. Archie just nodded and swooped them both back up and he was gone in a flash of light. Shit, I am sorry about your door Xander. No need to be sorry it was not you're doing but I will need to talk with Elfie's bodyguards and family later. Now let me speak to the men, before we console our loved ones. Xander, Marcus and Phillip went into the living room where all the men were talking amongst themselves, all the men went silent when Xander entered the living room. You were all warned were you not, the next person to disrespect my family in my home will not die so quickly believe me, I will keep you alive long enough so Archie can peel the skin from your body and hack bits off you before he kills you very painfully and slowly, is that clear enough for everyone. They all nodded and with that Xander left the room and went upstairs with Marcus and Phillip.

Jessie was laid on the bed with Leah and Archie was sat on the bed with his wing covering them. Archie stood up and folded his wing back, Phillip could feel that Archie was calmer. Thank you, Archie, Marcus said. Can you change back or do you need to stay near Jessie. I need to be close for a little and I cannot change back just yet. That's ok Archie stay as long as you need. Marcus walked around the bed and sat on next to Leah, he stroked her hair, come on honey give daddy a big hug as I need one. Daddy love's you and with that Leah let go of Jessie and turned over and hugged Marcus, he pulled her on to his lap and hugged her, then stood up and said look uncle Phillip was worried about you as was grandpa, do you think you could give uncle Phillip a big hug, so grandpa can help Mummy by giving her a give hug. Marcus passed Leah to Phillip, Xander can you give Jessie a hug she needs energy now. Yes, of course. Marcus pulled Jessie up in the bed and lifted her up, Xander sat on the bed and Marcus placed Jessie on to his lap.

Marcus took Leah back from Phillip and sat down next to Xander, after ten minutes or so Jessie woke up and Archie changed back to his human form. Phillip, Marcus said would you take Leah down stairs with Victor and Morgan and get her something to eat and drink, Archie would you go with her to make sure that no one approaches her. Archie looked at Jessie. She's fine Archie I don't want her to worry about Leah. Yes, I will go and he left with Phillip and Leah. Xander passed Jessie back to Marcus who gave her a hug and kiss. Where

369

is Leah? She's fine she just left the room with Phillip and Archie to get a drink. And Elfie? Archie killed him when you put your shield up. Are they all still hear Jessie asked Xander? Yes. Well let's get this over and done with, can you get them to line up again as Leah needed to check a few things first.

Do you think she is up to it Jess she looked so frightened earlier asked Marcus? Yes, if you can get them to behave themselves. Jessie you have my word and I apologize for what happened earlier said Xander. It's not your fault Xander, he has paid the price for what he did and thank you for helping. Now shall we go down and try again! Xander was the first one into the kitchen, Archie he said would you come with me as we are going to try again and I think having you closer to Jessie will deter anyone form doing the same thing again. Of course, I will, would you like me to change form. Yes, if you think that would help. Ok Archie said and walked out into the hallway and changed form, he went back into the kitchen. Phillip, Xander said if you would like to come with me, Archie and Marcus and then if the girls give us a few minutes with the men and come in everyone will be ready. Marcus kissed Jessie and Leah, don't worry everyone will behave. Xander walked into the living room with Archie, Phillip and Marcus. Joshua closed the door. Everyone stood up and everyone went silent. Everyone this is Archie just in case you did not get his name earlier, he will stand in that corner while my great granddaughter try's again, now does anyone not understand the brief you were all give. No one moved. Joshua opened the door and Leah and Jessie came back in Archie opened his wings slowly just for effect. Leah did not stand so close to the men this time, Jessie put her arm around her. Even Jessie had to admit they all looked good stood in a line in their black suits. Once again Leah stopped at Adele, Jessie looked at Adele, hold your hand out. He did it very slowly and Leah stepped forward and touched Adele's hand, Archie let out a little hiss of disapproval. Adele felt Leah draw some of his energy, he gave it willingly, he was trying not to look into her eyes just in case it triggered his calming influence. Leah let go of his hand and stepped back next to her mother, they walked past the rest of the line and then left the room. Archie put his wings back and walked from the room. Xander said gentleman you may sit we will be back.

Jessie was speaking to Leah in the kitchen when Marcus knocked the door and walked in followed by Xander. Leah would like to speak to Adele, she has chosen him and I think we should all sit down and have a chat at mum's house away from everyone here. I don't like her choice but she has chosen him willingly said Marcus. Yes, she chose him of her own free will. Xander remarked, I think she has been very clever and chosen well and it's her free will. If it wasn't Archie would have acted. Xander can you tell Adele that he is her choice. Leah give grandpa a hug and kiss as we are going home, Marcus can I speak to you in the hallway please. I need you to speak to Adele with Xander before you bring him over.

What about? He may be a king but in our house he will know his place and respect mum and dad, he will be expected to do every day house hold things like, lay the table and come on family days out, he must except that as a given and he must never ever use his influence over woman again in any way, nor must he have any lovers or girlfriend's. He must love and want Leah, if he does not then he must say now. She must come first and he must wait till she is of age. If he agrees to that then bring him over and if he does not then don't bring him. I will take Leah back now, is an hour enough time? Yes, and kissed her gently on the mouth. Come Leah let's check on nan and grandad, Jessie and Leah left with their security.

When they got home, Jessie took Leah into her bedroom and told her everything she knew about him, his past, his powers and his power over woman. Jessie said I am telling you this so you know everything, then you can't say I didn't tell you or warn you, also Leah he is a man and he will want you sexually and everyman has his limits so do not push him, he must also respect your age and if you don't want to do anything that makes you feel uncomfortable then tell him and me and if you feel frightened then use your power, Archie will not be far if you should ever need him, ok? Yes, mum. She had taken everything her mother had told her in. Right, let's go downstairs and get ready for our guest. Marcus and Xander had a quick chat in the hallway and they both agree that Tobias should be the second back up mate for Leah as he already shared a small bond with her. They both entered the living room and Xander said Adele and Tobias l would like you both to stay, we thank you all for coming you may all go. When everyone had left Joshua closed the door, leaving the four men inside the living room. Xander spoke first, Leah has made her choice of her own free will she has chosen you Adele to be bonded with, but because of her young age we have chosen a second, and that is you

Tobias as she already shares a bond with you. I am honored, Tobias said. Adele still looked shocked from what Xander had said.

Adele my wife wishes me to relay a few things to you and this will also apply to you Tobias if you are to be a second to Adele. First as you can see, she is not of full age so she cannot and will not be fully bonded until such time when she is ready because of her growing and her ability it could harm her. The second we will all be a family in every sense of the word and that means Xander is the head of our family, share's a very big and very close bond to Leah and it upsets her to be away from him, so no matter what even when you marry, she will need time with him. Second, Christine and Kirk are mum and dad to Jessie and Phillip and nan and granddad to Leah, you will respect them in their home, there are no titles there and they run that house, if you're asked to lay the table or take the rubbish out or make the tea then you do it, you will know you place. We are a family so everyone will come to family events and days out. Third you must want and love Leah and no one else ever, she needs pure energy just for her, that means no sex with other woman, no lovers and no girlfriends. You once told me that you would give everything up to find and have true love, well now you have your one and only chance, there will be no second chances.

You have waited nearly three thousand years for this one chance so don't fuck it up and don't use your power over or on woman ever again, that is the price you will pay. Now you will start to feel lots of things, you may use your calming but that is it because you could hurt Leah or she could kill you and I know you are our king but that means nothing to Jessie and Leah. So, we will try and allow you time to do the things you need to but whatever you do it should never affect them in any way. Oh yes and you have to live in England here with us in Southampton. Second you even look twice at my wife, I will end your life, that is if I get to you before Archie does, as not only does he protect Jessie but Leah to. So, if you agree then we will go back to our home and talk with Leah, Jess, Kirk and Christine. Well is it yes or no Adele? Marcus could tell Adele was taking everything that he said in. Calmly he agreed to all of it. Tobias! Yes, I agree. Good you may bring a bodyguard each when you visit and we will work security out later. Both men nodded at Marcus. Xander we will say goodbye for now and they will be back later. Robert opened the front door to let Marcus and his visitors in. Everyone is in the kitchen Marcus.

Leah had her hand on Christine's tummy feeling the baby kick and Kirk was hugging Jessie when Marcus walked in. How is my brother in law today? He has been kicking me all day and last night, Leah is calming him, Marcus walked over and kissed Leah and Christine. This is Adele and Tobias, yes, I remember them, Christine went to get up. No, mum don't get up you rest and dad you know Adele and Tobias. Yes, welcome and he let go of Jessie and went over to them and shook their hands. Of course, you know my wife Jessie and our daughter Leah, they both bowed to Leah. This is Sam, Adele said he is my personal bodyguard and the man next to him is Roberto he is Tobias's bodyguard. Would anyone like a cup of tea or coffee? Kirk asked. Yes, coffee please no sugar. Black coffee one sugar please. Sam, Roberto would you like to go with Robert he is Jessie's bodyguard, he will show you around and talk you through our security protocols. Adele waved his hand and they both went with Robert. Shall we go into the living room where we can all sit down in comfort and talk Kirk suggested when he handed Adele and Tobias their drinks? Leah, here is your tea.

Thank you granddad and she took the tea and held his hand, they walked into the living room together, Marcus and Jessie helped Christine into the living room, followed by Adele and Tobias. Every one sat down and all spoke about what everyone had been doing since there visit to Italy. After an hour or so Phillip and Sarah came in, Adele and Tobias stood up. Hello again Phillip said and nodded at Adele and Tobias, they both nodded at Phillip. Dr Adams Tobias said. No, please call me Sarah, again Adele nodded. How about we all go into the kitchen and see what we can find for tea as we have enough Christmas food to sink a battle ship, Jessie said as she got up and put the Christmas tree lights on. We can leave Leah and Adele to have a talk alone. Jessie asked Victor to come into the living room. Leah would like you in here while she and Adele are alone together, so please stay while we make tea. Victor nodded to Jessie and stood in the corner of the room. Jessie kissed Leah on the cheek and said now is the time to start to get to know Adele, ask him anything and tell him what you want, but listen to what he tells you, Victor will be here and we are in the next room, Jessie kissed her again and left the room closing the door behind her.

Adele sat on the other end of the sofa to Leah, he

turned sideways slightly to get a better look at her. He could see that she looked very young and very beautiful and he knew she was a virgin and he knew he could not rush her. He was going nowhere, she was going to be his life from now on, he knew she would be worth the wait after all he had waited nearly three thousand years and had every woman, he wanted but she was different and could only make him stronger. Leah moved closer to Adele so she could speak to him without talking loudly and looked into Adele's brown eyes, she felt the butterfly's in her tummy again, Adele spoke first, you have very beautiful brown eye's Leah, so do you, Adele smiled back at her.

Leah can you tell me why you chose me to be your mate, its ok if you don't know. Leah took her time, when I walked into the room, I was drawn to you, I felt butterfly's in my tummy and my heart beat got fast, I felt funny. I just wanted to touch you, and you're very good looking and your energy feels hot and sparks inside me. Leah went red in the face and looked at the floor. You don't have to be ashamed of telling the truth about how you feel or about what need's you want or desire, it will all come in time and thank you for being very honest with me. What about you, how do you feel about me? Adele looked at her, I am very taken with you Leah, I feel heat inside me when you're close to me even now and when you touched my hand you stirred many things up inside me, I want and desire you. I can start to feel emotion from you, I feel very protective of you as well Leah. Leah looked back up into Adele eyes again and smiled. He wanted her and he could feel the bonding heat building up inside him. Victor could feel an unease a feeling coming from Adele and stepped closer to Leah and said be at ease brother. Adele had never felt like this before. There was a knock at the door and it broke their gaze, come in Adele said and looked away from Leah. Sam, Adele's bodyguard entered the room.

Leah sat back and put her red flame on as she felt the bodyguard's unease. Stop where you are Adele said to his bodyguard. Victor spoke, you frightened Leah she feels that you are uneasy, its ok Leah Victor said as he came to stand in front of her. Just then Jessie came back into the room feeling Leah's unease. What is going on Jessie asked Victor. Leah has triggered the bond process in Adele and Sam must have felt the change and unease in Adele as did I. So, when Sam came into the room to check on Adele, he used his calming influence and Leah did not like it, it frightened her. Right ok thank you Victor. Stop that at once Sam. He did. Right tea is nearly ready, Leah be at ease, everything is fine, now Sam please leave the room so Leah can calm down. When Sam left the room Leah's light changed to white and then went. Did I hurt you Leah asked Adele, she sounded worried? No, you did not Leah and you have nothing to be sorry for darling, please don't worry. Leah go and give uncle Phillip a hug you will feel better and wash your hands for tea. Yes, mum she said as she left the room with Victor. Jessie said it's not your fault nor is it Leah's. Please speak to Marcus and dad as they went through the same thing. Your bodyguard needs to know what to expect and he is not to use his influence around us. Come tea is ready. Adele found that a place had been set for him next to Leah, he felt that he had been accepted into their family, another first and he settled down and enjoyed Christmas with wine and music and his new family.

When it came time to leave Adele felt Leah's unease as they walked to the front door, Adele thanked everyone and made arrangements to see Leah tomorrow. Jessie said you have two minutes alone to say goodbye and closed the hallway door. Don't worry Leah we will see each other every day, Tobias can you wait outside with Sam please. They left the hallway and closed the door leaving Adele and Leah totally alone for the first time. Adele took Leah's hand and kissed it and looked into her eyes, until tomorrow Leah. Leah asked if she could touch his face. Yes, he said Leah stepped closer to him and put both of her hands on his face, she looked into his eyes and closed hers and drew power from him. He felt his heat rise within him again and he could feel the need and power in her. Leah stopped drawing power from him and let go of him and stepped back. Sorry! Don't ever be sorry for needing to touch me, good night Leah and he kissed her on the head and left, leaving her alone in the hallway.

Jessie and Marcus took Leah to Xander for 8 .30 am the next day so she could have her time with him. Xander re booked the next ceremony of light for New Year's Eve in the morning and now they would use Xander's New Year's Eve party to announce Adele engagement to Leah, as all the elders and others were already there and it would give everyone a chance to meet Leah. Which also meant more shopping, Leah needed dresses and shoes, make and anything that they did not get the other day. We will need to get to London for a big shopping trip today and maybe stay overnight and come back tomorrow. But there are all the arrangements for the party, don't worry Jessie please leave it all to me, I would love to do this for Leah. Thank you Xander said Jessie and hugged him, Leah also hugged Xander, he felt over whelmed with love. Joshua and Marcus felt it to as did Adele when he walked into the room. He stopped and looked at Xander, Marcus said be at ease, it will take a bit of getting used to. Adele nodded at him and stood back a step and just waited till Jessie and Leah finished. Jessie turned to Adele, we have had to change our plans we have to go to London today shopping, Leah needs dresses and things for the engagement.

We will be staying in London tonight and go out to dinner this evening, would you like to come, I understand if you don't, I know shopping is not a man's thing but it will just be the four of us. I want to be where Leah is and I would love to indulge her, yes, I would like to, thank you. We will be staying at our house in London so security will not be an issue, we have a team there, we will leave in half an hour as the girls have to pack an overnight bag, is that enough time for you asked Marcus. Yes. Two and a half hours later they were all in London. Jessie spent the whole time grinning to herself in the car trying not to look at Marcus as she remembered her last trip to London with him. Marcus could not take his eyes from Jessie; he could see she was remembering to and he wanted her. The first stop was to designer dress shops where Adele paid for all of Leah's things then they went into Harrods where Jessie got Leah some make up and Adele brought Leah a few handbags and perfume. Jessie said, we are going to the lady's department, so you two can find something to do for ten minutes. They have a bar Marcus said to Adele, yes, I think I need a drink and pulled his credit card, out. No, that's ok I've got this.

Sam go with Robert and Morgan please, Adele said. Marcus and Adele went in search of the bar. Jessie let Leah choose some under ware for herself and Jessie chose something's for herself. Robert noticed two business men watching Jessie and Leah and as Jessie went to queue to pay the two men tried to get closer. Robert told Morgan to stand behind Jessie and Leah, while he and Sam stopped the men from advancing. Roberts Phone rang and he answered it not taking his eyes from the two men, it was Marcus wanting to know if the woman had finished their shopping, yes, I have to go. Ok, we are on our way and closed his phone. Adele and Marcus must have run because they were at Roberts and Sam's side before all of Jessie's and Leah's stuff where in the shopping bags. Is there a problem with my wife gentleman? The two men looked at each other, Adele took one step closer and smiled at the two men who were now backing away? Dad, Leah said I am hungry and me and mum have brought loads of stuff so can we go now. Yes, darling we can. Leah took Adele's hand and he smiled at her and said are we ready and took Leah's bags form her other hand.

They all walked back to the car hand in hand and went back to the Dewdney estate where once again William greeted them at the door. They all went into the kitchen where William made them all a late lunch and showed Adele to his room, he had a room next to Leah. Marcus and Jessie had their old room. Jessie told Leah to have a sleep for two hours as they would be out late, then have a bath or shower and put one of the dresses on and I will give you a hand with your hair and makeup if you need it. Leah asked if it was ok to spend some time with Adele before she went to sleep and Jessie agreed a short time on trust. When Leah went into Adele's room he was on his phone. Leah went to leave but Adele waved at her to come in, she sat on the bed while he finished his call. Leah said mum said I have to have a sleep as we are having a late night but I don't want to be a lone, Victor normally sit's in the room with me or Archie or grandpa. Oh, I see would you like one of the bodyguards to sit with you or would you like me to get your mum. No, Leah said mum and dad are bonding. Adele knew she meant they were having sex.

Ok, you can stay with me but we leave the bedroom door open and I had better tell Robert and Morgan. Leah smile and nodded. Ok, he said and went out the room and told Robert and Morgan what was going on. The door was to stay open and to come in and check on her if they needed to. Adele went back into his room and wedged the door open. Leah had taken her shoes off and was now laid on the bed, Adele took his jacket off and his shoes and laid on the bed next to Leah, he could tell she wanted him to cuddle her so he pulled her up the bed a bit more and pulled her to him so her head was on his chest, she put her hand on his chest and sound asleep within minutes, he pulled the blanket over them. He felt totally loved and peace with her there on him, he stroked her hair. The second Jessie walked back into the bedroom everything came back to her, Marcus had not forgotten as he was on Jessie the second, she closed the door, pulling her to him, kissing her, pulling her clothes off, touching her, he could hardly breath he needed her so much. Before she knew it, she was naked and under Marcus.

She kissed him back hard and ran her fingers down over his body, scratching him gently and making all the little noises that made him want her more. Marcus was breathing very fast and saying her name, he tried to enter her but she wiggled to tease him and he growled at her with want and need. She kissed his neck and pulled the back of his hair gently then slid her hands over his back and squeezed his bum. Jess please honey, he bent his head and took her breast in his mouth and sucked gently, Jessie pushed her body up against him and this time she let him take her with everything in him.

Adele could not sleep he had never just laid on a bed and held a woman. He found it very peaceful, he could feel Leah move on his chest in her sleep and loved it, he wondered what she would be like as a lover and wife, he would be honorable and give her everything. She moved again holding him tighter. He rubbed her back gently to soothe her and kissed her head, he felt very protective over her and the feeling filled him because when Morgan came in to check on her an hour later, Leah must have felt his protectiveness and her light came out of her body and covered them both. Morgan nodded at Adele and withdrew from the room slowly.

Jessie woke up with a sharp pain in her chest and

gasping for breath, after a second or two it passed and she grabbed Marcus who had now sat up in bed. What is it? something is wrong! Are you ok? Yes, its' not me. Marcus pulled on his trousers and ran from the bedroom and into Leah 's room, Robert where is Lea? She is safe, she is with Adele with the door open, why what is wrong? Marcus had to see for himself, he went into Adele's room to find Leah asleep cuddled up to Adele, with her light on. Adele sat up holding Leah to him so not to wake her. What is it? Danger, wake her up, stay with her and don't let her out of your site, keep your bodyguards close to you. Robert go to Jessie now, make sure she is ok and get security to check the house, be ready for anything. Marcus went back to his room. Robert was holding Jessie, comforting her. What is it Jessie? because you're starting to worry me and where is Archie. This is not good! Marcus went to his night stand and picked his phone up and called Kirk there was no answer. Marcus new this was bad. He then called Xander. Joshua answered Xander's phone.

What is happening here, Jessie is very upset. Christine's security alarms went off and then within a few minutes the house panic alarms went off, we believe that they were attacked, we don't know what's happened or who is hurt yet we are on are way now. We are coming back from London now, keep me up dated and he closed his phone. Jessie honey get dressed we are going home. Robert tell Adele we are leaving in five minutes. Marcus picked the house telephone up next to his bed and said William, we are leaving make sure all the girl's stuff is packed up and sent to Southampton and keep the house on full alert. Yes, sir and Marcus put the phone down and finished getting dressed, Jessie came out of the bath room dressed but she still looked upset. Ready, Marcus said to Jessie. Yes. Ok let's go, he took her hand and went to Adele's room, everyone was ready to go. What is the danger Adele asked, I will tell you in the car, Adele knew not to say anything else? Come we must go now!

They made it back to Southampton in under an hour and a quarter. Joshua had called Marcus and asked them to go back to Xander's, as they would know more by the time, they arrived home. All Marcus had told the others was that there had been a break in at mum's house. When they arrived at Xander's everyone could see the guards everywhere Marcus told them to stay in the car. Adele you come with me. Victor came out of the house to greet them. Marcus and Adele went into the house and closed the door. Victor what the hell happened and what is going on now? Be at ease Marcus, I have very bad news, about two hours ago Christine's house security set off their alarm to say they had intruders in the grounds of the house. Within two minutes they were in the house, the panic alarms where triggered by the bodyguards, there were two of our security teams there and shooting broke out, by the time we got there it was over and they had gone.

We reviewed CCTV footage of the house and grounds and it looks like there where at least thirty men, they went in over the walls a small army. Our men shot at least six of their men going into the house and internal CCTV, showed Kirk had killed the first three men through the front door, he was over powered, Phillip and the bodyguard 's killed another eight men at the back door. Archie in his human form killed another three trying to protected Christine and Sarah. Victor went silent. Then what Victor. Crispin shot Archie in the chest at point blank range, in his human form he died instantly as the bullet's went threw him and we just got word as you pulled up outside Christine died from her injuries, our doctors are trying to save the baby. Crispin injected Sarah with something and took her and Kirk was taken captive as was Simon. Phillip used his light and killed another three before they left the house. Phillip is in shock and is with Xander, Tobias and Akim and the other elders at our medical facility. Their death toll is at 23 and ours is now 10, we only had so many losses because everyone was in different parts of the house. Phillip could not protect them with his light and you can hear Archie say on the CCTV that he was forbidden to change form. Marcus could hardly breathe he bent forwards and held his knees. Adele asked what was being done to recover Kirk, Dr Adams and Simon. Our priority was the family but two of our men followed a van to Winchester the same address as before, we have had a surveillance team watching the house for some time and we have the two men outside the address as well. Come Adele said to Marcus and Victor, let's go to the medical facility, Marcus I am very sorry for your loss, the woman doesn't know yet. you must tell them before we get there, come we have no time. Victor and the extra security followed in the other cars.

Marcus and Adele got back into the car. What is it,

what has happened and where is Xander asked, Jessie? Jess, I have some very sad news to tell you honey, I need you to listen and remember that Leah and others are in the car, so I ask you to control your light for their safety. Jessie started to shake with fear and tears welled up in her eyes. Their car was now speeding to the brother hood medical facility. Mum and dad's house was attacked by the man Crispin, he broke into the house and kidnapped dad, Dr Adams and Simon, he killed Archie, as he could not change form and the bullets went threw him into mum and she died a few minutes ago, the doctors are trying to save the baby now, Xander is there with Phillip and the others. Jessie honey, I am so very sorry. Jessie thought back her feelings of shock, hurt and pain for Leah's sake, she couldn't talk, tears rolled down her face, her chest felt tight and she found it hard to breath.

Leah felt very uneasy and distressed at the news, her nan and the angel had been killed and now her mum was so upset, she felt frightened. Mum, Leah said and took her seat belt off and threw herself at Jessie and tried to cuddle her for comfort. Marcus just put his arms around them both. Robert opened his phone and called Joshua, we are about to arrive, I think Xander and Phillip should come to the car, we will need their assistance and closed his phone. Adele was still in; shock he was trying to keep it together for everyone but the feeling's coming from Leah and Jessie were killing him. He was failing to protect his new family and felt totally useless, some mate, some king he was. When the car pulled in Adele asked, what can I do Marcus, what do you need me to do? Take Leah for me please, she may want to cuddle Xander or Phillip. they need to calm down, they are in shock and they will want to see Christine and Archie.

Adele scooped Leah up pulling her from Jessie gently, she was crying her heart out. Xander opened the car door when the car came to a stop. Marcus lifted Jessie up and passed her to Phillip so he could get out of the car, Phillips light shot out of him and surrounded him and Jessie. He did not turn back, to hand Jessie back to Marcus, he just kept walking with her into the lift and Marcus let him. Adele handed Leah to Xander so he could also get out of the car. Little one I am so sorry Xander said, come let us be strong for mum and Uncle Phillip. Xander carried her into the lift with Adele and Marcus. They got out and walked to the operating room, where the doctors had just finished operating, the doctor came out, we managed to save the baby, he will need to stay in intensive care for at least two months if not longer. We could not save the mother. If you wish to go in now you may. Phillip carried Jessie into the operating room and closed the behind them. Xander sat down outside the room with Leah and tried to comfort her, Marcus sat next to them. He was in total disbelief. His life was falling apart and his wife had lost her family again, she had already lost her mum and dad 19 years ago because of the brother hood of the knight. Jessie and Phillip must hate him or at least blame them for what has happened, he was totally gutted and empty. Adele could see flashes of light coming from under the operating room door.

Tobias and Akim walked up the hallway towards Xander, Marcus and their family. What is happening Adele said to Marcus? Marcus took his head out of his hands and looked up at see the light, there trying to bring her back to life. What! Yes, they heeled Kirk when he was shot in the chest, but I think Christine is beyond all help now said Tobias. Let them try Marcus said they need to feel they tried. Xander stood, Adele take Leah, they will need my strength, Akim and Tobias come with me. All three men went into the operating room. After ten minutes Marcus went into the room. That's enough Jessie, Phillip, she's gone, you're draining yourselves and the others. If you have anything left in any of you, then please try Archie if anyone could help it would be him. Phillip took the men with him to the room that held Archie's body. Phillip could see that there was no hope, Archie's body had turned to a pile of dust. Phillip went back into the hallway he felt drained and tired he sat down, Victor stood next to him and put his hand on Phillips shoulder so Phillip could draw power from him and recover.

Marcus tried to drag Jessie away from Christine's body but she clung to the bed and would not move. Jess honey she would not want this, come on honey please, don't let Leah see you like this, Jessie she's out in the hallway with everyone. Jessie let out a loud cry, she could no longer keep the pain inside her, everyone in the hallway turned and looked towards the room that now held Christine's dead body. They all felt Jessie pain as it came flooding out of her. Jessie slid down onto her knees and cried, sobbing out loud screaming, no, over and over she was totally inconsolable. All everyone could do was to stand there and feel her pain and listen to her breaking her heart.

After twenty minutes Jessie had run out of steam and was slumped on the floor. Marcus scooped her up and took her out of the room, nobody said a word when the door opened and Marcus did not look at anyone, Jessie's face was buried in Marcus's chest, Marcus looked like he was carrying a rag doll. He took Jessie upstairs to the apartments only Morgan and Robert followed them. Marcus laid Jessie down on the bed and wrapped her in a blanket and told Robert and Morgan to stay in the room with her, she is not to be left alone. Robert, I will send the doctor up and I will check on Leah. Robert nodded, Marcus kissed Jessie and left the room. He wanted to die, his family had been ripped apart by a madman and he could not console his wife or protect his family. Marcus went back downstairs, where more of the elders and other brother hood had gathered. Marcus said to Xander I need a doctor to go to Jessie now and I want an update as to where we are and what plan we have to recover the rest of my family and I want it now. Levi went for the doctor and Joshua gave him an update, when that was done, they came up with a plan, which was for him to drive to Winchester break down the door and get his family back and kill everyone there. Let's go. Marcus, Xander said you're in shock I don't think that you're in any fit state to go anywhere.

My wife lost her mother and father 19 years ago

because of us, now she finally had a mum and dad and she loses them again because of us, if I don't get Kirk and Sarah I am afraid I will not have a wife or family anymore and there is a tiny baby in there that does not have a mother and may not have a father because of us. Be at ease Marcus, you are upset and feeling Jessie's pain right now. Leah wiggled on Adele's lap, stood up and said, dad I want to go with you to get grandad and auntie Sarah back, I can help shield you and granddad, she walked over and held her dad 's hand, so you all will be safe. Oh darling, Marcus hugged her to him, I think mum needs you more darling and we have Uncle Phillip. I am not scared dad. Marcus looked at Xander and then back to Leah. Ok, I tell you what darling I need someone who is not scared and someone who is strong, I know it's a lot to ask but if you think you're up to it. Marcus, Xander said nervously, I urge you to think about what you are about to say, I will not allow you to put Leah in any danger

. Marcus gave Xander a look that said, shut up. Adele stood up and looked at Xander. Marcus then looked back to Leah, Leah I am taking all of our strongest men with me and that will leave grandpa, Adele and mum alone with no one to protected them and I don't want to worry about them while I am gone, I need someone who can use there light to protect them as mum cannot use her light right now, so can I trust you to watch them all for me, I will understand if it is too much for you. Do you think you can do that job for me Leah?

She looked at Xander and then at Adele and nodded, yes, dad I can protect our family and hugged Marcus. Leah's light burst out of her body and wrapped itself around her and Marcus. Enough of that now, you will need all of your energy for when I am gone. Sorry dad and she stopped her light and gave Marcus one last hug and then went over and held Adele's hand. Marcus looked at Adele and Xander, be ready for anything. Come, he said to Akim and Tobias, let us get our loved ones back.

Marcus left the brother hood of the knight Medical facility with fear and pain in his heart, anger and revenge in his brain and weapons on his body and his brothers at his side. They all drove towards Winchester in a fleet of car's, speeding along the motorway. By the time they arrived at the house in Winchester the surveillance team, who had been watching the house for weeks had given them a strategic update on the best entrance into the house and where everyone was being held. Akim was the first man through the front door with Phillip and four other men. Phillip used his shield to protected Akim and the other men with him. Tobias went in the back door with another four men and Marcus went through the downstairs window with two men, Levi had climbed to the upstairs window and entered the house with three of Adele's men.

Within three minutes of the men entering the house in a haze of noise, screaming and blood shed they had taken one prisoner and killed anyone left and recover their loved ones. Marcus had found Sarah stripped naked and handcuffed to a bed, she was still unconscious and looked very pale, she had a black eye and looked like she had taken a beating and may have even been raped. Marcus had decapitated the man in the room with her. Marcus wrapped her in a sheet and removed the hand cuffs with another strong swift blow of his machete, he handed her to one of the men that was with him, he told him to guard her with his life and take her back to the car. In the meantime, Levi had killed two men in the room that he had gone into, they had Simon strung up naked, they had been torturing him badly. Levi shot the first one in the head and the second man with the knife in both of his knees then the head. It took all three of Adele's men to get Simon down as they had to take his weight before they could cut him down, Simon had been cut very badly all over his body. Akim, Phillip and their men went down the hall to the first room, there were plans on the wall, photos of his family, map's and time tables. Akim told two of the men collect all of that and any computers, cameras and phones.

They continued through the house, they could hear gun fire from other rooms in the house, they moved quickly down the hall to another room, where Kirk lay naked tied to a table, they could not tell if he was alive, his eyes were puffed up and closed as he had been very badly beaten up, he had burn marks all over his body and had chucks of flesh missing on his arm, stomach, legs and from the soles of his feet, he was covered in blood. Dad, Phillip cried out and surrounded the table with his light, he took off his jacket and placed it over Kirk. Quick Akim, give me your hand, Phillip pulled a knife from his pocket and cut his hand and Akim's hand, then put them both on Kirk and pushed his light and energy into Kirk as fast and hard as he could, but Phillip knew he would need Jessie as Kirk was so badly damaged. Akim took his jacket off as well and covered Kirk up, as Phillip lifted him up in his arms as gently as he could. Akim get dad stuff, there on the floor and his bracelet. Akim picked up Kirk's bloody belongings.

They left the room and went back to the cars with Kirk. Tobias team were met with the most resistance. Tobias was the second man in the backdoor, Roberto was the first, he killed the two men sat down in the kitchen, another man ran into the kitchen shooting and Roberto got hit in the arm, Tobias shot the man in the head without even flinching. Crispin ran pass the kitchen and into the hall, he tried to run down the steps to the basement but Roberto and Tobias gave chase and wrestled him to the ground, there was more shooting behind them. Tobias hit Crispin over the back of the head with his gun, knocking him out, they handcuffed him and carried him out of the house and the rest of the team killed anyone who was left alive.

They all left and made their way back to the brotherhood of the knight's apartments and medical facility. Everyone got out of their cars and went into the medical facility where Xander and Adele were waiting for them. Xander looked horrified at the state of his family. Phillip said to Xander, we need Jessie and Leah here now. Joshua opened his phone and called Victor and Robert. The doctors and nurses were cleaning and assessing each victim by the time Leah and a very tired and upset looking Jessie walked in to the medical facility. Everyone turned to look at her; she was way past even caring about what she looked like, with her blood shot eyes, from crying so hard. Phillip was in the hall outside of Kirk's room. Sis its dad he needs us both, he is in a very bad way.

Where is Marcus, Jessie asked. He is with Sarah. Leah take Adele and go and help Simon, he is in need of your help, he is in a bad way. Leah took Adele's hand and Victor followed them into Simon's room. Xander, we will need you, Akim and maybe Tobias as well, as we will need lots of energy. They all went into the Kirk's room. Jessie was not prepared to see the state of Kirk, never in all of her live had she seen such an act of mutilation. Oh god, let's start, Jessie pushed all the light that she could into Kirk as did Phillip, when Jessie had drained all of her power she just fell to the floor without any warning. The others felt weak, all Xander could do was call for Robert, who came into the room and could see what had happened, he picked Jessie up and laid her on the bed next to Kirk's. Marcus came into the room after Robert. Is he going to be ok? Yes, Phillip managed to say, but dad will still need treatment. Leah came into the room. Dad how is grandad? Leah saw Jessie on the bed and ran over, mum, what's wrong with mum? Nothing darling, she's very tired she just needs to rest. Adele picked up on Leah's anxiety and went into the room after her as did Victor. Marcus put Kirk's bracelet back on his wrist. Phillip asked Leah, do you think you're up to helping auntie Sarah on your own? Yes, I am up to it and went into Sarah's room to help her recover. Adele and Victor went back outside to wait in the hall. Joshua, where Crispin is now asked Marcus. He is hand cuffed to a medical bed in the same room Archie was in and there is an armed guard in there with him. Ok, let me move Jessie to another room and you all need to rest.

Before Marcus could say anything, else there was a blinding blast of light that filled the room, nobody could see anything for a few seconds, then the light faded to a glow and there stood Archie in his angel form, he was stood next to Jessie's bed. He looked crazed and did not seem to know them, he looked different he now had one black wing and he looked very upset as if he did not know what was going on. He opened his wings fully and let out a loud screaming hiss towards them all. Its ok Archie, no one is going to hurt her and Marcus slowly put his hands up in front of him.

Marcus told everyone to move away, out of the room, slowly. Archie did not take his eyes from Marcus. When everyone had left the room Marcus said, she is fine, Jessie is tired out, that's all, she is just sleeping, she tried to help Kirk and it was too much for her. She is still very upset, she thinks you're dead, Archie you died trying to save Christine, she to is dead the pain is too much for Jessie to bear. Marcus put his hands down very slowly. Archie this was not our doing, the man who did this is from father, an immortal, he is crazed, he just wants to go back to father. He has killed too many people including you and Christine and very nearly Kirk, now you know that we cannot kill him because he will be re born and be even more crazed. He cannot go back to father via Jessie not now.

So, I think I might know a way around all of this, father gets what he wants and that is to stop Jessie's pain so her light can shine, Marcus nodded at Archie and you will be back in fathers good book, so to speak because you look like you have been punished enough, I can see you have suffered Archie. I know you love Jessie as I do and that is why you did not want her to suffer and why you tried to stop Christine from being killed. Now I know that there must be a balance in heaven as here on earth. Yes, Archie! Marcus said as he nodded his head again to make sure that Archie was following everything that he was saying. So, I propose an exchange, a sole for a sole. You take Crispin, the man who killed you and Christine, the man who did this to Kirk and the same man that wishes to hurt Jessie and you return Christine to her body. That way everybody wins. If he is not enough then I gladly will go with you and leave this life on earth so Jessie can have her family back. Archie, I love her so much I cannot live with her pain, I love her so much that I will willingly give my life up, so that she may have hers back, please Archie I am begging you. Make this right for her.

Archie, seemed to be thinking about what Marcus had said he lowered his wings. Archie moved towards Kirk's bed and looked down at him, he then touched his bracelet and ran his finger over the word dad. Archie then touched Kirk's chest pushing light from his hand in Kirk's chest until his wounds were fully healed. Thank you, Archie. Archie stepped back and turned to Jessie, he bent over the bed, kissed her on her lips, he touched her cheek with his hand and pushed his light into Jessie, he stroked her hair and picked up her hand kissing her wedding ring and laid her hand back down. Archie turned to face Marcus and fully opened his wings, light shot out of Archie and filled the room, Archie's wing went around Marcus and in a flash, they were stood next to the bed where Christine's body was. Archie bowed down next to her body, he folded his wings away and stood up again, he looked at her bracelet it said mum, it was the same as Kirk's. Archie touched it and remembered things that had happened, love, family bonding, faith, fun, games, smiles a touch and her child. Archie knew that Marcus was right. Archie opened his wings and lent forward and whispered into Christine's ear, then kissed her forehead, put his hands on her and pushed a blast of light into her lifeless body and then covered her with a shroud. Archie turned and put his wing around Marcus and they were next to the bed that Crispin was handcuffed to. Marcus said to Levi who was stood guard. Be at ease brother, please give me the key and stand down now, Levi gave Marcus the key to the cuffs and withdrew from the room slowly.

Leah had finished with Sarah and walked back out into the hall, she asked Adele for a cuddle, so she could draw some power, then she asked Victor what was going on and why everyone was in the hall. Victor replied, I don't know. Leah went over to Xander, grandpa what's wrong, where is dad? Leah, Xander is very weak, your dad is fine he is talking to someone Tobias informed her, Who? Everyone's out here, anyway dad's not in there, I can sense he is not. What! said Phillip and went into the room. Phillip could see that Kirk was fully healed, he could also see that Marcus and Archie were not in the room. Phillip went back out into the hall where Levi was walking towards them. Joshua asked Levi why are you not at you post? Levi looked at Leah and could feel Xander's influence on her, Marcus ordered me to stand down, he and his visitor are with Crispin now. Take me to my farther now. Yes, Levi takes us to Marcus. Everyone turned to see Jessie coming out the Kirk's medical room.

Brother, I sensed your worry, dad is fully healed. Jessie walked past everyone and touched Xander on the shoulder and gave him some of her light. Right Levi, lead the way. Levi did not know what to do, he looked at Xander and Joshua. Take them Phillip said and Levi nodded and lead them to the room where he had left Marcus and Archie with Crispin. Levi stopped, please be careful and he stepped back, so Jessie and Leah could go in followed by Xander. Levi stopped anyone else from entering. Archie, Jessie exclaimed, as she entered the room. Archie looked up as he was bent over the other side of the bed, looking at a man, Marcus was near to the door. Jessie honey, take Leah and leave, Archie is not himself. I can see, Archie what happened to your wing, I saw what was left of your human body, how are you here? Archie looked at Jessie, then looked at Leah and Xander. Archie then spoke for the first time. I am here to put things right, I have returned your father to full health and I am returning your mother, the price for that is free will, so your mate has agreed to come with me, and this sole wishes also to return to father. What, no Marcus and she stood in front of Marcus, no, you cannot take him, Marcus please don't go, don't leave us, I won't let you take him and Jessie's light burst out of her chest and surrounded her and Marcus. Marcus put an arm around Jessie's waist and pulled her to him, then turned her around, Jess honey I have to go, I made a deal to get mum back and end all of this, I am doing this because I love you so much, I will give up my life so you may have your life with mum, dad and Leah, please honey it's ok.

Marcus kissed Jessie hard on her mouth, pulling her tighter, holding her. Leah ran over to Jessie and Marcus, she started to cry as did Jessie. Leah flung herself at Marcus, no dad, stay, I love you, please don't go dad. Archie took a step back. Xander said Leah, daddy's not going anywhere. It is my time to go, I am very old and tired, I will gladly take my grandsons place as I love you all, Archie is this agreeable to you. Everyone looked at Archie he nodded. I have seen my family grow and my great grandchild and I am at peace. The holy messenger told me this day would come and I am ready, come child give me one last hug and lets us say our goodbyes. Oh no, grandpa, I love you, please don't go. Don't cry Leah, be at peace, now I will miss you and love you very much but it is my time to rest, now my family are safe.

Xander gave her a big hug and kiss, be good little one. Leah hugged Xander tightly around the neck and buried her head in his neck, trying not to cry, so hard. Marcus let go of Jessie. Jess say goodbye to

Archie and Xander, then take Leah outside please, I will be out soon and he kissed Jessie on the mouth. Jessie let her light fade and stepped away from Marcus and took two steps towards Archie, thank you Archie and goodbye, she reached out with her hand and touched his face and then stepped one step closer and kissed his cheek, she stepped back and said thank again and went to say goodbye to Xander. When Xander had finished saying goodbye to Jessie and Leah they left the room. Marcus hugged Xander and kissed him on the head. Goodbye father and a tear fell from Marcus's eye. Enough child, come unlock Crispin, we must go now.

As Marcus unlocked Crispin's handcuff's Xander took his ring and necklace off, when Marcus had finished Xander gave them to him, they had one last hug together. Goodbye my grandson and kissed his cheek, you are now their Knight, their holy man as you are truly blessed, goodbye my son and with that Xander stepped towards Archie.

I am ready Archie, let us start our journey together. Archie nodded and picked Crispin up with his black wing and scooped Xander closer to him with the other wing. Archie looked at Marcus and Marcus said thank you and nodded, Archie winked and nodded back to him, a burst of bright white light filled the room and in a flash they had gone.

Printed in Great Britain
by Amazon